I0591294

WHAT'S AN EARL GOTTA DO?

BOOK TWO IN THE ASTLEY CHRONICLES

COURTNEY MCCASKILL

HAZEL GROVE BOOKS

THE ASTLEY CHRONICLES

Book 1: How to Train Your Viscount
Book 2: What's an Earl Gotta Do?

Coming Soon:
Book 3 (Available Spring 2022): The Sea Siren of Broadwater
Bottom
Book 4: The Duke's Dark Secret

For more information, visit www.courtneymccaskill.com

THE ASTLEYS OF HARRINGTON HALL

Edward Astley IV, Earl of Cheltenham
Georgiana Astley, Countess of Cheltenham

Edward Astley V, Viscount Fauconbridge, age 26
Harrington Astley, age 25
Anne Northcote (née Astley), Countess of Wynters, age 23
Lady Caroline Astley, age 19
Lady Lucy Astley, age 18
Lady Isabella Astley, age 18
John Astley, deceased at age 2
Frederick Astley, age 13

First published in 2021 by Hazel Grove Books.

What's an Earl Gotta Do?, Copyright © Courtney McCaskill, 2021.

Excerpt from *The Sea Siren of Broadwater Bottom* Copyright © Courtney McCaskill, 2021.

All rights reserved. The moral rights of the author have been asserted. No part of this book may be used or reproduced in any manner whatsoever without written permission except in the case of brief quotations embodied in critical articles and reviews. All inquiries should be made to the author.

Paperback ISBN: 978-1-63915-003-8

Kindle ISBN: 978-1-63915-004-5

eBook ISBN: 978-1-63915-005-2

This is a work of fiction. Names, principal characters, events, and incidents are the products of the author's imagination. One real historical figure, Lord Hobart, makes a cameo appearance. Although I attempted to make this cameo appearance generally consistent with Lord Hobart's activities in 1802, the scene in which he appears has no factual basis. As discussed in the author's note, there is also one scene that was inspired by George Smart and the manner in which he invented his "Chimney Cleansing Machine." Any other resemblance to actual persons, living or dead, or actual events is purely coincidental.

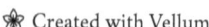 Created with Vellum

WHAT'S AN EARL GOTTA DO?

PROLOGUE

$\mathcal{L}$ondon
March 1798

MICHAEL CRANFIELD LEAPT from the carriage before it came to a full stop in front of the white stone town house on Cavendish Square. His legs, cramped after the overnight journey, were unprepared for this sudden exertion, and he almost went sprawling face first onto the pavement. He managed to keep his feet and sprinted up the steps of the Astley family's London residence, ignoring the footman's bewilderment.

"Is Anne here?" he asked, panting as he crossed the threshold. "I must speak to her right away."

An older man who had a butlerish look about him, between his ramrod-straight posture and air of silent disapproval, raised a single eyebrow. His expression was that of a man who had smelled something exceptionally unpleasant, and he seemed to be pondering which was the graver offense, the fact that Michael looked every bit as rumpled and dusty as one would expect after spending eighteen hours on the road, or that he'd had the audacity to refer to the Earl of Cheltenham's daughter by her first name. He lifted his chin high enough that Michael could see right up his nose. "Could you possibly be referring to *Lady* Anne?"

"Yes—Lady Anne, of course. It's just—I've known her all my life, so I—" Michael swallowed. He didn't have time to explain. "Is she here? I need to speak with her. Urgently."

"She is not. Perhaps you could leave your card, Mr.—"

"There isn't time for that." *Oh, God.* The most important conversation of his life, and he was going to miss her. "Where did she go?"

The butler puffed out his chest. "This is most irregular, sir. You may leave your card. *If* Lady Anne wishes to receive you—"

"In two hours, there is a ship sailing for Canada, and I must be on it," Michael bit out.

The butler looked him up and down. "Rather urgent business for a man of your years. Do tell what it might be."

"I am not at liberty to disclose it. But suffice to say, the matter is urgent enough that my father just pulled me out of Oxford." Michael detected the tiniest sliver of interest in the butler's stony expression. "Please, sir," he begged. "I have to be on that ship, and I must speak to Anne before I go. I could be gone a full year, and I—I've never told her that I—" He swallowed, unable to believe he was admitting this to a complete stranger. "I mean, I'm fairly certain she already knows, but—" Lord, this was mortifying. The butler's mouth was hanging open in a most unbutler-like fashion. But Michael plowed on because he had to convince the man somehow. "But I haven't actually asked her to—to be my—"

The butler's eyes sharpened. "You are the boy next door. *Lord Morsley.*"

"Yes. Yes, I am." Michael felt his face reddening, all the

way to his large, sticky-outy ears. He shouldn't be surprised. Everyone back home in Gloucestershire seemed to know he was hopelessly in love with his best friend, that he had been for years.

But it was lowering to discover that his feelings were so openly discussed that someone had mentioned them to this man whom he had never met, who lived a hundred miles away.

At least his confession had the desired effect. "A thousand apologies, my lord. Carter!" the butler snapped at the man posted at the door. "Gather the footmen, as well as Lady Anne's and Lady Cheltenham's maids."

"Yes, sir!" Carter said, already sprinting toward the back of the house.

It was quickly ascertained that Anne and her mother had gone out to pay a round of social calls. Nobody knew their precise itinerary, although between Yarwood (this proved to be the butler's name) and the ladies' maids, they were able to put together a list of several dozen possibilities.

Footmen were dispatched at a run to inquire at the houses on the list. Michael was pacing past a drawing room when a gentleman with short brown hair peppered with flecks of grey appeared in the doorway. Michael started, and the man laughed.

"I'm sorry. I probably should have made myself known earlier. I've been waiting for Lord Cheltenham." He extended a hand. "I'm the Earl of Wynters."

"Lord Wynters." Michael pumped his hand. "I am the Earl of Morsley."

"Come, sit." Lord Wynters gestured to a chair before the fire. He strolled over to a decanter in the corner and filled two glasses. "I daresay you could use a spot of this," he said, handing one to Michael.

Michael was raising the glass to his lips when a great clattering sound almost made him spill his drink. It proved to be Lord Wynters's walking stick, which he had knocked over as he resumed his seat on the sofa. As the earl leaned it against the couch once more, Michael noticed that the shiny black lacquered stick had a silver handle shaped like an icicle.

"I could not help but overhear your predicament," Lord Wynters said.

Michael cringed. "I… er…"

The earl laughed. "Come now, there's no need to feel embarrassed. I, too, was once"—he paused, studying Michael assessingly—"seventeen?"

"Nineteen," Michael said, unable to keep a hint of defensiveness from his voice.

"Nineteen. My apologies." Lord Wynters sipped his drink. "Lord Morsley—that would make you Redditch's heir."

"Yes, sir."

"Then you've nothing to worry about. Your father is tall, as was your mother, God rest her soul. I'll wager that, within the next year, you'll grow into those hands and feet."

"Thank you," Michael muttered, even though he felt the opposite of grateful. He was all too aware that, unlike his friends, who had shot up dramatically in the last few years, he remained on the shorter side of average. Not only that, he was scrawny and *terrifically* awkward, with hands and feet so large they looked like they could not possibly go with the rest of his body.

Throw in his gigantic ears, and he wasn't exactly a fairytale prince.

But Anne wasn't shallow. She didn't care about things like that.

At least, he hoped to God she didn't.

The earl was shaking his head, looking wistful. "You remind me very much of myself when I was not too much older, when I began courting my first wife. You've chosen well for yourself, if you don't mind my saying so. Lady Anne actually bears a striking resemblance to my Clara." He gazed across the room, lost in thought. "A very striking resemblance indeed."

"I see," Michael said. He was so anxious, it was difficult to attend to what the man was saying, but he was trying not to be rude.

There was a rush of footsteps in the foyer as the first footman returned. "Excuse me," Michael said, already halfway across the room.

"They were at Lady Grenwood's house earlier," the footman said, hands on his knees, breath coming in gasps. "But they left a half hour ago, and her ladyship didn't know where else they were heading."

Yarwood gave the man no quarter, handing him another slip of paper. "We've thought of three more houses."

"Yes, sir!" the footman said, hauling in one last breath before rushing out the door.

Time passed both agonizingly slowly and all too quickly. Somehow every time Michael checked his pocket watch, another five minutes had disappeared. Soon all the footmen but two had returned, and still there was no news.

Michael sighed and turned to Yarwood. "If I am to make my ship, I must depart in ten minutes. As much as I hate to convey such a message in a letter, it appears it has come to that."

"I believe you are right, my lord," Yarwood said, leading Michael back into the drawing room, where the earl was still waiting before the fire. Yarwood opened a writing desk and gestured for Michael to sit.

Over the years, Michael had imagined proposing to Anne in hundreds of different ways. On the balcony at a ball. In the Greek folly behind her house. On the pond where, years ago, they had whiled away many an hour playing pirates (Michael had quickly rejected that one. They had been prone enough to overturning the skiff without anyone attempting to go down on one knee).

But he had finally decided that he would propose in the meadow next to Cranfield Castle, the glorious old ruin that had been in his family for almost five hundred years. This happened to be the spot they had been picnicking the summer they had both been fifteen, when Michael had come oh so close to kissing her.

Proposing in a letter therefore tasted like the bitterness of defeat, and what Michael was able to compose in the space of ten minutes left much to be desired. But at least he was able to cover the essentials: that he loved Anne, that he had for years; that he wanted no one but her for his wife; that he never wanted to be parted from her; and that if she would but wait for him, he would rush back to her side just as soon as he had completed the task his father had set before him.

"There," he said, putting a final crease in the paper and rising to his feet. He consulted his pocket watch and was dismayed to discover that he should have left five minutes ago. "I must hurry."

"I will ensure that Lady Anne receives it," Yarwood promised.

"Thank you, Yarwood," Michael said with feeling. "For everything."

The earl had crossed the room to shake Michael's hand. "Good luck to you, young man."

Michael accepted his hand. Plague take it—he was in such a state he had entirely forgotten the man's name. "Thank you, my lord."

And so Michael hurried down the steps as quickly as he had rushed up them, anxious for Anne's answer and knowing he would have to wait months to learn what that answer might be.

LORD WYNTERS GLANCED about the drawing room. The house was still aflutter following the excitement caused by young Lord Morsley's unexpected arrival. The footmen were chattering amongst themselves in the foyer.

Yarwood, the only one who seemed to recall that they still had a guest, had taken up a position just outside the door.

"Yarwood," Lord Wynters called, "I suppose I won't wait any longer. But I wonder if I might ask a favor before I go."

"Certainly, my lord."

He raised his empty glass. "I happen to know that Cheltenham keeps a bottle of Martell up in the library. Would you mind fetching me a glass?"

"At once, my lord."

As soon as the butler was out of the way, Wynters crossed to the writing desk and seized Lord Morsley's letter. He didn't bother to open it; he knew well enough what it said.

He threw it straight into the fire.

He then scrawled a quick note of his own, which he positioned on the desk at the precise angle of Lord Morsley's missive.

By the time Yarwood returned with his drink, Wynters was back in his seat, arm draped across the back of the sofa, looking for all the world as if he had never moved.

CHAPTER 1

*L*ondon
July 1802
Four Years Later

ANNE NORTHCOTE, the Countess of Wynters, crept into the foyer of the Falmouth mansion, naked but for a sheet of black lace net.

At least, she mused grimly, that was how she appeared.

In truth, the black net was fully lined with beige muslin. But the muslin matched Anne's skin tone so closely, at first glance it gave the illusion that... that...

That she wasn't wearing *anything* beneath the net.

Oh, this dress was a terrible idea. Her little sister Caroline's terrible idea, to be specific. Anne's husband, Lord Wynters, had died in his sleep precisely one year ago, and tonight was her reentry into polite society. Anne never had time to keep up with the latest styles, and after a year spent in mourning, her wardrobe was badly out of fashion. Asking her stylish little sister to commission a few gowns for her had seemed like the perfect solution.

This scandal of a dress was apparently Caro's notion of half mourning. Anne felt her cheeks flush beneath the rouge her maid had applied.

Rouge! She never wore rouge, but she was wearing it tonight, and *lip pomade*, too. Along with a crimson hothouse rose tucked behind her ear, and a black lace mask to match her gown.

Halfway across the foyer, Anne decided she couldn't go through with it.

Really, considering the day she'd had, who could blame her?

Her shoulders slumped as she thought of the messenger who had called upon her earlier, bringing tidings of her impending humiliation. No, pasting on a false smile and pretending to enjoy herself, knowing that everyone here would be laughing at her tomorrow morning, would only make things worse. She would make an excuse to Lady Falmouth and—

"Just where do you think you're going?"

Anne steeled herself before she turned. "I'm feeling unwell, Mama."

"Are you?" Georgiana Astley, the Countess of Cheltenham, circled Anne like a shark, eyeing her from behind her peacock-feathered lorgnette mask.

Anne wrung her hands. "It's nothing, just a headache—"

Lady Cheltenham snapped her mask down. "Stop slouching. We both know your discomfort has nothing to do with your head and everything to do with that dress."

"It's not the dress."

Her mother cocked a skeptical eyebrow.

Anne sighed. How like her mother to see right through

her. "At least, not entirely. I do feel a bit ridiculous. But I—I received some bad news."

"What happened, dear?"

Anne closed her eyes. "I am to be the subject of a cartoon."

The countess frowned. "A cartoon? What do you mean, a cartoon?"

"This morning I intervened on behalf of a chimney sweep's apprentice stuck in a flue in Holborn. The boy survived," Anne said, seeing consternation fill her mother's eyes. "I was able to persuade the building's owner to open up the wall to cut him out."

"Of course you did." Her mother puffed out her chest. "That's my girl."

"But the owner was very resistant to damaging his building on account of a lowly sweep, and in order to sway him, I had to be a bit"—Anne waved a hand, searching for the right word—"fervent."

The countess arched an eyebrow. "Fervent?"

"You might even say vehement."

"What did you say, darling?"

Anne knotted her hands. "I might have shouted that he should be ashamed of himself, that he had no right to call himself a Christian, and if he didn't let us open up that wall, I would make sure his name was on the front page of every newspaper in London tomorrow. In front of a crowd of two hundred," she added in a rush.

The countess flipped open her fan. "Considering a child's life was at stake, I think you had the right of it."

"Yes, and in truth, I wouldn't do anything differently, if that is what it took to save the boy. But a cartoon is to be printed tomorrow, picturing me dressed in a Roman helmet, towering over a cowering man. I am shown prodding him with a spear and reciting a version of my speech. The caption reads, 'Lady W, London's very own virago.'"

"How do you know this?" her mother demanded.

"A messenger came by the Ladies' Society's offices today."

"Darling, perhaps it's not as bad as you—"

"It is. I saw it." Anne looked away, feeling tears forming in her eyes.

Her mother stepped forward and took her hands. "Oh, darling, I know it's unpleasant. But this cartoon will be forgotten in a week's time. You'll see. Besides, you should wear this as a badge of honor. If *someone* isn't saying something nasty about you, it only means you aren't worth remarking upon."

Anne sighed. Her mother would have considered it an honor, just as her mother could have worn this dress with her head held high. Anne had always marveled at her mother's (and sister's) unwavering confidence.

But she just wasn't like that.

"The point is," Anne said, "I'm not much in the mood for a ball."

"Have you considered," Lady Cheltenham said carefully, "that a little diversion might be exactly what you need?"

"I doubt I'll find any tonight. I'll probably spend most of the evening standing in the corner, as usual."

Her mother snorted. "You do not *stand* in the corner so much as *hide* in the corner. If you would stop doing that, your dance card would be full every night."

"Mama," Anne protested, "my dance card has never been full. Not even once."

"That's because when you came out, you spent all of three weeks on the Marriage Mart before accepting the first proposal you received. And you spent most of those three weeks hiding in the ladies' retiring room."

This was a difficult point to argue, as her mother's facts were essentially correct. Not that she had drawn the right conclusion. "Are you saying I shouldn't have accepted Lord Wynters?"

"Not if that was what you truly wanted. Just that there was no need to be so hasty about it."

Anne struggled to keep a note of accusation out of her voice. "It's just that—*you* were the one who always used to comment on how I was going to be a countess someday. Or sometimes you would say marchioness." She bit her lip. "I understood my duty. When Lord Wynters proposed, I knew it was my only chance to marry someone of the rank and standing you and Papa expected—"

"Oh, my darling child." Her mother's eyes were full of sorrow as she took Anne's hands and pressed them. "How I wish I had never said a word. Had I known how thoroughly you misunderstood me—" The countess broke off, looking down. "The point is, had you given it a little more time, you would have had a dozen proposals from which to choose."

"No, I wouldn't have. I'm not like you, Mama. I'm... boring and plain."

Her mother had been hailed as the most beautiful woman of her generation, with her honey-blonde hair and her stunning blue eyes. The *Astley* eyes, they were called, as five of Anne's six siblings also had them.

Anne, on the other hand, had plain brown hair and plain brown eyes. She was the only daughter not to inherit her mother's beautiful eyes.

And she knew vanity to be a sin, but sometimes she felt like a plow horse in a family of unicorns.

"You are neither of those things," her mother insisted.

But with the prospect of having to re-enter the Marriage Mart hanging over her like an axe, Anne had spent the past year musing upon the many things that rendered her unmarriageable, and now they came pouring out. "I'm boring. I'm plain. I spend too much time on my charity work. I didn't produce a child in three years of marriage—"

"No one will hold that against you. Everyone knows Lord Wynters didn't father a single child in any of his three marriages."

"—I'm a *virago*—"

The countess huffed. "I, for one, would consider that a compliment."

"—and I'm too tall," Anne concluded.

Her mother scowled. "You most certainly are not."

"Of course I am." Anne laughed. She was only two inches shy of six feet. How her mother could even suggest—

The countess fanned herself dismissively. "Your figure is elegant."

"I'm taller than most of the men in that ballroom!" Anne hissed.

"Many men don't care about that, Anne."

Anne shook her head. A lifetime of experience had taught her differently. "No man wants a wife who makes him feel unmanly."

"Well," her mother said, snapping her fan closed, "you don't have to marry every insecure fool in that room. You just need one man smart enough to know a thoroughbred when he sees one."

"A *thoroughbred*? I'm not a thoroughbred—"

"That is exactly what you are." Her mother peered at her. "Really, Anne, I don't understand what happened to you. You were always so confident growing up."

Anne sighed. It was true. Growing up in the Cotswolds, she had been best friends with the boy next door, Michael Cranfield, and had spent most of her childhood riding hell-for-leather across their fathers' adjoining lands, climbing trees and having adventures. Anne had been an unrepentant tomboy, and it had never occurred to her to doubt herself.

She sometimes wondered where that confident girl had gone. Perhaps Michael had taken her off with him when he left for Canada. He'd never returned, and Anne hadn't heard a single word from him in four years.

Of course, as soon as she had arrived in London, she'd realized that the rules were all different here. The qualities she used to prize in herself, the same ones Michael had valued in her as a friend—her courage, her determination, and her sense of adventure—were the worst sorts of liabilities on the Marriage Mart.

So she had adopted a new identity, as the most respectable woman in all of England. It had been necessary to get her charity off the ground, as no one would donate to an organization run by a hoyden. That was what made her rare slip this morning especially galling—she had more on the line than just personal embarrassment. If people stopped donating to the Ladies' Society because she had lost her temper—

Her mother interrupted her train of thought. "You, my dear, are about to be pleasantly surprised. Besides, you want to find a new husband, do you not?"

"I do." And that was the rub of it. Anne needed a husband if she was to have children. And Anne wanted children. She wanted them just as much as she wanted the air that filled her lungs.

And Lord Wynters had not given her any.

"You're dressed to find one tonight," her mother said, seizing her by the shoulders and steering her across the foyer. "Do look for someone more stimulating this time, dear."

Anne bristled. "As I mentioned, *you* were the one who said I needed to marry an earl—"

"I know I did. But you married the wrong earl, darling."

"Surely the words *wrong* and *earl* do not go together. They are inherently nonsensical."

"Hmmm. Well, I'm sure you'll do better this time. Now, quit slouching, and for God's sake, *smile*," her mother said, all but shoving her into the ballroom.

Well, there was no helping it. Anne threw her shoulders back and cocked up her chin. Two gleaming marble staircases curved down to the parquet floor below. The Falmouth ballroom, normally sedate in tasteful shades of cream and gold, had been transformed into a lush fantasy for the occasion of the masquerade. Purple velvet flounces draped the balconies overlooking the ballroom below. Wine-red roses overflowed from vases perched on pedestals. The candelabras had been draped with wisps of gold netting. Even the stand where the musicians were setting up had been transformed into a sumptuous grotto. Half the guests had come in full costume—Anne saw Helen of Troy, Oberon, and the usual assortment of nuns and friars—and the other half had simply added a mask to their usual evening finery.

As she reached the bottom of the stairs, a gentleman wearing a green Highland kilt passed in front of her, bearing two glasses of lemonade.

She watched his jaw drop. He swiveled his head so he could continue to gape at her as he crossed the room...

... until he crashed at full speed into a column and went sprawling on his backside.

Oh, dear God. She glanced around and saw people openly gawking at her. Her dress must be even worse than she'd feared. Every instinct demanded that she flee, but... why wasn't anyone checking on the fallen gentleman? What if he were truly injured? She couldn't just leave him lying there on the floor.

Tamping down her annoyance, she hurried to his side,

relieved to see that his kilt had settled modestly. "Are you all right, sir?"

He stared up at her, looking rather dazed. "That depends upon your answer."

"My answer? I—I don't understand."

She extended her hand to help him up, only to find it firmly seized. The man kissed the back of her gloved hand (actually kissed it—Anne had never been so scandalized in her life!) "Tell me at once—do I stand a chance?"

"I... I don't know what you mean, sir—"

"I mean," he said, "that tonight I have seen beauty such as I never dreamed could exist. Say you'll take pity on me, fair goddess, and grant me the favor of a dance."

Oh dear, Anne mused. He must have hit his head. "I apologize, sir," she said, struggling to free her hand, "but I... I don't even know you, and—"

"Alexander Fitzroy, at your service, Madame. May I know the name of my enchantress?"

A tall man who wore his blond hair in the sort of casually windswept style that probably took an hour to arrange spoke. "She is Lady Wynters. And I would like a dance as well."

Anne stared at the masked man for a beat, then realized it was the Viscount Scudamore.

Strange. Lord Scudamore was the treasurer of the Royal Military Asylum. They were both actively involved in the charity world, so Anne knew him fairly well. He'd been showing more and more interest in the Ladies' Society over the past year, and Anne had him on her short list of candidates for a vacant position on her board as vice president.

But he had never asked her to dance before. He was precisely the type of man who never asked *her* to dance. He was rich; although the estate he had inherited had been mired in debt, Lord Scudamore had worked a miracle, turning it around in three short years. He was also young. Titled. Handsome, even.

Anne blanched, realizing that Lord Scudamore was awaiting her response. "Um, certainly, my lord. And you as well, Mr. Fitzroy," she added hastily, seeing his woeful expression.

She penciled their names onto her dance card. "You look surprised, my lady," Lord Scudamore said.

"A bit," Anne admitted. "You've never asked me to dance before."

"You were never available before," Lord Scudamore countered.

She was blinking at him in surprise when a man dressed as Sir Walter Raleigh drawled, "We've all been waiting for *you* to come out of mourning." Anne's mouth fell open, and chuckles broke out from the cluster of men surrounding her.

That cluster was growing in size and increasing in volume.

"Lady Wynters, would you do me the honor—"

"May I have the pleasure—"

"I would particularly like to request the supper dance—"

Anne quickly surrendered her dance card. She recognized most of the gentlemen in spite of their masks, but not all, and it seemed simpler to let them write their own names.

After penciling in his name, Nathaniel Bartindale smiled. "Just one dance left," he said, holding the dance card aloft.

A half-dozen arms shot out at once, and three men managed to take hold of it.

Augustus Mapplethorpe gave it a sharp pull. "Come on, you two, give it here."

"No, you give it here," William Davison retorted.

"Let go, the both of you," grunted Baron Gladstone, who was dressed as Julius Caesar.

Gracious, this was the strangest night of her life! None of

these men had ever shown her the slightest interest before. But now they were scrapping after her dance card like a pack of starving dogs. Anne took a hasty step back as Mr. Davison's elbow came within inches of grazing her ribs.

And then, at the top of the stairs, she saw him.

He was difficult to miss, towering as he did over every other person in the room. His black hair had the windswept look that was so popular, a wave falling artfully across his forehead. She could see little of his face, as he wore one of the plain black masks their hosts had been handing out to those who needed one. But she felt a strange certainty that underneath that mask, he would be handsome; surely only an exceptionally handsome man could carry himself with such confidence. She knew that if her sister Caro had seen him, she would have huffed, because he was wearing *boots and buckskin trousers*, which were fine for riding, but completely inappropriate at a ball. And just as horrifying, even Anne could tell that his coat was several years out of fashion. But gad! That coat looked marvelous on him.

Goodness, Anne never had such thoughts about men. She valued character over appearances. The most important qualities she required in her future husband were that he be kind, meticulously respectable, and supportive of her charity work.

But it was just so hard not to notice a man's appearance when he had shoulders that were so broad and so... firm. His stomach had none of the paunch most gentlemen had, it was as flat as a board. And those trousers...

Those trousers fit him to *perfection*.

Oh, gracious, he was headed right this way! Had he noticed her gaping at him? At his *trousers*? Oh, how mortifying, whatever was she going to do?

Anne had been so distracted by the handsome stranger, she had scarcely been paying attention to her more immediate surroundings, and she saw that the struggle for her dance card raged on. Lord Gladstone jerked his arm suddenly to the right, and Mr. Davison lost his grip. He gave a yelp of surprise and began to topple backwards.

Unfortunately, Anne was standing in exactly the wrong place; Mr. Davison was going to crash into her. She closed her eyes and braced herself for the impact...

... only to feel herself *swept off her feet*, high into the air.

There was a firm arm behind her shoulders and another under her knees, and she felt her right side pressing against a rock-hard chest. She was suddenly enveloped in the scents of smoky cedarwood and leather, and... something strangely familiar she couldn't quite place. Just as quickly as he had picked her up, her rescuer swung her around and set her down. Off-balance, she grabbed his arms. They felt like a pair of tree trunks, they were so thick and firm. She jerked her hands away as if she'd been burned, and promptly swayed backwards. He grabbed her around her ribcage, steadying her, and not only were his hands deliciously warm, they were so big they almost encircled her waist.

Anne squeezed her eyes open and found herself staring directly into a cravat.

There was only one gentleman in attendance who was tall enough that Anne would be at eye level with his cravat. She glanced down, and the buckskin trousers confirmed it. *Oh, God.* It had to be the beautiful, dark-haired man she had been gaping at moments ago.

Heat rose to her cheeks. His hands were still wrapped around her waist. Up close, she saw that he was even more ridiculously gorgeous than she had imagined from across the ballroom. At least, from the neck down he was—she wasn't at an angle to make out much of his face, to say nothing of the fact that he was wearing a mask. But if a better-proportioned man existed in all of Christendom, she had yet to see him.

She suddenly thought of a sketch she had seen of a statue of Hercules. It was really just a headless torso reclining on a pedestal, a barrel chest and rippling stomach covered with ridge upon ridge of thick, bulging muscles, with the barest scrap of linen draped across his hips.

Hercules, that would be the perfect costume for this man.

Anne would quite like to see him in that loincloth.

Oh, gracious heavens—where had *that* thought come from?

A rich baritone rumbled above her head. "Have a care, Davison. You almost injured her."

To his credit, Mr. Davison did look horrified. "My deepest apologies, Lady Wynters. I hope you won't hold it against me, as I was dearly hoping to lead you out—"

"She's not dancing with you," the deep voice snarled.

"But I—"

Her mystery man didn't say a word, but turned to glare at Mr. Davison, who recoiled under the man's ire as if it were a physical blow.

"I... I... of course not. Please accept my most abject apologies, Lady Wynters."

"Of course," she whispered.

The orchestra was starting to tune up. Tristan Bassingthwaighte, dressed as Shakespeare, stepped forward, a smug smile upon his face. "I believe the first dance is mine."

"You're mistaken, Bassingthwaighte," her rescuer growled. "She's dancing with me."

"Now see here," Mr. Bassingthwaighte protested, snatching her crumpled dance card from Lord Gladstone and holding it aloft. "Lady Wynters promised this dance to me. It is my dance, and if you take it, then I will—"

"Then you'll what?" Her rescuer leaned in, towering over Mr. Bassingthwaighte by almost a full foot. "Are you challenging me? Because if you are, I accept."

Mr. Bassingthwaighte had turned a peculiar shade of green. He glanced mournfully at Anne, then back toward the tall man. "My apologies, sir. Enjoy your dance."

"Believe me, I will. Come, Anne."

Anne? Had he just called her *Anne?* There wasn't a single man in London, save her own brothers, whom she had given leave to address her by her first name. She had never been more confused in her whole entire life!

Her partner took her hand and towed her toward the center of the ballroom. Everyone, absolutely everyone, was staring at them. And no wonder—she was wearing the most scandalous dress imaginable, she had almost incited a *duel*, and now she was being dragged across the ballroom by a perfect stranger, as if she were the spoils of war. She, the most respectable woman in all of London! Well, not anymore, clearly, but still.

She spied her two older brothers standing near the refreshment table and shot them a beseeching look. *Help*, she whispered. As expected, Harrington was laughing at her. Honestly, she hadn't expected any differently, Harrington thought everything was a joke. But to her surprise, her eldest brother, Edward, also ignored her entreaty. He was smiling broadly, his dimples flashing, and he raised his glass in salute.

That was strange because Edward was the most honorable man she knew. It was completely unlike him to stand by when any woman was in distress.

Oh, but there was her Mama. Surely she would save her. She shot her mother a desperate look, but the countess wore a smirk that rivaled Harrington's, and carried on fanning herself in smug satisfaction.

Well, there was no helping it, she was going to have to dance with the man. She took up her place in the set and forced herself to smile.

The music began. Their first turn was unremarkable, but

on their second, the man leaned down and whispered in her ear, "You look beautiful tonight, Anne."

She shivered, actually shivered, as his deep voice rumbled up and down her spine. Goodness, he had called her Anne— again! And she still had no idea who he even was. She felt certain they had never met before.

This man she would have remembered.

And yet clearly, he knew her. She peered up at him, baffled. The mask fit him poorly enough that she couldn't make out his eyes. But what she could see of his face was every bit as handsome as she had suspected it would be from across the ballroom. He had a strong jaw, freshly shaven but already showing a hint of a dark shadow. His ears stuck out a bit, but somehow it suited him, balancing out the broadness of his shoulders.

He also had the most perfectly shaped lips she had ever seen.

W*hy* did she keep thinking these things, about… lips and loincloths? What was *wrong* with her?

As they circled each other a third time, the deep voice returned to her ear. "Let's go somewhere where we can talk."

"Talk?" she sputtered.

He was already leading her toward the open balcony doors. If there had been any doubt that everyone was staring at her before, they certainly were now! What on earth were they going to talk about? She didn't even know the man. Oh, this was a disaster, of the most epic proportions.

He led her out onto the deserted balcony. Anne managed to extricate her hand and took up a place at the balustrade overlooking the garden.

She cast about for a topic. "It's chilly tonight, isn't it?"

"Funny," the deep voice replied, "I feel positively warm."

What on earth did *that* mean? She was trying to think of a response when the man took her by the shoulders and turned her to face him. "Anne," he said, laughing, "you don't recognize me."

It was true, but she could hardly admit as much. "Of course I... erm... that is to say..."

"I know it's been four years, but I didn't think you would have forgotten me entirely," he said, reaching up to unhook his mask.

Anne froze, her heart suddenly pounding. Four years? There was someone she hadn't seen in four years. Someone she had missed every single day, so much it *hurt*. But it couldn't be...

The mask came off, and she found her gaze riveted to his eyes. Even in the dim torchlight of the balcony, she could see they were a deep, emerald green.

There was only one man in the world who had eyes that green.

"Michael!" she gasped, and without thinking, she threw her arms around his neck.

CHAPTER 2

*A*nne had sometimes wondered how she would feel when this moment finally came, the moment she saw Michael again. She had honestly never been sure. There were times when she had missed him so much, she would have given anything to have him with her, even for just an hour.

But then there were times when she had cried herself to sleep, wondering why her one-time best friend, the boy who used to write her twice a week from school without fail, wouldn't answer any of her letters.

There were moments when she thought of Michael warmly, as her dearest friend. But if she was being honest, there were also moments when she felt hurt. Confused.

Even angry.

And so she had never been sure what her reaction would be. But now that he was here...

She was glad to see him. *So* glad.

It was such a relief to find that she felt that way.

Michael embraced her warmly. When Anne drew back,

they were both smiling, even if she had tears in her eyes. He reached up and carefully removed her mask.

Standing mere inches from him as he unfastened the ties, Anne felt shy. Her first instinct had been correct: without the mask, Michael was everything that was tall, dark, and handsome.

Sometime in the past four years, the little boy she'd grown up with had turned into this magnificent specimen of the male species. It was going to take some... getting used to, that was all.

She took a hasty step back once he finished with her mask. "It's so good to see you."

"It's wonderful to see you, too." He gave her a look. "And I'm relieved to see you still remember who I am."

Anne laughed. "I can't believe I didn't recognize you! In my defense, you were wearing a mask. And you must know, Michael, how much you've changed in the last four years. Why, you must be a full foot taller than you were when last I saw you."

"Not quite. Only eight inches. I now stand six feet, five inches."

"Well, you look marvelous." Anne's voice broke on the last word, and tears formed in her eyes anew. "I'm so sorry, I..." She looked away, unable to continue.

Suddenly she was in his arms again. She found herself flush against a warm, solid expanse of chest. Those tree trunk-thick arms enveloped her completely, and it felt *wonderful*. She could feel his breath in her hair and the slight scrape of his jaw when it brushed her forehead.

Her breath was shaky, and her heart was racing like a hummingbird's wings. Which was ridiculous! This was... this was nothing. It wasn't as though Michael *meant* anything by it. Why, this was just like all the times she'd hugged him right before he left for school, the exact same hug she had given her brothers.

This felt distinctly unlike hugging her brother.

"It's all right," he murmured into her hair.

"I just..." She swallowed, squeezing her eyes shut. "I missed you so much, Michael."

His voice was rough when he replied, "I know, Anne. Believe me, I know."

They remained there for a moment before it dawned on Anne that anyone might come out onto the balcony and discover them in what appeared to be a compromising position. Not that it was, of course! Michael wasn't interested in her in that way.

Her face fell a trifle as she recalled the day she had learned that with absolute certainty.

Anne stepped back. "Look at me, crying when I'm happy." She dabbed at her tears with the back of her glove. "Tell me all about Canada."

"Canada is..." The corners of his lips turned up and his green eyes sparkled. "Do you remember how when we were younger, you and I could always dream up the best adventures?"

"Of course, I remember. Pirates and sea monsters. Knights and dragons and damsels in distress."

"I don't recall you ever having been in distress."

She strove to make her voice light. "I was referring, of course, to Caro. And occasionally to Harrington."

He laughed, a full-throated sound that made her heart squeeze, she hadn't heard it in so long. "Indeed! And that's what Canada is like. I had adventures there. Real adventures." He paused, and when he looked at her again, his eyes were very... intense. "When I was there," he said carefully, "I felt like I had *almost* everything I've ever wanted."

Her cheeks flushed. This is Michael, you dolt, she reminded herself. He didn't mean that the way it sounded.

And yet, the look in his eyes when he said it... Anne and Michael were so close growing up, they'd joked that they could read each other's faces. Her siblings even had a rule that they weren't allowed to be partners in whist, because he would take one look at her face and throw down a trump card, able to intuit when she couldn't pick up the trick. Sometimes Anne felt like she could glean more from the quirk of Michael's eyebrow than she could from an hour of someone else's conversation.

And the way he was looking at her right now... Why, if Anne didn't know better, she would have said his expression was... ardent.

She shook herself. That was the crux of it, she *did* know better. "I look forward to hearing about every one of those adventures." She forced a bright smile.

But she found she couldn't hold it.

"Michael," she said, dropping the mask of false cheerfulness, "what happened?"

IT FELT UNREAL TO MICHAEL, after four years of struggling to accept that Anne would never be his, to be standing on the balcony of this fancy London town house, different in every way to the square log cabin he had inhabited out on the Canadian frontier, with Anne standing close enough to touch.

He was so glad her mask was off and he could finally see her. She looked much the same as he remembered—perhaps a touch paler than she'd been four years ago and missing the spray of freckles that typically appeared across her nose in the summertime, which made him wonder if she spent too much of her time stuck indoors. Her figure had ripened a bit since last he saw her, and although she couldn't be described as anything but slender, she'd lost the slightly coltish quality she'd once had. Michael didn't much mind either way—he'd thought she looked perfect before, and she looked every bit as perfect now.

Those were the only changes he could detect. She wore her warm brown hair the same way, piled atop her head, highlighting her long, elegant neck. As for her eyes... Michael knew Anne wished she had blue eyes like her sisters, but he'd never understood it. He could stare into Anne's big, rich, gorgeous brown eyes for days.

He drew in a breath, and there it was: a hint of strawberries. She had always smelled like strawberries; he happened to know it was from the hand cream she used. He'd caught the scent the second he swept her into his arms, and his knees had gone slightly weak, so much did that sweet, familiar scent remind him of her.

He felt the way you did after a bad chest cold, the kind where no matter how desperately you gasped and struggled, you could never get a satisfying lungful of air.

Seeing Anne again... it was as though he had drawn his first full breath in four years.

He found his gaze drifting to her lips. Anne's lips were naturally rose-pink, and they were full and wide enough that when she smiled, that smile had a way of taking over her whole face. No one could smile at you like Anne Astley. When she did, it all but knocked him flat.

Notably, she was not smiling at him at the moment. And he couldn't say that he blamed her.

He cleared his throat, recalling that she had asked him a question. "I'm so glad I can finally tell you. I've been wanting to explain everything for so long. Although—" he broke off, inclining his head toward the crowded ballroom "—perhaps not right here."

Anne nodded. "I understand. Your father told me... well, nothing detailed. But he implied that you were on some sort of mission for the Crown."

"I was. Although the details shouldn't get out, at this point, there's no reason I might not confide in you. And I will, Anne. I swear, I'll tell you everything, just as soon as we're somewhere we won't be overheard."

"It's not so much that. I mean..." A guilty look crossed her face. "Of course, I want to hear about it. But it's more..." She looked down, and he watched her steel herself. "Did you receive my letters?"

He had known this was coming, too. How could it not? They had corresponded regularly for all the years he was away at school, first at Eton and then at Oxford. It must've been jarring when he stopped writing altogether.

The problem was that it was impossible to write a coherent reply when one hadn't read the recipient's original missive. After Michael had completed the task that brought him to Canada, he'd made his way to his father's farm near Lake Simcoe. There he'd found a small mountain of correspondence waiting for him. He could remember searching through the pile for Anne's hand and struggling to open her letter with fingers that shook, his heart in his throat at the prospect of reading her answer to his proposal.

But it contained no answer, no mention of his proposal at all. It was as though she'd never received his letter. And what was more, it contained such unexpected, horrific news that he fell to his knees when he read it: she had married someone else.

He hadn't opened any of her letters after that. He couldn't bear to. If they had contained one word of her happiness with another man, it would have gutted him.

Anne was waiting for him to respond. He decided to tell her the truth.

At least, some of it.

"I did receive them," he said.

It was physically painful to see the heartbreak steal over her face. She swallowed. "Then may I ask why you didn't reply?"

Michael froze, scrambling for a response.

After a moment, Anne continued, "I wondered if it was something I'd done, if you were mad at me, or—"

"I'm not mad at you," Michael said. That at least was true.

To be sure, there had been moments when he had been furious, not with her but with himself (*why* had he let her go to London without declaring himself first? How could he have been so stupid as to assume she knew?) He had also been mad at fate, which had seen fit to separate them at the worst possible moment, when Anne was making her debut upon the Marriage Mart.

But as he worked his way through the rest of his mail, it became clear that something had gone terribly wrong. That Anne had somehow never received his letter. That her parents had formed the impression that she had refused him and had therefore given their consent when she announced her wish to accept this Lord Wynters.

And by the time they realized she had never received his proposal it had been too late.

However miserable he had been, he'd always known deep down that it wasn't Anne's fault.

She was awaiting his answer. He studied her face, hating to see sadness in her eyes. "I hurt you. I mean—of course I did. How could it not have hurt?" He took both of her hands in his. "I am sorry for it, Anne. Because hurting you is the last thing I would ever want to do. There's a reason I didn't write back. That I couldn't. And I'll explain everything, I promise

31

you." He made a sound of frustration. "Just as soon as we're not surrounded by four hundred people."

She peered up at him for a moment, and Michael could scarcely breathe, so anxious was he for her reaction. Then he saw her brow slowly unknot, her shoulders relax, and he felt her squeeze his hands. "Thank you for that," she said. "I'm sure once you've had a chance to explain, it will all make sense."

It was such a relief to see the sorrow gone from her face. "So," he said, eager to redirect the conversation, "I've been travelling for the past three months. How are you?"

"I'm doing well, just focusing on the Ladies' Society, as always." A smile stole over her face. "The most wonderful thing happened recently. It's a long story, but I came into possession of this little bejeweled box that turned out to be an ancient Egyptian artifact. It sold at auction last month and fetched enough that the Ladies' Society will be able to double in size."

"That's marvelous. An Egyptian artifact—how on earth did you come by that?"

Anne's eyes went wide as guineas. "Oh dear, you probably haven't heard. My husband died a year ago."

Oh, he had heard, all right. "I'm so sorry," he said, which wasn't even a little bit true, but seemed like the correct thing to say.

"He won it at a hand of cards just before he passed away." She pressed a hand to her heart. "I hope I didn't imply I was glad my husband died!"

Michael for one wouldn't have minded. "Not at all." He cleared his throat. "So… you're a widow now?"

She tilted her head. "Well, of course. What else would I be?"

"Indeed, I was just wondering if you had perhaps remarried already, or were promised to someone else," Michael said, the words spilling out in a rush. This was his greatest fear. As soon as Wynters had died, everyone he knew had immediately written to him with the news.

His friends had been so prompt that their letters had all gone out on the same ship.

And that sack of letters had gone astray, moldering in some godforsaken corner for six months, so that he only received them twelve weeks ago. His father's more recent missives, asking what the hell was taking him so long, had suddenly made sense.

He'd rushed back as quickly as he could, feeling sick with worry that Anne would accept another man's suit before he got there. He peered at her, his heart in his throat. "Are you?"

"I am not. I only just left off full mourning."

"And are you planning to remarry?" Michael asked, striving to make his tone conversational.

"I am. You know I've always wanted a large family. And I didn't have any children. With Lord Wynters." She flushed, turning to rest her hands on the balustrade and gaze out over the gardens.

Michael took up a position next to her. "I see. Well, are there any leading contenders?"

"None so far. I've only just started my search. It's actually the reason I'm here tonight—to look for a husband."

Suddenly Michael felt better than he had in… about four years. "And you've found him," he muttered under his breath.

Apparently he hadn't spoken as quietly as he'd intended, because Anne's head whipped around and her mouth fell open. "What was that, Michael?"

"Er, nothing." Although, judging by the pack of men scrapping after Anne's dance card, the sooner he declared himself, the better. He couldn't risk waiting too long.

Again.

"Actually, Anne, the truth is…" He swallowed. *This was it.*

He took her hand in both of his, gathering his courage. "The reason I came back—"

"I say, Morsley," came the familiar voice of Anne's brother Harrington, "just how long were you planning to monopolize our sister?"

Michael gave the Astley brothers, who emerged from the ballroom, a look of incredulous annoyance. "A bit longer, as it happens."

"What's this scowl?" returned Harrington. "Is that any way to greet an old friend?"

"I would rather speak with your sister," Michael said pointedly.

"She is, after all, so much better looking than I am," Harrington replied.

"Better smelling, too," Michael muttered.

"Now, don't be silly, Harrington," Anne said. "Michael and I have catching up to do. You know we've always been best friends."

Harrington rolled his eyes. "Oh, yes, best friends. I have a best friend, too, yet I cannot recall the last time I scooped Thetford into my arms and—"

Without even looking at him, Fauconbridge reached out and cuffed his younger brother upside the back of the head. "Harrington. Behave," he intoned.

Harrington sighed. "It will go against form, but just this once, I suppose I could give it a try."

"Glad as I am to see you both," Michael said, giving them a glower that said he wasn't glad at all, "is there any particular reason you have interrupted my time catching up with your better-looking, better-smelling sister?"

"Indeed, there is," Fauconbridge replied. "As you may have noticed, Anne has caused quite a sensation this evening. The first dance is almost over, and Gladstone has the second. He has already vowed that, unlike Bassingthwaighte, he will call you out if you take his dance."

Michael was already turning back to Anne. "Fine. Let him call me out. Now, if you two will excuse us—"

"Michael! No!" Anne exclaimed. "I won't have you taking such a risk."

He rolled his eyes. "Oh, please, Anne. I was at school with Gladstone. He's the worst shot in the world. He probably doesn't even know which end of the gun to load."

She took his arm and began tugging him back toward the ballroom. "All the more reason not to duel with him. He's like to kill you by mistake while attempting to *delope*."

"I'm willing to take the chance," Michael grumbled, digging in his heels and pulling her to a halt just shy of the ballroom.

She turned to face him. "Well, I'm not. There will be no taking of unnecessary chances. Not when I've just gotten you back after such a very long time."

Her voice was tremulous with sincerity, which managed to penetrate his annoyance. "I suppose I can accept that."

"Morsley!" Fauconbridge called from inside. "Are you coming?"

"I suppose I should be calling you Lord Morsley, too," Anne mused, "at least when someone's around to hear." The rest of the Astley brood called him by his courtesy title, but he and Anne had always used each other's first names, as far back as he could remember.

"Don't you dare," he whispered. He still had her mask, and now he lifted it to her face, gently fastening the cord behind her head. He purposely swept his fingers along her hairline as he finished, framing her face. "Perfect," he said softly. He felt her shiver, which was immensely satisfying. "I take it your dance card is full for the rest of the evening?"

"I'm afraid so."

"I feared as much. So, when can I see you again? For more than two minutes between dances?"

"Tomorrow. I join Edward and Harrington for shooting practice once a week. You'll come, won't you?"

"I'd like nothing better."

"Meet me at my house at nine o'clock." Anne wrote the address on the cover of her dance card, then ripped it off and handed it to him.

"Nine o'clock. Perfect."

Anne left then to fulfil her promised dances. As anticipated, he found few chances to speak with her, and never for more than a minute or two.

But that didn't matter. Tomorrow he would find a way to shake off her brothers so they could be alone.

Tomorrow, at long last, he would propose.

CHAPTER 3

*E*xcept the next morning, Michael didn't go shooting with Anne. Just as Anne was preparing to leave, she received a note from Michael—apparently Lord Hobart had gotten wind of his return and requested that he present himself at Horse Guards to provide an update about the current situation on the Canadian frontier.

Anne sighed as she strode into her front parlor. She usually found its yellow silk wall hangings so cheerful, but today they failed to ease her disappointment. She took a seat at the rosewood writing desk and pulled out a sheet of foolscap to pen a quick reply. Michael could hardly refuse the Secretary of State for War and the Colonies. But this was the only free moment she had today, and she'd been hoping to spend it with him.

She was just putting the finishing touches on a note suggesting they go for a drive tomorrow when one of her footmen, Hugh, appeared in the doorway. "Mr. Samuel Branton," he announced.

Anne smiled as one of her closest friends came into the room. Samuel Branton was a barrister—her barrister, as it happened—and a fixture in London's charitable reform movement. Samuel was born in Jamaica but had lived in Britain for more than a decade. He was five years older than Anne and a bit taller, with warm brown skin and tightly coiled black hair he wore cropped short to facilitate the barrister's wig he wore when arguing before court. As always, Samuel was impeccably turned out, wearing a burgundy silk waistcoat beneath a perfectly tailored coat of charcoal grey.

"Thank you for coming," Anne said, rising from her desk. "Let me ring for some tea."

Samuel held a hand up. "Thank you, but no. As it is Wednesday, I know your brothers will be by to collect you any minute, so you can enjoy your one and only hour of leisure for the week."

Anne wrinkled her nose. "That's rich, coming from you. If you've ever taken the afternoon off, I'll eat my bonnet."

"Then I suggest you dress it in an oyster sauce, because I did so as recently as seventeen ninety-four," Samuel joked, settling into the Chippendale chair before Anne's desk. "If the crime lords of St. Giles don't take a day off, then neither do I. So, what's this news you mentioned in your note? I'm especially curious given your exploits yesterday morning. Does it have anything to do with—"

"Climbing boys," Anne said, finishing Samuel's sentence for him. Samuel's passion was the welfare of children, and one of his main initiatives involved the working conditions of climbing boys, sometimes called sweeps' apprentices. Samuel was both lobbying to strengthen the Chimney Sweepers Act and pushing for better enforcement of the paltry laws already on the books.

"I knew it," he breathed. "Tell me everything."

Anne proceeded to do just that. "I fear I raged at him,

right in front of a crowd of two hundred. They've even turned it into a cartoon."

"I saw it this morning. You were truly an avenging angel."

Anne shook her head. "I worry it will scare off donors to the Ladies' Society. How I wish I had bitten my tongue."

"You did the right thing, so hold your chin up."

Anne gave him a tight smile. "I learned several things of note. I ended up removing two climbing boys from their former master. Nick and Johnny are their names. Johnny was the one stuck in the flue, and Nick... how I wish you could have seen dear Nick exerting himself, doing everything possible to facilitate Johnny's rescue. When the building owner insisted there was no point in opening up the wall because Johnny was probably dead already, it was Nick who scrambled up that dangerously narrow chimney and confirmed he was still breathing. Then he climbed the gutter pipe like a squirrel to show the mason where to dig and scurried around the roof, stacking the loose bricks out of the way so the mason could work more quickly. Well, I wasn't about to leave any child in such a deplorable situation, and especially not after that. But the master sweep kicked up quite a fuss about me taking Nick, as apparently he's quite good at what he does." Anne picked at the sleeve of her riding habit. "I fear I shouted at him, too. He was trying to drag Nick away, but fortunately I had the crowd behind me—"

"I should say so," Samuel said, looking amused.

Anne cleared her throat. "Neither boy knows their precise age, but Johnny could not be older than five, and Nick looks to be about eight. Given that Nick told me he passed four Christmases with his master sweep, Mr. Smithers..."

"They both started when they were underaged," Samuel said.

"Precisely." The Chimney Sweepers Act did not offer

nearly sufficient protections, but it did mandate that climbing boys be at least eight years old.

"So where did this Smithers fellow get not one but two underaged boys?"

"I asked him precisely that. I asked what workhouse apprenticed out a boy so young. His face turned scarlet, and he said it was none of my affair. But then he said something revealing."

Samuel leaned forward. "Do tell."

"As I was taking Johnny and Nick away, Smithers offered a parting shot. He said it didn't matter because he would have two new boys *from his lordship* by that afternoon."

"From *his lordship*?" Samuel asked. "You're certain that's what he said?"

"Absolutely certain. I asked him what he meant by *his lordship*, and a look of panic crossed his face. He rushed off after that, but I thought you should know."

Samuel steepled his fingers, lost in thought. "It could be a nickname. This person might not actually be a lord."

"It could," Anne agreed. "But whoever he is, it sounds as if he funnels a steady stream of underaged boys to the master sweeps of London."

"It certainly does." Samuel shook his head. "What could Nick and Johnny tell you?"

"I haven't interviewed them yet. They both had quite the ordeal yesterday, and I wanted to give them a chance to get settled."

"They're staying at your lodging house?"

"Yes." The Ladies' Society's primary initiative was running a lodging house that provided two hundred women and children with a safe place to live for a price that didn't constitute extortion. Most of Anne's residents were widows with children and now and again she could find someone willing to take in an orphaned child. There was a particular resident Anne had immediately thought of, a widow named Mrs. Briggs, who had raised five boys of her own and liked nothing better than having a whole pack of them underfoot. As Anne had hoped, Mrs. Briggs had been delighted to look after Nick and Johnny.

"If they feel up to it," Anne continued, "I'll speak to them today."

Samuel rubbed at his forehead. "Those poor boys. How are they faring? Did Johnny suffer any permanent injuries or—"

"He seems to be recovering remarkably well," Anne hastened to reassure him. "I sent for a physician and, although it's early, he could find no signs of lasting damage."

Samuel sagged back in his chair. "Thank God. Whenever I see something like this, I always wonder if that's what happened to Robbie, and—" He broke off, running a hand over his face.

Robbie was Samuel's little brother. Their father was a physician, and Samuel had been sent to Britain at the age of fourteen to complete his education just as his father had gone to Edinburgh years before to obtain his medical degree. Samuel was nineteen years old and training at the Inns of Court when he received word that his parents had both been killed in a carriage accident. He set sail for Jamaica to retrieve his little brother, Robbie, who'd been eight years old at the time. But when he arrived, he found that an unscrupulous cousin had seized his father's property and packed his brother off to England to work as someone's servant.

Samuel immediately turned around and sailed back to London. But he had never been able to find out what became of Robbie.

Not that he had ever given up his search. But that had been eight years ago, and at this point, finding his little brother would take nothing short of a miracle.

This was why she and Samuel were such kindred spirits. Samuel would never stop fighting against dangerous working conditions for children. Never. He had taken his sorrow at being unable to rescue his brother and channeled it into saving other children from lives of exploitation and misery. To Samuel, it wasn't just a cause. It was *personal.*

Just as Anne's cause was personal to her. She swallowed, thinking of her childhood nursemaid, Bridget, and the incident in which Anne had learned just how fragile a woman's place in the world truly was…

"Has there been any news?" Anne asked. "Did anything come of that possible lead in Manchester?"

"It wasn't him," Samuel said. "Believe me, you'll be the first to know when I find him."

"I'm sorry," Anne said quietly.

"As am I." Samuel cleared his throat. "Well, I'm going to head over to Bow Street. I'll tell all of this to my contact, Mr. Charles Hoskins. He's one of the good ones."

Anne knew precisely what Samuel meant by that. Unfortunately, it was all too common for constables and even magistrates to be in the pocket of the criminals they were charged with policing, and even the Bow Street Runners were not entirely immune. You had to be careful to whom you reported a crime. "And I will speak to Nick and Johnny."

"Perfect." Samuel stood, and Anne rose to accompany him to the door.

They encountered her brothers in the foyer. "Mr. Branton," Edward said, offering Samuel his hand. "Will you be joining us this morning?"

"I wish I could, but I'm due at court."

"Another time, I hope." Edward glanced around. "Where's Morsley? I thought he'd be here first thing."

"Alas," Anne said, "Michael had to send his regrets. He's

been summoned to Horse Guards to give an update on the situation in Canada."

"Wait—Morsley?" Samuel said. He turned to Edward and Harrington. "As in, *the* Lord Morsley?"

Harrington wagged his eyebrows. "The very one."

Anne cocked her head. "I didn't realize you knew Michael."

"Oh, er…" Samuel tugged a glove on. "Only through what you've told me. He's your childhood friend, correct?"

Anne smiled. "What a memory you have—I know it's been years since I mentioned him to you."

"Yes, I, uh—" Samuel nodded as he accepted his hat from Hugh. "Well, I must be going. The Admiralty Court waits for no man."

"Of course. I'll let you know what I learn from Nick and Johnny."

Samuel bowed over her hand. "Thank you, my lady."

$\mathcal{A}$cross town, Michael exited Horse Guards and was immediately enveloped in the stench of the Thames. His visit with Lord Hobart had taken only a quarter of an hour. Given how fraught the situation with France remained, Michael understood that the Secretary of State for War and the Colonies had more pressing concerns than the Canadian frontier. Still, it was hard not to feel annoyed, given that his morning with Anne had been dashed for something so brief.

At least he'd received one piece of good news, something he'd been hoping might come to pass: Lord Hobart had confirmed that Michael was to begin training to one day assume the post of Governor General of Canada.

Michael set off for home on foot, glad for the chance to stretch his legs after weeks cooped up on a ship. Those weeks in a cramped cabin had been particularly torturous because Michael had never been any good at sitting still. This had made his school years a challenge at best. Michael was a dutiful son, and he'd tried to acquit himself well in the class-room, but although he knew he wasn't stupid, he just wasn't bookish. To make matters worse, he had little facility for languages, making Eton's curriculum of unrelenting Latin and Greek a daily misery. Michael thought best when he was moving around, preferably out of doors.

The army would have been a tempting path, had his father not absolutely forbidden it. When Michael was nine, his mother had died in childbirth, along with the little girl she'd been struggling to bring into the world. Losing his wife had been a crushing blow for the marquess, and Michael could understand why his father was loathe to let his only remaining family member take such a risk. But his father's edict had left Michael floundering, dreading the future looming before him of being stuck inside the library all day, poring over endless ledgers.

But then he'd been sent to Canada, and it had been a breath of fresh air (literally, Michael thought, shooing a fly as he stepped around a pile of rotting garbage). In Upper Canada every day was an adventure, and the things he was required to do happened to be precisely the things he enjoyed: riding, shooting, and building. The fact that he was heir to a marquessate was actually a strike against him, as his neighbors had assumed he would be soft. But he was able to win their respect the same way every man won respect out on the frontier—by the sweat of his brow. In Canada, no one cared that he hadn't memorized the complete works of Aristophanes. A man was judged by how hard he worked and how well he cleared the land, and Michael thrived on that physical labor.

What was more, out on the frontier, Michael's three terms at Oxford had been sufficient to make him a man of letters. He'd been asked to join the Legislative Council of Upper Canada at the age of nineteen. Then the army had written asking for his help—could he find them a supply of walnut wood, which was desperately needed to make stocks for guns? Michael could, and he did. A request followed from the Royal Navy, Upper Canada being the ideal location from which to secure the hundred-foot poles they needed for ships' masts.

Michael might not be bookish, but here was a task suited to his qualities. Whereas ninety-nine men out of a hundred would've pulled out their pen to explain to the Royal Navy that getting mast poles out of the Upper Canadian wilderness was impossible because you would have to recut the entire road to move something that long, Michael had pulled out his axe. He'd hired a crew of ten men and had joined them in the grueling work of straightening the road. It had taken the better part of spring and summer to get those poles out of the woods and to wrestle them downriver, but it had been worth it. The boy who'd once been dismissed by his teachers as a bit slow was suddenly regarded as a man of ability, the one who got things done. Michael found he liked that quite a lot.

Then had come the commission from the Crown itself.

Michael was proud of what he had done. Three years earlier there had been a horrific famine in Britain. When the Crown asked Michael to buy up as much Canadian wheat as he could and have it shipped back home, he had spent three exhausting months canvassing the countryside, doing nothing else. As bad as the famine had been, he knew it wasn't boasting to say that it would have been ten times worse were it not for his efforts. He had done something important. He had made a difference. He had—

Michael's reverie was broken by a trio of young Corinthians, staggering home still in their evening dress and smelling like a distillery. One of them lurched into Michael's path, forcing him to leap out of the way. He narrowly missed stepping in a pile of pig excrement lying right in the middle of the pavement.

God, how he hated London. Why on earth would anyone

want to live here? It was bad enough that it was noisy, crowded, and stinking. But the worst part, he thought, glaring after the three drunkards, was the triviality of it all. Michael enjoyed a night out with his friends as much as any young man. But for most men of his age and rank, that was *all* their lives amounted to, an endless round from the tailor —a waste of time and money, as far as Michael was concerned—to the club to some seedy gaming hell.

In Canada, Michael had felt such a sense of purpose. He could still recall his heart swelling in his chest as he watched that first ship sail away with a load of hundred-foot masts, knowing that the Royal Navy was going to be able to repair their fleet because of him.

He had received a letter of thanks from Lord Nelson himself. How could he go from *that* to the useless life of a young London buck?

He couldn't.

And he wasn't going to.

He was going back to Canada just as soon as he could, the only place on the face of this earth where he could acquit himself admirably with the skills that he had. He was going to do something important with his life. He was going to be Governor General.

He was going to make his father proud.

Everything was going to be perfect. Because this time when he sailed for Canada, he would have Anne with him.

As his wife.

Michael nodded to the butler as he entered Cranfield House, his family's London residence on Hanover Square. "Good morning, Hoyle. Did any messages come for me while I was out?"

"Yes, my lord," Hoyle said, presenting two letters on a silver tray, "one from Lady Wynters and another from Lord Fauconbridge."

There was no question which one he was going to read first, but his shoulders slumped as he scanned Anne's brief missive. He'd hoped that the morning's shooting would be a prelude to them spending the rest of the day together, but Anne wrote that she was busy with her charity work all day and all evening.

She did suggest they go for a drive tomorrow afternoon, so at least he had that to look forward to.

Fauconbridge's letter was a suggestion that, as he was suddenly free, he pay a visit to the tailor.

Michael groaned. He knew he needed to go. Last night no less than seven people had hinted with a remarkable lack of subtlety that his jacket did not pass muster. He had no wish to embarrass Anne on their wedding day, so he knew he'd have to do it sooner or later.

Still, visiting the tailor on his first full day in London... it felt like an ill omen.

He sighed. "Hoyle, let me have my hat again. It would appear I'm going back out."

CHAPTER 5

"*Y*ou're in fine form today, Anne."

Anne smiled at Edward as she took up the powder horn and began to reload her flintlock pistol. They were just outside of town at the home of Anne's friend, Mrs. Wriothesley, who served as the Ladies' Society's treasurer. Mrs. Wriothesley had issued an open invitation for Anne and her brothers to make use of their shooting range, and they had gotten into the habit of practicing together each Wednesday morning.

"Thank you," Anne replied.

"Not bad," Harrington allowed.

"Not bad?" Edward said. "She's hit every target. What more would you have her do?"

"Sure, she's hit every target," Harrington agreed. "But the real test is not whether you can hit a painted bull's-eye. The real test is whether you can make the shot when everything is on the line."

Anne groaned. "Not this again."

"Yes," Harrington said. "This. Again."

"Do we have to do it this week?" Anne asked as she

rammed the ball into place, perhaps a bit more forcefully than was strictly necessary.

"We will do it this week, and the week after, and the week after that, until you get it," Harrington replied.

"I wish Michael were here," she grumbled.

"Believe me, so does Michael," Harrington returned. "Although it wouldn't help you get out of my exercise, because he would agree with me."

"You think so, do you?"

"I do. If Morsley didn't know that being able to make a shot under pressure can mean the difference between life and death before, he certainly found out after getting charged by that bear." Harrington gave a low whistle. "I'm almost jealous it wasn't me. What a chance to test yourself!"

Anne snapped the ramrod back into place, even more annoyed because her brothers had heard this story while she had not. For all that Michael was supposed to be her best friend, it was Edward and Harrington who'd gotten to spend half the night catching up with him, while she was stuck dancing with Augustus Mapplethorpe, whose breath smelled of pickled cod.

"Go on, then," Harrington said.

Deep down she knew her brother had the right of it. Harrington was by far the best shot in the family. Truth be told, Harrington was one of the finest shots in all of England, and Anne was grateful that he took the time to help her.

Usually.

"Fine," she said with a sigh, taking up her position before the target.

She settled into her shooting stance, and Harrington came to stand just behind her. "Close your eyes," he said. "Now, picture it—you're at your lodging house. And that new family, the one you were telling us about—where the husband used to beat his wife, and she only left him after he started hitting her daughter?"

"The Hoves," Anne said.

"The Hoves," Harrington said. "Imagine yourself there in the dining hall for the midday meal when who should show up but Mr. Hove. He's discovered where his wife and children have gone, and he's not the least bit happy about it."

Anne swallowed. The scenario was all too plausible.

"He has a knife," Harrington continued, "and he grabs his wife by the hair and jerks her to her feet. He presses the knife to her throat. You are just across the room with your pistol. You have a clean shot. You're the only one who can save her."

"My footmen—" Anne began.

"He would slit her throat before they could take two steps. You are the *only one* who can save her."

Anne's heart raced, and her hands were shaking.

"Picture her standing there, the knife at her throat," Harrington said relentlessly. "Picture the fear in her eyes, the desperation. Picture her looking at her children for what she believes will be the last time. *Picture it.* And take the shot!"

Anne opened her eyes. She checked her stance. She focused on the target...

... and she watched her shot fly a good foot and a half outside, and too high to boot.

She had missed.

As she always did.

Her shoulders sagged.

"Don't be so hard on yourself," Edward said.

"Be hard on yourself," Harrington said. "You do hard work, in hard neighborhoods, amongst hard men. You cannot afford to do otherwise."

Anne sighed. "I understand. "

"I would not hold you to such a high standard," Harrington continued, "if I wasn't confident you could do it.

Your form is perfect, Anne. You've always been an excellent shot. But something's happened in the last few years. You don't believe in yourself. If you can just—"

"What time is it?" Anne asked.

Edward consulted his pocket watch. "Half eleven."

"I must get back," Anne said.

They packed their weapons away and started toward the stables.

"You must be glad to have Morsley back," Edward said.

"Of course," Anne replied. "His return was a wonderful surprise."

"And his timing is... fortuitous," Edward added.

Anne peered up at him, brow furrowed. "Fortuitous? How so?"

"It's just that, well, you're looking for a husband, and he is unwed," Edward said. "You two get on so well together. Have you never considered that you might..."

Anne laughed. "Oh, no! That is to say, certainly Michael has every quality I would seek in a husband." She looked down. "But I know he doesn't think of me in that way."

She caught Edward and Harrington exchanging a look. Edward cleared his throat. "What makes you say that?"

"Oh," Anne said, feeling heat rising to her cheeks, "it's nothing."

There were a few beats of silence, then Harrington said, "It doesn't look like *nothing*."

Anne waved him off. "Just something he once said."

"And that would be?" Edward pressed.

Anne cringed. How could she describe that horrifically awkward encounter? She had never told anyone about it. But it appeared her brothers were not about to let it go. "It was the last day of summer," she began haltingly. "I remember you were heading off to Oxford, Harrington, so Michael and I would have been fifteen. We were having a picnic over by

Cranfield Castle, and… um… my bonnet started to blow away, and we both reached for it, and we somehow ended up in an… an awkward position."

The last part was a lie, but she could hardly tell them the truth—that she and Michael had been teasing each other, and for reasons Anne still could not understand to this day, she had reached out and started tickling him. And then he had started tickling her back, and they had started rolling around on the picnic blanket and somehow Michael had wound up *lying on top of her*.

No, clearly she couldn't tell her *brothers* that.

They reached the stables. A groom was already leading Anne's mare out, so she headed toward the mounting block.

Edward's brow was wrinkled. "So, you both reached for your bonnet. Did you bump heads or—"

"Yes!" Anne lied.

"And what happened next?" Edward asked.

It felt like her cheeks were on fire. "He apologized and made sure I understood that he had not meant for it to happen. That he was not interested in me in that way. And that he never would be," she added in a small voice.

She swallowed thickly, recalling her mortification. Looking back, she could not fathom what had possessed her to touch him in such an inappropriate manner. Of course, having grown up together, Anne had felt comfortable with Michael in a way she could never have imagined being with another boy. How many times had they boosted each other over a fence, or pulled each other into a tree? Gracious, after Michael's mother died when they were nine, he'd spent hours just lying there with his head in her lap. They had even tickled each other before, but it had been altogether different when they were both *seven*. At fifteen, she should've known better.

But it was the strangest thing—although tickling him was

entirely out of character for her, at the time it had felt so... natural. Even when they started rolling around, and he wound up on top of her, she... hadn't minded.

Be honest, Anne. You thought he was going to kiss you.

She'd even closed her eyes.

But instead of kissing her, Michael had scrambled off her. She could still picture him sitting on the blanket, knees to his chest, his back to her.

That was when he said it.

"I'm so sorry, Anne."

She pushed herself up to sitting. "It's all right, Michael."

"I did *not* mean for that to happen," he continued, still refusing to look at her.

"I—I see." She started to redo her braid, which had come undone in their tussle.

"I hope you know that I would *never*—"

She ducked her head. She could have sworn he was at least *thinking* about kissing her. "N—never?"

He slashed his hand for emphasis. "Absolutely never."

"Oh." Anne was glad he was facing the other way because her face felt like it might crumple.

"Not in a *million* years—"

Now she was just annoyed. "Thank you, Michael! I understand. There is no need to keep explaining."

He lumbered to his feet. "Excuse me," he said, stumbling into a nearby copse of trees.

He returned five minutes later, looking sheepish. Anne found it difficult to meet his eyes. He sat beside her on the blanket.

"Anne, I—I'm so sorry."

"You mentioned that," she muttered.

"You're not mad at me, are you?"

She sighed. She was embarrassed, and, if she was being honest, disappointed.

It was normal for a girl to feel excited about receiving her first kiss. That was probably all it was.

But it wasn't Michael's fault if he didn't want to kiss her.

She looked up at him and did her best to smile. "No, Michael. I'm not mad at you."

"Good." She could still recall his expression in the split second before he dropped his gaze to the blanket. His eyes, emerald-bright in the afternoon sun, held anxiety, relief, and... something else she had never been able to pinpoint. He added in a rush, "Because I hope you know that you mean everything to me."

She did know that.

They were best friends, after all.

"I do," she said. "And you mean everything to me, too."

They packed up the picnic, and Michael escorted Anne back home.

They never spoke of it again.

With time, Anne had come to see that Michael was right —they were friends. Nothing more than that. That moment on the blanket had been nothing but a passing midsummer madness. It didn't matter that Michael felt nothing for her beyond friendship, because that was precisely what she felt for him, too.

Of course it was.

When Michael returned for Christmas break, it had occurred to someone that they were no longer eight years old, and that Anne needed to be chaperoned. And so that horrible picnic was the last time they'd been alone together.

Which was fine. She certainly wasn't planning on tickling him again.

Anne blinked. Edward was speaking. "He said that?"

"He did," Anne said.

Edward held Anne's mare while she mounted, then they started toward the main road. "Did you ever consider,"

Edward said, "that he might have said something reflexively to diffuse an awkward situation, but perhaps he did not mean it?"

Anne glanced over her shoulder at her brother. Why wouldn't he let it go? "No. He was clear about it. Inescapably so."

"I understand," Edward said. "But sometimes a man will, uh, prevaricate. Perhaps he didn't know what to say and he…"

Anne turned in the saddle to look at him. "Am I truly having this conversation with my brothers?"

"It's a perfectly reasonable thing to ask," Edward said. He glared at Harrington. "Help me out, will you?"

"Oh, no. You're doing so well." Harrington chortled.

They had reached the turnpike. The day was beautiful, with a crisp blue sky dusted with puffy white clouds. Anne had always loved to ride, although she found so few chances to do so these days. And her brothers were the best company.

Usually.

"I think," Edward said, "you should at least consider—"

Anne had had enough. "If you want to continue this conversation, you'll have to catch me first. And fortunately for me, neither of you can do that."

As she urged her mare into a gallop, she could hear her brothers behind her, laughing as they gave chase.

CHAPTER 6

Three hours later, Michael staggered out of a shop on Saville Row. He turned to glare at the doorway through which he had come. When next he saw Fauconbridge, he was going to give him a piece of his mind.

"Morsley?" The object of his ire had materialized there upon the pavement, along with his brother.

"What in God's name were you thinking?" Michael burst out.

Fauconbridge's brow wrinkled. "I don't know what you—"

"Sending me to that—that—" Michael gestured toward the shop, unable to summon words sufficiently heinous to describe it.

"Look, Morsley, I know you've never much liked going to the tailor—"

"How could any man like it? It was *horrific*."

"You're blocking the pavement," Harrington said, seizing his upper arm and towing him along.

"That Pinkerton fellow all but had a fit of vapors over my

jacket," Michael grumbled. "He went on and on *and on* about how he'd make me a new one straight away because he'd never 'suffer' me to be seen wearing something so 'grotesque' in public."

"Hmm," Fauconbridge said.

"I was tempted to tell him I wore it to a ball last night. With *buckskin trousers*. The only reason I didn't is because I honestly thought he might suffer some sort of thrombosis."

"Gallant of you," Harrington said.

"And have you seen how tight the latest fashions are? How am I supposed to chop down a tree or paddle a canoe or field dress a moose, if I can scarcely move?"

"Conveniently," Fauconbridge said, "in your future role as the Marquess of Redditch, you will be doing precisely none of those things."

"There's also a real dearth of moose in London," Harrington observed.

"I tried to leave after that, but they wouldn't let me. No, first I had to look at three dozen spools of identical blue fabric, then it was three dozen spools of identical black fabric, and then—well—you know. And he kept asking me all these ridiculous questions I couldn't answer about buttons and swallowtails and something about an M-knock—"

"M-notch," Harrington said. "It refers to the shape of the collar."

"Why couldn't this Pinkerton fellow just decide what was suitable?" Michael fumed. "Isn't that what I'm paying him for? Do I look like the sort of man who knows what kind of coat to order?"

"No," the Astley brothers replied in unison.

Michael paused long enough to narrow his eyes at the both of them. "And the worst part is, he made me promise I'd visit the shoemaker straight away. To get fitted for a pair of *dancing pumps*."

Harrington steered him into a left turn. "Perhaps they'll write an ode someday to commemorate your sacrifice."

"Well, they should. I've got to present myself at the shoemaker in one hour, and…" Michael glanced around. "Say, where are we going?"

"We were just on our way to White's." Fauconbridge nodded toward the building they were approaching. "You look like you could use a drink."

"White's, you say?" Michael squinted at the building's columned façade. "I'm not a member."

"You're the future Marquess of Redditch," Harrington said. "Of course you're a member."

"I'm not. I—"

"We were both there when you were voted in, Morsley," Fauconbridge said, steering him up the short flight of white stone steps.

They led him to a room upstairs. Michael's impression of White's improved considerably when he learned that he could obtain not just a drink, but a beefsteak.

He ordered three. After all, he hadn't eaten in five entire hours.

"It certainly is good to have you back," Fauconbridge said as they settled around a corner table.

"It's good to be back," Michael said.

"Your father must be beside himself," Harrington said.

"Gad, I forgot to send him word of my return." Michael started to rise. "I'll have to arrange for a messenger straight away."

"I took the liberty of dispatching someone to Ravenswell last night," Fauconbridge said.

Michael sat back, surprised. "That was good of you."

Fauconbridge shrugged. "He's missed you."

"And I have missed him." As he said the words, Michael realized how true they were. He'd been raised to be stoic about such things, as had every man in the room, no doubt. But his father was his only living family, and Michael was suddenly struck by how good it would be to see him again after four years.

"How is my father?" Michael asked. "I've had letters from him, of course, but—how is he really?"

Fauconbridge nodded his thanks as the waiter set a brandy in front of him. "He's well enough. Much the same as you remember."

"About as well as he's been for the past fourteen years," Harrington said.

Michael understood Harrington's meaning perfectly. It had been fourteen years since Michael's mother's death.

As horrible as it had been to lose his mother, Michael had eventually recovered in a way that his father had never quite managed. His parents had been a love match, the kind the poets wrote of, and Michael's father showed no interest in moving on. He never remarried and, from what Michael could tell, he hadn't so much as looked at another woman in fourteen years.

Whenever Michael walked by the family plot, he always found fresh-cut flowers lying atop his mother's grave. And he couldn't count the number of times he'd walked into the gallery to find his father standing before his mother's portrait, gazing at it with unabashed longing. Once he even observed his father dabbing at his eyes with his handkerchief (an unheard-of display for an Englishman), prompting Michael to slip silently from the room. He'd known better than to say anything. Whenever Michael mentioned his mother, the marquess, who was usually the best of fathers, warm and interested in his son's life, would rise and leave the room.

But Michael understood his father's feelings, far better

than he'd ever wanted to, because four years ago, the same thing had happened to him.

He'd lost Anne.

He didn't like to think back on those early days, when despair had consumed his every thought, and just being awake had been a form of agony as his bleak, Anne-less existence loomed before him for the length of a lifetime. He'd eventually not recovered so much as become inured to the pain. That trite old truism that time healed all wounds was a bunch of rot. He had never gotten over Anne, and he knew with absolute certainty that he never would.

It seemed that the inability to love more than one woman in a lifetime was a family trait.

That was why he couldn't leave anything to chance. He *had* to marry Anne this time. The alternative was unthinkable.

And once he did, he was going to wrap her up in cotton gauze and make sure nothing bad ever happened to her. The thought of how rough and tumble they'd been as children now made him break out in hives—what if she'd fallen out of a tree and broken her neck?

And when the time came for her to give birth, he was going to have a half-dozen accoucheurs on hand, all the best ones in England. He didn't care if it cost him a king's ransom.

"He'll be so glad to have you back," Fauconbridge said, interrupting his reverie.

"For a few weeks, anyways," Michael said. He nodded his thanks to the waiter as he set a trio of plates before him.

"A few weeks?" Harrington frowned. "We were all hoping you were here to stay."

"No," Michael said, sawing into his first beefsteak, "my future is in Canada, for many years to come. It's what Lord Hobart wanted to discuss with me this morning. He wants me to start training to take over for Sir Robert Milnes." He speared a hunk of meat and shoveled it into his mouth.

"Sir Robert Milnes?" Fauconbridge said. "Am I to understand that you're to be the next Governor General of Canada?"

Michael swallowed. "It won't be for some years. I'm sure I wouldn't even be a candidate were it a position anyone else wanted. But the Crown wants a peer for that type of post, and most peers are unenthusiastic about life on the frontier. That I have a title and that I'm willing to do it are my only qualifications."

"Not so," Fauconbridge said. "Such a position requires a man of unimpeachable character and sound judgment. Both of which you have in spades. To say nothing of your"—he tapped the side of his glass, searching for precisely the right words—"decisive, authoritative disposition."

Harrington leaned forward. "What he means is that you're bullheaded and overbearing."

Michael laughed. "I fear I can't deny it. Well, I'm fairly certain that 'bullheaded' and 'overbearing' are both requirements of the position. I grow more qualified by the minute."

"So, if you're only staying for a few weeks, why did you bother to come back?" Harrington asked.

Michael swapped his now-empty plate for one that held a beefsteak. "I may as well tell you. Not that I need either of your permission. But I'm going to marry your sister."

"We know," the brothers replied in unison.

Michael sighed. "I had a feeling you probably did."

"*Everyone* knows." Harrington paused, then added brightly, "Except for Anne, of course."

"Superb," Michael grumbled, sawing into his beefsteak.

"So," Harrington continued, "when are you going to propose?"

Michael pointed his fork at Harrington. "It happens that I

was attempting to propose last night. But *someone* interrupted me."

"Aw, bad luck, Morsley," Harrington said, his voice annoyingly chipper.

"I'm starting to think you don't want me for a brother-in-law," Michael said.

"Of course we do," Fauconbridge said. "We want Anne to finally be happy, after all."

Michael gave him a sharp look. "And was she not happy? With Wynters? If he mistreated her—" Michael wasn't sure what he was going to do, given that the man was already dead.

But if his suspicions about what happened four years ago proved to be correct, he would require only the slightest pretext to go out and desecrate his grave. If that two-faced lying snake had laid a finger on Anne...

"Nothing like that," Fauconbridge said. "Come, Morsley, I would have met him at dawn."

"We both would have," Harrington said.

Michael sighed. He knew they would have. The Astleys looked after their own. "My apologies. I didn't mean to suggest otherwise."

"What I meant was..." Fauconbridge trailed off, considering his words. "It's not that Anne was unhappy with Wynters, from what I could tell. He was nice enough to her, allowed her to do her charity work, that sort of thing. But it also wasn't the case that he made her... particularly happy. If that makes any sense."

"I will make her happy," Michael vowed, raising his glass to his lips.

"At least you'll be able to get some children on her," Harrington said cheerfully, causing Michael to come alarmingly close to spewing port across the table.

Michael won his fight with his drink and came up coughing. "Harrington," Fauconbridge said in a tired voice as he began pounding Michael on the back.

"That is," Harrington continued, ignoring his brother, "I presume you'll be able to. Everything's in working order and what not, isn't it, Morsley?"

"Dear God," Fauconbridge muttered, taking a fortifying sip from his own glass.

"Surely," Michael replied once he had regained the ability to speak, "you do not expect me to dignify that with an answer."

"I for one," Fauconbridge interjected, "would very much prefer that you not."

"We're of one mind on that." Michael went to spear another bite of meat, only to have his fork clang against an empty plate. As he pulled his final beefsteak close, Michael saw the four men who had been occupying the adjacent table rise and depart. He glanced around. They were now the only ones in this end of the room.

There was a question that had been bothering him for four years, one he hadn't had the opportunity to ask in the crush last night. He leaned forward, dropping his voice. "Listen, there's something I need to ask you two. I've always wondered how it came to pass that Anne didn't receive my proposal."

"We've wondered that as well," Fauconbridge said. "Yarwood swears she read your letter. Says he placed it in her hands himself. But it eventually became clear that Anne had no idea you had proposed."

"I have a theory," Michael said. "Perhaps you can confirm something for me. The man she married, Wynters—did he carry a walking stick with a silver handle in the shape of an icicle?"

"Took it with him everywhere he went," Harrington

confirmed. "Because he was 'Lord Wynters.'" The exaggerated eyeroll with which Harrington accompanied this statement conveyed his opinion of the late earl's sartorial choice.

Fauconbridge's eyes had sharpened. "I didn't realize you'd met Wynters."

Michael stared unseeingly across the room. It didn't really come as a surprise. Deep down, he'd known it all along. "Apparently I did. You see," he blinked out of his trance, and found both Astley brothers staring at him intently, "he was there. That morning four years ago, when I scrawled out my proposal for Anne, then hurried off to board my ship. He was there, and I think he must have—"

"Fauconbridge, thank God you're here." Michael turned and saw the speaker's eyes narrow as he noticed Harrington. "Oh. It's *you*."

It was the Marquess Graverley. Michael remembered Graverley from school, and he looked much the same—lithe, blond, and haughty, with preternaturally high cheekbones and boots so shiny Michael could have checked his teeth in them.

An argument ensued about whether Fauconbridge would be willing to join Graverley for a drink. "*Alone*," the marquess clarified, glaring at Harrington.

It happened that Fauconbridge was unwilling to abandon his brother. Michael sighed. He'd finished his beefsteaks and, glancing at his watch, he saw that he needed to get going if he was going to make his horrifying appointment with the shoemaker. It appeared that he had learned as much as he was going to about Lord Wynters.

Well, no matter. He had learned what he needed to know.

He excused himself and wandered down the stairs and out onto St. James's Street in a daze. Yes, he had learned what he needed to know, had confirmed what he'd suspected all along: that it had been no unfortunate happenstance that Anne never received his proposal. That he had been sabotaged, and the man who had done it had gone on to become Anne's husband.

Now he just had to figure out what he was going to do about it. Should he tell Anne? After he proposed, she was bound to ask how his decision came about. He didn't want to lie to her. Hell, he doubted he *could* lie to her convincingly (growing up, they always joked that they knew each other so well they could practically read each other's faces).

He wanted to tell Anne that he loved her. He wanted to laugh with her about that picnic they'd had when they were fifteen, when he'd wound up lying on top of her and still somehow managed not to kiss her. He didn't want to give her some nonsense about how it was a smart match, and about how they would get on well because they were "such good friends."

The problem was, telling her the truth, that love had struck him down like a bolt from the blue when they were fourteen, when he'd returned home from Eton for summer break and had suddenly seen his best friend with the eyes of a young man, rather than those of a boy, was bound to lead to a whole series of questions. Questions like, *Why didn't you propose before you left?* that had answers like, *Actually, I did.* Answers that led inexorably to the dishonorable act carried out by her first husband.

It wasn't hard to guess that Anne would have strong feelings about being informed that her marriage had been built on a lie. Would she blame Wynters? Or would she resent Michael for telling her an uncomfortable truth? Hell, a lot of women would probably refuse his proposal on the grounds that he had besmirched the honor of their dearly departed husband.

And so he had a decision to make.

It wasn't as if much was riding on it.

Just his future happiness.

He shuddered as he mounted the steps to the shoemaker's shop, but not for the reasons he would've supposed an hour ago. How remarkable. There was something he was dreading even more than getting fitted for that pair of dancing pumps.

CHAPTER 7

*A*nne spent the afternoon hunched over her writing desk at her charity's lodging house in St. Giles. The Christmas when Anne had been fourteen, there was an incident in which the Astley family's longtime nursemaid, Bridget, fell pregnant. Bridget had sworn up and down that she had been raped by one of Lord Cheltenham's houseguests, a Lord Fitzhenry. Anne's father hadn't wanted to believe this and had dismissed Bridget. Anne had pleaded with him on Bridget's behalf. She had begged. She had even cried. But nothing she said had swayed him.

It was Michael who saved Bridget in the end by going to his own father and persuading the marquess to intervene. When Lord Redditch told Anne's father that he believed that Fitzhenry fellow to be the worst sort of cad, that personally he believed Bridget when she said it had been rape, and that he thought Cheltenham was being overly harsh, Anne's father had finally yielded.

The incident had shaken Anne's sheltered existence to its very foundations. This wasn't some whispered tale about a neighbor's cousin's maid, it was *Bridget*, someone Anne loved.

It had opened Anne's eyes to how fragile a woman's place in the world truly was, and how easily a woman could find herself cast out and abandoned through no fault of her own. After that, Anne had become determined to assist those women upon whom society had turned its back, and the Ladies' Society for the Relief of the Destitute was the result.

When Anne first came to London and began planning her charity, she had been shocked to discover the extent to which the cards were stacked against the poor, and especially poor women. One could be forgiven for assuming that a fancy West End mansion with marble floors and gilded plaster-work cost more to rent than a dilapidated shed in St. Giles, but you would be wrong—tenement housing rented for four times the price per square foot, and often more.

It was expensive to be poor. If you couldn't afford to buy a full haunch of meat, you had to settle for scraps that were mostly gristle and bone, paying the same price per pound and getting little nutrition in return. It didn't end there—the reputable shops wouldn't sell tea in quantities of less than a pound, and thus the poor were forced to pay unscrupulous dealers twice the price per ounce for adulterated products. The same principle applied to everything from coal to oats to potatoes to sugar (sugar! As if Anne's residents could afford *sugar*). If you couldn't afford to buy in the quantities sold by the high street shops, you had no choice but to get your daily bread from the disreputable. And thus, those who could least afford it ended up being charged the dearest prices for their daily necessities.

The situation was bad for all the working class, but it was worse for poor women than for poor men, because women's wages were on average one-third to one-half lower than men's, even when they were performing the exact same work. Wedgwood paid the women who painted flowers on its china sixty percent of what it paid men to perform the same task. Male weavers were paid decent wages to knit stockings, but the women who seamed those same stockings by hand worked for pennies. And male tailors were paid a living wage, while women received an absolute pittance for their sewing.

The rationale behind this discrepancy was that men were the breadwinners, and that women shouldn't be working at all. Well, even if one were to accept that as true, where did that leave women who were on their own with children to support? Society's prevailing sentiment was that charity should be limited to the "deserving" poor, and that to aid unwed mothers would only promote licentiousness. It galled Anne to have to turn away women trying to provide a better life for their children because they had once sold their body to put food on the table. She was hard pressed to understand why society deemed the counsel of Jesus to "judge not" unapplicable. But, as much as she hated it, to maintain her status as a respectable woman and attract donors to the Ladies' Society, Anne was forced to only accept applications from the "deserving" poor.

The good news, if one could call it that, was that even with the prospect of opening a second lodging house, there were more than enough respectable widows and legitimately born orphans to exhaust her budget a thousand times over. It seemed clear to Anne that the problem was structural: when women were paid such miserably low wages, their families inevitably faced destitution. And however much society might squawk were she to suggest raising wages for all women, surely everyone could agree that the situation was unfair to respectable widows struggling to support their children, especially when so many of their husbands had lost their lives in service to king and country.

And so Anne had written a pamphlet proposing to raise wages for widows with children to support. It had seemed logical at the time, but it had proved to be an unmitigated disaster. She had been mocked by polite society and had quickly learned that men didn't appreciate a woman making even the gentlest suggestion as to how they should run their businesses.

Although her pamphlet had been a failure, the lodging house run by the Ladies' Society was an unqualified success. It was simple in principle: treat its residents with basic fairness. Charge them a reasonable rent instead of the exorbitant rates charged by the slum owners to the east. Have a communal kitchen so groceries could be bought in bulk. Provide schooling for the children for their own benefit, but also so their mothers didn't have to dose their little ones with laudanum so they could get some work done, an all-too-common practice.

People often lavished praise upon Anne for her charity toward these "wretched creatures," which made her feel uncomfortable. Most of what she was doing didn't even qualify as charity, although she supposed the twice-a-week meat-and-potatoes program for the hungry and the Christmas initiative she'd started last year to give plum puddings to poor children might count as such. But her lodging house charged rent, the only thing that set her apart from other landlords was that her goal was to break even, not to make a fortune upon the backs of the poor. And in Anne's experience, there was nothing wretched about her residents. They were hard-working women who weren't looking for a handout; all Anne really did was remove a few of the obstacles that made their situation untenable.

Anne smiled at the shout of children playing in the streets below. It had taken a while to accustom herself to the noise and bustle of London, having grown up in the idyllic countryside of the Cotswolds. But over the past four years, London had become her home. It was here in London that she had found a sense of purpose, something more mean-ingful than the endless rounds of balls and parties. And London was where the Ladies' Society could do more good than anywhere else.

That made London precisely where she belonged.

She returned to her stack of correspondence. Toward the bottom, she found two pieces of good news. One came in the form of a letter from Mr. Archibald Nettlethorpe-Ogilvy, whose family ran an iron manufactory. He was requesting a meeting. Anne had no idea what that was about, but the Nettlethorpe-Ogilvys were one of the richest families in Britain, so she penned a delighted response, hoping she might be about to gain a new patron.

Anne's heartbeat kicked up a notch as she read the sender's name on the final letter in her stack: Marquess Graverley. For the past few weeks, she had been searching for a new vice president for her board of directors. And although all of the board members of the Ladies' Society up until this point had been, well, ladies, it had occurred to her that every eligible young miss in London would flock to her events if one particular man was guaranteed to be in attendance...

And so yesterday she had swallowed her qualms and braced for almost certain rejection, and sent a letter to Marcus Latimer, the current Marquess Graverley and future Duke of Trevissick, who was without question the most eligible bachelor in all of England, asking if he would consider serving as her vice president. Lord Graverley did not have a reputation for his charitable works; much to the contrary, he was known for being every inch the rakehell. Yet, much to Anne's astonishment, in the past three months he had become a fierce advocate for her society.

As she popped open the wax seal, Anne reminded herself to keep her expectations in check. Lord Graverley would surely decline, just like the last three candidates she had asked. Except... he hadn't declined. He wrote that he would be honored to serve on the board of such a worthy organization.

She read the marquess's note a third time, still not quite able to believe it. In addition to being a rich future duke, Lord Graverley was almost absurdly handsome, with pale hair, ice-blue eyes, the sort of cheekbones that would make a sculptor weep, and an elegant fencer's physique.

Had someone asked her yesterday, Anne might have named Lord Graverley as the most handsome man of her acquaintance. Today, however...

A tremor ran across her shoulder blades at the memory of how Michael had looked last night. Although most women would probably still prefer Lord Graverley's refined features, Anne found Michael's newfound combination of tall, dark, and hulking far more affecting.

She shook her head to clear it. Gracious, what was this? Handsome was nowhere near the top of the list of qualities she sought in a husband. What she needed was a good man, of excellent character, and of the rank and position her family expected her to marry. Someone who would treat her kindly, help her start a family, and support her rather than limit her in her work for the Ladies' Society.

Michael has every one of those qualities, a little voice whispered in the back of her head. *Why should you not have it all?*

It was the voice of a young Michael that answered, as clear and sure as the day he'd uttered the words. *Absolutely never... Not in a million years...*

She sighed. It did her no good to dwell upon such things. She needed to find a man who might actually consider marrying her.

There was a knock at the door. Anne looked up to see Mrs. Godfrey, who lived on-site and oversaw the day-to-day operations of her lodging house, flanked by two boys and bearing a tea tray.

"Good afternoon, Lady Wynters," Mrs. Godfrey said. "I have Nick and Johnny here, just as you requested."

"Thank you," Anne said as Mrs. Godfrey set down the tea tray, curtseyed, and took her leave. Anne smiled at the boys. "Please, have a seat."

She poured for the three of them and gestured for the boys to help themselves to the plate of currant biscuits, which they did with obvious delight.

"How are you settling in?" Anne asked.

"I wuv id here," Johnny said through a mouthful of biscuit. Nick elbowed him and he swallowed, then cleared his throat. "Beg pardon, m'lady. Mrs. Briggs said I wasn't to do that no more. That I need to swallow first."

Anne nodded, taking care to keep a straight face. "That's quite all right. And how about you, Nick? How do you like your new home?"

Nick blinked incredulously. "Are you bamming me? We get meat every day, and *two* rolls at breakfast, and I mean with butter." He shook his head. "I never heard the like."

Anne's smile was bittersweet. Nick's enthusiasm for something as simple as a roll was charming, even if the reason for it was distressing. Master sweeps were notorious for underfeeding their climbing boys so they could fit themselves into the tiniest of flues. Nick and Johnny had been so filthy they'd had to wash them in a tub out in the courtyard, and Anne had been distressed to see arms as thin as matchsticks and chests that were practically concave emerge as they peeled off their squalid clothes.

She cleared her throat. "And how do you boys find Mrs. Briggs?"

"Mrs. Briggs is grand," Nick said as he selected another biscuit.

"Hasn't clouted us once," Johnny added.

"I should hope not," Anne said, setting aside her teacup. "I was wondering if you two could tell me how you came to be working for your former master sweep."

"You mean Mr. Smithers?" Johnny asked.

"The very one."

"Well… uh…" Johnny scratched the side of his nose. "My papa was in the army. My mum went with him. But they both died. This was…" He screwed up his face in concentration.

"Smithers took Johnny on about two months ago," Nick offered.

"Yeah, two months, I guess. I went home on a ship. One of the officers said I'd live with a new family. A carriage came and took me to Mr. Smithers."

"A carriage?" Anne leaned forward. "Do you mean Mr. Smithers came to collect you in a hackney carriage?"

"No, there wasn't no one inside," Johnny confirmed. "And it wasn't no hackney. It was a fancy carriage. Black and shiny with a golden crest on the door."

"I remember the crest, too," Nick said. "That sounds just like the carriage that came for me."

A crest would make it possible to identify the carriage. Now they were getting somewhere. "What was it on the crest?" Anne asked.

Johnny said, "It was two pigs," in the same instant Nick said, "A pair of elephants."

"It weren't no elephant," Johnny said. "Aren't they the ones with long noses?"

"It was elephants," Nick insisted. "They did have a long nose, and tusks."

The two boys fell to arguing about it. Anne sighed. This was a good reminder that the memories of small children were fallible. Not that she had spent hours memorizing every crest in *Debrett's Peerage* as her mother had desired, but she felt fairly certain no noble house would select a lowly pig for its emblem, and elephants seemed only a little less far-fetched.

Anne cleared her throat. "You say this same carriage came for you, too, Nick?"

"Yes, m'lady. My father was in the army, too. The 18th Royal Hussars." Nick puffed out his chest. "My mum followed the drum, too, and my parents were both killed. There was an officer, maybe a lieutenant..." Nick bit his lip, thinking. "I don't recall his name, but he'd lost his leg and was being sent home. He's the one who looked after me. Said he was going to get me some kind of ship, a print ship, maybe?"

"An apprenticeship?" Anne asked.

Nick snapped his fingers. "That's the one. The carriage came for me twice. The first time it was empty. I remember my lieutenant got really mad. Said he wasn't just going to send Robert Palmer's only son off to God knows where in some empty carriage. So he wrote a letter, and a few days later, the carriage came again."

"And was Mr. Smithers in it this time?" Anne asked.

"Not Smithers," Nick said. "A gentleman. Talked like you do. So the lieutenant shook my hand and let me get in the carriage, and then the gentleman took me to this house. I stayed there a few days before Mr. Smithers took me away."

"Do you remember this gentleman's name?" Anne asked.

"No, ma'am, I don't think he said. He was a real strange cove. It was dusk when he came to collect me, and he refused to get out of the carriage. Shook the lieutenant's hand through the window. He had this big tricorn hat pulled down over his face, and he hunched back in the corner of the carriage. But at one point the lights of another carriage came straight through the window, and I got a look at his face. He caught me staring, and he clouted me."

"What did he look like?" Anne asked. "What color was his hair, his eyes?"

Nick screwed up his face. "I... I couldn't say. It was dark, and he had that hat on."

Anne tamped down the hope that had been rising in her chest. "Then you wouldn't recognize him?"

Nick bit his lip, considering. "I think I would, m'lady. I've a good memory for faces, and I can still picture his. It's hard to describe on account of his face being so plain. He didn't have a hook nose, or a scar, or anything like that."

"How long ago was this?" Anne asked.

"Uh... I passed four Christmases with Mr. Smithers. So sometime thereabouts."

"You said something about a house," Anne said. "Can you describe it?"

"It wasn't nothing fancy. Just a room, and about eight or ten boys sleeping on the floor. The master sweeps would come and take one of us away, another boy would arrive, that sort of thing."

This house was another potential lead. "Do you remember whereabouts it was?" Anne asked.

"I don't, but I do recall it was near a kiln," Nick said, waving a hand in front of his nose.

Johnny perked up beside him. "That's right—I remember the smell!"

"A kiln?" Anne asked. "You're sure?"

"Dead sure." Nick puffed out his scrawny chest. "As a sweep, I consider myself a bit of an expert on chimneys and their smells."

"You mentioned there was a steady stream of boys," Anne said. "How old were these boys?"

"Right around Johnny's age, m'lady."

"I see. And did this gentleman from the carriage come inside with you?"

"He didn't. There were three or four men inside who watched us," Nick added. He screwed up his face in concentration, then shook his head. "That's about all I can recall."

Anne thanked the boys and sent them back to Mrs. Briggs with a handkerchief-full of biscuits.

Anne pulled out paper and quill to write everything down before she forgot it. Johnny and Nick had provided several pieces of information—the crest on the carriage door, the kiln, and the lieutenant from the 18th Royal Hussars—which had the potential to be a break in the case. The crest suggested that "his lordship" might indeed be a lord.

She next dashed off a note to Samuel, then rubbed her temple as she considered whether she should write one more letter. You always had to be careful before you started asking questions. You never knew who might be conspiring with a criminal organization. But from what Nick had said, it sounded like the officer who brought him home had genuinely cared what had happened to his fallen soldier's son and had thought he was placing Nick in a legitimate apprenticeship.

Anne decided the risk was worth it. She pulled out a fresh sheet of foolscap and dashed off a note to Horse Guards, asking if they had any record of an officer of the 18th Royal Hussars who had returned home about four years ago after losing a leg.

She sealed the letter, placed it on her stack of outgoing correspondence, and said a silent prayer that this lieutenant could be found.

CHAPTER 8

*T*he following afternoon, Anne found herself pacing the length of her front parlor while she waited for Michael.

She glanced out the window just as a handsome black phaeton picked out in yellow pulled up to the curb. Anne grabbed her basket and was striding out the door before a groom had even arrived to hold Michael's horses.

But then she was brought up short.

She had thought Michael had looked unbearably handsome at the Falmouth ball, even if he was wearing last season's jacket and buckskin trousers.

But nothing could have prepared her for the sight of all that masculine perfection displayed for her viewing pleasure in a coat of impeccable dark blue superfine that fit his shoulders like a second skin.

And then it got a thousand times worse.

Because then he smiled at her.

That smile... did things to her. To her insides, to be specific. Take her heart, for instance: it was hammering in her chest as if she'd been running. There was a fluttery feeling in her stomach, as if a family of finches had taken up residence. And lower than that, between her legs, she was feeling…

Warm.

She suddenly became aware that she was gaping at him. That her feet had come staggering to a halt in the middle of her front steps, and her cheeks were warm, and… Oh gracious, was her mouth hanging open? Her mouth was hanging open, wasn't it?

She managed to close her mouth. A groom finally appeared and, as Michael climbed down, Anne ascertained that the view from behind was every bit as impressive as the view from the front.

She closed her mouth. Again.

"Michael!" she sputtered as he jogged up the stairs. He stopped one step below the level on which she stood and was still a good two inches taller than she was. As a woman who was taller than most men, she was unused to feeling delicate. *Feminine.* He took her hand in both of his and raised it to his lips.

"Is everything all right, Anne?"

Oh dear, he had noticed! That is, of course he had noticed, how could he not notice that she'd been staring at him with her mouth hanging open? She shook her head and laughed. "Of course. I was just noticing—is that a new jacket?"

"It is."

She could feel her cheeks burning. "It looks… it looks very well on you."

"Thank you." In his expression she detected amusement, and… satisfaction?

She didn't have time to ponder that, because he tucked her arm in his and escorted her to the carriage. It was one of those high-flyer models that were all the rage. Anne was busy enough with her society that she rarely found time for the afternoon promenade through Hyde Park, so she had only ridden in such a high vehicle on a handful of occasions. Let's see, there was usually a step somewhere…

Without warning, Michael's big, warm hands encircled her waist and he lifted her into the carriage with no apparent effort. This did nothing to restore Anne's composure, and she found herself closing her mouth for the third time in the space of two minutes.

Michael climbed up beside her. "So, where are we off to?"

"Hyde Park."

"And here I thought you had a surprise for me."

She laughed. "I do, and the location of your surprise is Hyde Park."

"Fair enough." He clucked to the horses, and they were off.

"So," Anne began, "what did you do this morning?"

"I paid a visit to your brother's tailor," Michael said with an unmistakable shudder.

Anne laughed. "That explains this handsome jacket. Was it that terrible?"

"You have no idea."

"Oh, but I do. You've never visited a French dressmaker. With *Caro.*"

"I will admit, that does sound horrifying, but I beg you not to make light of my ordeal."

"If you've survived… whatever it is you've been doing in Canada—wrestling bears, or some such—then surely you can endure a visit to the tailor."

"I would take the bears over this any day. But speaking of Caro, where is she? I thought she would've made her debut this year."

"Caro is away on her bridal trip. The wedding was just

last week, and you'll never guess whom she married—Lord Thetford!"

Michael turned his head and gaped before breaking into a broad grin. Anne knew he remembered the rather obvious infatuation Caro had developed for Harrington's best friend when he had come for a visit some four years ago. "Did she truly?"

"She did. And I am pleased to report that this time around, Lord Thetford is completely besotted with her."

Michael laughed. "Good for her."

"I'm so happy for her." Anne sighed. "A touch envious, if I'm being honest."

"Envious? What do you mean, envious? It's not as if you wanted to marry Thetford." Michael gave her a sharp look. "Did you?"

"Gracious, no. Lord Thetford and I would never suit. I just envy her for having made a love match." They had reached the entrance to Hyde Park. Rotten Row wasn't yet packed, as the fashionable promenade wouldn't begin for another hour and a half, but it was crowded enough near the gate that Michael had to slow the horses. "Drive all the way to the end of the row, then keep going," Anne instructed.

"You will make a love match," Michael said quietly, his eyes fixed on the path ahead.

Anne sighed. "I hope so. But you have no way of knowing that, Michael."

"Oh, yes, I do," he muttered.

Anne was about to ask what he meant by that when she heard someone calling, "Lady Wynters! Oh, Lady Wynters!"

She turned to see a familiar face approaching on horseback. Augusta Wriothesley was not only the most dedicated volunteer for the Ladies' Society, she was also one of Anne's dearest friends, for all that she was old enough to be Anne's mother. "Mrs. Wriothesley, good afternoon."

Mrs. Wriothesley steered her horse into a trot alongside them. "Did you see the article in *The Times* yesterday? The one about the Ladies' Society? I almost fell into a fit of vapors!"

Anne flushed, thinking not about the article so much as the cartoon that had accompanied it. "I... I did see it." She cast about for a change of subject. "Oh, forgive me. I forgot to perform introductions. Michael, this is Mrs. Augusta Wriothesley, my dear friend and the treasurer of the Ladies' Society. Mrs. Wriothesley, this is Lord Morsley, whom I know I have mentioned to you before."

"Mrs. Wriothesley, what a pleasure," Michael said, inclining his head.

"Oh!" Mrs. Wriothesley's mouth had fallen open. "Do you mean to say *this* is Lord Morsley? Your childhood friend?"

"The very one," Anne said.

"Oh my gracious, I..." Mrs. Wriothesley's eyes were keen as they travelled from Michael to Anne and back again. "I hadn't realized Lord Morsley had returned from... Canada, was it?"

"That's correct," Michael said. "I only returned two days ago."

"Well, it is a delight to meet you, my lord, and an even greater pleasure to have you back in England." Mrs. Wriothesley wheeled her horse around. "Well, I'll let you two young people enjoy yourselves," she called, already cantering away. "Good afternoon!"

"Good... good afternoon," Anne called after her, perplexed.

"Anne," Michael asked, "did an article truly run in *The Times* about the Ladies' Society?"

Anne cringed. "You could say that."

"That's wonderful! Do you have a copy?"

"Um, why do you ask?"

He gave her a strange look. "Because I want to read anything relating to the charity you founded, naturally."

"I would rather you didn't see it." He glanced at her, confused, and Anne sighed. "It wasn't just an article. There was also a cartoon. And…" She squeezed her eyes shut. "It wasn't flattering."

$\sim$

"WHAT DO YOU MEAN, it wasn't flattering?" Michael took his eyes off the horses to sneak a glance at Anne. She was looking down at her hands, which were twisted into knots around the handle of the basket she held in her lap. His chest tightened. "What kind of jackass would criticize you for helping the poor?"

Anne's knuckles were white on the handle of her basket. "You would be surprised."

Michael didn't care for the sound of that. "I should like to know what that means."

"Whereas I would prefer not to discuss it," she muttered.

"I insist you tell me." She said nothing, so after a moment he added, "It would appear you have forgotten how bull-headed I can be."

Her eyebrow twitched, and Michael knew he was treading on dangerous ground, because an eyebrow twitch was one of Anne's signature expressions. It meant that, no matter how placid a face she might be presenting to the world, she was getting annoyed. "Oh, no. I haven't forgotten."

"Come on, Anne—"

She sighed. "I fear I've been a popular subject of mockery for the past three years. It all started with my pamphlet."

"Your… your pamphlet?" *What pamphlet?* When had Anne authored a pamphlet?

Anne turned to him, incredulous. "Surely you recall it. I know I sent you a copy."

And he had probably received it, too, but seeing as he hadn't opened any of Anne's letters, he had no idea what it was about. He cleared his throat. "Of course I recall it, I just... I cannot comprehend what someone might find objectionable about it. It was so, er, well-reasoned, and—"

This seemed to be the right thing to say, because Anne's expression softened, and she reached out and squeezed his forearm. "Thank you, Michael. Although I'm sorry to report that your opinion was in the minority."

"What exactly do you mean by that?"

Anne bit her lip. "I probably didn't describe what happened next in my letters. I suppose I was trying to forget it ever occurred. But... well..." She swallowed thickly. "I was roundly mocked."

"Mocked?" One of the horses snorted and pulled at the bit, and Michael noticed that his fists had hardened to iron. He forced himself to relax his grip upon the reins. "What do you mean, mocked?"

"Oh, it was mostly of the theme of, look at this silly woman, who fancies she understands economics."

"And who was doing this mocking?"

"A lengthy question to answer, as it was said behind my back, to my face, in the press—"

"Why did your husband not put a stop to it?" Michael snapped. "He should have called out the first man who said such a thing."

"He—" Anne broke off, looking down at her hands.

The suspense was killing him. "He what?" She murmured something he couldn't make out in response. "What was that?"

"He didn't read it," Anne said, her voice tremulous.

"He didn't *what*?"

"I was trying to arrange meetings with businessmen, with factory owners and the like, to see if I could convince anyone to try out my plan. It wasn't going well. At all. And I thought I might have more luck if Lord Wynters helped broker a meeting with someone of his acquaintance. But..." She looked away.

"But?" Michael asked, making an effort to gentle his voice. It wasn't Anne he wanted to throttle, after all.

"But when I asked for his help, he revealed that he hadn't read my pamphlet. And when I asked him to read it, he..." She swallowed thickly, steeling herself. "He refused. He said he had 'matters of importance' to attend to."

Michael could read Anne's face well enough to see just how deeply this refusal had wounded her.

That settled it. Michael was *definitely* going to desecrate Wynters's grave.

With a *sledgehammer*.

He felt rather than saw Anne lay a hand on his arm. "Michael, calm down." She chuckled nervously. "There's a painting in the gallery at Ravenswell depicting your ancestor, the Third Marquess of Redditch, at the Battle of Agincourt, in which he's about to put a battle-axe through someone's head. You are making precisely the same expression."

Michael gave her a sideways glare. She was closer to the truth than she realized. "He upset you," he grumbled.

"That doesn't matter."

"It matters to me."

Anne closed her eyes, tilting her head toward his shoulder. "Thank you, Michael. But there's nothing we can do about it now."

"Not so. What about the author of this cartoon? We've any number of battle-axes moldering around Ravenswell. There's even one at Cranfield House, now that I think on it—"

"Michael!" She poked him in the shoulder. "No battle-axes."

"It's above the mantelpiece in the first-floor parlor—"

"Absolutely not! You need to take the right fork up ahead, by the by."

"Humph," he huffed as he complied with her instruction. "May I at least maim whoever it was?"

"No!"

"I could do so very lightly—"

"There will be no maiming, lightly or otherwise." Anne managed to keep her features stern for about four seconds, before the corner of her mouth twitched, then curled upwards. "But thank you, all the same."

They emerged from a copse of trees. One of her grooms, who was waiting by the banks of the Serpentine, stepped forward and waved. "Ah," Anne said, "here we are. Stop the carriage anywhere."

CHAPTER 9

*M*ichael reined the horses in. Beside him, Anne asked the groom, "Is everything in readiness, Harold?"

He inclined his head as he took charge of the horses. "All according to plan, m'lady."

Michael lifted Anne down, and she led him toward the riverbank. Her mood seemed to be restored, as she was tugging his arm to hurry him along. "Are we having a picnic, then?"

She snorted. "A picnic isn't much of a surprise."

"I thought since you had that basket, that perhaps…" He trailed off as he caught sight of a white skiff arrayed on the grassy riverbank. "Anne, is this for us?"

"Well, of course."

"You mean we're—" He broke off, glancing around. They were right at the point where the Serpentine bent to extend into Kensington Gardens, and this early in the afternoon the waters were deserted, save for a pair of swans.

The gardens were lush and green. There was even a little

grey stone summerhouse adorning the verdant sweep of lawn.

Michael was no expert, but he would say the setting was picturesque. Romantic, even.

It was *perfect*. And Michael decided right then and there that this was where he was going to propose.

"Welcome to the latest installment of Anne and Michael's Pirate Adventures," Anne said, sounding pleased with herself.

That was when Michael noticed that someone had hastily painted the word *Misery* upon the boat's prow. He threw his head back and laughed. "I see that you managed to get the name right this time."

"I capitulated just this once, in honor of your return. I still maintain that there is no finer name for a pirate ship than the *Queen Anne's Revenge*."

"That one is already taken. Besides, I'm the captain, and the captain gets to name the ship."

"Remind me, Captain Cranfield, which is the higher rank —captain or admiral?"

"Admiral Astley. As if you would ever let me forget."

"Although I'm not Anne Astley anymore. I suppose it should be Admiral Northcote now."

Michael attempted to disguise his instinctive growl as a mere clearing of his throat. He was never going to refer to Anne using that blackguard's name. The mere thought of saying it aloud was revolting. "Doesn't have the same ring to it. I believe I will continue calling you Admiral Astley."

Anne responded with a sweeping gesture. "So long as you acknowledge my superior rank."

Michael was laughing as he moved the front end of the skiff into the canal, then offered Anne his hand. Once she was settled, he gave the boat a good push and climbed aboard in one smooth motion, and then they were drifting along in the bright afternoon sunshine.

He couldn't help but smile as he watched Anne. For all that she'd taken up the white parasol that had been waiting in the boat, she wasn't making much use of it, instead tipping her head back to enjoy the sunshine upon her face.

After she'd finished basking, Anne smiled at him. "This is just like old times."

"The only thing missing," Michael said, giving a pull at the oars, "is the strawberry tarts."

Anne smiled, her nose crinkling, and Michael knew immediately that something was afoot, because that was Anne's other signature expression, one he liked to see much better than the eyebrow twitch of doom. Whenever he saw that nose crinkle, it meant that Anne Astley was about to get up to some mischief.

She reached for the basket she'd brought along. "Who said they were missing?"

Michael grinned. "You do not have strawberry tarts in there!"

"I most certainly do," Anne replied, pulling them out.

They drifted along, enjoying their tarts. Anne tossed a few bites to a pair of ducks, one of whom tried to climb right into the boat before Michael shooed him away with the oar. Strawberry tarts were Anne's favorite, and she'd brought them on their afternoon adventures literally hundreds of times. Drifting along with Anne in a boat, on this perfect summer afternoon, eating strawberry tarts... Michael's throat constricted.

This feeling, this contentment, this was precisely how his life was meant to be.

Precisely how it would be from now on.

"Delicious," Michael declared, licking the last few crumbs from his fingers. He took up the oars again. "Now let's see, what else did we used to do on our pirate adventures? We've argued about the name of the ship, as well as over who holds the superior rank, and we've eaten our strawberry tarts. The only thing left to do is to come up with some harebrained scheme, the ultimate result of which will be both of us falling in."

"I have been pleased to see," Anne said, "that this vessel is proving to be more seaworthy than the original pirate ship *Misery*."

"I have a feeling that our previous difficulties lay less with the ship and more with the crew manning her. I recall one incident in particular—"

Anne rolled her eyes, but she was smiling. "You would bring that up."

"—in which our fearless admiral screamed in a manner unbecoming His Majesty's Royal Navy."

"We sail under the black flag, so let us leave His Majesty out of it. And you know very well that there was a spider, a great, black, hairy spider, that had crawled upon my leg!"

Michael shook his head, every bit as unimpressed by this explanation as he had been at age nine. "And that scream was accompanied by the most comedic flailing of arms, to which no description could possibly do justice. Perhaps I should demonstrate."

"I should very much like to see that," Anne said, gesturing for him to proceed.

Michael sighed. "And she's called my bluff."

"Indeed, she has," Anne said cheerfully. "Besides, you were the one who caused us to capsize, with your ostensible attempt to 'help' by charging into my end of the boat."

"So you're saying it was my fault? I suppose next time I'll leave you to the mercy of the great, black, hairy spider."

She smiled sunnily. "Of course you won't. To do so would go against every fiber of your nature as a Cranfield. You're not happy unless you're bashing some evildoer over the head with your battle-axe."

He laughed, hauling at the oars. "You have me again."

"So," Anne said, "do I finally get to learn what it is you've been doing in Canada?"

Michael glanced around. The water was deserted. "I suppose you do."

Anne leaned forward. "Well?"

Michael let off rowing for a moment, allowing the boat to drift. "You may recall that three years ago, my Uncle Charles was stationed out on the Canadian frontier."

"I remember it well. That would have been just before his brigade was transferred to the Continent. We had the pleasure of Major-General Cranfield's company for several months while they resupplied."

"That transfer was the reason for my mission. You see, a coded message was intercepted indicating that the French knew my uncle's brigade was to be recalled to the European theater. It further indicated that a traitor within our ranks had been dispatched to Canada to present him with a false set of orders, instructing him to lead his men deep into the Canadian wilderness."

"Oh, my gracious!" Anne frowned, tilting her head. "But how did any of that involve you, Michael?"

"The traitor bearing the false set of orders was my uncle's former batman. A man by the name of Jeremiah Derrickson."

"Ah," Anne said, her brow unfurling. "Your uncle would have trusted him."

"My uncle would have trusted him," Michael confirmed. "There's no one you can confirm your orders with, out there on the frontier. Given two sets of contradictory orders, and one is coming from your former batman, well, it's not difficult to imagine which set he would have followed. They needed someone he would trust implicitly."

"So that's why they sent you."

"Indeed." Michael gave a couple of pulls at the oars, to

keep them from drifting into the bank. "I had to depart quite hastily. Father pulled me out of Oxford midterm, and the next day I was on a ship. I was six days behind Derrickson. I'll tell you the whole story another time, but the long and short of it is that after weeks of hacking my way through the wilderness, I managed to beat him there by six hours."

"You did it." Anne's smile was a touch tremulous. "You had an adventure, a real adventure. A quest, even!"

It struck Michael that Anne understood better than anyone how much that moment had meant to him, the moment he had staggered into his uncle's camp at one in the morning, more exhausted than he'd ever been in his life, but equally exhilarated to have succeeded.

Anne laughed as she dabbed at her eyes with the back of her glove. "It's everything you've always wanted."

Michael said nothing as he leaned forward to offer her his handkerchief. It was bittersweet even now, to think about that moment. At the time, it had felt like the culmination of a dream.

But he could not now think of that triumph without immediately recalling what it had cost him: a future with the only woman he had ever loved, the only woman, he felt certain, he would ever love.

At least, he had thought it had cost him that future. It turned out the Fates had seen fit to give him this second chance.

"So," Anne continued once she'd finished dabbing her eyes, "that accounts for the first few months. How do you explain the following four years?"

Michael cleared his throat. "My father's holdings near Lake Simcoe have grown to about ten thousand acres. I spent some time there, taking things in hand. Then I started getting requests from all over. If it wasn't the Royal Navy begging for mast poles, it was the army, desperate for walnut for gunstocks." He smiled ruefully. "I was everyone's man in Canada."

"It sounds as if you were much in demand. But were you truly so busy you couldn't spare a half hour to pen a letter to your best friend?" Anne asked the question lightly, but Michael could read her well enough to tell that it was no triviality.

He swallowed. The time had come to tell Anne the truth. He wasn't likely to get a better chance than this, after all.

He laid the oars aside. This chance had come about so unexpectedly, he hadn't planned out quite what he was going to say.

But he knew one thing: whatever he said, it was going to end in his proposal. And for a proposal, a man was supposed to go down on one knee.

It was just good form.

He rose halfway and inched forward slowly and deliberately. The boat swayed, but not dangerously so. He carefully started to lower himself down.

He glanced up at Anne to find her brow creased. "Michael? Is anything wrong?"

He sought the bottom of the boat with his knee. As he touched down, it slipped on something round. *The handle of Anne's basket.* The basket slid out of the way, but the unexpected jolt caused the boat to shudder. Anne flinched.

This caused the rocking to increase—a precarious situation, considering Michael was on one knee. *"Don't move,"* he hissed. After a moment he gained some semblance of balance and released his grip on the hull to slowly reach for Anne's hand.

"What is it?" she whispered. Her gaze dropped down to her lap, following the direction of his hand.

That was when she screamed.

CHAPTER 10

*W*hat on earth was Michael up to? One minute they'd been having a simple conversation, and the next thing she knew, he was crawling around the bottom of the boat.

"Michael?" she asked. What was he *doing*? "Is anything wrong?"

"Don't move," he whispered in response, which was not precisely reassuring.

"What is it?" she murmured. That was when she noticed his hand reaching out ever so slowly. His gaze was fixed upon a spot on her lap—the same direction his hand was travelling, and...

She glanced down and there it was: something huge and black and furry, right there on her leg! Anne screamed, rose halfway to standing, and began smacking at her skirts with both hands.

"Anne!" Michael was flailing at her skirts, too. "Hold still!"

"Get it off me!" she shrieked, struggling to flick it away.

Michael leaned forward and caught one of her hands. "It's all right, it's not a spider, it's a—"

The boat was already rocking perilously, but that was the moment their combined weight in the aft became too much. The skiff shuddered, and then the prow slowly began to rise out of the water.

Anne squeezed her eyes shut. They were going to fall in. It shouldn't have come as a surprise. At least half of their pirate adventures had ended precisely this way.

Although she had thought that, at twenty-three, they might have done better.

But instead of falling in, Anne was enveloped in a pair of tree-trunk-thick arms, lifted off her feet, and pressed into a rock-hard chest.

And then, the world tilted off its axis.

She meant that quite literally, because it turned out that Michael had snatched her up in his arms and thrown himself down into the bottom of the skiff in an effort to keep it from capsizing. She found herself lying on top of him, her head cradled on his shoulder, her breasts pressed against his chest, her skirts hitched up around her calves, and her legs tangled with his, as the boat pitched and roiled around them. His arms held her tight and, after a moment, as the boat slowly calmed, she noticed the rapid thud of his heartbeat beneath her ear. Her breath was coming in pants, and she could feel her body trembling. She felt dizzy… disoriented… *wonderful*.

Wonderful? That couldn't be right. This should feel… awkward. She and Michael were friends. Nothing more. Although… from her vantage point lying on top of him, she could feel an extremely prominent bulge that had formed in the front of his trousers, pressing into her stomach.

She had been married before. It wasn't as if she didn't understand what *that* was.

Oh, but what was she thinking? There was no point in deceiving herself. That was merely the reaction any young, healthy man would have, finding himself in such a position with *any* woman. It didn't *mean* anything.

Yes, this should feel awkward. It should feel mortifying.

But Anne found that she felt none of those things. Instead, she was overwhelmed by a feeling of rightness, a feeling not dissimilar to the way she had felt when Michael rolled on top of her at that picnic all those years ago. It was as if this was an inevitable conclusion. As if the universe itself had conspired to throw them on top of each other, right here in this boat.

Almost as if they were meant to be together.

Gracious, she needed to stop thinking these ridiculous thoughts and get off him! She struggled to sit up, but only managed to lift her head, and to her horror, Michael immediately caught her eye.

Oh, sometimes it was a curse that she could read his every expression. She steeled herself to see his discomfiture, his disgust, his eagerness to disentangle himself.

Instead, she saw... adoration?

That couldn't possibly be right.

Could it?

"Anne," he whispered, and there was a rawness to his voice that made her tremble all the harder. And then his hand came up and *framed her face*, and he was tipping his head toward hers. Her arms were sliding up around his neck, her own lips were craning toward his, her eyes were squeezing shut, and—

"I say, is anybody in there?"

"Check the water, Robert." A pair of voices, one male and one female, penetrated Anne's brain as if through a dense fog. It was the woman who was now speaking. "This is where the scream came from, I'm sure of it. They must've fallen in."

Suddenly Michael was looking at her with a regret so pure, it bordered on pain.

The woman continued, "Oh, how I hope they haven't drowned! I don't want to see a dead body."

"No, look, Margaret! Someone's there, in the boat. They're, er, they're lying down, and—oh my."

That jolted Anne into action. She tried to scramble off Michael, but her foot slipped and she ended up collapsing back onto his chest.

"I'm sorry," she called to the couple regarding them with their mouths set in identical grim lines. "It's not what it seems. Our boat started to capsize, and we lost our balance!"

"Come away, Robert," the woman said crisply. "I, for one, don't want to witness this licentiousness."

"Quite right, dear." The man squinted as he began rowing away. "I say, isn't that Lady Wynters?"

"Lady Wynters?" The woman raised a lorgnette to peer down her nose at Anne. "It can't possibly be. Lady Wynters is the most respectable woman in all of London."

"Well, she looks just like the woman in that cartoon..."

"Anne." Michael punctuated her name with a gentle squeeze. She dragged her gaze back to his, and found his eyes were intense. "There's something I need to ask you. Will you—"

"Yoo-hoo, anybody in there?"

This time, Anne's attempt to scramble off Michael was more successful, and she managed to regain her seat. The person who had called out proved to be a milkmaid standing on the near bank, accompanied by her cow.

"Oh, good," the milkmaid said brightly. "I heard somebody scream."

"Yes," Anne babbled, "we lost our balance for a moment, but everything's fine, everything is just fine!"

At this point, Michael emerged from the bottom of the skiff looking rumpled, frustrated, and utterly delicious.

The milkmaid appeared to agree because she gave a low

whistle. "Good for you," she stage-whispered to Anne as she turned to lead her cow back to the meadow.

Michael was staring off into space, by all appearances unaware of his surroundings. Gracious, but this was awkward. Anne looked down and began adjusting her skirts.

That was when she noticed something in the bottom of the boat. Now that the skiff was still, she recognized it for what it was—a large black feather.

"Oh, look at this," she said, picking it up. "This must have been what was clinging to my skirts. It must've come from that duck who tried to steal my strawberry tart."

Michael did not seem to have heard her. He was still staring blankly across the water. "I always knew that wouldn't work," he muttered to himself.

Anne frowned. "What was that, Michael?"

He shook his head, then looked at her, a rueful grin spreading across his face. "I'll just stay in my seat this time, and I daresay it will go much better." He cleared his throat. "Anne, I—"

"Ho there, is everything all right?" a male voice called. "We heard someone scream."

At this point, Michael said a word he wouldn't normally use in Anne's presence, although she had heard her brothers say it before. (Well, she had heard Harrington say it. Obviously Edward would never curse in front of a lady).

"Yes," Anne called to the pair of young men approaching in their own skiff, "that was just me. I thought I saw a spider."

Both men grinned. "Ah, I see," one of them called. "Jolly good, then."

Anne turned back to Michael. He was surveying the Serpentine. There were now a half-dozen other boats, as well as a family playing by the riverbank.

Anne cleared her throat. "I'm so sorry about that, Michael."

"Hmm?" Michael blinked, distracted. "Sorry about what?"

"You know." Anne flushed. "Landing on top of you."

"I'm not."

"Wh-what?"

"I'm sorry about a few other things. But not that part."

Anne shook her head. "I don't understand."

Michael looked her square in the eye as he took up the oars and began pulling them toward shore. "You will. Tonight."

Anne was left to ponder that for the rest of the afternoon.

CHAPTER 11

hat evening, while Anne's maid Sarah was getting her ready for the Sunderland ball, Hugh knocked at her door. "You have a visitor, my lady."

Anne had just finished her preparations, so she hastened downstairs, wondering who could be calling at such a late hour.

She found her visitor in the front parlor. He was a young man, probably around Edward's age. He was handsome, his blue eyes set off nicely by his bright red coat.

He stood to greet Anne, and that was when she noticed that he had an artificial leg.

Her heart rate ratcheted up a notch.

"Lady Wynters," he said, bowing over her hand with military precision, "forgive my intrusion. I am Lieutenant Phillip Avery. This afternoon I received a letter from Horse Guards regarding a boy I accompanied back from the Continent. His name was—"

"Nick Palmer," Anne finished for him as she curtseyed. She laughed at his startled expression, pressing a hand to her heart. "Forgive me, Lieutenant Avery, I just... you cannot imagine how pleased I am to see you."

She gestured for him to sit on the yellow-striped silk sofa before the fireplace, taking the facing chair for herself.

"I wish I could say I was pleased," Lieutenant Avery said. "I beg you not to mistake me, I am not displeased with you, and I am grateful beyond measure for what you have done. But..." He squeezed his eyes closed. "Am I to understand that Nick has spent the last four years as a *climbing boy*?"

"I'm afraid so."

He rose to pace before the fireplace. "I never would have let him get in that carriage, had I known. I thought he was going to be placed in an apprenticeship—a *respectable* apprenticeship," he clarified. "A good trade, where he could —" He broke off with a sound of disgust.

"Of course you did," Anne hastened to say. "Nick explained how you refused to let him get in the empty carriage. How you insisted upon meeting the man who came to collect him. I am hopeful that you will therefore be able to provide us with the break we need in this case."

Lieutenant Avery sat. "I will gladly tell you everything I know."

"How did you arrange for Nick's apprenticeship?" Anne asked.

"I wrote to the Royal Military Asylum. I know their building is still under construction, but I thought perhaps they might have some sort of program already in place."

This made sense. Founded by the Duke of York, the Royal Military Asylum's mission was to provide care for soldiers' children orphaned by the war with France. "May I ask with whom you corresponded?"

His shoulders slumped. "How I wish I could recall his name. I tore my rooms apart looking for one of his letters, but I must've discarded them. I do recall that he was on the board of the R.M.A., and he was lord something or the other."

"I see." Anne's mind was flying. Being well-connected in the charity world, she knew everyone on the board of the R.M.A. "Let's see, Viscount Scudamore serves as the R.M.A's treasurer, Baron Gladstone is its secretary, and the Earl of Aylsham its vice president. Do any of those names sound familiar?"

"Aylsham does. He's a lieutenant colonel in the Royal Marines. It couldn't have been him. He was fighting with Lord Nelson in Egypt at the time."

"Not Lord Aylsham, then. That leaves Lord Scudamore and Lord Gladstone." Anne knew both men, although she knew Lord Scudamore better than Lord Gladstone. Lord Scudamore was more deeply involved in charitable work; in the last year, he had volunteered to organize some small fundraisers for the Ladies' Society and had expressed an interest in joining its board someday. Anne hated to think it might be him, but given the evidence, she had to acknowledge the possibility.

Lieutenant Avery had been staring at the wall in concentration. He shook his head. "Neither name rings any bells. I've never had a good memory for names. But whoever he was, he wrote that, as their facility was still under construction, they were finding individual situations for the children. He asked about Nick's age and what not and said he could find an apprenticeship for him. Arranged to send his carriage 'round to collect him the following evening."

Anne leaned forward. This was precisely what Nick had described. "What happened next?"

The lieutenant shook his head. "It was most irregular—the pickup time was at dusk. A carriage arrived, all right, but it was empty. I questioned the coachman, and..." He waved a hand, struggling to explain. "Do you ever get a feeling that something is off?"

"I know exactly what you mean."

He sank back onto the sofa. "Would that I had gone with my gut. I refused to let Nick get in the carriage that night. I wrote again, explained what an exemplary soldier his father had been, and that I wasn't going to pack his son away into some empty carriage. I insisted upon meeting this Lord, well, Lord whoever, first. He made a fuss about it, let me tell you. We exchanged three of four notes that day before he finally agreed that he would come to collect Nick personally."

"And did he?"

The lieutenant frowned. "I... I think so. The same carriage pulled up. I remember the crest—two wild boars."

"Wild boars," Anne murmured. That made sense. It was closer to Johnny's description of two pigs, but Nick had been right about the tusks.

"So the carriage pulled up," Lieutenant Avery continued, "but the man inside wouldn't even get out. Just rolled down the window to shake my hand. I was trying to ask him where Nick was going to be placed, he said something about a wheelwright's apprentice in Sussex, and pulled him inside. I asked where in Sussex, but the carriage was already pulling away." His shoulders sagged. "I should have followed my instincts. I should never have let Nick go with him."

"Please, don't be so hard on yourself." Anne stood and walked to a corner pedestal, where she poured the lieutenant a brandy. He accepted it with a nod and she resumed her seat. "Whoever took Nick, it appears he has an operation funneling underaged boys into work as climbing boys. Your information will be crucial toward stopping him. Can you tell me what this man looked like?"

"I'm afraid I can't. It was dusk and, as I said, he refused to get out of the carriage. He had a large hat pulled down low over his face. Ugh." He clenched one hand into a fist. "It sounds so suspicious in retrospect. *Why* did I let Nick get into that carriage?"

"At least we now know of an apparent connection with the R.M.A. The Ladies' Society took in two former climbing boys the other day, and both are army orphans. It cannot be a coincidence. Think, Lieutenant—can you recall anything else about this man?"

"As I said, he reached his hand out through the window," the lieutenant said slowly, "and he wore a signet ring. It was a gold ring with a dark red stone—garnet, perhaps, or carnelian. It was carved with some sort of crest. I didn't get a close enough look to see if it was the same as the one on the carriage." He squeezed his eyes shut a moment. "That's all I can recall."

Anne rose. "Thank you so much, Lieutenant Avery. You've been tremendously helpful. Would you mind if I put you in contact with my friend, Mr. Samuel Branton? He's a barrister who can put you in touch with someone at Bow Street."

The lieutenant agreed, and Anne wrote out Samuel's direction.

Once he had departed, she set off for the Sunderland ball, with far weightier matters on her mind than an evening of dancing.

CHAPTER 12

*M*ichael somehow managed to survive yet another visit to the tailor and arrived at the Sunderland ball smartly attired in his new evening kit.

His thoughts were consumed with Anne. Although his attempted proposal had been by any reasonable measure a complete, total, and unmitigated disaster, he couldn't help but smile when he thought of it. After all, he'd gotten to hold her, to savor the feel of her sweet weight on top of him, to enjoy the way she trembled in his arms.

And he'd come within a hairsbreadth of kissing her. *Again.* But unlike that picnic all those years ago, this time she hadn't been terrified.

He'd seen desire in her eyes. She had wrapped her arms around his neck, craned her lips toward his. Had they not been interrupted she'd have kissed him back.

And when he asked her to marry him tonight, she was going to say yes.

He spotted Anne in the foyer and hastened to her side.

"Good evening, Anne," he said, raising her hand to his lips.

"Good evening, Michael."

"May I have the first dance?"

"Oh, dear." She retrieved a dance card from her reticule. "I already promised it to someone."

Michael was alarmed to see that her dance card was completely full. "Don't worry," Anne said, "I already put you down for two. See?"

He was somewhat mollified to see that the supper dance and the final dance of the evening were his. Still, that left four dances before he would have any meaningful time with her.

"Wait a minute," Michael said, pulling the dance card from Anne's grasp. "You're not dancing the first with Alexander Fitzroy, are you?"

"Indeed, I am."

"He almost knocked you over!"

Anne shook her head. "That was an accident."

"And Augustus Mapplethorpe."

"What's wrong with Augustus Mapplethorpe?"

Michael stared at her incredulously. "Does his breath still smell of pickled cod?"

"Um… well…" She cleared her throat. "I'm sure it will hardly be noticeable."

Michael rolled his eyes. "I'm sure it won't. And then it's Gladstone. You don't want to dance with him, either."

"Am I truly dancing with Lord Gladstone?" Anne asked, snatching her dance card back. "And Lord Scudamore," she whispered, then fell silent, staring blankly across the ballroom.

"I know Gladstone from school. He's as dumb as a box of rocks. And his estate is on the brink of insolvency."

Anne was gazing across the foyer, lost in thought. "So it is."

"Scudamore's estate is bankrupt, too," Michael noted.

This seemed to snap Anne from her trance. "It was four years ago when you left, but it's not anymore. He's performed quite the feat turning it around."

"Has he, now? You should still avoid him. When we were at Eton, he was one of those fellows who delighted in torturing the younger boys. Not me," Michael added as Anne's eyes crinkled with concern. "I was under your brothers' protection. But he once tied Clotworthy Elphinstone to a tree deep in the woods and left him out there overnight. The squirrels got to him. Have you never wondered why he only has the one eyebrow?"

Anne was busy scanning the crowd. "Help me, Michael. You have the superior vantage point. I need to find my mother, and... I don't suppose you know Mr. Samuel Branton?"

"I do not. But Anne—"

"He's a Black gentleman, a bit taller than me, with close-cropped hair and impeccable tailoring."

Did she really think *he*, of all people, would recognize impeccable tailoring? "Anne! Did you hear anything I just said about Scudamore?"

She spared him a brief glance. "Of course I heard you. And yes, that does sound despicable. But isn't that sort of thing fairly common at Eton?"

"Not to the extent Scudamore took it. He used to whip any boy who didn't perform the task he assigned them 'correctly,' and I mean hard enough to leave welts. Those who didn't have someone to look out for them used to spend all day outside, just to avoid him. If it was a downpour, they would huddle under a bridge rather than risk encountering him in Long Chamber."

She squeezed his forearm, craning her neck, and nodded toward the doors. "Is that Mama who just came in? With the scarlet ostrich feather?"

"Anne!" Michael stepped in front of her. This earned him a frown. "The point is these men are unsuitable. You don't want to dance with a great bully, nor someone whose estate is insolvent."

"I will admit that Lord Scudamore's schoolboy behavior sounds regrettable. But people can change. Today he is hailed as a paragon of charity and virtue. Why, just last month he organized a subscription sermon for the Ladies' Society that brought in forty-seven pounds. And as to someone whose estate is insolvent"—she gave a dark laugh—"I have to marry *someone*, Michael."

He blinked at her. "I should like to know what you mean by that."

She was back to scanning the crowd. "Papa structured my marriage contract with Lord Wynters such that, if we didn't have any children, my dowry reverted back to him. Now he's re-dowered me, which means I come with thirty-five thousand pounds. It gives me hope that I might get a proposal or two."

"You are *not* marrying any of these scoundrels," Michael said, biting back the words, *the only man you're going to marry is me.*

Anne looked up at him, exasperated. "It's no use pretending that my dowry won't serve as an inducement."

He took both of her hands in his. "Your dowry is not your greatest inducement. Only a fool wouldn't want to marry you. Anne, I—" He glanced around. The foyer was packed; not exactly the romantic prospect he had envisioned for his proposal.

He drew in a slow breath. It wasn't as if Anne was going to accept someone else in the next hour. He could be patient. His opportunity would come. Soon.

He held her gaze. "You deserve a husband who understands your worth. Which has nothing to do with your dowry. You deserve someone who'll treat you like a queen, who will dedicate his life to making you happy. And I'm going to be honest, Anne, I know those first few men on your dance card, and not a one of them is worthy of you."

Her annoyance melted away. "What a kind thing to say. But I must be practical, Michael. Not that I think he's truly interested in me, but I don't think it's fair to judge Lord Scudamore based on his youthful foibles. After all, you're the one who once walked around all morning with a bladder of cherry brandy in your mouth so you could pop it and make Harrington think you were bleeding."

"You know full well I only did that because he wouldn't stop stealing up behind me, grabbing my waistband, and yanking my trousers up to my ears."

Anne shook her head. "Your shirt was soaked with it. I've never seen him in such a frenzy. He thought he'd killed you."

"Yes, well, the point is, he never tried that maneuver again now did he?"

"Then there was the time you drizzled Mrs. McGillicutty's Tincture of Aphrodite over everything in his trunk. Edward said he went around Eton for a week smelling of apricot and orange blossom."

Michael groaned. This was the problem with falling in love with someone who knew everything about you. They knew... everything about you. "Harrington deserved that one, too. And he later agreed it was hilarious. But still, there's a difference between a childish prank and cruelty."

"I don't disagree. My point is merely that we have all done regrettable things in our youth that don't necessarily have any bearing on who we are as adults. And I've got to be realistic. My dowry *is* an inducement. If I should receive a proposal from some man whose debts are not too great and who is otherwise suitable—"

He squeezed her hands. "Say no. You'll receive a better offer. I promise you will."

Anne bit her lip. "I don't know, Michael. I might have to settle for a fortune hunter. I might not get another offer, and you know how much I want to have children—"

"You won't have to settle," he said quietly. "Trust me."

She sighed. "I'll think on it. Oh!" Anne was looking through the doors leading to the ballroom. "There's Mama. Over by the refreshment table." She pressed Michael's hand and slipped away.

He was watching her weave nimbly through the crowd when someone slung an arm around his shoulder. "Morsley! By gad, it is you!"

It proved to be Andrew Tomlinson, an old friend from Eton.

Michael sighed. Well, he had done his best. Hoping Anne would heed his warning, he turned to greet his friend.

CHAPTER 13

"*M*ama," Anne said, "I need your help. Whose crest features two wild boars?"

The Countess of Cheltenham heaved a dramatic sigh and looked heavenwards. "I tried. I really tried with you, Anne."

"Do you know whose it is?"

Her mother shook her head. "I tried to get you to study DeBrett's. But it's difficult to make any progress with a pupil who spends all her time running wild with the boys—"

"I don't see what that has to do with—"

"—more often than not wearing a pair of your brother's old trousers so you could ride astride. Oh, yes. I knew all about the trousers."

Anne sighed. "Please just tell me, Mama."

"You cannot imagine my astonishment that my little tomboy is now regarded as the most respectable woman in all of London. You gave no indication of it growing up."

"Lady Wynters!" a voice called. Anne turned and saw her first partner, Alexander Fitzroy, approaching.

"Please, Mama," Anne said. "It's urgent. Two wild boars. Whose is it?"

The countess fanned herself. "Had you spent even a quarter of the time I asked you to spend studying DeBrett's—"

"Lady Wynters," said Mr. Fitzroy. He was mere feet away, but a trio of passing debutantes impeded him.

"Mama!" Anne hissed.

"—then you would know that it is the Barons Gladstone whose crest features two wild boars," Lady Cheltenham concluded.

Baron Gladstone.

It... it all made sense.

He was the secretary of the R.M.A. All of its correspondence would therefore go through him. Lieutenant Avery had requested help from the R.M.A. via letter.

Opportunity.

His estate was insolvent.

Motive.

And it was his carriage that had taken Nick and Johnny away.

Evidence.

And she was going to have to dance with him. In less than an hour, she would have to paste on a smile and dance with the man who had... who had...

"Lady Wynters."

Anne all but jumped out of her skin as Mr. Fitzroy claimed her hand and bowed over it. She tried to disguise the shriek she'd just given as laughter.

Mr. Fitzroy did not seem to notice her discomfiture. As he led her away, Anne's thoughts were a thousand miles away from the bright, sparkling ballroom.

❧

MICHAEL WAS ANNOYED to see that his friend Andrew Tomlinson was accompanied by not one, but two of Anne's suitors, the very gentlemen they had been discussing earlier: Scudamore and Gladstone.

Delightful.

Scudamore had been two years ahead of Michael at Eton, and Michael had never much liked him. He was fairly certain the feeling was mutual. At Eton, it was a tradition for the younger boys to wait on the older boys, but in Michael's mind there was a difference between asking someone to make your morning tea and forcing someone to spend all morning polishing your boots, then whipping them because they still weren't shiny enough.

As to Anne's claim that Scudamore had changed for the better, he would believe that when he saw it.

Tomlinson didn't seem to notice the glare Michael was exchanging with Scudamore. "It's deuced good to see you, Morsley."

"And you as well," Michael replied.

"Was that Lady Wynters you were just speaking to?" Tomlinson asked. "She's caused quite the stir lately hasn't she?"

Michael eyed him warily. Not Tomlinson, too. Was every man in this ballroom dangling after Anne? "What do you mean?"

"Well, wasn't there an article in the paper about her the other day?" Tomlinson asked. "I didn't see it, but it's all anyone can talk about."

"I fear I missed it, as I just returned from Canada," Michael said.

"I read it," Scudamore said.

"Oh?" Michael said. "What did it say?"

Scudamore's grin was smug. "Oh, you know. This and that."

Michael tried to mask his annoyance. He wasn't about to give Scudamore the satisfaction.

Tomlinson screwed up his face. "What is it her charity does again?"

"Well," Michael said, tugging at his cravat. Given that he hadn't opened any of Anne's letters, the truth was that he had no idea what the Ladies' Society did, beyond his father's assurances that it was a "magnificent success." He knew the possibilities Anne had been contemplating before his departure, but he had no idea whether she had been able to found a model lodging house, as she had hoped, or had ended up starting with something more modest, such as a soup kitchen. "It's, uh, a bit complicated," he prevaricated.

"They knit scarves for the poor," Scudamore said.

"They what?" Michael's head jerked toward Scudamore. The man was regarding him evenly.

"They knit scarves for the poor," Scudamore repeated. "Isn't that right, Gladstone?"

"What?" Gladstone blinked at Scudamore three times. "Oh, right—Lady Wynters runs a knitting circle. Of, er, great esteem."

Michael made an effort to relax his brow, which he realized was furrowed. A *knitting circle*? Anne had never expressed any interest in that sort of thing. "Is that all they do?" he asked, striving to sound casual.

"Of course not," Scudamore said. "They also knit stockings and caps. And every year at Christmas, they distribute plum puddings to the poor."

Michael was studying Scudamore, trying to decide if he and Gladstone were bamming him, when Tomlinson perked up. "That's right, there was an item in *The Gentleman's Magazine* about the plum puddings last Christmas. I did read that one." He laughed. "My godmother, Mrs. Wriothesley, is on the board of her charity. That explains why she's constantly knitting."

"I… I see," Michael said. He didn't trust Scudamore and Gladstone as far as he could throw them, but Tomlinson wouldn't lie to him.

It must be true. Anne ran a knitting circle.

He felt a keen disappointment for Anne, who had dreamed of accomplishing so much, and had clearly had to settle for something much more modest. Of course, it must be difficult to start a charity out of nothing. Michael was sure Anne was doing the very best work she was able to do, given the circumstances she had encountered. And if the most she'd been able to accomplish was organizing a ladies' knitting circle, there was no shame in that.

The orchestra started to tune up. "Well," Tomlinson said, slapping him on the shoulder, "I'd best go find my partner. Welcome back, Morsley."

Scudamore and Gladstone had turned their backs on him and were already walking away. Well, the feeling was mutual —it wasn't as if Michael wanted their company.

Yet he found himself stuck directly behind them as a small crowd formed before the doors to the ballroom.

"So," he overheard Scudamore say to Gladstone, "which dance do you have with her?"

"The third," Gladstone returned.

Scudamore grunted. "I have the fourth."

Michael realized they were talking about Anne. He'd seen her dance card, after all.

"Ha," Gladstone said, "looks like I'll get to ask her first."

Ask her? Michael didn't like the sound of that one bit.

"She won't accept you, you know," Scudamore countered. "Not with the debts your father ran up."

Gladstone shrugged. "Probably not. Still, it's worth a try. There aren't many girls who come with thirty-five thousand pounds who can fill out a dress like that. Believe me, I've looked."

Scudamore wagged a finger. "Have a care. That's the future Viscountess Scudamore you're talking about."

Michael fumed. The *hell* Anne was the future Viscountess Scudamore.

"You mean to ask her tonight, then?" Gladstone asked.

Scudamore nodded. "I do. Have you seen the way Morsley looks at her? Like he wants to eat her. I've got to get in there before he does."

The throng before them shifted, and they made their way through the ballroom doors. Gladstone and Scudamore drifted away, unaware they'd been overheard.

God. He'd told himself he was being absurd, worrying someone would propose to Anne in the next hour, but here was confirmation that not one but *two* men were planning on doing precisely that!

He felt his throat constrict. He'd lost her once to Wynters. If he lost her again...

Darkness rose up and threatened to consume him. Suddenly his heart was racing, and the back of his neck felt sticky with sweat. He couldn't lose her again. He just... *couldn't.*

He gazed across the room and was annoyed to see Alexander Fitzroy kissing her hand as they took up places near the top of the set.

His jaw clenched. He was going to have to watch Anne like a hawk.

He needed to formulate a plan. That, and find some way to pass the next hour without losing his bloody mind.

CHAPTER 14

Stalking across the ballroom, Michael spied an old friend. Cecilia Chenoweth was the daughter of the local rector back in Gloucestershire, and he had known her his whole life. She was of an age with Caro, and the two of them had always been thick as thieves. Michael and Ceci were both only children and had always joked that they were honorary Astley siblings, so much did they run with the Astley brood growing up.

Now there was someone with whom he would genuinely like to dance.

He crossed the room and bowed over her hand. "Miss Chenoweth, how wonderful to see you."

Ceci smiled. "Lord Morsley, it has been far too long."

"Indeed. Might you be free for the first—"

He was cut off by the sound of a woman clearing her throat. He turned and saw a dark-haired girl eyeing him up and down. She looked vaguely familiar, but Michael couldn't place her. "Miss Chenoweth," the girl said, her eyes fixed on Michael, "perhaps you might be so good as to introduce me to your friend."

"I believe you are already acquainted," Ceci said. "Lord Morsley, do you recall Miss Araminta Grenwood? She's attended a number of Lady Cheltenham's house parties over the years. Miss Grenwood, this is Lord Morsley."

Araminta Grenwood. Michael hadn't thought of her in years, but he remembered her well enough. He'd once asked her to dance at one of Lady Cheltenham's gatherings, trying to be courteous to a young girl who knew few people in the room. He'd been about ten inches shorter at the time, and that was the year his face had tended toward spots. Although Miss Grenwood had danced with him, she had made it abundantly clear that she would prefer he not ask her again. She wanted to keep her dance card open so that the handsome Viscount Fauconbridge, whom the girls were already starting to call "Prince Charming," could ask her instead.

"Lord Morsley, I cannot believe I have forgotten," Miss Grenwood purred. "Were you planning on dancing this evening, my lord?"

Not with you. "I was just asking Miss Chenoweth if she would grant me the pleasure of a dance."

"Of course I would," Ceci replied.

"I would wager Miss Chenoweth has a number of dances free," Miss Grenwood said. "I, on the other hand, am available for only the supper dance and the Sir Roger de Coverley."

He turned to Ceci, ignoring Miss Grenwood's rather pointed invitation. "Are you available for the first dance?"

"I am," Ceci replied.

Michael extended his arm. "Excellent."

Ceci's grin was a bit wicked. "They're still tuning up. There's no need for us to depart quite so hastily."

Michael cast her a glare. "Yes, but I find that I am parched. Perhaps you would be *so good*, Miss Chenoweth, as to accompany me to the refreshment table." He grabbed

Ceci's hand, placed it on his arm, nodded to Miss Grenwood, and beat a hasty retreat.

He could hear Ceci chuckling beside him as they crossed the room.

"I suppose you think that was funny," he said.

"Oh, I'm not laughing at you," Ceci replied. "Well, perhaps a bit—I couldn't resist teasing you. But mostly I'm laughing at Miss Grenwood."

"Why is that?" He collected two cups of lemonade and handed one to Ceci.

"Because Araminta Grenwood has been absolutely horrible to me ever since the day I met her. And it might not be the most Christian sentiment, but I found it immensely satisfying to be asked to dance right in front of her by the most handsome man in the room."

Michael had just taken a sip of his lemonade, and almost spit it right back out, just as he'd almost done yesterday. He glanced at Ceci in shock and found that she was laughing at him.

"Oh, Morsley, if you could see your face! Don't panic, I promise I'm not setting my cap for you." She arched an eyebrow. "After all, we both know you didn't just cross an ocean for *me*."

This sent Michael into a fresh fit of coughing. He eyed Ceci with resignation. "You too? I'm starting to think everyone knows."

Ceci clucked sympathetically. "Not everyone. After all, your dear, sweet Anne has no idea. And if it makes you feel better, I don't believe Freddie is aware."

Freddie Astley was thirteen, so that came as little surprise. "I rather thought Lucy was in the dark, too," Michael said. Lucy was one of Anne's youngest sisters. She and her twin, Isabella, would have just turned eighteen.

"She was," Ceci agreed, "but she figured it out quickly enough after you fled to Canada."

Michael glowered, which sent her into a fresh fit of laughter. "Remind me again why we're friends," he muttered, offering her his arm so they could join the set. "First you jest about me being the most handsome man in the room—"

"I wasn't jesting. Not one bit. Just look at you, Michael Cranfield—all grown up and every bit as handsome as Fauconbridge and Lord Graverley." She pressed his arm. "It could not have happened to a nicer person."

Michael ducked his head, and she laughed at his discomfiture.

"So," she continued, "are you going to propose tonight?"

"I am. I've been trying to propose since the moment I got back. We keep getting interrupted." He dropped his voice. "I just overheard Gladstone and Scudamore talking. They're *both* planning to ask her tonight. And they've dances with her before I do."

Ceci's eyes widened with understanding. She squeezed his arm. "Don't worry. You told precisely the right person. I'll make sure nobody gets a chance before you do."

"But"—Michael grimaced as, across the room, Anne's partner kissed her hand *again*—"how can you be sure?"

Ceci's eyes sparkled. "I have my ways."

ANNE CURTSIED to Mr. Fitzroy as their dance drew to a close. As they came out of the Allemande position, the back of his hand brushed against her breast. *Again.* Her smile felt brittle as she struggled to extricate herself without appearing obvious.

"Come with me to the gardens, Lady Wynters," he said, seizing her hand and giving a suggestive flick of his eyebrow.

Gracious, if he was this forward with half of the *ton* looking on, Anne didn't want to find out what he would try should she repair with him to the gardens. As if she didn't have enough to worry about this evening! She still wasn't sure what she was going to say when the time came for her to dance with Lord Gladstone. "Oh, um…"

"Lady Wynters!" Anne turned and was immensely relieved to see her friend Mrs. Wriothesley bearing down upon her. "Oh, Lady Wynters, you'll never believe what has happened!" She turned to Mr. Fitzroy. "Terribly sorry to interrupt, but it's an emergency." She seized Anne's arm and began dragging her across the room.

"Oh, dear." Anne strove to make her face a picture of regret she did not feel. "I'm so sorry, Mr. Fitzroy," she called over her shoulder.

To her friend, Anne whispered, "Thank you for rescuing me! That man is like an octopus—" She broke off, glancing around. "Where are we going?"

"We're going right here," Mrs. Wriothesley said, scurrying behind a potted palm. She ducked down so her head was all but concealed and gestured for Anne to do the same.

"Um." Anne hesitated before copying her friend's posture. "To be sure, Mr. Fitzroy is more tenacious than one would like. But I don't think it's necessary to hide in the shrubbery—"

"Hang Mr. Fitzroy," Mrs. Wriothesley hissed, peering between the fronds. "Who cares about him? Why didn't you tell me your 'best friend' looked like *that*?"

Anne felt her cheeks flush. She peeked out from behind the palm, and surely enough, there was Michael, chatting with Cecilia Chenoweth.

She cleared her throat. "Michael has grown up quite a bit since last I saw him. He's been gone for four years."

"Well," Mrs. Wriothesley said, inspecting Michael as if he

were on the auction block at Tattersall's, "his timing could not be better."

Anne blanched. "His timing? I... I don't know what you mean."

"You've just come out of mourning and are in search of a new husband, is what I mean." Seeing Anne's panicked expression, Mrs. Wriothesley's expression softened. "Now, dear, you must grant me a mother's indulgence. Sometimes the impulse to matchmake is impossible to suppress."

"It's not that. It's just—"

"I was at the Falmouth ball, you know. I didn't know who he was then, but I saw him scoop you into his arms when that man almost knocked you down."

"He was merely looking out for me, as a friend."

The snort Mrs. Wriothesley gave this pronouncement was something less than ladylike. "I saw the way he looked at you. Take it from someone who's married off eight daughters —that is *not* how a man looks at his good friend."

Anne swallowed. And that was the rub of it. Because a little nagging voice in the back of her head had been saying the same thing, ever since their incident on the Serpentine.

Anne still didn't put much stock in his physical response. The hardness she'd felt pressing against her stomach was just an involuntary reaction, one that a man would have in close physical proximity with any woman.

But what happened next, she had no explanation for. Because he had reached out and framed her face, and his lips had been craning toward hers, and the look in his eyes...

Oh, God, she would never forget the look in his eyes.

How could she explain *that*? She couldn't. It flew in the face of everything she had always known about Michael Cranfield, which was that he would never, *not in a million years*, want to kiss her. But what if...

What if everything she had always known was wrong? What if there was a chance that he... that he...

She reminded herself that she was specifically and demonstrably bad at determining whether Michael Cranfield was thinking about kissing her. That her attraction to him was clouding her judgment.

Because Anne could no longer deny that she was attracted to Michael, not after the way her body reacted when he took her into his arms in the boat. Although who could blame her? Just *look* at him!

Anne felt her shoulders sag as she did just that. She was being ridiculous. Just look at him, indeed. There was absolutely no chance that the majestic demigod Michael Cranfield had become would ever be interested in the likes of her.

Mrs. Wriothesley's voice emerged as if through a fog. "Lady Wynters? Lady Wynters? Is everything well?"

"I'm so sorry." Anne shook her head to clear it. "You caught me woolgathering."

"From everything you've told me, he is a man of outstanding character."

"Yes." Anne swallowed. "He is the very finest man I know."

Those were the words she had said to him after she found out that it had been Michael who had pressed his father to intervene on Bridget's behalf. She knew she had embarrassed him when she said it; his ears had turned positively vermillion.

Well, it was still true, even after all these years. Just thinking about his recent words, about how she deserved a husband who would treat her like a queen, made tears spring to her eyes.

What a shame that husband wouldn't be Michael.

Mrs. Wriothesley's expression had turned peevish. "You cannot expect me to believe that you wouldn't like to have 'the very finest man you know,' who also happens to look like *that*, for your husband."

"Any woman," Anne said carefully, "would be lucky to have Michael as her husband. But," she held a hand up as her friend tried to interrupt, "it won't be me."

Mrs. Wriothesley seemed genuinely confused. "Why ever not?"

"Lord Morsley doesn't feel anything for me beyond friendship."

"But—"

Anne laid her hand upon her dear friend's arm. "I know it for a certainty," she said quietly. "It is so very kind of you to dream of such a fine match for me. But..." She had to look away. "I know it will never happen."

She felt her friend place her hand over her own, and when Anne looked up, Mrs. Wriothesley's expression was... a bit patronizing, truth be told. She patted Anne's hand three times. "We'll see now, won't we?"

"Mrs. Wriothesley!" Anne protested.

"I would advise you not to bet against the woman who's married off eight daugh—"

"Lady Wynters?"

The aroma of pickled cod announced Augustus Mapplethorpe, who either did not notice or preferred not to ask why Anne was hiding in a shrubbery. And so Anne excused herself and went off to fulfill her promised dances, feeling more confused than ever.

CHAPTER 15

A quarter of an hour later, Anne's dance with Augustus Mapplethorpe ended. She'd paid scant attention to Mr. Mapplethorpe, truth be told, so concerned was she about her looming dance with Lord Gladstone.

She reminded herself for the twelfth time that although the matching carriage crest was suspicious, it was only one piece of evidence. She mustn't assume Lord Gladstone's guilt without further investigation.

Still, Anne's stomach roiled as she watched the baron approach. Lord Gladstone was a brown-haired, barrel-chested man, perhaps an inch shorter than her. There was a countrified quality to him that made you expect a hunting dog or two to be trotting at his heels even in a ballroom.

He looked so ordinary, so unassuming, yet this was the man who might be selling tiny children to their almost-certain death. Anne's smile felt brittle, but she made sure it was firmly in place, determined to give nothing away.

As he kissed the air above her knuckles, her eyes fixed upon his hand. Of course he was wearing gloves, of the standard York tan kidskin. But Anne could just make out a bulge over his fourth finger that looked suspiciously like a signet ring.

She drew in a steady breath. At least now she had a concrete goal—to somehow get Lord Gladstone to remove his glove so she could determine if his signet ring matched Lieutenant Avery's description.

She tried to mask the shudder that swept between her shoulder blades as she laid her hand upon his arm. "So," Anne said as he led her toward the top of the set, "how are things at the Royal Military Asylum?"

The stare the baron gave her was a bit... blank. "Well, it's, uh. It's not open yet."

"Of course, but I'm sure the planning must keep you very busy."

"Indeed. We meet once a month. *Deuced* long meetings." Gladstone shook his head. "If they're not arguing over what to serve for breakfast, it's what the uniforms will be, or whether the bedstands should be wood or metal." He shrugged. "I'm the secretary, so I just write it all down."

"I... I see." Anne found herself at a loss, but she was saved from having to make a more substantial response by the start of the dance.

It was a country dance and lively enough that Anne found little opportunity to question Lord Gladstone further as they worked their way down the set. Once they reached the bottom and got a short reprive, Anne leaned in. "Do you think you will be quite overrun with applications? Once the R.M.A. opens, that is."

This was the most innocent segue Anne had been able to come up with into whether the R.M.A. was already overrun with applications. Lord Gladstone tipped his head to the side and blinked at her once... twice... three times. "Well, uh... we're planning for two hundred children to start."

"A handsome number," Anne said. "Do you think that will be sufficient to meet demand?"

The baron looked baffled. "I... I couldn't say."

Anne bit her lip as the dance swept them up again. She hadn't learned anything of value, but perhaps that wasn't surprising. She'd hardly been expecting a full confession.

As they circled each other, Lord Gladstone cleared his throat. He did it again, then a third time, and then he coughed into his fist. He fell silent a moment, then burst into a fit of coughing when they were halfway through the figure.

An idea occurred to Anne. She caught Lord Gladstone's arm and drew him out of the set. "Shall we get you something to drink?"

"If you"—he turned his head to cough again—"wouldn't mind."

The refreshment table was on the far side of the room, and they had to circle around the outskirts to avoid the dancers. The worst of Lord Gladstone's coughing had subsided, so Anne cast around for a topic. "What sort of education will the R.M.A. be providing to its charges?"

"It's going to be practical, I can tell you that." The baron cleared his throat. "It's not as if these are officer's children. They're destined for the subordinate situations of life, and they will be made to understand that. They'll learn to read, and a little arithmetic, but it wouldn't do, educating such children in a way that would give them airs of being above their natural place in the world." He shook his head. "They're going to have to earn their bread by the sweat of their brow for the rest of their lives. They need to get used to that from an early age."

Anne couldn't disagree more, but she wasn't about to argue with him when she was finally getting somewhere. "I see. What sorts of jobs will you be preparing them for?"

It seemed Lord Gladstone had finally warmed to a topic.

"The idea is that most of the boys will enlist in the army themselves when they turn twelve, and the girls will go into service. There will be daily drill for the boys—we'll have a drummer on staff—and the girls will work in the kitchen and laundry, in addition to the usual sewing and whatnot."

"It sounds like you have it all planned out." Anne paused, considering how to phrase her next question. "Are you considering any other trades for the boys? If they, say, did not want to go into military service?"

"Har-hem!" Lord Gladstone was still struggling with his lingering cough. "You've hit upon one of the challenges. However much we might wish otherwise, we cannot force the boys to enlist. Of course, we will provide every inducement for them to do so. But should some refuse, we'll have to find some sort of apprenticeship for them."

As a chimney sweep's apprentice, perhaps? Anne tried to make her voice casual. "And what trades have you identified as most fitting for these sons of common foot soldiers?"

Lord Gladstone was back to blinking at her in the slightly bovine way he had. "Well, uh, we'll cross that bridge when we come to it."

They had reached the refreshment table. Lord Gladstone stepped forward to obtain two glasses of punch. Anne was turning over what he had said. He was certainly a vocal proponent of child labor. Had his silence when she asked what apprenticeships they would seek for the boys been a guilty one?

"Here you are, my lady," he said, holding out a glass of punch.

Anne swallowed. This was it. If she wanted to see his signet ring, it was now or never.

"Thank you." As soon as the cup was in her hand, she made a show of fumbling it, and managed to spill half its contents onto his left glove.

"Oh, my gracious, I'm so terribly sorry!" She began digging in her reticule for a handkerchief, but kept her eyes fixed on his hand.

Lord Gladstone grunted, and, just as Anne had hoped, peeled off his sodden glove.

She held her breath as his wrist came into view, then the back of his hand, then his knuckles, then—

A gold signet ring, set with a red stone that looked to be carnelian. From this close, she could just make out the etching: the head of a wild boar, just like the crest on his carriage.

The truth swept over her. However mundane he appeared, this man—this *monster*—had been selling four-year-old children into working conditions that would kill nine out of ten of them before their twelfth birthday.

Lord Gladstone grunted again as he took the handkerchief Anne hadn't realized she was proffering. The movement jerked her back to the present. Oh, God, she needed to stay calm, to pretend nothing was wrong. But how could she smile and make small talk with the man who was… the man who…

"Lady Wynters, is everything all right?"

"Oh!" Anne jumped as she looked up and found Samuel peering at her in concern. "Mr. Branton—just the person with whom I need a word." She hastily drank what little punch she hadn't spilled, set the glass down, and snatched up Samuel's arm. "Thank you so much, Lord Gladstone, for the dance, and the punch, and the—er—conversation. A fascinating conversation, I learned so much about the R.M.A., so much indeed." She knew she was babbling but couldn't seem to stop. "I apologize again, about your glove and the… the punch."

"Lady Wynters, wait," Lord Gladstone said. "Your handkerchief—"

She had already dropped a curtsey and was leading Samuel across the ballroom.

Samuel leaned down to murmur in her ear. "I take that as a no, everything is not all right."

"No indeed. There have been developments in our investigation. Several of them." Anne swallowed and glanced about the room. The ball was an absolute crush, but the balcony didn't look to be crowded. She led him toward the French doors. "Let's go out here, where we won't be overheard."

"Very well," Samuel said, and they stepped out into the night.

ACROSS THE BALLROOM, Michael was on the verge of losing his mind.

It was bad enough that he'd had to watch Augustus Mapplethorpe kiss Anne's hand *seven times* during their set (Michael knew it was seven. He had counted). Then it was Gladstone giving her what he no doubt thought were seductive glances (which really made him look like a constipated tortoise).

Now he had to watch her repair to the balcony with another man.

Michael made an incoherent sound of anguish to Fauconbridge, Harrington, and Ceci, who had given up on dancing in favor of trying to help him get through the evening without murdering one of Anne's partners.

"Relax, Morsley," Fauconbridge said. "That's Samuel Branton. He works with Anne on a number of charitable initiatives. They're only friends."

"Friends," Michael huffed. He had difficulty believing any man could look at Anne and want to be just friends with her.

"No, really," Fauconbridge said. "Harrington and I ran into him yesterday morning. He seemed genuinely pleased when he learned that you were back. He wants what's best for Anne, and that includes her marrying a man who worships the ground she walks on."

"Oh. Well, then." Michael paused, then cut his eyes to Fauconbridge. "And how exactly does this man I've never met know that I worship the ground she walks on?"

Fauconbridge ducked his chin, rubbing the back of his head. "Oh, uh—"

"We told him, naturally," Harrington said. He laughed at Michael's expression. "As Anne's friend, Mr. Branton is naturally concerned that she find a husband who will treat her with the respect she deserves. You should be grateful we told him you were her best prospect."

"I hope you're not expecting a letter of thanks," Michael grumbled.

He watched Lord Scudamore approach the balcony doors, pause, then slip outside. "Huh, why is Scudamore going out there alone?" Harrington asked.

"He has the next set with her," Michael said. "I expect he's going to claim his dance."

"Speaking of dancing," Fauconbridge said, "why don't you go and look for a partner? You don't look so well. I can watch Anne, and the time will pass more quickly if you have some occupation other than standing around brooding."

Michael's glower was sufficient to convey what he thought of that idea. He crossed his arms and settled in to watch the French doors for Anne's return.

CHAPTER 16

"*A*nd so you see," Anne concluded, "all the evidence points to Lord Gladstone."

"It certainly does," Samuel agreed. They were out on the balcony, and Anne had just described everything she had learned, from her conversation with Nick and Johnny to Lieutenant Avery's unexpected call and concluding with her dance with Lord Gladstone.

Samuel consulted his pocket watch by the light of a wall sconce. "My contact at Bow Street mentioned that he's supervising the first half of the Night Patrol shift. If I leave now, I should just be able to catch him. I believe there is enough evidence to arrest Lord Gladstone right now." Samuel started to turn toward the ballroom, then paused. "Would Gladstone really be stupid enough to collect the orphans using his own carriage?"

"Yes," Anne said at once. "He would. If you had but two minutes' conversation with him, you'd understand. A criminal he might be, but a criminal mastermind he is decidedly—"

"Lady Wynters?"

Anne and Samuel froze, then slowly turned to face the French doors, where Lord Scudamore stood outlined by the light from the ballroom. Anne swallowed.

"I'm sorry, I was just coming to collect you for our dance, and—you were talking about Gladstone. You said… he was a criminal." The viscount shook his head, as if unable to conceive what he had just heard. "What do you mean by that?"

Anne forced a brittle smile to her face. "N-never mind. Is it time for our dance? Shall we—"

"You said something about orphans," Lord Scudamore insisted as he strode forward. "Orphans and a carriage."

He must have been standing there for some time. Anne's mind was scrambling for something, anything she could say to diffuse the situation. She exchanged a quick glance with Samuel, who seemed to be similarly at a loss.

"You said you were going to Bow Street." Lord Scudamore was growing flustered, his voice rising in both tone and volume. "You said he was a *criminal*. That is a serious accusation. A very serious accusation, and about my dearest friend—"

"Please, my lord." Anne turned to Samuel. "Do you think we should explain?"

"I don't see any way around it," Samuel murmured.

Anne had to agree. Although she was loathe to bring Lord Gladstone's *dearest friend* into their confidence, she could not imagine a scenario in which Lord Scudamore would hold his tongue without being told the reasons for their suspicions. Even then, he might still tip off Lord Gladstone, but Anne knew based upon the viscount's charity work that his interest in the welfare of children was sincere. Perhaps his moral compass would win out over blind fidelity to his friend.

Anne nodded to Samuel. "You can go and meet with your contact. I will explain to Lord Scudamore."

Samuel cut his eyes to the viscount. "You're sure?"

"Completely sure."

"Very well." Samuel bowed over her hand. "Let's speak again tomorrow."

"Indeed," Anne murmured. She turned to Lord Scudamore. "Come away from the doors, my lord, and I will explain everything."

As HIS GAZE had not strayed once from the French doors leading to the balcony, Michael marked the moment Anne's friend Samuel Branton returned to the ballroom.

Michael expected to see Anne and Lord Scudamore right behind him. But as the seconds ticked agonizingly by, they kept… not appearing.

"Ooh, looking bad, Morsley," Harrington said, sucking in a breath. "Very bad, indeed."

"Thank you for mentioning it," Michael muttered. He was trying to put on a calm front, but he felt physically ill. If he missed his chance with Anne, again…

The thought was so horrible he couldn't even bear to think it.

"Shut it, Harrington," Fauconbridge said. "The next set is just forming. They'll walk through those doors any second now. You'll see."

Michael stared at the doors almost without blinking as the musicians finished tuning up. He tore his gaze away just long enough to see that the dancers arranged into squares for a cotillion.

He all but jumped out of his skin as the orchestra played a

jaunty introduction, and still Anne and Scudamore did not appear.

Cold dread pierced his chest, growing deeper as the seconds ticked agonizingly by.

They weren't returning for their dance. Scudamore must have asked her to take a turn about the balcony instead.

Scudamore was going to propose. He was going to propose before Michael got a chance to speak. *He was going to lose her again.*

"Morsley, stop!" Fauconbridge was clinging to his arm; Michael was startled to realize that he'd been dragging his friend across the ballroom.

"I'll head out there and play the overprotective big brother." Fauconbridge said, straightening his coat. "That way if she's furious with someone, it will be with me."

"You'll do no such thing," Ceci said. Michael, Harrington, and Fauconbridge all turned to gape at her. "She's a widow," Ceci continued, "she doesn't need an overprotective big brother. She'll know at once Morsley put you up to it." She peered around Harrington's shoulder toward the balcony doors. "It will be much more convincing if I do it."

"*Hurry,*" was as much of a response as Michael could muster.

"I need a knife," Ceci said.

Harrington produced a pen knife. Michael watched in astonishment as Ceci sliced open the seam connecting her sleeve to her bodice. The cut was only an inch, but had she taken her hand off the seam (which she did not), her bodice would have gaped.

"*Ceci,*" Fauconbridge hissed.

She gave him a quelling look. "It has to be an emergency." She thrust the knife back into Harrington's hand and squared off her shoulders. "Wish me luck."

Anne and Scudamore had been out there alone for at least

five minutes, and with the dancing underway, Ceci had to skirt all the way around the edges of the ballroom. Michael could scarcely breathe as he watched her picking her way through the crowded clusters of matrons and wallflowers ringing the room.

Someone pressed a drink into his hand. It proved to be Harrington. Michael downed it without even looking to see what it was.

Fauconbridge placed a hand on his shoulder, and they stood in silence as Michael steeled himself for the most agonizing minutes of his life.

"AND SO YOU SEE," Anne said, "the crest on the carriage door points to Lord Gladstone."

Lord Scudamore squeezed his eyes shut. "I know it looks bad. But a carriage alone isn't proof. It could be his coachman who's in league with these villains."

"There's more. I was able to track down the officer who brought one of the boys back from the Continent, a Lieutenant Avery. He confirmed that the place he wrote looking for assistance was the R.M.A."

Lord Scudamore raked a hand through his hair. "The R.M.A. is not yet accepting applications."

"No," Anne agreed. "But if someone were to send one, to whom would it go?"

The viscount swallowed. "The secretary. Gladstone."

Anne nodded. "I thought as much. Lieutenant Avery recalled that the man who answered his letter was a lord. They met at night, and although he could not make out his face in the darkness, he recalled that he wore a gold signet ring with a dark red stone."

"Bloody—" Lord Scudamore spun away, making a sound

of frustration. "I apologize, my lady. I just—Gladstone has been my dearest friend. My dearest friend, ever since our school days. There must be some mistake, because I cannot *imagine* that he... that he..." He clenched his hands into fists as he stood at the balustrade, looking down.

Anne came to stand beside him. Lord Scudamore seemed sincere in his distress, and of course it would be devastating, to receive such news about one's dearest friend. "I quite understand. I am so very sorry to have to tell you this."

He sighed. "It's better that I know."

Anne swallowed. "I must now ask something of you, my lord. Something that I know will go against your sense of loyalty to your friend. But I hope that you agree, in light of what I have told you, that there are greater loyalties. To right and wrong and to basic human decency."

"You are going to ask me to say nothing to Gladstone." The viscount's knuckles were white upon the stone railing of the balcony.

"Yes," Anne said. "Mr. Branton is on his way to Bow Street right now. They will arrest Lord Gladstone tonight."

He squeezed his eyes shut. "I know it's the right thing. I know it has to be done. It's just so difficult for me to believe that Gladstone could do such a thing. Surely there must be some mistake."

"We will know soon enough. If the eyewitness confirms it was him, there will be no doubt."

"Eyewitness?" Lord Scudamore said slowly, raising his head to meet Anne's gaze. "I thought you said this Lieutenant Avery didn't get a look at his face."

"Lieutenant Avery did not," Anne said. "But one of the boys I rescued—"

"Anne?"

They both whirled around at the sound of a voice from the ballroom's entrance.

It proved to be Ceci, clutching her shoulder and looking wretched. "I'm so sorry to interrupt. I just... I couldn't find your mother, and I've had a bit of an emergency." She moved her hand just enough to reveal that the side seam holding the bodice of her dress in place had split.

"Oh, my gracious!" Anne said, hurrying over. She gave a nervous laugh. "We can't have you walking around like that."

"Indeed, no," Ceci said.

Anne wrapped an arm around Ceci's shoulders, then turned to Lord Scudamore, who was still standing by the railing. "Can I trust that you will keep this in confidence, my lord?"

The viscount placed his hand across his heart. "You have my word of honor."

"Thank you," Anne said.

She steered Ceci back through the French doors, leaving Lord Scudamore standing alone on the balcony, staring out into the darkness.

CHAPTER 17

*A*nne emerged from the ladies' retiring room and almost plowed into Michael, who stood rooted three feet outside the door like a fir tree, tall and unmovable.

She laughed as she pressed a hand to her chest. "Michael, I was just coming to find you."

He said nothing as he took her hand and placed it on his arm. He bowed deeply to Ceci, who had followed just behind Anne, then turned and began striding toward the ballroom.

Anne almost had to jog to keep up. Gracious, why was she so nervous? This was *Michael*. She had danced with him dozens of times over the years. Hundreds, if you counted the dancing lessons they'd shared growing up!

He glanced down at her then, and his green eyes were filled with such longing that Anne tripped over her own foot. Longing—that couldn't possibly be right. What had they put in the punch, that caused her to believe the man who had made it inescapably clear he saw her as nothing more than a friend might be *longing* for her?

They reached the ballroom. Instead of leading her to the top of the set, he proceeded across the floor at a rapid clip.

"Um, Michael." She squeezed his arm. "Should we not head over there?"

"I thought we might talk," he said, his deep voice causing gooseflesh to break out on the back of her neck. "If you don't mind?"

"I don't mind. That actually sounds lovely." After the strain of the last hour, having to question Lord Gladstone, then being overheard by Lord Scudamore, she could use a reprieve.

She'd had quite enough excitement for one evening.

Michael led her out the French doors and straight down into the garden. The night was cool, pleasantly so, after the crush of the ballroom. The moon was full, and it cast the gardens in the most gorgeous light. Moonlight suited Michael beautifully tonight, with his glossy black hair and spotless white linen. Even in the moonlight, she could make out the green of his eyes, so intense was the color.

He led her all the way to the back corner of the garden, over to a secluded stone bench. They sat down, and Michael took her hand in his. He closed his eyes.

Anne tipped her head back, enjoying the soft night sounds of the garden. She caught a whiff of jasmine on the breeze and closed her eyes to breathe in the sweet smell. *Delicious.* She was still tense following her conversation with Lord Scudamore, and she forced her shoulders to unknot and lower. It was a gorgeous summer night, and here she was, with her favorite person in the whole world. She should enjoy it.

"So," she said, "what was it you wanted to talk to me about?" She opened her eyes and turned to face Michael on the bench.

Except, Michael was no longer beside her on the bench. He was still holding her hand, but while she'd been enjoying the night air, he had moved.

He was now directly in front of her.

Kneeling.

Her heart began to race like a runaway carriage.

"Anne," he began, pressing her hand. He lifted his eyes to hers, and they were intense, and sincere, and she felt color rising in her cheeks.

He squeezed her hand again. "There's something I want to ask you."

"Yes?" she whispered.

He swallowed. "Will you marry me?"

She felt her mouth fall open. She... she hadn't been imagining things after all. Michael wanted her. He—he wanted to marry her!

But then she remembered their conversation from earlier that evening.

"Oh! That is very kind of you, Michael. But... *you* do not want to marry *me.*"

He blinked at her a few times. "I assure you that I do."

"It was what I said earlier, wasn't it? About how I might have to settle for a fortune hunter." She shook her head. "I shouldn't have said anything about it. I should have known it would make you feel sorry for me, but you don't have to—"

"Feel *sorry* for you? I don't feel sorry for you—"

"Oh, Michael, you are the dearest friend to ask me. But I could never allow you to throw away the chance of finding future happiness with someone you could truly love just to help me out of my predicament."

He was back to blinking at her again. "Have you any other objection," he began slowly, "other than this absurd belief that I do not truly wish to marry you?"

"Of course not. There isn't one thing about you that is objectionable. But my feelings are not absurd. You're the son of a marquess, and you're kind, and intelligent, and honorable, and... and..." Anne felt herself blush still deeper as she made a sweeping gesture. "Just look at you!"

His expression turned a touch smug. "You find me handsome, then?"

"Of course I do. As does every other woman in that ballroom. But that's not important. The point is, you're a wonderful man. Every single thing about you is wonderful. Why would *you* want to marry the likes of *me*?"

He didn't answer but posed a question of his own. "So, what you're saying is that you would marry me, if you believed it was what I truly wanted?"

It was her turn to blink at him. "Well—er—yes."

His eyes were very intense. "Then let me prove it to you." He slid onto the bench and his big, strong hands moved up to frame her face.

He pressed his forehead against hers. His voice was a ragged whisper. "May I?"

Her whole body fluttered with anticipation. She wasn't sure she could speak, but nodded as she mouthed a silent, "Yes."

And the next thing she knew...

Michael Cranfield was kissing her.

The groan he gave in the instant his lips contacted hers rumbled through his body before passing into hers. He kissed her as gently as if she were spun glass, the softness of his lips a tantalizing contrast to the scrape of his jaw when it brushed hers.

He broke contact and his green eyes drifted open, dazed. His fingertips traced the edges of her face as if she were the most precious treasure on the face of this earth, and Anne realized that his hands were shaking.

"God, Anne," he moaned before his lips descended on hers again. This time his kiss was not gentle, which wasn't to say it was rough. It was more... intent. He immediately delved into her mouth with his tongue, and Anne was so startled she parted her lips with a squeak.

Michael groaned again, not seeming to notice her discomfiture, but Anne felt a trace of panic. Her husband had never kissed her this way. Lord Wynters hadn't been much for kisses in general, preferring to get straight to the business at hand, and she felt embarrassed, to be a widow and not really know how to kiss him back.

But it turned out that didn't matter, because Michael took charge, sweeping his tongue around the insides of her lips, then moving it to tangle with Anne's. She found it surprisingly easy to follow his lead and, judging by the pleasurable rumbles rising from his chest, Michael didn't find her attempts lacking.

Anne began to relax. She looped her arms around Michael's neck and twined her fingers in his glossy black hair. This type of kissing was new to her, but... she found she quite liked it. It made her feel giddy, as if she'd had one glass of wine too many. A buzzing sensation began to build throughout her body, and her nipples in particular began to tingle. The image sprang into her mind of Michael putting those big, strong, warm hands on her breasts, an image her body apparently loved, because her nipples tightened almost painfully, longing for his touch.

Suddenly the kiss wasn't enough, and Michael seemed to agree with her, because he scooped her up and placed her in his lap. Now their heads were at the same level and Anne had much better access to his beautiful, sculpted chest. Beneath her leg where it rested in his lap, she could feel a bulge that was as hard as steel, the same one she had felt that afternoon in the boat. Now it wasn't just her nipples that longed for his touch—Anne felt an unfamiliar pulse start up between her legs, one that grew stronger with every passing beat. She squirmed in his lap, longing for... something.

Michael was kissing her in earnest, not only kissing her but running his hands over her body. He stroked up her arms and then down her back, pausing to tease her waist. He even caressed her bottom, pressing her ever closer against him. Anne found herself wishing he would touch her breasts with those big, warm hands…

By now his mouth was devouring hers and she was shaking so hard that she could not breathe, nor could she think. All she could do was cling to his shoulders, hanging on for dear life in this kiss that was as frustrating as it was magical.

Just when she thought she was going to crawl out of her skin, he pulled his head back. They were both panting, and Michael looked like he was struggling for control. He lifted his eyes to hers, then took hold of her hand and slowly drew it up to his chest where he placed it, palm side down, over the pounding of his heart.

"Do you feel that?" he asked, his voice deep.

"Yes."

He flexed his hips, pressing his arousal against her leg. "And do you feel *that*?"

This time her voice was a squeak. "Yes!"

"*Good*. And do you still not believe that I truly want you?"

"No," she replied, breathing hard. "I believe you."

He gave her one of his characteristic Michael Looks then, one she recognized as his Obstinate Face. Whenever she saw that expression, she knew that her choices were to give in or to prepare for a very long argument, because he would never give up until he got his way. "Then you'll marry me?" he asked.

She swallowed. "Yes."

"Now see here, Anne—wait, you will?"

"Of course I will. So long as it's what you truly want and, although I don't pretend to understand why, it seems that it is. You're exactly the type of man I've always hoped to marry." She shook her head. "More than that, even. You, Michael Cranfield, are the very finest man I know."

Anne knew she would never forget the smile that broke over his face when she said that. As many years as she'd known Michael, she had never seen him look happier than he did in that moment.

She didn't have long to behold the expression, because the next thing she knew, he was kissing her again. This kiss was rather less successful than their first attempt, largely on account of the fact that neither of them could stop smiling. And then Michael threw his head back and laughed. He surged to his feet as he grabbed her around the waist and began spinning her around in a circle. She threw her arms around his neck, and their laughter echoed off the stone walls of the garden that surrounded them.

He eventually settled them both on the bench, her again on his lap. She rested her head against his.

"I'm so happy," he murmured.

"I am, too."

"I wish we could stay here forever, just like this."

Anne wasn't so sure. Her skin was tingling. *Everywhere.* And that spot between her legs was still throbbing. With Lord Wynters, the act of making love had never taken more than five minutes, even on her wedding night. Anne had never felt this way before, but she suspected she knew what was going on. After she became a married woman, it was almost as if she'd been initiated into a club, and the ladies around her didn't filter their conversation in quite the same way they once had. They were just little comments and jokes made in passing, but they were enough for Anne to conclude that she was missing out on... something. And she was starting to suspect that things might be different with Michael.

So, as nice as this was, when she thought about sitting together on a *bench* for the rest of their lives?

She could suddenly think of someplace she would *much* rather be.

"I don't," she muttered, almost without thinking.

He sighed. "I suppose you're right. No doubt our absence has already been noticed. We should probably head back inside."

Anne bit her lip. She might as well be honest. They were to be married, after all. And judging by the still-present bulge in Michael's trousers, he was feeling more or less the same way. "That's actually not what I meant."

Michael cocked his head. "Oh?"

"It's just…" Anne swallowed. "I am a widow after all, and we're to be married, and… um…"

Michael's eyes were growing intense. "Yes?"

"And I see a gate behind us, and my house is actually just around the corner, and… and…" She ducked her head.

His eyes had turned glassy, his jaw slack. When he spoke, his voice was disbelieving. "Let me make sure I understand. Are you suggesting that we leave this ball right now, go back to your house, and… and make love?"

Oh, dear God, *why* had she suggested it? She wondered if she would fit beneath the bench. It seemed like a good enough spot to curl up in a ball and die of mortification. "I… er… yes?"

He stood so quickly Anne didn't even have time to find her balance before he grabbed her hand and towed her toward the garden gate. "That," he said over his shoulder, "is the best suggestion I have ever heard."

CHAPTER 18

*I*t appeared that the garden gate had not been opened in some time, for its seams were overgrown with moss, and it did not yield to the firm push Michael gave it. Anne was about to suggest they circle back through the house when Michael lowered his shoulder, took three running steps, and rammed it.

Anne was still gaping at the clumps of moss hanging from the edges of the gate when Michael grabbed her hand and pulled her through. He broke into a run.

"Michael," Anne protested, tripping over her skirts, "I can't run in this."

He scooped her up in his arms midstride and continued at his desired pace.

Her house truly was just around the corner, so he didn't have to carry her far. At the top of the front steps Anne motioned for him to set her down and held a finger to her lips. Perhaps they could slip inside without being noticed.

They had no such luck. Her footman, Hugh, emerged from the shadows. His eyes went wide and his mouth fell open.

Anne squared her shoulders. A widow could take as many lovers as she wished, and society would not so much as blink. She had faithfully mourned her husband for a year, and she and Michael were getting married. She had nothing of which to be ashamed. "Hugh, I know you will recall my mentioning that my friend, Lord Morsley, was back in England."

"Of course, m'lady," Hugh replied.

"You may be the first to congratulate us. Lord Morsley has proposed, and I have accepted."

A genuine smile came over Hugh's face. "Congratulations, m'lady. M'lord," he said, bowing.

"Thank you. We did not stay for supper at the Sunderland ball. If you would be so kind as to have someone make us up a tray and leave it in the hall outside my room."

"At once, m'lady," Hugh replied, retreating.

Anne tugged Michael's hand, leading him up the stairs toward her rooms. It was only once they had entered her sitting room that she noticed he was laughing.

"What?" she asked, confused.

"'Have someone make us up a tray. Leave it in the hall *outside* my room,'" he said, mimicking her voice. "If the world could see the spotless Lady Anne Astley right now—"

She smacked him on the shoulder. "Well, they can't. Although I suppose they might as well. Everyone is bound to notice that we've both disappeared. But I'll not concern myself with idle gossip. We're to be married, after all."

"Yes. Yes, we are."

"Besides, I'm not Lady Anne Astley anymore. I haven't been for years. I'm Anne—"

"You're going to be Anne Cranfield, is who you're going to be. The Countess of Morsley. And then someday, the Marchioness of Redditch."

"Hopefully not for a good long while, as I am excessively

fond of the current Lord Redditch. Anne Cranfield, Lady Morsley, will do just fine for me."

He closed his eyes and made a sound that was somewhere between a sigh and a groan. His smile when he opened his eyes was a trifle unsteady. "I do like the sound of that."

Then he pulled her into his arms and started kissing her. But he was doing more than just kissing her this time—a rush of cool air on her back announced that he had unfastened her gown.

Michael proceeded to use his big, strong, warm hands to strip Anne down to her shift and stockings, tossing everything in a heap on the carpet. She gave him a shy smile as she began unbuttoning his coat.

In short order, Michael's garments joined hers in the pile on the floor. Anne felt her mouth go dry as he peeled off his shirt and his torso came into view. His arms were as thick as her legs and bulging with muscles. His chest seemed to go on forever, it was so broad, and it was covered with a liberal dusting of black hair. His stomach was covered with ridges of muscle. Anne lifted her hand, wondering if it was as hard as it looked.

She froze when she realized what she was doing and glanced up guiltily. Before she could withdraw her hand, Michael grabbed it and pressed her palm against his chest.

"Yes," he said.

"Y-yes?" she squeaked. His chest certainly was as hard as it looked, and his skin was surprisingly smooth, almost satiny beneath her fingers...

He scooped her up in his arms. "Yes to you touching me," he said as he carried her through the doorway that led to her bedchamber and set her upon the bed. "Believe me, I'm going to be touching you." He kicked off his shoes and sat beside her. "You also have my permission to continue ogling me."

She pretended to bristle but couldn't conceal her smile. "I don't know that *ogling* is the term that applies."

"Ogling," he insisted, peeling off one of her stockings. "It felt wonderful. Have you ever been ogled before?"

"I couldn't say."

"Well, you're about to be," he replied, tossing her other stocking on the floor. Anne flushed as she tucked her bare legs beneath her. She was now wearing nothing but her shift, which was made of whisper-thin white linen. The rosy pink of her nipples was just visible through the delicate fabric. She ducked her chin, unable to meet his eye.

Michael grasped the hem of her shift, then paused. "Would you take down your hair?" he asked. "I want to see it hanging down to your waist, the way it looked..."

She was already reaching up to undo the pins. "The way it looked when?" she asked, surprised.

He cleared his throat. "Nothing, just... I'd like to see you with it down."

She didn't have time to contemplate this further, because as soon as her hair came tumbling down, Michael began to draw her shift up. He pressed her back onto the bed as he peeled it over her head, so that she ended up lying naked before him, her arms splayed up over her head, her hair spilling around her on the pillow. Up until this point, Anne had been amazed by how natural it felt, being with Michael. Kissing Michael. Undressing Michael, even. But being completely bare before him suddenly made her feel intensely vulnerable. She squeezed her eyes shut.

"Anne. Look at me."

She opened her eyes just a slit. And what she saw was... ogling. There really was no other word for it. She could read Michael Cranfield's face, and what she saw in his eyes in that moment was arousal. Fierce joy. Wonder. And *worship*. All for her. She began to relax.

"You're perfect," he murmured, stroking his hands up her legs, as if he couldn't help himself.

"I am not," she protested.

"*Perfect*," he insisted, groaning as he caressed her hips.

"I'm not. I'm too tall. It's... unwomanly."

"Too tall." He snorted. "You look like a *goddess*. Just look at your legs—" He trailed off as he caressed her from her ankles all the way up to her hips, drawing a groan from them both. "I've always thought you were the most beautiful woman in the world."

Anne could hear the longing in his voice, and his eyes held nothing but sincerity. Which was shocking, because... Michael thought she was beautiful? And what did he mean, he'd always thought so? That... that didn't make any sense...

She didn't have time to contemplate that, because Michael lay down beside her and took her into his arms, and everything resembling a coherent thought fled as his bare chest pressed against hers. She imagined this was what it felt like to be struck by lightning, if being struck by lightning were the most pleasurable sensation on the face of this earth. She began to tremble.

Then he started kissing her again, and this time, his hands were everywhere. She'd thought her skin was starving for his touch back on the bench, but that was nothing compared to the craving she felt now. He took her breasts in his hands, and the pleasure was so acute, her whole body jerked. "Yes— oh, God, Michael! P-please—"

He kissed her jaw, then worked his way down her neck and collarbone. Anne lay there panting, wondering if it was possible to die of longing as he kissed the soft swell of her breast. Just when she was sure she couldn't take it anymore, he sucked a nipple into his mouth.

It was every bit as good as she had imagined it would be. She cried out and her hips bucked off the bed. Her response seemed to please Michael because he gave a growl as he redoubled his efforts.

She realized that she hadn't been touching him, which seemed like a waste, given that those broad, gorgeous shoulders were within arm's reach. So she began running her hands over him. Admittedly, there was little art to what she was doing, as she was halfway out of her mind, but Michael didn't seem to care. He'd moved his lips to her other breast, and his hands were stroking down over her stomach. She knew it was time, that any second now he would reach down and remove his breeches and take her. For the first time in her life, she was eager for what she knew was about to happen. She spread her legs for him.

But instead of reaching for his waistband, Michael groaned and settled his hand between her thighs. Anne stiffened. What was he doing? His fingers searched between her folds until he found whatever he'd been looking for. And he started to rub her, gently at first, but then with slowly increasing speed. And... oh, *God*... that felt good, that felt really, *really* good. But... why were her legs shaking? Her pleasure was mounting so quickly she felt almost... out of control. Was... was this supposed to be happening?

"Michael?" she asked.

"Yes, darling?"

"I... I think something's wrong."

He immediately froze. "Do you want me to stop?"

Her body was already protesting. "No! Please don't stop. It's just... I think there's something wrong with me. I'm worried that I'm... going to explode. I've... I've never felt like this before."

His expression suddenly became one of pure masculine satisfaction. "Good," he growled. He slid down her body and buried his face between her legs. And oh, oh, *oh*—if she had thought his *hand* felt good, it was nothing, *nothing* compared to the pleasure of his *tongue* swirling over that sweet little spot! She didn't even have time to contemplate what he was doing before her world came apart. Her hips surged up off the bed and she started writhing as everything between her legs began to pulse. She heard herself crying out as Michael gave her the most pure, unadulterated pleasure, sensations so beautiful she had never imagined they could even exist.

As she came down, he slid up beside her and took her in his arms. She was beyond words, but she made some contented babbling sounds as she snuggled against his chest, running her hands across his warm, smooth back, down to the waistband of his breeches.

His breeches?

That was when Anne realized that she had been so far gone, so lost in the pleasure he was giving her, that she had done absolutely nothing for him. He hadn't even taken his breeches off yet!

She began fumbling for the buttons of his placket. He rolled onto his back and smiled, seeming to enjoy the sight of her ministering to him.

Or at least, attempting to minister to him. She wasn't making much progress with those buttons. To be fair, it was tough going—the breeches were fitting him rather snugly due to the extremely large bulge in front.

"Perhaps you could assist me," she murmured.

He barked out a laugh. "That would probably be wise. Another minute of you stroking me like that, and I'm likely to finish before we even get started."

She flushed. He made quick work of the buttons and flexed his hips, pushing his breeches and drawers off together and tossing them aside.

She gaped at him. He was... he was *huge*, there was no other way to put it. He was long, and he was so, so *thick*, and even though she hadn't been a virgin in years, she was not at all certain that this was going to work.

"Anne, look at me." She did, and she saw such tenderness in his eyes. He took her in his arms and started kissing her again, and it felt so beautiful, being with Michael like this, it felt more than beautiful, it felt...

Right.

He lifted his head. "Better?"

"Yes," she said, and she meant it. "Michael, I... I want you."

He rolled her onto her back and positioned himself above her. "You have no idea how much I want you, Anne. *No idea.*" He snagged a pillow and slid it underneath her hips.

She felt him aligning himself at her entrance. He paused, his forehead resting against hers, his eyes closed. Then he opened them, and the look in Michael Cranfield's eyes, just before he made love to her for the first time... she recognized it as the inscrutable face he had made after that awful picnic, just before he told her that she meant everything to him. Only in this moment, when he was on the cusp of making her his own, it was a thousand times more poignant. Tears welled in her eyes, threatening to spill over. Slowly he began sliding into her. She spread her legs and tried to relax. And before she knew it, he was seated fully inside of her.

As he began to move, Anne felt her neck and shoulders, which she hadn't even realized were clinched, relax. She'd been half-expecting their joining to hurt because of Michael's extraordinary size, but there was no pain, none at all.

She glanced up at Michael. He was studying her intently, his jaw clenched. "Maybe more like this?" he said, adjusting the pillow to raise the angle of Anne's hips.

"Oh! Wh-whatever you like."

"I'm more concerned with what *you* would like," Michael muttered.

He continued his gentle thrusts for a minute, then reached down to shift the pillow again. "How does that feel?"

Anne swallowed. Part of her wanted to tell him that he needn't trouble himself, that she just wasn't one of those women who derived pleasure from the act of lovemaking. She couldn't bring herself to be quite so bold, so instead she said, "Don't worry about it, Michael. It's fine."

"No, it's not." She watched a vein pop out on the side of his neck. His shoulders beneath her hands could have been made of iron. "*Fine* is not fine." He reached down and began fumbling with the pillow again. "I mean, maybe it is, but I'm at least going to *try* to make it good for you."

"Really, Michael, it's—oh!"

He froze, holding her at the precise angle he had just found. "Oh?"

That place he was now rubbing, that felt... interesting. "Oh... Oh *my*."

Michael was studying her face intently. "Does that feel good?"

It felt better with each passing stroke. "It does. I just—I need—" Anne had no idea what she needed, but suddenly she was acutely aware that she needed *something*.

"How about this?" Michael asked, starting to circle his hips slightly instead of just thrusting back and forth. "Does that feel good? Or am I too big?"

"*Oh, Michael!*" And just like that, she had discovered the thing she needed, which was for Michael Cranfield to rub that magic spot inside of her. Just. Like. *That*. "You're not too big. You're just the right size. You're absolutely *perfect*." She groaned and her head lolled back onto the pillow.

Above her, Michael grinned, although his brow remained knotted. "Good."

Anne became aware of things she's been too tense to notice just moments before. Michael's body, gorgeous beneath her hands, rubbing against her best and most sensitive spots. The delicious sensation of all of his skin pressed up against all of hers. How much she loved his weight on top of her, pressing her into the mattress. The adoration in his eyes as he looked down at her.

Or maybe it was some mysterious combination of those things. But whatever it was, Anne felt her thighs began to tremble anew, and that feeling returned, the one where she felt like she was about to explode. She heard herself babbling his name, and then he started circling his hips faster, and then... Oh... oh... *ohhhhhhhh!*

Her world shattered a second time, and somehow the pleasure was even sweeter than before. Michael caught her eye, and she found herself unable to look away from the unbridled joy in his eyes as he watched her reach her climax.

He switched from the circling motion to the in-and-out thrusts he'd started with, and moments later, the pleasure was upon him. His thrusts became frantic, then his entire body grew as hard as stone above hers, and then it was his turn to shake and to call out her name. She felt him spasming inside of her, and she was treated to the sight of a face she had never seen from Michael before, a face that said he was experiencing the most pure, overwhelming pleasure.

He collapsed on top of her, breathing hard. She cradled his head against her neck and traced her fingers over his back. "Mmmmmm," he murmured.

After a few minutes he lifted his head. "How are you?" he asked with a crooked smile. His hair was sticking up in the back. He looked *adorable*.

"I'm wonderful! I... I liked that," she said biting her lip.

He laughed, rolling off and settling her head upon his shoulder. "I suspected as much."

"What gave me away?"

"Mostly the way you were screaming, 'Yes, Michael! Yes, Michael! Yes, Michael!'"

She flushed. "I didn't realize I was doing that."

He ran his fingers through her hair. "Oh, but you were."

She smiled, stroking her fingers over his chest. "I guess there's no point in denying it, then. But that wasn't what I was referring to, when I said that I liked it."

"Oh?" He raised his head to look at her.

"I mean," she hastened to explain, "of course I liked the 'Yes, Michael! Yes, Michael!' part."

"You mean the 'Yes, Michael! Yes, Michael!' *parts*, plural," he said, that look of supreme masculine satisfaction settling over his features again.

She tickled his side and he squirmed beside her. "Parts, plural. You are correct. But what I meant was that I liked it when you... when you..." She felt her cheeks heating again, and looked down.

He brought a finger to her chin and tipped her head right back up to meet his gaze. "You mean the part where I came inside of you?"

"Yes. That part," she replied, laughing. "I liked knowing that I had made you feel good. Seeing it on your face."

He kissed her tenderly. "That was what I liked, too."

"The part where you came inside of me?"

He laughed. "No, silly. Although you just gave me the most intense pleasure I've ever felt. By far. But my favorites were the 'Yes, Michael! Yes, Michael!' parts. Knowing that I made *you* feel good. Seeing it on *your* face."

She smiled and closed her eyes, enjoying the feeling of his arms around her. After a few minutes, she felt the rumble of his chuckle beneath her ear. She propped up her head. "What?"

"I have some good news for you."

"Oh?"

"You did say your favorite part was when I came inside you. What kind of gentleman would I be if I only allowed you to have your favorite part once in the course of the evening?"

She peeked down and saw that he had already grown hard. *He wanted her again.*

She certainly liked the way *that* made her feel.

She smiled, rolling onto her back. "Yes, please. I only hope I'll be able to give you your favorite part again, too."

He smiled tenderly, brushing a lock of hair off her forehead. "Parts plural, my darling Anne. Parts plural." He slid down and buried his face between her legs.

And indeed, Michael was right. It was parts, plural.

CHAPTER 19

*M*ichael awoke the next morning with a smile on his face.

Needless to say, it had been the best night of his life. Everything about it had been perfect. Anne was going to be *his wife*. He had made love to her. He had just awoken with her in his arms. And it had all been better than anything he could have imagined.

Michael had known some women over the past four years. Not so very many—unmarried women were few and far between on the Canadian frontier. But after he found out Anne had married someone else, there hadn't been much point in saving himself any longer. So when a widow in the nearest town offered to relieve him of his virginity, he accepted. That woman, Mrs. Fitzherbert, had taken it upon herself to teach him exactly how to please a woman.

He was feeling grateful to Mrs. Fitzherbert right about now.

Those encounters had meant nothing to him, but he had thought at the time they were all he would ever have.

But last night... that had been something else entirely.

He'd always known that making love to Anne would be special. He had expected the joy and the pleasure to surpass anything he'd experienced before.

What he had been unprepared for was the magnitude of his feelings. He had meant it when he said that she had given him the most intense physical pleasure of his life. But he had also meant it when he had said that his favorite part of their lovemaking was watching her reach her peak. When he thought about her face, in the moment that he had given her the first taste of pleasure she had ever experienced...

Just... joy. Gut-wrenching, heart-bursting, joy.

And there had been quite a few opportunities for him to enjoy watching Anne climax. After her fifth orgasm, she put on her dressing gown and snuck out into the hall to retrieve the supper tray. He made her take the dressing gown off again before they ate, which turned out to be a stroke of genius, because after they made their way through the meats and cheeses, Anne discovered a plate of strawberry tarts. That prompted Michael to confess how much he had always loved the smell of strawberries, because it reminded him of her.

This led to her teasing him, which led to him tickling her, which led to her tickling him right back, which in short order led to them both becoming extremely aroused. Which, in turn, led to him declaring that there was only one thing he could think of that was even more delicious than strawberry tarts. He proceeded to dress those areas of Anne's body with the cream that adorned the aforementioned tarts and demonstrated how very delectable he found those parts of her to be. All of which culminated in orgasms numbers six and seven for Anne. And what kind of gentleman would he have been, if he had not allowed her to enjoy her favorite part?

Afterwards, Anne began drifting off to sleep, so he settled

her in his arms. But he couldn't resist pointing out that she would never again be able to look at a plate of strawberry tarts without imagining him with his head buried between her legs—a significant problem, considering how much she enjoyed strawberry tarts. She blushed very prettily when he said that.

As he came fully awake, Michael saw that light was just breaking through the windows. Anne was still in his arms, but she had turned in the night so that her back was facing to his front.

This meant that some of her best and most sensitive areas were literally at his fingertips, and it was tempting to avail himself of that access. But they'd had a late night, and he didn't want to wake her.

As he lay there, struggling to resist temptation, she moaned and muttered something he didn't catch.

"Anne?" he asked. "Are you awake?"

Her response was another string of babble, but there were two words he caught.

They were *Mmmmmmm* and *Michael.*

He smoothed her hair aside and began kissing her neck in hopes that she was waking up. She groaned and arched her back, which had the effect of pressing her bottom into his eager cock. It also caused his arm, which was draped over her, to brush against her breasts. She purred and grasped him by the wrist, placing his hands there more firmly. He was glad to comply and began teasing first one nipple, then the other.

He was enjoying the incoherent sounds of pleasure she was making when she grasped his wrist again, this time to pull his hand down across her stomach. Even halfway asleep, she gave a wiggle of anticipation, and then she *spread* for him and positioned his hand exactly where she wanted it. He found her wet, as he knew he would. He began giving her slow, gentle, teasing little rubs. Within a few minutes, she was writhing in his arms and moaning his name. He kept his touch deliberately gentle. Her eyes blinked open, and he saw the moment she realized it wasn't a dream.

"Michael," she said in a breathy voice, "that feels sooooo good! I need... I need..."

He kept his strokes deliberately slow and gentle. "What is it you need, Anne?"

"You..." She trailed off as he gave her sweet spot a particularly delicious swirl. "Oh, Michael!"

"Perhaps some of this?" he asked, continuing to pet her just where she needed it most.

The sounds she made next did not qualify as English words, but to Michael, they were the sweetest music in the world.

"What do you want, Anne? Do you want to come like this?" he asked, momentarily increasing the pace of his hand. "Or do you want my cock?"

"Oh, Michael, I want them both!" she cried. "But I suppose I can't have that. I want... I want your cock," she confessed, ducking her chin as she said that word for the first time.

She was trying to roll over onto her back, but Michael had an idea. "Stay there, darling. Your wish is my command."

He lifted up her top leg, parting her, and tipped her torso forward just a bit. He continued stroking her between her legs with his free hand. But from this angle, he thought he could make this work...

Anne groaned as she realized what he was doing. As he flexed his hips to slide his cock inside her, she pushed back, until he was fully seated while they both lay on their sides. "Oh, Michael!" she cried out. "That feels so good!"

He began pumping into her, gently at first, keeping his hand working her little sweet spot. His cock and his hand proved to be an excellent combination for Anne. She was out of control within seconds, and an orgasm ripped out of her on his fifth thrust.

He enjoyed that, he enjoyed that very much. Was there anything better than watching the woman he loved taking such sweet pleasure from his cock? But, having come four times in the past eight hours, it was going to take him a little bit longer to achieve his own release. He continued thrusting into her gently, but moved his hands up to her breasts, worried that her little rosebud might be too sensitive so soon after her peak. He need not have worried, for although she was clearly enjoying his ministrations to her breasts, after a couple of minutes, she grabbed his hand and pulled it back down between her legs.

He *loved* that. He loved having her so eager for his touch that she was demanding his hand. And so he rubbed her with renewed effort, and pumped into her from behind, and to his immense satisfaction he was able to give her orgasms nine and ten. His own release soon followed, and it was every bit as powerful as his previous four.

She turned around and snuggled up to him. "Good morning," she said.

"It certainly is." They fell into a companionable silence. After a few minutes, he said, "Could I ask you something?"

"Of course."

"Had you really never had a climax until last night?"

She blushed. "I had not."

He ran a thumb over her flushed cheeks. "It's just that... you're so good at it."

She laughed. "I think you're the one who's good at it, as you put it."

"Believe me, you're good at it too. Very good. You made me forget myself. I didn't take any precautions, didn't wear a sheath, or even remember to withdraw. You could conceive," he said carefully.

She sat up, her hands going to her stomach. She was *beaming*. "I hadn't thought of that! Do you really think so?"

"You never know." He smiled. "You would be excited about the possibility—here I was thinking you would be worried about a scandal."

She laughed. "What scandal? I've an appointment this morning, but we can be married by special license this very afternoon, as far as I'm concerned."

"I love the way you're thinking," he replied. "Although perhaps we should allow a few days so we can send word to our families. I know my father would be disappointed to miss his only son's wedding."

"You're right, our families must be there. Although I don't know that we should wait for Caro. I almost don't even want to send her word. She would feel she had to come back, and I hate to interrupt her bridal trip."

"We'll figure it out," he said, pulling Anne down to lie with her head upon his chest. "We'll have the ceremony sometime in the next week. Then we can leave for Canada the week after."

ANNE BLINKED and lifted her head from Michael's chest. Surely she must have misheard. "Canada? What do you mean, leave for Canada?"

He grinned at her. "You're going to love it there, Anne—it's so beautiful, and every day is an adventure. I can't wait to show you everything I've built."

Oh, thank goodness—he just wanted to show her what he'd been doing these past four years. "You mean as a bridal trip?"

He laughed. "We'll be there a bit longer than your standard bridal trip."

Of course, it took so long just to cross the Atlantic, it would only make sense to stay for a few months. Such a long trip would require extensive planning. She would have to find friends to oversee the various functions of her charity while she was gone.

She would need at least a month to prepare.

"How long did you have in mind?" she asked.

"That depends, of course, but I hope we won't be coming back for thirty or forty years."

"Thirty or forty *years*?" she cried, sitting up. "What do you mean, thirty or forty years?"

"My father is as healthy as a horse and thank God for it. I'm in no hurry to ascend to the marquessate. But of course, we'll have to return to England once I do."

"But Michael, surely you cannot be thinking to move to Canada until you inherit? You're the heir. You belong in England. Your father needs you. I need you—we all need you!"

His smile was fond as he tucked a lock of hair behind her ear. "And I need you too, Anne. But you'll always have me. You need never worry about that. We'll always be together. In Canada."

"But I cannot move to Canada!" she cried.

Michael had been so excited imagining what the next couple of weeks held that he'd been paying scant attention to Anne. He looked at her now and was surprised to see that she was genuinely in distress. He sat up and took her hands, and said carefully, "I see that this has come as a surprise. It will be a big adjustment, to move away from all your family and friends. I see that now. But give yourself a few days to get used to the idea and it won't seem so daunting. After all, the only thing that matters is that the two of us are together."

"No, Michael, that is not the only thing that matters!" she exclaimed. "It's not just a matter of my family, although I cannot imagine leaving them for *thirty or forty years*. My society is here. There are so many people depending on me."

"Now, Anne, I know your society is important to you. But I need to be in Canada. So you're going to Canada, too."

Anne swallowed and looked sadder than he could ever remember seeing her. "If that's the case, Michael, then I cannot marry you," she said, her voice breaking.

Michael couldn't believe what he had just heard. It was a sensation he had felt only once before, when he found out Anne had married someone else—a sledgehammer to the center of his chest. Suddenly he couldn't breathe, he couldn't think, he couldn't—she couldn't—she had to...

"You have to marry me," he said, the words emerging rougher than he would have liked.

"I cannot. Not if you insist on moving to Canada."

"You *have to*," he repeated, his panicking brain not functioning well enough for strategy or finesse. "You promised that you would."

"That was before I knew you were going to drag me off to Canada!"

"You *have to*, Anne," he said again. "You could already be carrying my child! If you would just think rationally—"

He saw her eyebrow twitch and realized *that* hadn't been the right thing to say.

"I am thinking rationally!" she hissed. "You're the one who's not thinking rationally! So many people are counting on my society, are counting on me. I cannot abandon them, I cannot—"

"I cannot believe," he snapped, "you would even *contem-*

plate refusing me so you can stay here, and… and"—he gave a contemptuous flick of his wrist—"knit scarves for the poor!"

She froze, then slowly raised her head. Her expression held the wrath contained in a single eyebrow twitch, multiplied ten thousand-fold. Even though he stood a full head higher than her, Michael found himself recoiling.

"Knit scarves for the poor?" she said slowly. *"Knit scarves for the poor?"*

Oh, God. He had always imagined that when he died, it would be in his own bed at the age of ninety. Or perhaps he would be thrown from his horse, or mauled to death by a bear. Something manly.

But no. Judging by Anne's expression, he was about to be murdered.

By the kindest, most saintly woman in all of England.

He tried to backtrack. "I did not mean to imply that it was not important work—"

"I have never once *knit a scarf*, in my *whole entire life!*" she exploded. "Is that how little you think of me? Knit scarves for the poor!"

She shot off the bed and began tearing around the room. It took him a second to realize that she was gathering up his discarded garments. She strode through the door that led to her sitting room.

He hurtled off the bed as he realized her intention. He reached the door as she flung it open and threw his clothes out into the hall.

"Anne!" he thundered, hurrying to retrieve them. "Be reasonable! We need to discuss this calmly." He spun back toward the door. She stood framed in the doorway, naked and irate, holding his drawers in her hand. As he stepped forward, she threw them square in his face.

He ripped them off his eyes, but it was too late. She

slammed the door in his face, and he heard the tell-tale click of a key turning in the lock.

He pounded on the door. "Anne Astley, you open this door right now!"

"Go away!" was the muffled answer he got in return.

"We have not finished!" he thundered, only to be interrupted by the sound of someone clearing his throat.

He looked up and saw the footman he had met last night, Hugh, striding down the hall, flanked by four of his fellows. Michael hastily moved his drawers in front of his groin.

"Uh… m'lord…" Hugh blinked, and Michael could almost see him struggling to figure out the proper decorum for addressing an irate earl who was naked in the hallway. "Her ladyship has an appointment this morning."

"Hang her appointment," Michael snapped. "I need to speak with her."

Hugh began rolling his shoulders, as if he were loosening up. That was when Michael noticed that Anne's footmen were… unusual. Footmen were usually selected for their height, their fine figure, and their elegant bearing. These fellows met the height requirement, perhaps, but 'elegant' wasn't the word Michael would have chosen. They were huge, hulking men. Three out of the five looked to have had their noses broken, probably more than once. And judging by the way they were glaring at him, they weren't above roughing up a peer of the realm, if that was what Lady Anne required.

Michael sized them up. He could likely take any one of them in a fight, but not all five together. He sighed, recognizing defeat when he saw it.

Hugh perked up as he marked Michael's capitulation. "Come, m'lord. There's an empty bedroom right there. I'll be your valet."

One of his fellows snorted, and Hugh rounded on him. "What? I can manage!"

Michael reluctantly accepted Hugh's offer, and fifteen minutes later, he found himself standing on the street, gazing up at Anne's window.

Well, this was a setback. He'd lost that battle.

But that didn't mean he was going to lose the war. He spun on his heel and headed back to Cranfield House to plot his next move.

CHAPTER 20

*A*n hour later, Anne found herself climbing the steps to the Nettlethorpe-Ogilvy mansion, a great Gothic pile of grey stone complete with crenellations and faux towers that stood out like a peacock in a henhouse amongst the sedate Palladian town houses that surrounded it.

How she was going to get through this meeting when her mind was flying in a thousand different directions, she had no idea. One minute she was furious (with Michael, obviously), the next crushingly disappointed (that she wouldn't be marrying Michael after all). She would then segue into terror (that she might now be pregnant with no prospect of a wedding on the horizon), then she would work her way back around to furious.

How dare he belittle her work. How *dare* he. For any other man to have said such a thing would not have surprised her. Indeed, she heard cutting remarks about her "little charity" every week, if not every day, and her placid smile never faltered an inch.

But she had never expected it from Michael, who knew

how hard she worked, who knew that the Ladies' Society meant everything to her.

"Lady Wynters." The Nettlethorpe-Ogilvy butler bowed as he held the door for her. "Please follow me."

Anne's footsteps echoed off the flagstones as she followed the butler across the spacious entryway. The foyer of the Nettlethorpe-Ogilvy mansion matched the building's Gothic exterior, with pointed arches above the windows and ribbed vaults crisscrossing the high ceiling. Suits of armor bearing halberds were arrayed along the walls, and... Anne squinted at the pièce de résistance displayed on a square pedestal in the center of the room. It was a partially ruined statue in black marble, depicting... a man's naked rear end? Anne peeked over her shoulder as they mounted the stairs, thinking she must be mistaken, but no, it was definitely a man's hindquarters. How very odd...

Instead of showing her into one of the stately public rooms, the butler led her up two flights of stairs and toward the back of the house.

The room he indicated was a cluttered space, more workshop than library, with a pair of long workbenches covered with strange contraptions made of brass running the length of the room. As she made her way down the row, she felt the crunch of metal shavings beneath her slippers.

The room was also, Anne could not help but notice, covered with a fine layer of what appeared to be soot.

A maid hurried over. "You can sit right there, m'lady," she said, gesturing to an elaborately carved shield-backed chair that had been positioned before the desk. "I brought that one in from another room, just to make sure it's completely clean."

"Er... thank you," Anne said, seating herself. The maid continued bustling about, wiping down everything in the room. After a moment, Anne asked, "Is Mr. Nettlethorpe-Ogilvy on his way?"

A great clattering arose from the room next door, followed by the sound of shattering china. The maid made a sound that was half chuckle and half sigh. "I warrant that's him right there."

Surely enough, Mr. Nettlethorpe-Ogilvy came bustling into the room. He was of around Anne's age, but this was no frivolous young dandy. He had left off his jacket and was clad in only a shirt and plain grey waistcoat. His brown hair was sticking up in what was not so much the fashionable windswept look, as the a-family-of-owls-has-been-nesting-in-my-hair look. And much like his workshop, he was lightly coated in soot

But in spite of these idiosyncrasies, it was the object cradled in his arms that drew Anne's eye.

She hadn't the faintest clue what it was, but it had a large bushy brush, almost like four brooms fitted together in the shape of a flower, connected to a series of short pipes, each the length of her lower arm and slightly flared on one end. A rope had been strung through the pipes, connecting them to the brushes. Mr. Nettlethorpe-Ogilvy had folded about a dozen of the pipes under his arm, but another dozen dragged behind him on the floor, clanking as he made his way down the length of his worktables.

"Ah, Lady Wynters," he said, circling around to deposit the mysterious contraption on top of his desk with a cacophonous clatter. He started to reach out to take her hand, then recoiled, seeming to recall that he was covered in soot. "Excuse me," he said, using his handkerchief to scrub at his face and hands.

Once he finished, he said, "I apologize for the mess. Probably I should have rescheduled and made myself presentable.

But I was so excited about this"—he gestured to the tangled heap on his desk—"and knowing how excited *you* will be about it, I couldn't bear to delay."

Anne was at a loss, but she forced herself to smile. "I... I'm sure I will be."

"I got the idea when I saw that article in *The Times*," he said, settling into the chair behind his desk. "That was marvelous, what you did for those climbing boys." He shook his head. "It started me thinking—why do sweeps even use climbing boys? I thought there had to be a better way, some device that could clean a flue just as well, without putting children in such a dangerous situation."

He began sifting through a pile of papers on his desk and pulled out an architectural plan. "I did a bit of investigation and learned that the real problem is that our chimneys are so convoluted. Look at this," he said, turning the drawing around so Anne could see it. "See how the flue makes three ninety-degree turns *and* has a U-bend?" He shook his head, genuinely affronted. "Appalling design. I should know—when you're in the business of making iron, you know how air moves around a fire. But the fact is, half the buildings in London have a flue that's not straight, and nobody's willing to tear down half the buildings in London to fix them. I realized that what we needed," he said, reaching for a pipe, "was a very long broom, with a handle that could bend through those corners."

Mr. Nettlethorpe-Ogilvy pulled the rope taut, and Anne watched in astonishment as the tangled heap on the desk transformed into a long-handled broom. "It can bend?" she asked.

"It can." He demonstrated how the handle could be straight or malleable depending on the amount of tension in the rope. "I was so excited, I stayed up all night building my prototype."

"Does it work?" Anne leaned forward to examine it more closely. If this contraption could truly take the place of a little boy squeezing himself into a chimney…

"It does indeed. Now, for the worst flues, like this one," Mr. Nettlethorpe-Ogilvy said, tapping the diagram he had showed her, "this alone won't work. What you'll need to do is insert a little door right here at the bend. But this should work well enough on ninety percent of the flues in London. I've been testing it all morning."

"On fourteen different fireplaces!" the maid called from the corner, where she was still scrubbing.

"Yes, hence the mess." Mr. Nettlethorpe-Ogilvy rubbed the back of his head. "I didn't realize you were supposed to drape a cover over the fireplace before you cleaned it. I am sorry about that, Maggie."

Maggie shook her head, but she was smiling fondly. "Now that's all right, Mr. Nettlethorpe-Ogilvy." She turned to Anne. "'Tis an honor to work for a truly great man. We don't pay no mind to the occasional inconvenience."

"Well, I think your invention is marvelous," Anne said. "You cannot imagine the wretched conditions from which it will save hundreds of young boys. Will you be able to produce them in your family's factories? Or do we need to find a manufacturer?"

"That was what I particularly wished to discuss with you," Mr. Nettlethorpe-Ogilvy said, digging around his desk. Anne blanched as he pulled out a copy of her old pamphlet. "I was so impressed after reading the article in *The Times*, I set out to learn more about your Ladies' Society, and I found out you'd written this pamphlet." He shook his head. "I'm ashamed to say I'd never before considered the rather obvious ramifications that paying women at a lower wage must have on widows with children to support. I thought this would be the perfect opportunity to try it."

"Try it?" Anne asked, blinking at him. "Try what?"

"Your plan, of course," Mr. Nettlethorpe-Ogilvy said, flipping to the appropriate page of the pamphlet. "To hire widows who find themselves in the role of breadwinner and pay them a living wage. I see no reason a woman couldn't make one of these." He glanced up at Anne, his eyes guileless. "Do you think you could find a dozen or so women who'd be willing to work in my family's shop?"

Anne found herself unable to speak. After all those years, all of those failed attempts to convince someone to give her proposal a chance, she had resigned herself that this moment would never come. Now that it was here, she should be elated. And she was, but she was also blinking back tears.

Oh gracious—she could not start crying in front of Archibald Nettlethorpe-Ogilvy.

She glanced up and found him peering at her with wrinkled brow. He pulled his handkerchief from his pocket and started to offer it to her, then blanched as he noticed it was covered in soot. "I'm sorry," he said, fumbling the handkerchief, "I—"

Anne chuckled, pulling her own handkerchief from her pocket. "You have absolutely nothing for which you need apologize. I am the one who is sorry. It's just..." She swallowed. "This is actually the first time someone has agreed to put my proposal into action."

Mr. Nettlethorpe-Ogilvy leaned a hip atop his desk. "You're joking."

"I'm afraid not." Anne dabbed at her eyes. "It seems that many men do not appreciate a woman making suggestions as to how they should run their businesses."

He regarded her for a moment. "If you will pardon my saying so, Lady Wynters, it is my impression that the world is full of stupid people. Not because they aren't engineers," he said, gesturing to his workshop, "but because they wouldn't know what's important if it came up and bit them on the nose." He held her gaze. "You do not share in their failing. And I hope you won't let those blowhards discourage you."

Anne gave him a watery smile. "You cannot imagine how much that means to me. How much this means to me," she said, gesturing toward the bending broom. "And to answer your question, yes, I am certain I can find a dozen respectable widows who would be thrilled to work in your shop."

Mr. Nettlethorpe-Ogilvy escorted her to the foyer. He cringed as they approached the statue of a man's buttocks. "Please pardon the... uh..." He cleared his throat. "A few months ago, Lord Ardingly sold some items from his Egyptian collection, and my parents purchased this, um... striking statue."

"Ah." Well did Anne recall it, as the sale had been orchestrated by her sister Caro, to restore the Ardingly estate to solvency so she could marry the earl's son. "That explains it."

They arranged to meet at the same time the following week to discuss the particulars of the jobs for her residents.

Once she was ensconced in her carriage, Anne sagged against the plush cushions, overwhelmed by waves of emotions. Someone had finally agreed to put her plan into action. And there was real hope that Mr. Nettlethorpe-Ogilvy's invention could eliminate the need for climbing boys to squeeze themselves into burning chimneys. She felt as though she could *fly*.

Yet at the same time, she was on the brink of crying or screaming or punching the velvet squabs upon which she sat, she wasn't quite sure which one. *That* was how she deserved to be treated. That was precisely how, and yet today was the first day a man had ever afforded her such respect. Usually she was dismissed, she was condescended to, she was lectured, as if those windbags knew a tenth of what she knew about the harsh realities faced by the poor.

She had grown so used to sitting through such remarks that she could do so without her smile wavering. After all, it served no one and nothing for her to show her ire. No one would donate to a society run by an angry harridan. She always had to be mindful of the bigger picture.

Everyone thought she was submissive to the point of being lily-livered. They could not have been more wrong. Her public demeanor was a calculated decision, one she had to make every single day. It took a great deal of backbone to sit through all that drivel with a placid smile on her face.

But Mr. Nettlethorpe-Ogilvy respected her. He thought her work was important. So what if a hundred blowhards dismissed her? Mr. Nettlethorpe-Ogilvy was smarter than all of them. He was one of the greatest minds of their age, and if *he* held her in esteem…

"Beg pardon, m'lady," her coachman called through the window, "but we're being followed."

Anne froze. Although most thought her meek and kind, she was not without her enemies. There was a reason she didn't go into St. Giles without at least two of her hulking footmen. And the recent business with Lord Gladstone was an ugly one. If he held no compunctions about selling four-year-olds into the worst imaginable conditions, who knew what the baron might be willing to do to avoid the consequences of his actions?

"What does he look like, Harold?" Anne asked.

"Uncommon tall fellow. Black hair. Dressed like a gentleman. Got himself a big bunch of flowers, he does."

Anne wrinkled her nose and dared a peek out the window. Surely enough, there was Michael some thirty feet back, following them on horseback.

"Try to lose him," she said, slouching against the squabs.

They had almost reached the Ladies' Society's lodging house. Anne still wasn't sure quite what this newfound swirl of feelings meant, but she did know one thing.

She wasn't about to put up with any nonsense from the likes of Michael Cranfield.

CHAPTER 21

*A*s soon as he returned to Cranfield House, Michael formulated a plan. It was a fairly simple plan: prostrate himself before Anne and beg for her forgiveness. Clearly Scudamore and Gladstone had been bamming him with all that rot about knitting scarves for the poor; they probably never imagined it would work so well, that he would turn around and make such a complete cake of himself. But what was just as bad, when he thought back to the specific words he had used... his behavior had been deplorable, and it was no wonder Anne was furious with him. He'd just been so undone by the thought of her not marrying him that he hadn't been thinking clearly.

He'd made a mess of the whole thing. He'd been in such a hurry to propose before someone else snatched her up, he hadn't given much thought to what he was going to say. Hell, he hadn't even told her that he'd been in love with her for the past nine years, nor had he mentioned his thwarted proposal, the fact that he hadn't read any of her letters, or—his personal favorite—that her former husband was a worthless, lying skunk.

He really had intended to tell her all of that, even if he'd been dreading the last point.

But then Anne had suggested they make love.

He also needed to explain what important work he'd been doing in Canada. Once Anne understood everything he'd been doing, and that he was going to be the next Governor General, she would understand why their future needed to be in Canada.

Because their returning to Canada was not negotiable.

And so he'd hurried home and changed, sent a footman out to procure the biggest bunch of flowers that could be found, borrowed a horse from the nearby mews and arrived at Anne's town house just in time to see her carriage pulling away.

He hadn't minded cooling his heels while she had her appointment. He needed to think through what he was going to say. But he didn't mean to let her escape.

After she departed, he mounted his horse and followed at a discrete distance.

They were heading east. Michael peered at the surrounding buildings. He didn't know London well, but the neighborhood was growing progressively worse. As he rode past a church, Michael called out to a pair of girls rolling a hoop along the pavement. "Say—what's the name of that church?"

They looked up, startled, the forgotten hoop clattering on its side. "'Tis St Giles in the Fields, m'lord," one of them called.

St Giles? St Giles was one of the most dangerous rookeries in London. What in God's name was Anne doing in *St Giles*?

The neighborhood continued to deteriorate. Michael tried to stop his racing thoughts, but everywhere he looked, he spotted a new source of peril. The trio of dogs sniping over a bone in the alleyway were likely rabid. That butcher looked a little *too* efficient with his cleaver. And there was no shortage of miscreants and ruffians, from the irate drunkard being tossed from a basement gin house to the seedy fellow leaning against a building's corner who was actually *twirling a knife* as he surveyed the crowd, no doubt in search of his next mark.

Michael could not lose her again. He pictured the past four years of his life, how the excruciatingly acute pain of those first few months after she married Wynters had slowly distilled into a dull ache right in the place where his heart used to be, one that never really went away. He thought of that horrible moment when he woke each morning, when he found himself lying in bed, struggling to find a reason to get up, to keep going without her. He knew what it was to live without Anne, and he *was not doing that again*. He couldn't. It didn't matter what he had to do, he was going to keep her safe, and he was going to start by getting her the hell out of this sad excuse for a neighborhood.

Anne's carriage halted in front of a large brick building and one of her footmen opened the door. Michael hurtled off his horse, thrust the reins into the footman's hands, and shoved the man out of the way, blocking her exit.

"What the devil are you doing here, Anne?" he demanded.

Her eyebrow gave a violent twitch. "I am running my society. If you would be so kind as to step aside."

Not a chance. "You're not disembarking. Not here. You obviously haven't noticed, but this is no neighborhood for a lady."

She rolled her eyes and proceeded to squeeze past him. "Whatever gave you that idea? Was it the flash-house across the street? Or the three drunkards passed out in the alleyway?"

He grabbed her by the arm. "You may think it a joke, but this place is dangerous."

A crowd had begun to form, drawn, no doubt, by their raised voices, and when Michael seized her arm, a heavyset, black-bearded man whose form of employment was probably *pirate* stepped forward. Michael immediately moved in front of Anne, but the man surprised him by saying, "You'll unhand Lady Wynters!"

Michael glared him. "This is none of your concern—"

"'Tis all of our concern," a reed-thin man with a face full of freckles said, stepping forward to join the first.

"I'm not some vagrant who is going to harm her," Michael continued, eyeing the ragged trousers of the second man, which had been patched in a dozen different places. "I'm the Earl of—"

"Do you think I give a toss?" Black Beard interrupted.

Michael gritted his teeth. "I am merely trying to assist her. She seems to have gotten turned around and doesn't understand where she is."

The small crowd burst into laughter.

"Poor wee lamb," a white-haired woman chortled. "All turned around and no idea where she be."

"Definitely wasn't 'ere yesterday," added a woman whose basket marked her as a flower seller. "Nor the day afore that, nor the day afore that."

Michael peered up at the building. What on earth could bring Anne here, of all places? Although, for all that the neighborhood was run down, this was a fairly imposing edifice: six bays wide, in a plain but serviceable red brick. He frowned. "Anne, do you... do you rent space in this building?"

"No, Michael, I do not rent space in this building." She wrenched her arm free from his grasp. "I own this building." She turned on her heel and strode up the steps.

Michael made to follow her, but found his way blocked. "And where do you think you're going, m'lord earl?" Black Beard asked.

"I need to speak with Anne. Let me pass."

"Oh," Freckles exclaimed, "*Anne*, is it? A bit overfamiliar with her ladyship now, aren't you?"

Michael was startled to realize that these… these *vagrants* didn't seem bent on harming Anne. Much to the contrary, they seemed to be trying to protect her. "Not at all, considering she is my betrothed."

This brought the two up short. Black Beard looked him up and down. "Her ladyship's betrothed, you say?"

"Yes," he replied curtly.

"Just a bit of a lovers' quarrel, then?" Freckles asked.

"Indeed," Michael muttered, gesturing to the flowers.

The two men exchanged a look. "I suppose that's alright, then," Black Beard said, stepping back so Michael could pass.

He started toward the building, then turned. "May I ask why you stopped me? What concern is it of yours?"

Black Beard shifted from foot to foot. "Me old gaffer was always a working man. Spent his days unloading ships from dawn 'til dusk. But last year, a cask of wine fell right on his wrist. The break didn't set right, and now he can't lift his own glass, not with his right hand, leastways. We try to do what we can for him, my brothers and me, but it ain't much. Somehow 'er ladyship got word of him, and now he gets meat and potatoes twice a week, he does. And he wouldn't get by without it."

Freckles nodded beside him. "Her ladyship took me sister in, along with her four children, after her husband died." He nodded toward the building. "They're in there right now. Me sister takes in some sewing. Her ladyship just got the oldest boy apprenticed to a shipwright. And the three little ones are in school, learning their letters and such. I don't like to think where they would've ended up had her ladyship not stepped in."

"I see," Michael said.

At least, he was starting to.

He entered the building. Anne was still in the entryway, kneeling amongst a flock of children who were clamoring for her attention. He saw her adjust the bow in one little girl's hair. Another pressed her rag doll forward for a kiss; dolly received one, as did dolly's owner. A little boy presented Anne with a bouquet. Truth be told, it was just a bundle of weeds, but you never would have known the way Anne sniffed it appreciatively.

"Thank you, Charles," she said. "I will tuck these in my pocket, so I can enjoy them for the rest of the..." She spied Michael, and her smile vanished. "Oh. Are you still here?"

"Yes. I'm here to apologize."

"You are doing a *magnificent* job of it," she hissed, rising to her feet.

"I would like to do better," he said, offering her the irises. She made no move to accept them. "Is there somewhere we could go to talk?"

"Lady Wynters!" A woman in a plain grey dress entered the foyer and curtseyed deeply.

"Mrs. Godfrey," Anne said, curtseying in return. "How are you this morning?"

The woman wrung her hands. "Oh, my lady, I'm so glad you're here. Mr. Branton just arrived, and—oh!" she said, noticing Michael for the first time. "I apologize, I didn't realize we had a visitor. A new patron, my lady?"

"No," Anne replied, "he's not a patron. He was just leav—"

"Allow me to introduce myself, Mrs. Godfrey," Michael interrupted smoothly. "I am Lord Morsley. I have the honor of being Lady Anne's betrothed."

Mrs. Godfrey gasped. "Betrothed! Why, I had no idea, Lady Wynters."

Anne was glaring at him. "I don't know that *betrothed* is the word I would use."

"That is the word one generally uses, *darling*, after one has promised to marry a man," he replied cheerfully, taking Anne's hand and tucking it into his arm. "As you did last night."

"That was before I knew you were planning to drag me off to Canada," Anne said through clenched teeth.

The room fell silent. "Canada?" Mrs. Godfrey said softly. "But—do you truly mean to move to Canada, my lady?"

Before Anne could answer, a little girl gave a great wail and threw herself at Anne's legs. "No, Lady Wynters! Ya can't, ya can't!"

"Now, Eliza," Mrs. Godfrey said, attempting to pry the girl off Anne, "this won't do. It is for Lady Wynters to make her own decision, and..."

"But without lady Wynters," the girl bawled, "Ma and me'll have to go back to Pye Street, where we was ten to a room and the roof leaked and there was never anything to eat. I'll not go back there. I won't. *I won't!*"

Michael saw dozens of pairs of wide, watery eyes staring at Anne beseechingly. Anne knelt down and wrapped little Eliza in her arms. "There, there, Eliza. Don't cry. Lord Morsley was just having a joke." She glared up at him over Eliza's shoulder.

After a few minutes, the little girl calmed down and Anne stood. "Now, what were you trying to tell me, Mrs. Godfrey?"

She bit her lip. "I'd best let Mr. Branton explain it. He's waiting in your office."

CHAPTER 22

*A*nne strode into her office, annoyed that Michael followed close upon her heels. She found Samuel seated at her writing desk. "Mr. Branton, good morning."

Samuel crumpled his half-finished note. "Lady Wynters, thank God. I was hoping I wouldn't have to convey this in a letter. I just received word that…"

Samuel paused as Michael squeezed into the room. She sighed. "Mr. Branton, allow me to present Lord Morsley, my childhood friend whom I know I have mentioned. Michael, this is Mr. Samuel Branton, who is a dear friend in addition to being my barrister."

Michael pumped Samuel's hand. "Mr. Branton, a pleasure. What Anne *meant* to say is that I am her childhood friend, and, as of last night, her betrothed."

Anne turned to glower at him. "I already told you, the wedding is off. Must you keep telling everyone that?"

Michael gave her his full Obstinate Face. "Absolutely everyone."

She rolled her eyes and turned back to Samuel. "What news, Mr. Branton?"

Samuel's eyebrows were raised, but he chose not to comment. "Last night I went to Bow Street. The runner I've been working with, Charles Hoskins, agreed there was sufficient evidence to arrest Lord Gladstone."

"Gladstone?" Michael asked. "What does Bow Street want with—"

Anne silenced him with a look, then turned back to Samuel. "Please continue."

"I called at Bow Street this morning to see if the arrest had been made. It has not. By the time Hoskins arrived at the ball, Gladstone had left, and he has yet to return to his house."

"Perhaps he moved on to a second entertainment," Anne said. Although it made her nervous that Gladstone was still at large, it was common enough for men of his class to stay out all night. "A gaming hell or some such. Did Bow Street set a watch on his house?"

"They did, and at first I thought that seemed sufficient. I was just getting ready to leave when the news arrived that a body was pulled from the Thames this morning. It belonged to Nick and Johnny's former master, Mr. Smithers."

"Who," Michael asked, "are Nick and Johnny, and who is—"

Anne held up a hand to silence him. Her heart was flying in her chest. "Could it have been an accident?" she asked Samuel.

Samuel shook his head. "The coroner's report is pending. But I'm given to understand there were stab wounds."

Anne started to pace the room. "He knows. He knows the net is closing in around him. Lord Scudamore must've warned him—" She turned and found Michael looming in her path. "What?" she asked, exasperated.

He looked slightly deranged; Anne had certainly never seen that eye tic before. "I demand to know what the hell it is you're mixed up in, that involves Bow Street and a stabbing and dead bodies being pulled from the Thames, is what!"

Anne sighed. He was never going to let it go. "Fine. What happened is this…"

WHEN ANNE'S tale began with her going into Holborn to square off with a criminal who bought four-year-olds to send up burning chimneys and the unprincipled scum who would employ such a man, Michael's blood began to simmer.

When she came to the part where she decided the best course was to question the prime suspect herself, his blood began to boil.

By the time she reached the not-exactly-startling conclusion that the type of man who sold children to their almost certain death did not scruple to commit murder in order to save his own worthless hide, steam was all but coming out his ears.

"So," Anne said, "our first concern is Johnny and Nick's safety. If Lord Gladstone is eliminating witnesses, he will surely target them next."

"Our first concern," Michael snapped, "is your safety and disentangling you from this mess."

Anne ignored him. "It would be tempting to move them to an undisclosed location, but we have to assume this building is under surveillance. We'd have to think of a way to sneak them out. Then comes the question of location. I would bring them to my house, but I fear that's too obvious."

"Don't be ridiculous, Anne! They can't go to your house."

Anne rounded on him, hands clenched into fists. "And where would you suggest they go?"

"You said Bow Street is involved. Turn them over to Bow Street. They'll know what to do with them."

"Bow Street? What will Bow Street do with two young boys?"

"They'll find an appropriate situation for them."

Anne's eyebrow twitched. "Perhaps with a charity that runs a lodging house for widows and orphans. If only we could find one of those!"

Michael leaned in. "Now see here, Anne—"

"I agree," Mr. Branton interjected, "that your house is too obvious a location, and that we should assume this building is being watched. Until arrangements can be made for a safe-house, the boys will have to stay here."

"I think you're right," Anne said. She crossed the room and leaned out into the hall. "Ralph, Joseph," she called to the two footmen who had accompanied them, "would you come in here, please?"

Anne briefed her footmen on the situation. "For the time being, those boys need to be guarded around the clock."

"I'll do it," Joseph offered. "I'm the oldest of seven. It won't be no bother, watching over a couple of boys."

"You must never leave them unattended," Anne said.

"Joseph can bunk here," Ralph suggested, "right in the same room with the boys. Another of us will stand watch outside the door at night when he's asleep. We can take it in turns."

"Perfect. We'll also need extra security for the front door."

"I know some likely fellows," Ralph said.

"Are they trustworthy?" Anne asked.

"Yes, ma'am. Most of them are my cousins."

"Good. Get them in place as soon as you can." Anne turned to Mrs. Godfrey. "Please speak to Nick and Johnny. They need to understand that they're not to go outside until this has been taken care of, not even to play in the alley."

"I'll go at once, my lady." Mrs. Godfrey stood, and Joseph followed her out.

Mr. Branton rose. "I should be going, too. You mentioned that Johnny and Nick thought the house they were taken to was near a kiln. I have a contact over at the Exchequer—I'll ask if he can do a little digging, see if Gladstone owns any property that would fit that description."

"An excellent thought," Anne said.

"A needle in a haystack, most likely, but we'll leave no stone unturned." Mr. Branton bowed over Anne's hand, paused, then grabbed Michael's arm and pulled him toward the door. "Walk me out, Morsley."

As soon as they were a little ways down the hall, Mr. Branton stopped, spinning to face Michael. "I've heard enough good things about you that I'm trying to give you the benefit of the doubt," he hissed. "But you are making it exceedingly difficult."

Michael glowered at him. "You cannot expect me to be pleased that my future wife is tangled up with a bunch of murderers."

"I can tell you this much—she's not going to be your future wife if you keep barking orders at her and treating her like a child. Aren't you supposed to be the person who knows her better than anyone? Do you truly believe she will respond well to such an approach?"

Michael pictured Anne's eyebrow twitching furiously. "No," he grumbled.

"No, indeed. Now, I suggest you get back in there and channel that anger in a better direction."

"And what direction would that be?"

Mr. Branton gave him a hard look. "Help her win. And for God's sake, take a calming breath the next time you find yourself tempted to open your mouth." He spun on his heel and strode off down the hall. "Good day, Lord Morsley."

Michael returned to the room to find Anne putting the finishing touches on a letter. She stood, ignoring Michael as she folded the letter, then turned to her footman. "Ralph, shouldn't you be seeing to that extra security?"

Ralph shifted uneasily. "It's just—I don't like to leave you unattended, m'lady. Not with someone out there dumping bodies in the Thames."

Michael decided Ralph was his favorite of Anne's footmen. Anne, on the other hand, did not seem to share his appropriate concern for her safety. "Harold will provide sufficient protection."

Ralph frowned. "Please, m'lady."

"I will watch over Lady Anne," Michael said.

Ralph started to perk up, but then paused, noticing the withering glare Anne was directing at Michael. "That won't be necessary," she said.

It was worse than he'd thought if Anne was so mad at him she would rather put herself in danger than endure a quarter hour of his company. Michael decided to heed Mr. Branton's advice and took a slow, deep breath. He crossed the room and took Anne's hand. "Let me at least see you home," he said quietly. "I know you're furious with me. I even understand why. Honestly, I don't blame you."

She was still frowning, but he could tell she was softening. "I don't know, Michael."

"I meant what I said earlier, about wanting to apologize. Please, Anne?" He held her gaze, bringing a hand up to frame her face when she started to look away. "Surely you know that I would never let anything bad happen to you."

He watched the warring emotions in her eyes and held his breath.

Anne gazed up at Michael, mesmerized. It was downright unsporting of him to be looking at her like that, with those jade-green eyes and that beseeching expression. What chance did a girl stand?

And, as annoying as it was to admit, his suggestion that he accompany her home was probably the wise course. Besides, she'd have to talk to Michael sooner or later. It wasn't as if she was going to stay mad at him forever.

He was her best friend, after all.

"All right," Anne said.

Anne led him out to the carriage. They were clearly going to have it out, and she didn't hold out any great hope that Michael would wait until they'd reached the relative privacy of her town house to do it. Surely enough, before Ralph had even closed the carriage door, Michael claimed both of her hands. "I'm sorry, Anne. I'm so, so sorry. I know I sounded dismissive this morning, and... and... generally awful. I didn't mean to, I just... when you said you wouldn't marry me after all, I couldn't think straight, and it all came out wrong."

The carriage lurched into motion. "I know you were upset, Michael. But still, I cannot believe you would disparage my work in such a fashion. You know how many hours I put in, and how much the Ladies' Society means to me. It's almost all I wrote about in my letters—"

"I never read them," Michael burst out.

Anne gasped. And to think, she had supposed him to be her best friend! She tried to jerk her hands free, but Michael refused to relinquish them.

"What do you mean, you never read my letters?" She felt a tear streak down her cheek. "It's bad enough that you never wrote back, but the fact that you couldn't even be bothered to—"

"I couldn't bear to read them," Michael said, clinging fast to her hands. "I..." He made a sound of disgust. "I'm explaining it all wrong. I'm doing every bit as badly as I did this morning."

Her voice broke as she replied, "There is no need to continue, as I cannot imagine anything you could say that would excuse—"

"*I love you.*"

Anne mouth sagged open. Her eyes flew to his face, and... and he looked sincere. But that couldn't be right, how could he possibly...

"I love you, Anne," Michael said, his voice shaking. "I always have. Ever since we were fourteen."

"No, no you haven't," Anne sputtered.

"I have. I swear I have. I—"

"But... but..." Anne shook her head. "There was something that happened. When we were fifteen. It was the day before you went back to Eton. We were having a picnic, and..." She rubbed her forehead. "You probably don't even remember it."

Michael's mouth had fallen open. "Did you just suggest that I don't remember the most erotic moment of my life prior to last night?"

Anne gaped up at him. Her brain was utterly confounded. He might as well have been speaking Urdu because none of this made sense, none of it made any sense at all. "But you... you leaped off me, and you said you regretted it! That you would never want to kiss me—"

"I never said that!" He looked affronted.

Now Anne was annoyed. "You most certainly did! You said you would never, not in a million years—"

"I said that I never meant to insult you! That, in spite of what was going on inside my trousers, I wasn't going to *violate* you in the middle of a *field*!"

Anne was back to blinking at him. "Your... your trousers? What are you talking about?"

194

"I didn't mean to have such a coarse response. But I was fifteen, Anne. Even today, well, you were there in that boat. You saw about how well I can resist you. I'm sure you can understand that at fifteen, there was absolutely no chance I could find myself lying on top of the girl I desperately loved without having an... an ungentlemanly response."

Anne's spine went ramrod straight. "Oh! You're saying you had a... an..." She gestured vaguely toward her groin.

He gaped at her. "You mean to tell me you didn't even *notice?*"

Anne's cheeks were positively aflame. "I was fifteen, too, Michael. A very innocent fifteen. I didn't understand there was anything *to* notice. I mean—" She swallowed. "At fifteen, even if someone had come along and pointed out exactly what was going on inside your trousers, I wouldn't have understood what it meant. I thought you were trying to explain that you would never be interested in me. In that way."

"Oh my—" Michael tilted his head back and gave a wordless growl. "I glanced down and you had your eyes squeezed shut. You were cringing, you were stiff as a board, and I suddenly realized that I was pinning you to the ground. I thought I must have terrified you, especially given, well, what happened to Bridget."

Another tear coursed down her cheek. "I wasn't terrified. 'Nervous' would be fair. I closed my eyes because... because I thought you were going to kiss me."

A look of pain crossed his face that was so acute, she could hardly bear to see it. "God, how I wish I had."

A silence fell. Anne felt about as disoriented as if the carriage had lurched into a ditch and turned onto its side. Michael loved her? And had done so ever since they were fourteen? This flew in the face of everything she'd believed.

Anne frowned. "Wait, Michael, if you were in love with

me, why didn't you say something before you left for Canada?"

"I did. I proposed—"

"No, you didn't!" Suddenly she was furious. She'd been having trouble enough believing him, but now Michael might as well have been telling her that left was right, and up was down, and one plus two equaled four. "I feel quite certain I would have remembered that."

He squeezed his eyes shut. "I'm explaining this all wrong. I *tried* to propose, would be more accurate."

"What do you mean, you tried to propose? It would seem that one either does or does not issue a proposal. There isn't any middle ground!"

"I—" Michael broke off, glancing out the window. He released Anne's hand to knock on the roof of the carriage. "Harold, take a right up ahead. Take us to Astley House."

"Yes, my lord," Harold said.

Anne peered out the window. They'd been driving past Cavendish Square and Astley House was already coming into view. "Michael, why do we need to visit my parents' house?"

The carriage pulled to a halt. Michael's face was set into grim lines. "You'll see."

CHAPTER 23

*M*ichael felt nauseous as he led Anne up the steps to her parents' townhouse. He hadn't been here since the day of his thwarted proposal—not the most comforting memory.

And now he was about to inform Anne that her former husband, the man whom she had pledged to love and to honor, and in favor of whom she had promised to forsake all others, was an outright villain, and that her marriage had been built upon a lie. And even though every indication was that Wynters hadn't treated her particularly well and that she harbored no deep affection for him, Michael, the man who'd stared down a charging bear without flinching, was terrified.

Yarwood was manning the door, and as soon as he spotted Michael, his stern features creased into a portrait of misery. "Lord Morsley, I am so glad you have come. I spoke to Lord Fauconbridge and Master Harrington the other day, and I beg you to allow me to express how horrifically sorry I am. I honestly thought I had delivered your letter to Lady Anne. But clearly I failed to safeguard it."

Anne's mouth had fallen open as she stared wide-eyed at

197

the Astleys' normally taciturn butler. "Yarwood?" she said softly. "What on earth?"

Yarwood did not seem to have heard her, for he soldiered on, wringing his hands. "I had entirely forgotten he was here that day. It was not until some months later that we came to realize that Lady Anne had never received your proposal, you see. And compared to your unexpected arrival, his presence was such a trifle, it was hardly even worth remembering. It wasn't until Lord Fauconbridge and Master Harrington questioned me that I recalled that you were not the only guest we had that morning."

Michael nodded sympathetically. "It's all right, Yarwood."

"It is not all right." Yarwood's voice was shaking. "It is not all right, and it never will be. I think—" He squeezed his eyes shut. "He asked me to fetch him a drink. I'm almost certain of it. And I left the room. I left the room, left your letter right there on the desk, and he must have…"

Michael clasped him on the shoulder. "You are not to blame. The blame lies solely with the man who acted with such dishonor."

"I am inexpressibly sorry for it," Yarwood said, hanging his head.

"There is no need." Michael gave his shoulder a squeeze. "We came here to speak with you, so please don't mention our arrival to anyone. I need to have a word with Lady Anne."

"Of course, my lord."

Anne had fallen silent. Michael released Yarwood's arm with a final squeeze, then led Anne into the same drawing room where he had scratched out his proposal all those years ago.

"Michael," Anne said as soon as the door closed, "am I to understand that you were here four years ago? And you—"

She shook her head, as if distrusting what she'd just heard, "—you wrote me a letter of proposal?"

"I did." He walked over to the writing desk. "The whole business with my uncle was so urgent, I had to depart on the first ship going out. But I stopped here, hoping to make my proposal first. You were out with your mother, and the footmen weren't able to track you down. When it reached the point that I had to leave or I would miss my ship, I sat down right here, and wrote out my proposal in a letter."

"A letter that someone took," Anne said. She had been staring into the fireplace, but she slowly turned. Her eyes were guarded as she whispered, "Who was it?"

Here it was, the moment he'd been dreading. "I think you know," he said carefully. "Think, Anne. Right around the time I left for Canada, did you come home from paying some calls, and find a letter had been left for you?"

"I did." She gave a bleak chuckle. "I daresay the only reason I recall it is because so many people have asked me a similar question over the years." She squeezed her eyes shut for a second, then opened them. "It was a note from Lord Wynters. That's whom you encountered here. Wasn't it?"

"It was."

Anne's voice shook. "Let me make sure I understand. You came here on the day of your departure and wrote me a letter of proposal. Lord Wynters happened to be here as well. After you departed, he sent Yarwood away on an errand, removed your letter, and replaced it with one of his own. Is that what you're telling me happened?"

Michael swallowed. His heart was pounding, and he thought he might be physically ill, but he forced himself to say, "That is what I believe must have occurred, yes."

For a horrible eternity that was probably no longer than five seconds, Anne stood perfectly still. Then she made the most wretched sound, like an injured animal, some combination of misery and fury. She whirled around to face the fire-place. Her head was bowed, and her shoulders were heaving and convulsing.

"Anne," he said, crossing the room in three steps. He reached out tentatively, unsure if she was crying with hurt or anger or something else, only to find that she wasn't crying at all. Instead she was... digging through her reticule? "What are you—"

"Here!" she said, pulling out a pocket mirror with a porcelain case. She pulled her arm back as if to throw it at the wall.

"Anne!" He covered her hand, trying to be gentle even as he pried the mirror from her grasp. In as many years as he had known her, he had never seen Anne like this. She was physically shaking with fury. He had no idea what it meant, no idea what to do, what to say. "I know you must feel very upset. But you'll regret smashing your mirror."

She glared up at him. "It was a gift from Lord Wynters."

"Oh. In that case." Michael hurled it straight into the fire-place, where it made a very satisfying sound as it shattered.

He turned back to Anne, to find her struggling to unclasp her garnet earrings with hands that shook.

"Did he give you those, too?"

"*Yes.*" She was breathing hard.

"Don't destroy those," Michael said as she started to draw her arm back again. At Anne's glare, he said, "They're worth something. You can sell them and donate the proceeds to the Ladies' Society."

Her voice was petulant. "*Fine.*" Wrinkling her nose and holding them between her thumb and forefinger, the way you would pick up a ball dropped by a dog that was dripping with slobber, she deposited them in her reticule.

When she lifted her gaze to Michael, her eyes were wary. "Why did you not tell me?"

He sighed, grabbing her hand and pulling her toward the sofa. "Because I wasn't sure, not until two days ago. It's a serious accusation, and not something to be made lightly." He ran his thumb over the back of her hand. "I was in such a state that day, I forgot the man's name as soon as he told it to me. The only thing I could remember was his unusual walking stick, with a handle in the shape of—"

"An icicle," Anne finished for him, looking down.

"Yes. It took me years to piece it together, and still I wasn't sure. Not until your brothers confirmed it was Wynters who carried that walking stick." They fell silent, Anne staring blankly into the fireplace. After a moment Michael said, "May I ask what the note you did receive said?"

"It was merely a sentence or two, explaining that he had stopped by in hopes of seeing me, and looked forward to dancing with me at, oh, whatever ball was being held that night." Anne brushed at a stray tear with the back of her glove. "It was nothing of any consequence, and those were the exact words I said to Mama when she came bursting in here, asking what my letter said."

Michael squeezed her hand but said nothing.

Anne continued, "I understand now why she was so excited. Yarwood must have told her what was in your letter. She asked to see it, but I... I was in a bit of a pique that afternoon, and I refused. She had been encouraging me to be more confident, you see, to stop hiding in the ladies' retiring room. And I knew she would interpret it as a sign that Lord Wynters was interested in me." She looked down. "Which I suppose it was. But I clutched it to my chest, and said, 'Please, Mama. Just leave me be.' Then I stalked out of the room."

"And she thought you had refused me," Michael said quietly.

"She must have, yes." Anne's face crumpled, and tears began to streak across her cheeks. "I could have married you," she said, her voice breaking. "I could have spent every single day with you. My best friend. My favorite person in the whole world. And instead, I... I..."

He pulled her into his lap. "I know, Anne. Believe me, I know."

They stayed that way for a while, with Michael stroking Anne's back while she cried on his shoulder. Eventually the worst of her sobs subsided, and she sat up, accepting Michael's handkerchief. "Come on," she said, sliding off his lap. "Let's go home."

CHAPTER 24

*T*hey made the short drive back to Anne's house mostly in silence. Anne did find the arm Michael wrapped around her shoulders comforting. She was still struggling to process everything he'd told her. It was probably a sin to think it, but a part of her was glad Wynters was dead. She could not imagine how she would have gone on with him as her husband had she found out about his deception while they had still been married. He had tricked her. He had taken her choices away. That *blackguard*.

Then there was the fact that Michael loved her! Anne peered up at him. He gave her a rueful half smile. She was starting to accept the truth of his feelings. It still felt unreal, but she knew Michael Cranfield almost as well as she knew her own self, and she could tell he was sincere.

What Anne was having a more difficult time processing were her own feelings. Did... did she love Michael, too? Of course she did, he was her best friend. But did she—

The carriage drew to a halt, and Anne shook her head to clear it. She could not dwell on these things right now.

She informed her two other footmen, Hugh and John, of

the death of Nick and Johnny's former master, then led Michael to the front parlor. She immediately pulled out paper and ink. She needed to write to a few of her contacts, ask if they'd heard anything…

Her train of thought was interrupted by the clearing of a throat. She glanced up to find Michael looming before her writing desk. "So. Anne." He drew in a deep breath. "Now that I've explained myself better, I will go ahead and obtain a special license so we can marry with all possible haste."

Anne sighed, laying down her pen. "I hope we can, Michael. But there are still things we need to discuss."

"Such as?"

She steeled herself. "Such as where we would live. Now that you've seen the Ladies' Society, surely you understand how critical my work is. That there are women and children depending on me."

"I understand."

Anne's eyes flew to his. She felt hope bubbling up inside of her. "Then… does this mean you're not planning to go back? To Canada?"

He set his jaw. "I do plan for us to go back to Canada."

She blew out a breath she hadn't realized she was holding and turned back to her letter. "Then we remain at an impasse."

"Look, Anne," he said, coming around the desk and taking her hand, "I know how important your charity work is. But my work in Canada is important, too. I'm going to be—"

"Lady Wynters." Hugh appeared in the door bearing a letter on a silver tray. "This arrived for you while you were out."

Anne unfolded the note.

. . .

I'VE HEARD you're asking questions about the R.M.A. The rot goes deeper than you realize. If you want to learn more, meet me tonight at midnight in the alley behind the Red Lion Inn. I won't speak to nobody but Lady Wynters, and don't do nothing that will draw any notice, or I won't come out.

"AN INFORMANT HAS COME FORWARD." Anne showed the note to Hugh. "Who brought this?"

"It was a boy," Hugh said. "Not in livery. Just your standard delivery boy. I'm sorry, I didn't question him, m'lady. I didn't think nothing of it."

"That's all right, Hugh. Would you please go and fetch Sarah?"

Hugh bowed. "At once, m'lady."

Michael wandered over to her desk and picked up the note. Anne rose and began pacing the library as plans started to form in her mind. "I'll need something very plain to wear. Sarah can find me something."

"Wait," Michael said, "tell me you're not even considering it."

She reached one end of the room and spun on her heel. "They say they have information regarding the 'rot' at the R.M.A. Of course I'm considering it."

"Anne," Michael fumed, "they just pulled someone's body out of the Thames! It could be a trap."

"Obviously. But it could also be legitimate. Besides, why would they want to harm me?"

"Because you're investigating them."

"Bow Street are the ones investigating them, and they already have every piece of information I do. I can see the value of eliminating a witness. It's why they killed Mr. Smithers, and why Nick and Johnny are in so much danger.

But what impact would harming me have, other than bringing all of Bow Street down upon their heads?"

"Yes, well, where is this… Red Lion Inn?" Michael asked, consulting the note.

"Holborn," Anne said as she paced past him. "Not far from Lincoln's Inn Fields. Let's see, I should probably go by hackney carriage…"

"Holborn?" Michael said. "That alone should be enough to dissuade you. You have no business being in Holborn at midnight."

"It's not far from my lodging house," Anne countered, "and in a very similar neighborhood."

"Which brings me to my next point. Your lodging house is in an unsuitable district."

Anne narrowed her eyes. "It will come as a great shock, but charity lodging houses are not generally found on Grosvenor Square."

"Your lodging house is in *St Giles*," he snapped. "St Giles is a *rookery*!"

"This from the man with whom I used to have all of my best adventures." Anne looked him up and down. "When did you turn into such a stick?"

His mouth fell open. "Did you just call me a stick?"

She cocked up her chin. "I believe I just did. And what right do you have to criticize? Aren't you the one who's been squaring off with angry bears in Canada?"

"It is a different matter entirely for *me* to do something risky—"

Anne felt her eyebrow give a violent twitch, and Michael froze midsentence, studying her face. He seemed to (correctly) sense that he needed to abandon that particular argument.

"Anne," he started again, "I just care about you, and I don't want to see you get hurt. Surely that's not so hard to understand."

She waved this off. "Your concern is misplaced. The neighborhood is not so bad as you suppose, and I never go there without at least two of my footmen."

"Which is better than nothing, especially if all of your footmen resemble the brute squad who threw me out this morning. Good God, Anne, where do you find such men?"

Anne decided to consider this a rhetorical question, on account of the fact that Michael would not like the answer. The types of men who made the worst criminals in St Giles hesitate didn't come with unblemished records. "I've gone there every day for the last four years, and nothing bad has ever happened."

"Well, that's going to change once we're married."

Anne rounded on him, hands on her hips. "*If* we're married.".

"*When* we're married," Michael insisted, looming over her and giving her his full Obstinate Face. "If you think I'm going to let you go traipsing about St Giles—"

"And if you think I'm going to tolerate you barking orders at me, treating me like a child—"

"Christ, woman! I'm just trying to protect you!"

Anne felt something snap inside of her. "Well, I don't want your protection! What I want is your respect!"

MICHAEL FELT as though he had just been slapped. They'd been shouting seconds ago, but his voice when it emerged was quiet. "How can you even say that, Anne? I respect you. I respect you more than any other person on the face of this earth."

Her voice shook. "You have a funny way of showing it. I

expect my future husband to support me in my charity work, not limit me. If you are unwilling to do that, then there is no possibility of us marrying."

These words caused a familiar red haze to settle over Michael's brain, obscuring any attempt at rational thought. He knew this was the exact opposite of what he needed right now. He took a slow breath before replying. "I intend to support you in your charity work by helping you stay alive to do it. And that means preventing you from going to Holborn at midnight, into what is almost certainly a trap."

Anne crossed her arms. "Name any three facts about Holborn."

Michael plumbed the depths of his brain. Nothing much rose to the surface. "It is in London. It is a bad neighborhood. And... you are not going there."

"It happens that I was there four days ago. It also happens that I know a thousand times more about Holborn, and whether or not it is a dangerous neighborhood, than you do. And yet you stand there, lecturing me!"

Michael tilted his head to the side and shook it, in hopes that a useful retort would fall out. Sadly, one did not. "It is a husband's duty to keep his wife safe."

"Well, you aren't my husband. And you aren't going to be, if this is how little respect you have for my judgment. But do you know who does respect me?" Anne drew herself up to her full height. "Archibald Nettlethorpe-Ogilvy."

Michael had no idea what she had just said. "God bless you?" he hazarded.

Anne narrowed her eyes. "What do you mean, God bless you? I didn't *sneeze*, Michael."

"Did you not? Who in God's name, then, is Archiwhat Kettlecorp Overtree?"

"Archibald Nettlethorpe-Ogilvy," she said haughtily, "is

one of the most brilliant inventors of our age, famous for making precision machine tools—"

"Oh, Nettlethorpe. Of Nettlethorpe Iron, I take it. That'd be the grandson. Yes, I read something about him."

"Indeed. *He* thinks my charity work is important. Not only that, but he wants to work with me, on a number of initiatives." She lifted her chin. "You would think that my supposed best friend, the man who claims he wants to marry me, would offer a similar level of support."

"Well, I don't care what Archibald Nettlethorpe-Ogilvy thinks. If you think I'm going to permit you to go traipsing through Holborn at midnight—"

Hugh reappeared in the doorway. He caught Michael's eye, and began shaking his head, waving his hands in front of him, and mouthing the word, *No*.

Apparently Hugh's analysis was sound, because Anne snapped, "Permit! No, Michael, you will not *permit* me to do anything, because I do not require your permission. You are not my husband and I do not answer to you."

Michael started to blanch but recovered quickly. "Well, let's see what your brothers have to say about it."

Anne leaned forward, uncowed. "Unlike some people, my brothers do not try to limit me. Harrington's response to my doing *hard work in hard neighborhoods amongst hard men*, as he put it the other day, is to teach me how to shoot."

"That's Harrington, but I know Fauconbridge would never condone you putting yourself in danger."

Anne huffed. "If you had read my letters, you would know that I never would have been able to found the Ladies' Society without Edward's help." At Michael's blank look, she continued, "Do you recall the translation he completed during his final year at Cambridge? Of Aeschylus's *Prometheus Unbound*?"

"Of course."

"He published it and donated the proceeds to the Ladies' Society. That's how I was able to make my start. My brothers know exactly what I do, and they support me. But even if they didn't, they have no authority over me. As a widow, I make my own decisions, and if I want to go into Holborn tonight, there is absolutely nothing you can do to stop me."

Michael blinked at Anne, horrified to realize that she was right.

Anne, his precious Anne, could march straight into the worst rookeries in London, and there wasn't a damn thing he could do to stop her. And if something were to happen to her...

The possibility was so horrible, his brain recoiled from even considering it. He had lost her once, to Lord Wynters.

He could not lose her again. He couldn't bear it.

He would rather die.

"Michael?" Anne had laid a hand upon his forearm. Her anger seemed to have melted away, and there was nothing but concern in her eyes.

Without thinking, he raised his hand to caress her cheek. "I cannot bear for anything to happen to you," he said, his voice guttural.

From the doorway, Hugh cleared his throat. "And that's why we need a good plan, we do."

Anne, who'd had her back facing the door, startled as Hugh entered the room, followed by a maid. She took a hasty step back from Michael.

"I grew up in Holborn," Hugh continued, "and the thing to know is it's uneven. There'll be a street I wouldn't walk down in broad daylight that dead-ends into a respectable shopping district. The Red Lion's a prosperous establishment. The owners aren't going to let that area go to seed."

Michael caught Anne's eye and found that she was giving him a very *I-told-you-so* look. "Nonetheless," Michael said, "I doubt there is any plan that would satisfy me."

"You should go with her, m'lord," Hugh said.

"Me?" Michael tore his gaze from Anne to look at Hugh. "But the note says she has to go alone."

"The writer says he'll only speak to Lady Wynters," Hugh countered, "and that she can't draw any notice. Well, you can stand a few feet back and keep watch if he insists upon it. And a man and woman walking together at that time of night won't draw no notice at all, especially if you act a bit, er, friendly."

"That's a good idea, that is," the maid said. "Too many people will recognize her ladyship, but nobody knows you, m'lord. If things don't look right, you can just back her up against a wall and block her face from view. It's a good thing you're already betrothed, because you'll have to make it look like you're about to—"

"Thank you, Sarah," Anne interjected. "We have the general idea."

"I'll find something for you to wear, m'lady," Sarah said. She turned to inspect Michael's coat, which was one of his new ones. "You won't want to dress quite so sharp, m'lord. Stands out too much. You'll want to look a bit shabby."

"I believe I have just the thing," Michael muttered.

"Good." Sarah beamed. "I'll go start preparing, m'lady."

After Hugh and Sarah had taken their leave, Anne returned to her desk and began drafting a letter, paying Michael no attention. He eyed her the way one eyed a tiger, then cleared his throat. "So. Anne. Are you still mad at me?"

She heaved a great sigh, then looked up. "Exasperated might be a better word. The way you've treated me this morning has been atrocious—"

"It has," he hastily agreed. "And I am extremely sorry."

"—but I'm not going to stay mad at you forever."

"You... you're not?" Hope flared in his chest.

"Of course I'm not," she said, turning back to her letter. "You're my best friend, after all."

"Good." He came around the desk in three quick steps and took both of her hands in his. "Because I cannot bear for you to be mad at me."

She narrowed her eyes. "In that case, I suggest you do better going forward. Because I have a right to be upset with you, Michael. 'Knit scarves for the poor' indeed!"

"I wish you would stop making arguments that are so difficult to refute," he grumbled.

"Not a chance."

He sighed. "So, what are we doing this afternoon?"

"*I* will be occupied writing letters to my various contacts, as well as preparing for this evening. I suggest you do the same."

"I was afraid that would be your answer," he muttered.

"You may return at half eleven."

"Half eleven," Michael agreed. He leaned in to kiss Anne, and she very pointedly offered him her hand. He settled for pressing a lingering kiss to her palm and took his leave.

AN HOUR AFTER MICHAEL DEPARTED, Hugh appeared in the doorway to Anne's office. "Lord Scudamore," he announced.

Anne scrambled to her feet. "Lord Scudamore. What an... an unexpected pleasure."

This, of course, was a lie. Considering Mr. Smithers' dead body had just come floating down the Thames, it appeared that someone had tipped Lord Gladstone off, and all the evidence pointed to Lord Scudamore.

"Lady Wynters," he said, bowing over her hand, "I wanted to let you know of a development since our conversation last night. An unfortunate development, I'm afraid."

"I... I see." Anne gestured for him to take the chair before her desk, then turned to Hugh, who was just heading out the door. "Hugh, won't you *stay* and pour Lord Scudamore a drink?"

Hugh's eyes went wide as he nodded, understanding her unspoken plea. He crossed the room to the decanter.

Lord Scudamore gave her a cringing smile. "You are nervous, I assume, because you've heard about the master sweep who was murdered overnight."

Anne blanched. "How do you know about that?"

"I called at Bow Street an hour ago, to see if they had arrested Gladstone and to offer my assistance with any questions regarding the R.M.A." He squeezed his eyes shut. "The news I received was of a most horrific nature, and I... I fear it is all my fault." He opened his eyes and held her gaze. "I wanted you to hear it directly from me."

Anne gripped the edge of her desk. "What is it?"

He squared off his jaw. "Gladstone has fled."

"Fled? What do you mean, fled?"

"Bow Street has patrolmen watching his house. He didn't return last night, nor this morning. When they questioned his servants today, they said he came in through the back entrance around two o'clock in the morning, hastily packed a trunk, then left. They've no idea where he went."

Anne tried to hold her voice steady but was unable to conceal its shaking. "So Lord Gladstone has gone to ground, and a key witness has turned up dead. I should like to know how he realized the net was closing around him."

"You think—naturally, I must own—that I must have told Gladstone of our conversation last night."

Precisely. "Well? Did you?"

"I swear, I did not." He stared at the carpet. "I fear it is my fault nevertheless."

"And why is that?"

Lord Scudamore set his drink upon her desk. "I swear to you, upon my word of honor, that I did not tell Gladstone." He regarded her steadily. "But I did confide in Lord Aylsham."

"The Earl of Aylsham?" Anne asked, startled. "Whatever for?"

"I thought he should know. Lord Aylsham is vice president of the R.M.A., after all. And I knew he couldn't be involved. From what you told me, this has been going on for some time, and, being in the Royal Marines, he only returned to the country six months ago. I thought he might be able to think of some piece of evidence that I had missed. Although, if I am being honest..." He raked a hand through his tawny hair. "Part of me wanted to believe it was all some terrible mistake. That Gladstone was truly innocent, and that Lord Aylsham would point out something that would clear him from blame."

The viscount rose to pace before the fireplace. "I spoke with Lord Aylsham in an empty sitting room on the ground floor. It overlooked the back gardens. The window was open, and at one point, I heard the sound of branches breaking nearby. I went and shut the window, but I didn't think much of it. Probably just a pair of lovers meeting in the garden. But given what has transpired since then..."

"You think it was Gladstone."

Lord Scudamore turned to face Anne. "Surely it must have been. What other explanation could there be for Smithers's death?"

Anne studied the viscount. He seemed sincere in his distress, and he might very well be telling the truth.

But it was also possible that he had forewarned his friend, then staged a conversation with Lord Aylsham to cover his tracks.

Lord Scudamore cleared his throat. "The most important

thing now, and the reason why I'm here, is because if Gladstone is eliminating witnesses, that places your two climbing boys in grave danger. You said one of them caught a glimpse of his face, correct?"

"Yes, that's correct."

Lord Scudamore sat down again. "I assume they are staying at your lodging house. You will need additional security. I would be grateful if you would allow me to provide it." He rubbed at his forehead. "Gladstone's escape is entirely my fault. I should have been more circumspect, but I... I just wasn't thinking clearly. My providing those boys with additional guards is the least I can do, given the circumstances."

"Thank you, but I already have additional men in place."

Lord Scudamore leaned forward. "Are you certain you have enough of them? What precautions are you taking?"

"I've placed one guard with them at all times, another at the front door, and a third to stand watch overnight."

"Are you certain I can't send a few more men to help? Through my connections with the R.M.A. I can access a network of former soldiers. Good, upstanding men, who are experienced at standing watch."

"No, thank you. I am happy with the arrangements that are already in place."

"Very well," the viscount said, standing. "Do send the bill for the additional guards to me, though. It would be a weight off my conscience."

"Very well, my lord."

Anne accompanied him to the door with Hugh trailing after them at a discreet distance. "I take it Morsley proposed last night?" Lord Scudamore asked as he pulled on his gloves.

Anne felt her cheeks reddening as she considered her answer. "Er... yes. Yes, he did."

Scudamore sighed. He took Anne's hand in both of his, but instead of bowing over it, he pressed it. "Morsley is a lucky man," he said, his expression rueful. "A very lucky man indeed."

Then he did bow over her hand, his lips grazing the backs of her knuckles. "Good day, my lady."

CHAPTER 25

*A*nne was ready when Michael knocked on her door that night. He came in a hackney carriage and was wearing his old jacket. The plain grey frock Sarah had found for Anne fit reasonably well, and the flaps on the cloth cap were large enough to conceal her face. The final accessory to Anne's outfit was tucked inside her pocket. In addition to the flintlock pistol she used for target practice, she kept a tiny Queen Anne pistol, the kind one loaded by unscrewing the barrel. It was only five inches long, which made it perfect for when she needed something discreet.

Once they disembarked from the hackney, Anne took Michael's arm and led him toward the alley behind the Red Lion Inn. Michael was on high alert, scanning their surroundings for any sign of trouble and occasionally turning to check behind them.

Anne sighed. "Michael," she said, tugging his head down so she could whisper in his ear, "you can't look around like that. It's too conspicuous."

Ignoring her, he whipped his head to the left to scrutinize

what turned out to be an alley cat. "Someone could sneak up on us."

"I understand, but you can't be so obvious about it."

"What do you suggest, then?"

"Act as if you've had too much to drink. Stagger a bit and, if you must turn your head, do so drunkenly."

Michael glared at her but made a visible effort to comply.

Soon they reached the appointed alleyway. The night was clear and, although the moon was nearly full overhead, the alley was narrow enough that little light filtered down to where they stood. Anne urged Michael to lean one shoulder against a wall and took up a position facing him, trying to pantomime a flirtatious conversation between a streetwalker and a potential customer.

Michael was back to obsessively checking their surroundings. "Relax," she whispered, smoothing his lapel in a manner she hoped looked coquettish. "Pretend you're enjoying yourself."

"I cannot enjoy myself while you are in danger," he said, his voice clipped.

"You've got to try. Come," she tugged at his coat, "look at me as if you want me."

He turned his head and did just that, raising a hand to frame her face. It was dark, but Anne could read his face well enough. His expression was one of adoration, but it was mixed with a ferocity that took Anne's breath away. It was a look that said he was ready to kill for her, ready to die for her, ready to do whatever was required to keep her safe. It was an expression that would not have looked out of place on his ancestors who built Cranfield Castle some five hundred years ago.

She gave a shaky laugh. "Now you're overdoing it. I don't think that's how a man looks at the woman he's just hired for the evening."

"This is the only way I know how to look at you," he ground out.

Anne's cheeks grew warm, and she was trying to think of a reply when they heard the sound of a man clearing his throat.

Michael spun around and stepped in front of Anne, both fists raised. A short man with dark hair and broad shoulders stood peering at them uncertainly, his hat clutched in front of him in both hands.

"Lady Wynters?" the man said, leaning around Michael to squint at Anne. "Oh, good, it is you." He shook his head, chuckling. "Blimey, you're even prettier than your cartoon."

Anne gave him a tight smile at the mention of the cartoon. She took Michael's arm and tried to move him out of the way. When he didn't budge so much as an inch, she stepped around him. "Thank you so much for meeting with me, Mr., er…"

"Price. Arnold Price." He looked Michael up and down. "Who's this, then?"

"A good friend," Anne replied. "He can be trusted."

Mr. Price frowned. "What I've to say is for your ears only."

Oh dear. There was no way Michael was going to step so much as five feet away from her. What was she going to—

"I am Lady Anne's betrothed," Michael said quietly.

Mr. Price's head snapped up to look at Michael. "Her betrothed, you say?"

"Yes," Michael said. "I'm sure you can understand my unwillingness to leave my future bride unprotected at this time of night."

Something softened in Arnold Price's expression. "Is that true, your ladyship? He's to be your husband?"

Anne didn't know how to answer. "I… er… yes."

Mr. Price considered for a moment, then shrugged. "I

guess that's all right, then." He glanced up and down the alleyway—much more subtly than Michael had, Anne couldn't help but note, then said in a low voice, "I'm a brick-layer by trade. Right now I'm working on the R.M.A. head-quarters."

"Is that so?" Anne said.

"It is." He dropped his voice to a whisper. "Someone from Bow Street came around the site today, asking questions. Had we seen anyone bringing young boys to the site, or a shiny black carriage coming to pick them up. Then they started asking about some cove they pulled out of the river this morning. They said it was the same master sweep you had a run-in with the other day."

"Mr. Smithers," Anne supplied.

"Smithers, yeah. They asked if we'd seen him coming around or if we'd seen anything else that was suspicious."

"I see," Anne said. "And did you have anything to report to Bow Street?"

"I ain't seen no boys being brought to the site, or no shiny black carriage or anything like that. But I can tell you, there's something fishy going on at the R.M.A." He shook his head. "I've been wanting to tell someone about it."

"So why," Michael asked, his voice clipped, "did you not tell the Bow Street runner who asked for that exact informa-tion? Why involve Lady Anne in this sordid business?"

"That's the problem with constables, ain't it? Three of them are fine, but then the fourth is in someone's pocket. You can cause yourself a whole world of trouble if you say something to the wrong man. But between them asking about little boys being sold and then about Smithers, I figured it must involve that same business you got tangled up with the other day, m'lady. And I thought, that's who I'll tell. Lady Wynters. Because I know you're not in anyone's pocket."

Anne was glad it was dark because she was fairly sure her cheeks were pink. "So, what exactly has been going on at the R.M.A.?"

"Someone's pilfering the construction materials. I know that don't sound like much, but they're not doing it in a small way." He leaned in. "Apparently about five thousand pounds' worth of bricks went missing."

"Is that sort of misappropriation not fairly common on a construction project?" Michael asked.

"Don't mistake me," Mr. Price said, "it is. Although not to the tune of five thousand pounds. Besides, Alexander Copeland is the overseer. The army always hires him because there's never any funny business on an Alexander Copeland site. 'The Emperor of Barrack-Builders,' they call him. I know Mr. Copeland got called before the R.M.A.'s board for questioning. He walked the foundation himself, calculating exactly how many bricks went into it, and he was at a loss to explain where the rest had gone. Looked right upset about it, he did." Mr. Price shook his head. "I think someone made off with those bricks, but I don't think it was Alexander Copeland."

"Do you have any idea who it might be?" Anne asked.

"I don't, m'lady. The thing is, five thousand pounds' worth of bricks is a lot to go missing. I doubt someone could haul that much off without being seen, even if they did it in the dead of night. And we'd have noticed that half the pile of bricks was gone." He paused to glance over his shoulder. "That's what makes me think the skimming happened on the front end. I don't believe those bricks were even delivered."

Anne caught Michael's eye and wondered if he was thinking the same thing.

Someone on the R.M.A.'s Board.

Someone like Lord Gladstone.

"Is there any other suspicious activity?" Anne asked.

"No, m'lady. Not since they started asking questions about the bricks. Which maybe isn't so surprising."

"Indeed," Anne said. "You've been tremendously helpful. I appreciate it more than I can say."

Mr. Price waved this off. "Just doing my part. Skimming a few bricks is one thing. But if someone's really been selling little boys as sweeps' apprentices—that's a nasty business, that is." He grinned. "But they'll rue the day they crossed our virago."

Now Anne was sure she was blushing. "Oh… er…"

Mr. Price glanced around. "Well, that's all I had to say. No use lingering."

He melted into the darkness.

Michael was already towing Anne toward the main road, where he flagged down a hackney carriage.

Once the door closed, Anne pulled off her cloth cap. "It all fits. It all fits perfectly. It's someone on the R.M.A.'s board. Who sits on the R.M.A.'s board, and is in dire financial straits? Gladsto—eemph!"

Anne gave a squeak as Michael scooped her into his lap and tried to kiss her. She held him at shoulder length. "Michael! I was talking."

"Have some pity. You've been rubbing up against me, pretending you were trying to seduce me, for the last half hour. It has had the predictable effect."

Surely enough, she could feel a familiar bulge pressing against her leg. "That can wait," she said, causing Michael to groan. Anne cleared her throat. "As I was saying, the evidence points to Gladstone."

Michael, who had settled for kissing her neck, paused long enough to say, "I thought Gladstone was the secretary. Isn't embezzlement more the treasurer's area?"

Anne shuddered. That did feel wonderful, what he was

doing. "You would think so," she managed to say. "But charitable boards are specifically set up to prevent that."

"How so?" Michael asked, moving up to Anne's ear.

"They—*God, Michael*—they require the treasurer to put down a... a deposit. Typically for five hundred pounds, as a guarantee. If there are any irregularities with the books, it comes out of their deposit. It removes temptation because they would only be stealing from themselves."

Michael kissed his way across her jawline. "Who is the treasurer of the R.M.A., anyways?"

Anne was now panting. "Lord... Lord Scudamore. And that's the thing—" She groaned, losing her train of thought mid-sentence, as Michael slid his hands up her torso and began to caress her nipples with his thumbs.

She felt a chuckle rumble through Michael's chest. "What's the thing?"

"M-motive," she gasped. "Lord Gladstone is—*God, that feels good*—in debt up to his eyeballs. Whereas Lord Scudamore—*oh, Michael!*—managed to turn his estate around years ago. Lord Gladstone is the one with the motive."

"An important consideration." Now Anne was the one leaning in to kiss Michael, and he was the one grinning wickedly as he held her back a few inches. "I thought you wanted to talk."

Anne decided turnabout was fair play and reached down to stroke the bulge that was still poking her in the leg. This had precisely the effect she desired, and Michael's head listed to the side on a groan. When she leaned in to kiss him this time, he met her lips voraciously.

Anne smiled into the kiss. Although she was still annoyed with him, she found herself starting to soften. After all, he had helped her tonight. She had to admit, their going together had provided a good cover, and although she would have been willing to walk down that alley alone, she'd been glad to have Michael by her side. He hadn't shown much talent for subterfuge, but he had tried.

This reminder of how pleasurable kissing Michael was also didn't hurt, and she found herself melting into his chest, her arms curling around his neck.

In the darkness of the hack, Michael's hands roved freely over her body, lingering over her best and most sensitive areas. By the time they crossed into Mayfair, Anne's body was humming pleasantly when she felt a rush of cold air against her legs.

"Michael," she laughed, "what are you doing?"

His hand was inching up her thigh, drawing tantalizingly closer to the place between her legs that was already throbbing for him. He pressed a kiss into her neck. "Reminding you how much you want to invite me in to stay the night."

His fingers were sifting through her curls in search of that sensitive little nub, and she shifted in his lap, spreading her legs to give him access. "Mmmmmmm," she groaned at the exquisite pleasure of first contact. "That does sound... very tempting. But I should—*oh!*—probably say no."

"No? Why 'no,' darling?"

Her head lolled onto his shoulder. "After last night, there's —*oh, Michael!* There's already a chance I could be pregnant. Truth be told I've... I've worried about it all day," she admitted. "I can't do anything that will increase those odds."

He frowned. "Don't worry about that Anne. We're getting married. Whether you're carrying my child right now or not."

"That's easy to say." She tipped her head back on a gasp as he swirled his thumb in *exactly* the right spot. "But... but our future plans are still completely at odds."

"We're going to figure that out," he insisted.

"I hope so. But what if we don't? I can't take another chance like we did last night." He opened his mouth to protest, and she placed her hand gently over his lips. "And please, don't argue. I can't possibly think clearly while you're... while you're..." She couldn't help but squirm against his hand. What had started as a few lazy caresses was rapidly growing in urgency. *God*, she wanted to come...

"How about this—we'll only do things that won't make you pregnant."

"Isn't there still a risk? Even if you use a sheath, or withdraw, or—"

"A small risk, yes. But that's not what I had in mind."

That made her curious. "Oh? Then what are you suggesting?"

He began to kiss her ear. "More of what I did to you last night. And what I'm doing to you right now. I'll use my hands on you, and my mouth."

That did sound... tempting. Very tempting, especially when he increased the pace at which his finger was swirling over that little rosebud between her legs. Oh, that felt good, that felt divine, and suddenly she was right on the brink of climaxing, right there in the hackney carriage.

Much to Anne's regret, that was when the carriage drew to a stop in front of her house. Michael pulled her skirts down and hastily set her on the seat next to him just before the driver opened the door. Anne wasn't sure if her legs were going to hold her as she climbed out of the hack, but somehow they did, and the next thing she knew, she was alone with Michael on the pavement.

"Well?" he asked, his eyes bright. The stress of the day— their fight, the murder of Mr. Smithers, the many revelations Michael had thrust upon her, the uncertainty that plagued their future—had all melted away, and he looked boyish and happy.

She made her decision. "Come inside," she said, taking his hand.

CHAPTER 26

*M*ichael knew he was grinning stupidly as Anne towed him through the front door of her town house.

Frankly, he didn't care. Nothing was going to wipe that stupid grin off his face.

Hugh, who opened the door, tried to keep a straight face. He succeeded for all of two seconds. "Good evening m'lady. Lord Morsley," he said with a bow.

They proceeded to Anne's rooms. Out in the hall, Michael made a show of examining the lock. "What are you doing?" Anne asked.

"Seeing if I can pick this in case you lock me out again. I'm not sure that I can, but no matter. Next time I'll just ram the door."

"That will make a fine show for the household staff," Anne said, removing her cap and placing it on her dressing table. "The housemaids were distressed to hear that the gorgeous Lord Morsley was naked in the hallway, and they all contrived to miss it."

He closed the door and turned the key. "How sad for the housemaids, because there won't be a repeat performance."

"That depends on whether or not you can stay in my good graces," Anne said as she pulled pins from her hair.

Michael crossed the room in three swift steps, caught her around the waist, and pulled her body flush against his. "After what I'm about to do to you, my darling Anne, I guarantee that I am going to be in the very best of your graces." He reached around and began undoing the ties of her dress.

"You sound very confident in yourself."

"I am." He shoved her dress to the floor and began working on her stays. "Nothing gives a man as much confidence as the knowledge that he made his lady love climax ten times the previous evening."

She flushed very prettily. "Was it ten times? Who was counting, anyways?"

"I was counting, and it most certainly was ten. Possibly your neighbors were counting as well, given how loudly you were screaming my name. Let's see if we can improve upon that tonight." He lowered his head to hers for a kiss.

She immediately melted against his chest. God, he loved it when she did that.

He tossed her stays to the floor and took a moment to enjoy the sight of Anne wearing nothing but her chemise. She managed to look sweet and seductive in equal measures in the whisper-thin white muslin. Reaching for the ribbon gather at the neckline, he noticed that the embroidered decoration was in the pattern of strawberries. That made him smile.

As much as he liked the strawberries, they had to go. He pulled the chemise over her head, leaving Anne wearing nothing but her silk stockings and garters. Those, he decided, could stay. He scooped her up in his arms and carried her to the bed, where he lay her gently down. He quickly divested himself of everything but his trousers and lay down beside her.

She immediately began stroking his chest. Her face held a touch of embarrassment, as if she weren't sure whether she was supposed to be touching him, but with a strong undercurrent of awe as she gazed at his chest. Would that he could somehow go back in time and tell his skinny-as-a-broomstick-handle, spotty-faced fourteen-year-old self that one day his beloved Anne was going to be lying naked before him, stroking his bare chest with *that* expression on her face. Without question, this would have been the best news fourteen-year-old Michael had ever heard.

He began kissing her again and running his hands up and down her front, and in short order she was squirming and purring for him again. He rolled a nipple between his thumb and index finger and was gratified when she arched her back in pleasure, her legs falling open.

That seemed like an excellent suggestion, so, as he took a nipple into his mouth, he stroked his hand down over her stomach, then lower to part her folds. She was wet, which he loved, and as soon as his hand made contact with her little rosebud, she groaned with pleasure.

"Ooooh, Michael! Yes! Right there—oh, that feels so good!"

He played with her for a few minutes, lavishing attention on one breast then the other, keeping his hand between her legs deliberately gentle. Every time she scooted her hips forward, he would subtly retreat, keeping his strokes soft and teasing.

After a few minutes, she realized what he was doing. "Michael!" she mewled in protest.

"Yes, darling?"

"You're doing that on purpose."

"Doing what on purpose?"

"Teasing me. I've been dying to come ever since we were in the carriage! Why won't you let me?"

He chuckled as he slid down her body. "Because, my darling Anne, I'm building you up. Although you want to throttle me right now, when you finally reach your peak it's going to be so high, and your pleasure so intense, you're going to thank me for the torturous way I got you there."

She looked partially mollified and partially intrigued as he began kissing his way down her stomach, still caressing her ever so gently with his fingers. He spent a few minutes worshiping the insides of her thighs while her legs twitched in anticipation beneath his lips. After several kisses that barely grazed the little pink nub that was swollen and begging for his attention, she cried out in frustration, then reached down and grabbed his head, and positioned his mouth just where she wanted it.

Michael smiled. Deciding he had tortured her enough, he gave her what she so clearly wanted, although he kept his tongue deliberately gentle as he teased her little sweet spot.

He glanced up and drank in the sight of the glassy pleasure in Anne's eyes. He kept his caresses light, but as her cries grew more and more desperate, he decided it was time. He paused and repositioned his mouth over her sweet little nub.

And then he began to suck.

He did so gently at first, but the effect was instantaneous. Anne froze, her eyes flying open. He could read her face, and her expression right now told him that she was feeling such pleasure as she'd never imagined existed.

"Michael?" she whispered uncertainly. He didn't answer but increased his suction just a fraction.

"*Michael,*" she moaned, and he could tell she was getting close. He increased his suction a hair more and looked up at her, and that was when she began to cry out.

"Michael... Michael... *Michael!* Oh, my God, yes, Michael!

Oh, my *God* that feels so good, please don't stop, don't ever, ever stop! Oh, my *God*, oh, my... Michael. Michael! *Michael!*"

Then the pleasure was upon her, and she exploded. There was no other word for it. Her back arched up like a bow and held for the space of a few heartbeats before crashing back down upon the bed. He kept sucking her as she screamed and thrashed on the bed and her legs shook and everything between them flexed for him in frantic pulses of delight. She continued screaming his name and thrashing and pulsing and trembling for a full minute before she collapsed on the bed.

Only then did he leave her, but just long enough to slide up the bed and take her in his arms. She was completely boneless, breathing hard, her eyes closed.

He thought she might fall asleep after such a powerful climax, but after a few minutes her eyes blinked open, dazed and full of wonder. "What did you just do to me?"

He smiled. "Is that a complaint?"

She poked his bottom. "You know full well it isn't. That was magnificent." She laughed, rubbing at her side. "I came so hard, I think I might have strained something."

"Good," he laughed, stroking her back.

"Give me just a minute for the room to stop spinning, and I'll attempt to do the same for you."

He froze. "But Anne," he said carefully, "remember what we discussed? You don't want to risk any chance of pregnancy. So there's nothing you can do for me, darling."

Her head popped up. "Oh, but there is!" she said brightly. "Did you not know? There's a way I can use my mouth on you, too." Michael's astonishment must have shown on his face, because she ducked her head and added, "I mean, I've never done it before, but I've heard other women make, um, passing comments and little jokes, and..." She laughed nervously. "In any case, I understand it's possible. Come on," she said, reaching for the buttons of his placket, "I'm sure we can figure it out."

"Anne," he said in a strangled voice, "I don't expect you to, er…"

"Oh!" She paused with half of the buttons on his trousers undone. "Would you not like that?" she asked shyly.

Michael groaned. "Of course I would *like* it." He gestured to his straining cock. "Just look at me. I'm about to explode. But you are a lady, gently bred, and I would never expect for you to do such a thing for me."

Anne's forehead crinkled. "You use your mouth on me. How is this any different?"

"But I enjoy doing that for you. I love worshipping you, giving you pleasure."

She smiled and crawled up his body, pressing her naked flesh against his as she went, and gave him a tender kiss. He cradled her face and kissed her back. He was so distracted that it took him a moment to notice that her hands had returned to the placket of his trousers, where she continued to undo his buttons.

"Anne?" he asked, trying to stifle a groan as her fingers teased his shaft through the layers of fabric.

She smiled. "You enjoy pleasuring me. I'll bet I'm going to enjoy pleasuring you, too." She started kissing his neck, working her way down his body the way he had done to her earlier. Her hands continued working at his placket, and as the final button sprang free, she began struggling to push his trousers and drawers down.

Michael groaned. He knew that, as a gentleman, he should resist. But there was absolutely zero chance that was going to happen. As Anne sucked one if his nipples into her mouth, his cock gave a pulse of approval, and the last thread of his resolve snapped. He lifted his hips and pushed his remaining garments off, tossing them on the floor.

Her nose crinkled in delight as she looked at his straining cock. She began to touch him tentatively, just with her fingertips—a delicious form of torture, when he wanted so much more. She jerked her hand back as she encountered the bead of moisture that had formed at his very tip, but she quickly realized how sticky it was, and began smoothing it over his head. Michael had propped himself up on his elbows so he could watch her, but as she began to tease him there, he let his head loll back as he groaned.

"Is that all right?" she asked.

He looked up, and she read the answer in his eyes. She looked delighted as she resumed her soft little touches.

"Am I doing this right?" she asked after a few minutes.

"You're doing great," he replied immediately.

"What I mean is, is this how you do it when you, um. You know." She was blushing, but she hastily added, "When you touch yourself." He froze, stunned but also unbearably aroused by the direction the conversation was taking.

She misinterpreted his silence. "But what am I saying—you probably don't do that—I didn't mean to suggest that you—"

He barked out a laugh. "Of course I do. I touch myself every goddamn day. Oftentimes more than once. What did you think I was doing after I fled into the woods during that disastrous picnic?"

She gave a startled laugh. Now she was really blushing, but she looked enormously relieved. "I believe we have previously established that I had no idea what was actually going on during that picnic. Did you truly…"

"I did. I was about to spend in my trousers. That was the other reason it was rather imperative that I get off you."

"Oh, my gracious! And to think that I had no idea." She paused, biting her lip. "Would you show me how you do it?"

He reached down, covering her hand with his, and

demonstrated how he liked to be stroked. "And do you know who I think about when I do this?"

"Who?" Anne asked in a small voice.

"You," he replied, looking her in the eyes. "Always you."

She managed to look both embarrassed and pleased, and continued stroking him as he removed his hand and leaned back against the pillows. "That's it," he encouraged. "God, that feels good. Yes—squeeze me tighter. You won't do it too hard."

She soon picked up the rhythm. "Now let me try it with my mouth," she said eagerly, sliding down toward him.

"You don't have to do that if you don't want to, Anne," he hastened to say. "What you're doing feels very good. It will make me come."

"But won't it feel even better with my mouth?"

"Um." He should lie. It would be the gentlemanly thing to do. He opened his mouth to demur, and found the word, "Yes," emerging.

So much for that plan.

"Then I want to use my mouth," she said, lowering her lips toward his shaft.

She kissed the head of his cock with those full, wide, petal-soft lips, and he was unable to contain a groan of pleasure. He was big enough that she had to make a few attempts before she managed to take all of him inside her mouth, each one giving him a tantalizing taste of the pleasure he was about to experience.

He was losing control, and fast. "It's just—*God, Anne*—if you do that, you're going to make me come."

She laughed, looking up at him. "That's the general idea."

"I'm going to come *in your mouth*, Anne."

She regarded him in silence for a few beats, studying his face. "And you would like that," she said slowly.

He cringed. "I... um..."

"Don't even bother lying to me, Michael Cranfield," she said with a smug smile. "I can read your face. You've been thinking about me taking you into my mouth. For a very long time, if I'm not mistaken."

A man should not blush, but he felt his face heating. "I, uh—"

"Here," she said, releasing his shaft and coming up beside him. She gathered up all the pillows and propped him up so he was half-reclining. "There!" she said with delight. "I can tell already that you like to watch me touching you. Especially when I'm touching your cock." She studied him again. "You like that, too, don't you? To hear me talk about your cock?" She lay down beside him, pressing her body against his, wrapping her hand around him and stroking his length the way he had shown her, and put her lips right next to his ear. "Your cock is so big, Michael. Your cock felt so wonderful last night, Michael. Mmm, just thinking about how much pleasure you gave me with your cock makes me want to come again, Michael."

He answered with a garbled string of desperate babbling that caused Anne to laugh. "Damn it, woman! You're going to make me spill on the sheets."

"After the way you tortured me, I'm not the least bit sorry." But she did take pity on him, holding his eyes as she slid down his body and positioned her mouth above his cock. "Now lie back and relax and enjoy the view." And finally, *finally*, she slipped her lips around the tip of his cock.

Oh, fuck. She had scarcely touched him, and he was already on the brink of insanity. Anne was right. He had been dreaming of her doing exactly this ever since he was fourteen years old.

He'd been dreaming about other things too, of course, but one of his favorite fantasies had always involved her taking him by the hand and leading him somewhere slightly secluded—maybe into an empty parlor, or around the corner of the stable. Or best of all, reimagining the picnic when they had been fifteen so that she had followed him into the copse of trees and wound up helping him with his "problem." In his daydreams she would drop to her knees and open his trousers. He always fantasized that she would smile up at him with that mischievous crinkle of her nose as she took out his cock, perhaps make a little cooing sound when she found him rock hard, just for her. And then she would look up at him with those gorgeous brown eyes as she took his cock into her mouth.

Deep down, he knew it was stupid. Fourteen-year-old Anne never acted that way, and even if they married some-day, he knew one didn't do such things with one's lady wife. It was just a dirty, delicious fantasy for him to think about while he was tossing off. He had always understood it was never going to happen.

Except... it was happening. And, *God*, her lips wrapped around his cock felt a thousand times better than his wildest imaginings.

Clever girl that she was, she had already mastered the way he liked his cock to be stroked. Her hands were so soft and so sweet, and she was using both of them to stroke up and down his shaft. And oh, God, the feeling of her mouth! Gad, she swirled her tongue right over his head, where it felt so, so good! *God*, he wanted to come.

As he watched Anne slide her mouth up and down his cock, she flicked her eyes up to meet his, and he saw her nose crinkle in delight at the sight of him feeling such amazing pleasure.

It was his every fantasy come true. His ballocks tightened and he felt the familiar twinge as he passed the point of no return. He knew he was going to come, any second he was going to come, and he felt the undiluted pleasure of being right there on the brink. He heard himself calling her name, and his hands went to the back of her head, urging her on. Then he felt a white-hot burst of pleasure as he climaxed in her mouth.

He saw Anne's eyes widen as his seed filled her mouth, but she didn't stop, game girl that she was. No, she kept stroking him, drawing out his pleasure, until all of a sudden it was too much, and he combed his fingers into her hair and gently drew her off.

Her mouth came off his cock with a pop. Her cheeks were flushed, and her eyes had that glassy quality about them that he loved to see. He kissed her deeply, and she moaned and squirmed against him.

Remembering her words about how just thinking about his cock inside of her had made her want to come again, he pulled her up so that she straddled his mouth and began working her nub with his tongue while he slid two fingers inside her and massaged that special spot on the front side of her inner wall. Apparently her words about wanting another climax hadn't been just for show, because her response was a desperate, "God, Michael, please!" and she began touching her own breasts. It only took a minute before she was screaming his name and pulsing above him as he enjoyed the sweet nectar of her pleasure.

Once her trembling subsided, he pulled her down to lie with him, propped up on the pillows together, her head on his shoulder.

"Mmmmmmm," he murmured, leaning over to blow out the candles on her nightstand. Only a trace of moonlight through the window illuminated the room.

Anne giggled as she snuggled into his warmth. "I enjoyed that. Torturing you," she clarified as he raised an eyebrow at her.

"Well, seeing as you enjoyed it so very much, I will graciously suffer through it again, as often as you would like."

"How magnanimous of you," she muttered, settling into a comfortable position on his shoulder.

He kissed her cheek. "I love you, Anne. God, I love you so much."

He felt her stiffen in his arms.

CHAPTER 27

"*I* love you, Anne. God, I love you so much."

Anne froze, unsure how to respond. After a moment, Michael gave her a gentle squeeze. "Is everything all right?"

She swallowed. Should she say it back? Because she loved Michael. Of course she did, he was her best friend. It was just that she wasn't sure if she was *in* love with him. Which wasn't to say that she wasn't, it was just that... her world had been turned upside down in the past twenty-four hours, then flipped around and shaken for good measure. She was still trying to wrap her head around the fact that Michael loved her, to say nothing of the news that her former husband had deceived her. Then there was the fact that Michael was going back to Canada.

Anne couldn't move to Canada. It was impossible. And it seemed that her brain was balking at even considering whether Michael, who held the distinction of being both her favorite person on the face of this earth, and the man who was going to leave her, might also be the love of her life.

Some things were too terrifying even to contemplate.

Michael was still waiting for an answer. "It is, Michael. I just... I can't quite believe you feel that way. About me. It's... a bit overwhelming, truth be told."

He propped his head on one elbow so he could look at her. "I know I bombarded you with it this afternoon. With that, and with everything else. I hope it doesn't make you uncomfortable to hear me say it. I've been longing to say those words to you for almost a decade, and I can't bear to hold them in anymore. I want to tell you that I love you a thousand times a day."

He reached out and tucked an escaping curl behind her ear. "If it makes you feel better, I don't expect you to say it back. I can see the uncertainty on your face. And honestly, I would rather you not say anything just yet. Because *when* you tell me that you love me," he said with a pointed look, a very *Michael* look, "because I know you will one day, I don't want it to be because you know how much I want to hear it. I don't want it to mean that you love me like your best friend in the whole wide world. I want to know that you mean it without a single doubt in your mind. That you mean it in the exact same way I mean it when I say it to you."

Anne sighed. How like him to have read her so well. "You're talking as if we're going to have the rest of our lives together. But I still cannot go to Canada. After everything you saw today, surely you understand that. I have hundreds of people relying upon me for the roof over their head and the bread on their table. Orphans and widows and children, Michael! I cannot abandon, them, I—"

"I do understand that."

Something that felt distinctly like hope bubbled up in the center of Anne's chest. "Then... have you changed your mind? About going back?"

He sighed, and lay back on the bed, staring at the ceiling. "No. I still mean to go back."

Anne ducked her head as she settled onto his shoulder, trying to conceal her disappointment. "Then it's impossible."

They lapsed into silence for a moment, then Michael said, "Do you remember the famine three years ago?"

Anne shuddered. "The Ladies' Society was overrun with applications. It was terrible, Michael—snow on the fields in May, frosts in June and flooding in July. The fields were so waterlogged, nothing would grow. People were literally starving by the thousands."

"I'm the one who broke it," Michael said quietly.

Anne startled in his arms. "You... you what?"

"Not entirely, of course," Michael said, still staring at the ceiling. "From everything I've heard, it was still awful. But it would have been ten times worse had I not been running all over Canada at William Pitt's behest, buying up as much wheat as I could and arranging to have it shipped here."

Anne swallowed. It was jarring how much she had missed, how little she knew of Michael's life over the last four years. "I-I didn't know that."

"There were also commissions from the army and the Royal Navy." He grinned ruefully. "I got a letter of thanks from Lord Nelson the first time I sent the Royal Navy a shipload of mast poles. But breaking the famine, that's the assignment I'm most proud of." Michael looked at her then, his eyes urgent. "I know you're doing important work here, Anne. I've seen for myself what a difference you're making. But please don't imagine that going back to Canada is some lark for me. I'm doing important work there, too. It's why Lord Hobart wants me to be Governor General one day."

"Gov-Governor General!" Anne exclaimed, sitting up. "Of *Canada?*"

He nodded. "It wouldn't be for some years, but I'm already on the Legislative Council of Upper Canada. And I'm to begin formally training so that whenever Sir Robert Milnes steps down, I'll be ready."

"Oh, my goodness, Michael. I... I had no idea." Suddenly she was blinking back tears. "I'm so very proud of you."

He pulled her back down to rest upon his shoulder. "*That* is why it's important for me to go back to Canada. Not just so I can have some frontier adventure."

Anne brushed at a tear that was threatening to slip loose. "I understand, Michael. But surely you must see that however much we might wish to marry, our futures are incompatible. You need to find someone else, someone who can go with you to Canada."

He shook his head. "No, Anne. There's no one else for me. I've loved you since I was fourteen years old. And that will never change. I didn't stop loving you when you married someone else. I didn't stop loving you when you were on the other side of the world. I didn't stop loving you when I couldn't bear to open your letters because I was terrified they would be filled with tales of how happy another man was making you. I still loved you with every fiber of my miserable, wretched, broken heart." He gave her a sad smile. "I don't think we Cranfield men have it in us to love more than one woman in a lifetime. Just look at my father—fourteen years since my mother's death, and she's still the only woman in the world for him. And that's exactly how I feel about you. So please, don't suggest I find someone else. There's no one else for me but you. And there never will be."

Anne's heart was pounding from the force of Michael's declaration, the sincerity in his eyes. "But Michael, what are we going to do? It's impossible," she said, unable to conceal a note of despair in her voice.

"I refuse to accept that. I won't be parted from you. Ever." He lay back to stare at the ceiling again. "There is a solution. And I'm going to find it."

"You mean you're going to try to wear me down," Anne said, a trifle annoyed, "until I give up my dream, and you get everything you want?"

"No." He huffed. "As if that would even work."

"Then what?"

"I don't know." He yawned, pulling the duvet up to cover them. "But I'll figure it out."

Anne wasn't convinced, but she was exhausted and comfortable enough snuggled up with Michael that she didn't have long to dwell on their problems, because she found herself drifting into a dreamless sleep.

CHAPTER 28

The first thing they did the following morning was send a note to Mr. Branton detailing what Arnold Price had told them about the misappropriated funds at the R.M.A.

Well, Michael reflected with a wolfish grin, strictly speaking that was the *second* thing they did the following morning. He felt his cock stirring as he fondly recalled the first thing they'd done.

Michael dispatched another note to Cranfield House requesting a fresh set of clothes be sent over. After an informal breakfast in Anne's rooms, he dressed and headed home, as Anne had a full day ahead of her. All Michael had to fill his day was another visit to the tailor, although Anne had promised to dine with him that evening.

It was a fine, sunny morning, and Michael opted to walk home. He always thought best when he was moving, and he needed to think if he was going to come up with a solution to his and Anne's predicament. He was quite lost in thought as he bounded up the steps to Cranfield House, so that he gave a start when the front door burst open.

Out flew his father.

"Michael!" the marquess boomed. "There you are, son."

Michael grinned. "Father!" He jogged up the last few steps, and they both came to a halt.

The first thing Michael noticed was that he was now taller than his father, by a good four inches. Of course, he had known this would be the case, but it was one thing to know something like that theoretically, and another to experience the strange sensation of looking down upon the man to whom he had always looked up. It was also jarring to witness the effects of the passing of four years in an instant. His father still looked robust, but he had probably shrunk an inch. He also had a lot more grey in his hair than Michael remembered, and more creases around his eyes to go with it.

The second thing he noticed was the expression on his father's face. To be sure, he looked elated, but Michael also detected a trace of moisture in his father's eyes. There was a moment of indecision when they finally came together, when Michael got the impression that his father was thinking about... hugging him?

Not that the marquess said anything about it, and he settled upon a vigorous handshake accompanied by a few thumps on Michael's shoulder. But still, this was about as much emotion as Michael had seen out of his father since his mother died. It brought him up rather short.

His father led him down the hall to the library, where he went straight to the decanter in the corner. "I don't care if it's half nine, we're having a drink." He handed Michael a snifter of brandy. "I won't ask why you came back, as the answer is obvious. Don't think I didn't notice that you weren't here when I arrived."

Michael tugged at his cravat as they settled into a pair of leather wing chairs. "Yes, I had some business early this morning."

"Ha! I'm sure you did, but I wasn't referring to this morning. I got in late last night, and I know full well you just came home. To say nothing of the fascinating note that arrived an hour ago, requesting that a fresh change of clothes be sent to a certain lady's house."

Michael was fairly certain he was blushing. "I... well... you see..." Gad, now he really did need a drink. He took a fortifying sip from his glass.

"I take it you got the job done this time?" his father asked conversationally.

Of course he choked, and came alarmingly close to spewing his drink across the room for the third time in three days. Oh, God, did he really have to discuss this with his *father*? "I... um... that is to say..."

His father laughed at his obvious discomfort. "I don't need to hear the details, son. Just tell me this—has Lady Anne agreed to be your wife?"

"Yes." Michael couldn't help smiling, as he recalled the moment Anne had said yes. "I proposed, and she accepted."

His father thumped the armrest with his fist. "That's my boy."

"Well," Michael quickly amended, "there are a couple of issues we're still trying to work out. Anne has some concerns about how she'll be able to run her society—"

"Well, of course, as well she should. Our Lady Anne has become an important patroness in her own right, as you have no doubt seen for yourself. We will put whatever conditions she requires into the marriage settlement. It will just be a matter of the attorneys figuring out the exact wording."

Michael decided not to enlighten his father that things were a bit more fraught. After all, he was going to marry Anne. That was not in question.

"We will have to make a worthy donation to Lady Anne's charity to mark the occasion of your marriage." His father paused, tapping his finger against his glass. "Do you think that twenty thousand pounds would suffice?"

Michael raised his eyebrows. "I am sure that twenty thousand pounds will do quite handsomely, and that Anne will put it to the best of use." He laughed. "I hadn't thought to be the one bringing twenty thousand pounds to my marriage. I didn't realize I had a 'dowry.'"

His father laughed. "That's the only advantage of just having the one of you. No daughters to dower, and no younger sons to set up. So there's plenty of money to go around." His father looked down, and Michael knew he was thinking about the daughter he had almost had, and about Michael's mother. But he didn't say anything. He never did.

Michael cleared his throat. "So, how is everything at Ravenswell?"

They spent the morning exchanging news regarding the family holdings, both in Gloucestershire and Upper Canada. It was so good to see his father again, Michael scarcely noticed the passing of time.

His stomach, by contrast, eventually announced the arrival of midday with a loud rumble.

His father laughed, consulting his pocket watch. "Noon already?" The marquess stood. "Come on, let's go to White's for a chop. I want to show you off a bit."

White's was largely empty. The fashionable dinner hour wasn't for a few hours hence, so the marquess was disappointed in his hopes of parading his strapping young son before his friends. But upon entering the dining room, they spotted the Astley brothers occupying a corner table.

Fauconbridge immediately stood and bowed. "Lord Redditch, how nice it is to see you in town."

"Good afternoon Fauconbridge, Harrington," his father said. "It was good of you to send me that note, Fauconbridge, letting me know that Michael had returned."

"It was my pleasure," the viscount replied. "Won't you join us?"

They accepted gladly. Additional drinks were obtained, and Michael ordered his usual three beefsteaks. Fauconbridge turned to the marquess. "Lord Redditch, how is your new grove of apple trees coming along?"

"Quite well, quite well, especially considering what a dry spring we've had. I think they'll take."

"I don't know how you contrive to get anything to grow in that loamy soil you have in your bottomlands," Fauconbridge replied. "We have some two dozen acres of it, too, and I can't get anything to grow there, other than rapeseed."

"The secret," his father replied, "is to select the right variety of apple. A Dymock Red will grow in the clay. A Foxwhelp or a Councillor, you're just wasting your time."

"What about a Longney Russet?" Fauconbridge asked.

His father considered. "A Longney Russet might do, but of course, those aren't any good for cider. You might try a Hen's Turd, but only if the spot has good drainage."

"How glad I am in this moment," Harrington said, "to be the second son. I have absolutely no idea what you two are talking about, and I have no desire to find out. Have I truly been drinking something called a Hen's Turd?"

The marquess laughed. "I regret to inform you that you have. At least it tastes better than it sounds. It's a bit of a mystery how it got that name."

"Are you getting all of this, Morsley?" Harrington asked. "You'll need to remember to plant Hen's Turd in all of that loamy, well-drained soil you're going to inherit one day."

"Perhaps I should make a few notes," Michael said. He made the comment lightly, but in truth, he was out of his depth. The farming he'd been doing in Canada had been relatively straightforward: clear some land, plant some wheat, then clear some more land, and plant some more wheat. He'd known that farming in England wasn't that simple, but he hadn't realized it was quite so complex.

He would need to learn all of this before the time came for him to take over the estate. People were depending on him, after all.

"My apologies," Fauconbridge said. "I must be boring you two. Let us speak of something else. I believe you have some news of a much more exciting nature, Morsley."

"Indeed he does." His father elbowed him. "Tell them, Michael."

Michael grinned. "Anne accepted me."

A round of congratulations followed. "Splendid, Morsley, splendid," Harrington said. "Although I would not say precisely that it comes as news."

"I suppose not. You did know I was planning to ask her, after all," Michael allowed.

"I was more referring to the fact that I watched you propose." Harrington shook his head. "Couldn't see a thing from the balcony, but I found a room on the second floor with an unimpeded view."

Michael blanched. "You... you were spying on us?"

"My favorite part," Harrington continued, "was when she said yes, and you picked her up and started spinning her around. I had no idea you were such a romantic, Morsley! Although I also enjoyed the part that followed soon thereafter, when you decided you needed to leave the garden *immediately*, and you rammed the gate with your shoulder. Somewhere you were eager to get to?"

"My apologies for my brother," Fauconbridge said. "As always." He turned to Michael's father. "Don't worry, my lord, Morsley made a good show of it. Got down on one knee and everything."

Michael sighed. "*Et tu,* Fauconbridge?"

"Naturally I was watching," the viscount replied. "That is

my little sister you were leading off into the garden. I was fairly confident Anne would accept you, but had she given any sign that your attentions were unwelcome, as much as I value our friendship, I had to be ready to charge down there and run you through." Fauconbridge delivered this threat of dismemberment with an amiable smile.

"It was a bit touch and go at the start," Harrington informed his father. "At first I thought she had refused him! But he started kissing her, and then he hauled her into his lap, and apparently he was able to persuade her of the size of his, let us say, regard."

Fauconbridge turned to Michael. "You're a brave man, Morsley. Marrying Anne means you'll have Harrington for a brother-in-law."

"I wouldn't have even considered it," Michael said, "were it not for the fact that there will be an entire ocean separating us from Harrington."

"What?" his father cried, his voice raw with shock. Everyone at the table froze, looking at the marquess's stunned face. "You… you mean to go back?" his father said after a few beats of silence. "To Canada?"

Oh, hell. "I… er… yes. Anne and I will settle in Canada. You know of all I've been doing there, for the army and the navy, and the Crown. And just the other day Lord Hobart asked to see me. He wants me to succeed Sir Robert Milnes. As governor general."

What his father said was, "Governor general. What an honor. I'm proud of you, son. I… I just hadn't realized you were going to leave again." But the marquess's voice was completely flat, and his expression could only be described as…

Crestfallen.

Fauconbridge was urgently signaling for the waiter to bring the marquess another drink. Harrington, on the other hand, was eyeing Michael skeptically. "I say, Morsley, has my sister really agreed to give up her charity and move to Canada?"

"Well," Michael replied, nodding his thanks to the waiter who placed his three beefsteaks before him, "not precisely. We're currently trying to figure out how she can continue running her charity while we're in Canada."

Harrington snorted. "Well, that's a 'no' if ever I've heard one."

Michael swallowed a mouthful of beef. "We're going to figure something out."

"I know my sister," Harrington said, "and she's not giving up her charity. I can tell you that right now. She's every bit as bullheaded as you, beneath her sweet-as-sugar exterior. You've seen the hours she has to put in to keep it running. There's no way she can do that from Canada." Harrington studied Michael's face for a few beats. "I'll warrant she told you she couldn't marry you after all, as soon as you sprung this whole 'Canada' business on her."

Michael almost choked. He didn't mind that Anne could read his face; it had certainly been convenient last night. But Harrington Astley reading him like a book was a most unwelcome development. "We're going to figure it out," Michael repeated. "And we're going to live in Canada. Because I say so. I'm the man, and the man is in charge."

"Oh, dear," his father said. "Keep telling yourself that, son." He laughed at Michael's glower. "I do know a thing or two about having a wife. And I can tell the three of you that a woman has a way of altering even your best-laid plans."

"Harrington and I know a little bit about that," Faucon-bridge said. "We do have four sisters, after all."

"Yes, you do," the marquess returned. "Unlike Michael here, who's accustomed to ruling the roost. But trust me when I tell you that if you find yourself a love match, your wife will be a hundred times better at bending you to her will than any sister." The marquess's eyes took on a faraway look. "It will be worth it, though."

"See, my lord?" Harrington said encouragingly. "You have nothing to worry about. He's not going back to Canada. There's no way he'd leave Anne behind. He's been besotted with her since he was twelve years old."

"That is not true," Michael said.

He attempted to spear another bite of meat, only to discover that his plates were already empty. Scowling, he glanced up to see that everyone at the table was regarding him with bald skepticism.

"Only since I was fourteen," Michael grumbled, reaching for his drink.

"Oh," Harrington said, rolling his eyes. "Well, in *that* case."

Michael glanced at his pocket watch. "As much as I'm enjoying this delightful conversation, I'm due at the tailor. You'll have to amuse yourselves as best you can by mocking me behind my back, rather than to my face."

"That will suit us perfectly," Harrington said cheerfully.

Michael stood, then turned to his father. "I promised to dine with Anne tonight. I hope that won't be a problem."

His father waved him off. "Not at all, my boy, not at all. Don't worry about me."

"I hope you'll dine with us tonight, Lord Redditch," Fauconbridge said immediately. "We're just having a quiet family meal, but you would be most welcome."

"I should be delighted," the marquess replied.

"Mother is planning something a bit more elaborate for tomorrow night, and I hope you'll join us for that as well," Fauconbridge said. "You and Anne too, Morsley."

Michael nodded. "I'll tell Anne."

He took his leave. The last thing he saw before he left the room was Harrington lean forward and say something that caused his father and Fauconbridge to burst into laughter.

Michael hurried outside, eager to get out of the firing line of Harrington's razor-sharp wit.

He shuddered.

He was looking forward to going to the tailor. Surely this was one of the signs of the end times.

CHAPTER 29

*A*nne spent the morning paying fundraising calls and arrived at her lodging house just after noon. She'd hardly settled down at her writing desk when Samuel came bursting through the door.

"Mr. Branton," she said, rising. "Good afternoon. Would you like some tea or—"

"They've stopped investigating," he declared.

"Stopped—who has stopped investigating? You don't mean Bow Street?"

"I do mean Bow Street," he said, wrenching off his hat and plunking it down on the tea table. He started to pace the room. "I received your note, and when I got a break at midmorning, I went down there to speak to the runner I've been working with, Charles Hoskins." He gave a bitter laugh. "Lo and behold, Mr. Hoskins had just been assigned a private murder investigation and was packed off on a mail coach bound for Cumberland before dawn."

"But… but surely someone else can take over for Mr. Hoskins." Anne paused, noting Samuel's grim expression. "Can't they?"

"You would think so, yet the clerk refused to let me speak to anyone else. Another runner I know, George Higginbotham, walked in while I was arguing with the clerk." Samuel shook his head. "I thought Higginbotham was one of the good ones, but he blanched when he saw me and hurried by." Samuel paused in his pacing, turning to face Anne. "Someone's paid them off. I'd bet anything."

Anne sank back into her seat. "Paid off? But... if Bow Street won't investigate, how can we—"

The door flew open, and Mrs. Godfrey rushed in. "My lady, I'm sorry to interrupt, but I've been awaiting your arrival."

Anne rubbed her temple. "Is it urgent? Mr. Branton has brought news of a serious setback in our investigation."

Mrs. Godfrey's knuckles were white as she twisted her apron into knots. "It could not be more urgent, nor more serious."

Anne blinked up at her. She was in genuine distress, her mouth drawn, her shoulders quivering. "Are... are Nick and Johnny all right?"

"Johnny is fine. He's up in his rooms with Mrs. Briggs. But Nick—" Mrs. Godfrey dabbed at a tear with her apron. "Nick was snatched off the street just before dawn this morning."

It was late afternoon when Michael mounted the steps to Anne's town house. He wore a bottle green jacket which he'd just been fitted for, paired with a grey waistcoat and buff trousers. He wasn't usually the sort to peacock about, but he'd been enjoying Anne's reactions to his new clothes, and he hoped she'd find his new kit handsome as well.

As he raised his hand to knock, the door swung open.

Anne stood there looking harried; Michael rather had the impression she'd just slid to a stop in front of the door.

"Good afternoon, Anne—"

"Thank God you're finally here," she said, cutting him off as she grabbed his arm and hauled him inside. "Hugh, have the carriage brought 'round," she called as she began towing him toward the front parlor.

"I'm glad to see you, too," he said, amused that she seemed to think it was possible for her to manhandle him.

"Where have you been? I sent you a note hours ago."

"I've been at the tailor," he said, gesturing to his new jacket.

"Oh. That explains it."

"What's your hurry? Surely supper's not waiting."

"No. We'll eat something in my rooms later."

Now *that* sounded promising. "I look forward to it, especially if we will be dining *au naturel.*"

"What?" Anne looked up at him and rolled her eyes at his lascivious expression. "Not like *that*, Michael."

"It's a perfectly good suggestion," he grumbled.

"There will be plenty of time for that later. Right now we have things to discuss."

Things to discuss—words that struck terror into the heart of any man. He sought to delay the inevitable. "I see you haven't noticed my new jacket."

"Your *jacket*? Who cares about your jacket? You look absurdly handsome in it. As usual!"

"Um. Thank you?"

They entered the parlor. Michael saw that Mr. Branton was there. He sat slumped on the yellow-striped couch, legs splayed out in front of him. He looked weary to the bone.

"He's here," Anne said.

"Thank God," Mr. Branton replied, running a hand over his face.

Michael frowned. "Anne, what's going on?"

"Lord Gladstone paid someone off, is what's going on, and now Bow Street has quashed the investigation."

"Quashed it?" Michael frowned. "But how can they quash it? A man has been murdered, for God's sake!"

"Yes, well, it gets worse—this morning, Nick was kidnapped."

"Kidnapped?" Michael all but shouted. "How was he kidnapped? He wasn't supposed to leave the building."

Anne stalked over to her desk. "It was a trap, is what it was. Joseph was performing bodyguard duty, but Johnny—the little one—forgot he needed to wait and went running down to breakfast while Joseph was performing his, er, morning toilette."

Michael tilted his head. "His morning toilette? Joseph didn't much strike me as the 'morning toilette' sort of fellow."

"He was having a piss," Mr. Branton called from the sofa, apparently well beyond the point at which he could be bothered to observe social niceties.

"Ah," Michael said. "I see."

Anne cleared her throat. "As soon as Nick realized Johnny was gone, he raced downstairs to make sure he didn't forget himself and go outside. Unfortunately, Johnny walked straight into Gladstone's trap. When he got to the dining hall, all the little ones were abuzz that there was a man outside handing out toffees. Johnny went out there without a second thought."

Michael frowned. "I thought someone was supposed to be guarding the door."

"They were," Anne agreed. "Most of them were Ralph's cousins, but a few weren't, so they didn't all know each other. Someone had showed up an hour earlier and told Ralph's cousin, Anthony, he was there to relieve him. Anthony didn't think a thing of it and left. It was the alleged bodyguard who grabbed Johnny the second he walked out the door."

Anne was now pacing the room. "Meanwhile Nick came downstairs and was immediately suspicious of this story about a man giving away candies. He went outside to check on Johnny, and lo and behold, he finds the fake bodyguard and the toffee man trying to wrestle him into a hackney carriage!"

"What did Nick do?" Michael asked, feeling physically ill.

Anne wheeled around. Her hands were shaking. "I'll tell you what Nick did, he went charging in and bit one of them on the arm. Johnny managed to get away. But they... they grabbed Nick instead. Johnny ran inside and raised the alarm. But by the time Joseph and Mrs. Godfrey got out there, Nick was gone."

Michael leaned against the mantelpiece. "We've got to think. Nick's been taken, and Bow Street refuses to investigate. The regular constables are probably even more corrupt than Bow Street—"

"*Much* more corrupt," Mr. Branton noted.

Michael squeezed his eyes shut. "There's got to be someone we can turn to for help."

Anne strode over to him. "Don't forget, Lord Gladstone didn't just kidnap Nick and have Mr. Smithers murdered. He also stole five thousand pounds of construction funds from the army. Which makes his arrest of great interest to—"

"Horse Guards!" Michael said. "Army headquarters." He cocked his head. "Why didn't you go there and tell someone what happened?"

Anne cast a glance to the heavens, as if asking the lord to grant her patience. "I did go there," she ground out. "We both did. But the clerk refused to let us speak to anyone."

Michael frowned. "Why did he do that?"

"Well, for one, because they do not grant audiences to

women at army headquarters, Michael," Anne said, speaking slowly as if to a small child.

"But…" Michael shook his head, struggling to understand. "But that doesn't make any sense. You're a public figure, what with your charity—you were even featured in *The Times*. You're highly intelligent. You're the daughter of an earl. And you were bringing them important information. Information they needed to know. It's idiotic, is what it is." He paused, frowning. "But wait—you said you both went. Did they refuse to admit Mr. Branton because… er…"

"Because I'm Black?" Mr. Branton rose from the sofa. "Not this time. This time I do believe it was because I prosecuted a case against the clerk's older brother last month. He was convicted of embezzling funds from the Royal Navy and is sailing for New South Wales as we speak." He shook his head. "In a way it was refreshing, to be treated poorly for something I'd actually done."

"It's hardly your fault that his brother is unprincipled scum," Michael began.

Anne stepped directly in front of him. "You are correct, but what we need right now is someone who can gain us an audience at Horse Guards."

Michael straightened. "Say, what about me? I'm acquainted with Lord Hobart. I'm—"

"—the next Governor General of Canada, yes," Anne said, taking his arm.

"I'll go down there right now," Michael said as Anne steered him toward the door. "We should summon the carriage."

Hugh appeared in the doorway. "Carriage is ready, m'lady."

"Ah. How fortuitous," Anne said.

They made their way to the foyer. "I'm going to yell at that mutton-headed clerk," Michael said, accepting his hat from Hugh, "until he's got the fear of God in him. Then you can tell Lord Hobart what's going on."

"That will be lovely," Anne said, "save for one detail. Mr. Branton will do the talking."

"That's fine, but why not you, Anne?"

Anne beamed up at him as she tugged her gloves into place. "Because Mr. Branton could convince people to buy frogs and locusts in the midst of a Biblical plague."

Mr. Branton nodded solemnly. "It's what I do."

"Excellent," Michael said. "We have our plan, then."

Once they were ensconced in Anne's carriage, Mr. Branton leaned forward. "Now, I need you to tell me every single thing you know about Lord Hobart."

CHAPTER 30

*A*lthough she was sick with worry about Nick, Anne couldn't help but enjoy what happened once they arrived at Horse Guards.

It wasn't merely the fact that he was six and a half feet tall and burly; Michael really did have a special talent for looming. He employed it to its full effect upon the hapless clerk.

"Lord Morsley!" the clerk said upon their entrance, brightening. "How can I be of assistance?" Anne marked the moment he noticed that Michael was flanked by the very pair he'd turned away earlier in the day. His smile froze, and he began to physically droop.

"Is this the man you spoke with this afternoon, darling?" Michael asked, speaking at full volume. "The one who refused to assist you?" Around the room, multiple men looked up from their work, craning their necks to see.

"The very one," Anne confirmed. "Mr. Thackery."

Mr. Thackery gulped. "Is... is there a problem, my lord?"

Michael began to loom. "That depends. Do you consider it a problem that my betrothed was dismissed, and was therefore unable to obtain the help she needed?"

"I… I didn't realize she was your betrothed—"

"Not that it should matter," Michael snapped. "Anyone of Lady Anne's unimpeachable character should always be granted the basic courtesy of a hearing. To say nothing"—he placed his hand in the center of Samuel's back and drew him forward—"of my personal barrister."

Mr. Thackery narrowed his eyes at Samuel, then turned to Michael. "Your personal barrister? I was unaware your lordship had business with the Admiralty."

Michael froze for a second, but he recovered quickly. "As it happens, I have been assisting the Royal Navy, sending them shipments of raw materials from the Canadian frontier."

Anne made a point of laying her hand upon Michael's upper arm as she smiled up at him fondly. "Did you not tell me that you received a letter of thanks from Lord Nelson himself after the first delivery of mast poles?"

"Why, yes. Yes, I did."

Samuel pressed a hand to his heart. "It is an honor to act as Lord Morsley's liaison."

The clerk's face had taken on a greenish cast. "I… I see."

"But let us return to the matter at hand," Michael said, looming even harder. "Do you have anything to say for yourself?"

Mr. Thackery's posture by now was what Anne would describe as cowering. "I'm terribly sorry, my lord—"

"It is not *I* who am owed an apology."

"That is—my lady. And Mr. Branton. I… I should've let you speak to—er—someone." Anne didn't feel quite ready to offer her absolution, and apparently Samuel felt the same way, because they both maintained a stony silence. After a moment, Mr. Thackery cleared his throat awkwardly. "Shall I tell Lord Hobart you're here, then?"

"You should've done so four hours ago," Michael said. "So yes."

The clerk led them back to Lord Hobart's office. The baron scowled as he looked up from the piles of papers that littered his desk. "This had better be important, Morsley."

"It is," Michael replied. "Allow me to introduce my betrothed, Lady Anne Astley—"

Lord Hobart barked out a laugh. "You work quickly, Morsley. So that's why you came back."

Michael cast Anne a quick smile. "Indeed. And this is Mr. Samuel Branton, a barrister working primarily in the Admiralty Courts. He will explain."

"Very well," Lord Hobart grumbled. "I suppose I should ring for some tea."

Samuel held up both hands. "That is very kind of you, my lord, but it is not necessary. We will not take up one minute more of your time than we absolutely must."

Samuel launched straight into the case, laying out the facts clearly but concisely. Anne knew Samuel had a knack for reading people and tailoring his approach to the person to whom he was speaking, but she was accustomed to seeing him begin with more of an effort to charm his audience. As Lord Hobart listened in stony-faced silence, she could not help but wonder if Samuel's tactics were sound.

Once he finished his account of the malfeasance taking place at the R.M.A., Lord Hobart rose and went to the door. "Get in here, Thackery."

Anne's heart kicked up a notch as the clerk entered the room. "I'll be dictating a letter," Lord Hobart informed him.

"Yes, my lord," Mr. Thackery replied, hurrying to a writing desk in the corner and pulling out a sheet of paper. "To whom shall I address it?"

"To the Chief Magistrate at Bow Street," Lord Hobart said.

"Is—is there a problem?" Mr. Thackery asked.

Lord Hobart rounded on him. "Five thousand pounds of the army's money has been stolen. Does that strike you as being a problem?"

Anne was careful not to let her face fall at the baron's concern for the embezzled money, but not for the children in harm's way. But her smile felt tight. Lord Hobart must have noticed, because he hastily added, "And the children. Absolutely deplorable, what's being done to those children."

Lord Hobart proceeded to dictate a note that was inescapably clear, for all that it was only four sentences long. "If I find out that you did not deploy every resource available to you in order to get to the bottom of this, I will not hesitate to bring the questionable circumstances under which your investigation has been conducted to the attention of Mr. Addington," he concluded.

There was a scratching sound as the clerk's quill skidded off the edge of the page. "Mr.—Mr. Addington?" he asked, eyes huge. "You don't mean the prime minister?"

"Of course I mean the prime minister," Lord Hobart snapped. "And the next time someone comes to tell us that five thousand pounds of the army's money has been stolen, don't send them away. Now get out of my office, all of you."

It happened that Samuel was happy to wait for the clerk to finish transcribing the letter. "I cannot wait to see the look on their faces when I walk into the Bow Street offices with a letter from the secretary of state himself," he mused.

"We'll all go together," Anne said, squeezing Michael's arm. "That way you can loom some more. You're so good at it."

Michael puffed out his chest. "At the risk of sounding like an outrageous braggart, I also have an innate talent for glaring and shouting, should the situation require it."

Such a brief missive took very little time to transcribe,

and within a quarter hour they were climbing out of Anne's carriage at Bow Street. The reaction at Bow Street closely mirrored that of the clerk at Horse Guards. Cowering gave way to outright panic after Lord Hobart's letter was read.

"A thousand apologies, Lord Morsley," the clerk, whose name was Mr. Hewitt, said. "We will make sure this is thoroughly investigated going forward."

Mr. Hewitt began shuffling through some papers, apparently assuming this reassurance was sufficient and the conversation over.

Samuel leaned his elbow against the counter. "Excellent. When will this thorough investigation begin, and what will it entail?"

Mr. Hewitt bristled. "What did you just ask me?"

It turned out that Michael could loom quite effectively even when separated from his quarry by a counter. "What my *personal barrister* just asked is what you're going to do to about Lord Gladstone. Tonight. Because, in case it didn't penetrate your thick skull, a boy's life is in danger."

"This is the same boy who caught a glimpse of the baron's face?" Mr. Hewitt asked.

"The very one," Anne said.

Mr. Hewitt shook his head. "He's probably dead already. The whole reason Gladstone took him was to eliminate a witness."

Anne felt her chest constrict. This was precisely her fear, that she was already too late.

But she could not give in to that despair. She lifted her chin. "We must try. There is still a chance that Nick is—"

Mr. Hewitt cut in. "Although a tender heart is a credit to a woman—"

Michael leaned forward. "Did you just interrupt Lady Anne?" he all but shouted.

Mr. Hewitt physically recoiled. "I... I'm sorry, my lady."

"So what you are arguing," Michael continued, "is that there is no need to act tonight because Nick has already been murdered. Refresh my memory, what entity is responsible for tracking down and apprehending the murderers of children?"

"That would be the Bow Street Runners," Samuel said conversationally.

"That's what I thought," Michael said. "So. What's your plan?"

Mr. Hewitt looked taken aback. "It will take time to formulate a plan, to find the manpower to—"

"What were Lord Hobart's exact words?" Michael asked.

Samuel made a show of scanning the letter. "Let's see. Ah, yes, here it is. 'If I find out that you did not deploy every resource available to you—'"

Michael shook his head. "What a shame I'll have to tell Lord Hobart his instructions were ignored."

Mr. Hewitt scowled. "Be reasonable. Lord Gladstone's current whereabouts are unknown. We don't even know where to begin looking."

"How marvelously convenient," Samuel said. "In our earlier interview, both Nick and Johnny reported that, based on the smell, the house where Lord Gladstone was keeping the boys was near a kiln."

Mr. Hewitt threw up his hands. "Who even knows how many kilns there are in London, or where they are!"

Samuel reached into his breast pocket. "Fourteen. That's according to my friend over at Exchequer. I have a list of them right here."

The clerk glared at him. "So you're suggesting we just send men out to these fourteen kilns, and check the surrounding buildings for a bunch of kidnapped orphans?"

"Precisely," Michael said. "Finally, you're catching on."

"And who is going to check these kilns?" Mr. Hewitt asked.

"Forgive me if I've been misinformed, as I've spent the past four years in Canada," Michael said, "but does Bow Street not employ a Foot Patrol? What for, if not tasks of this nature?"

"It is a wild goose chase—" the clerk began.

Michael gave him a hard look. "Better than sitting around doing nothing."

Anne stepped forward and took Michael's arm. "Did Lord Morsley mention that he's going to be the next Governor General of Canada?"

"Hand-picked by Lord Hobart himself," Samuel noted.

Mr. Hewitt gave an aggrieved sigh. "*Fine.*"

In the end, ten pair of men from the Foot Patrol were mustered to initiate the search. "I'll take Pottery Lane in Notting Hill," Samuel offered.

"Give the rest to me," Anne said. "I'll divide it up amongst my footmen."

As they left the Bow Street offices, Anne still felt sick with worry about Nick.

But at least she now had the tiniest sliver of hope.

CHAPTER 31

*T*he sun had set by the time they reached Anne's house. A maid brought a tray of cold meats and cheeses into the library, and Michael tucked in while Anne went to give assignments to her footmen.

Anne didn't return until twenty minutes later. Michael had managed to save her some chicken and a bit of the ham, and, of course, a strawberry tart.

The first thing he noticed as she strode into the room was that she had changed into the same plain gray gown she had worn last night when they went into Holborn.

The second thing he noticed was that she was carrying his old coat, which he had left there that morning.

"Good, you saved some for me." Anne handed him his jacket. "Put this on, and we'll leave in five minutes."

Michael frowned. "Leave? What do you mean, leave? And why are you dressed like that?"

Anne swallowed her bite of ham. "With the extra guards who've been set at my lodging house, I only had enough footmen to check two out of the three remaining kilns. So we'll be searching around the Coade Stone manufactory in Lambeth."

Michael crossed his arms. "The hell we will."

Anne, who had been in the act of spreading butter on a slice of bread, glanced up at him. Seeing his expression, she gave an exasperated sigh. "Not this overprotective nonsense again."

Nonsense? He didn't want the woman he loved to *die*, and she called it nonsense? "It's not nonsense."

"Lambeth isn't such a bad neighborhood. The Coade Stone manufactory is just a little ways upriver from Vauxhall, and absolutely everyone goes there."

"Still, there's no need for you to go—"

"Of course there is!" Anne set aside her plate and stood, her eyebrow twitching. "Were you paying no attention this afternoon? Nick has been *kidnapped*. I will leave no stone unturned."

"I will go. Alone," Michael said in his Voice that Brooked No Argument.

Apparently Anne was proof against the Voice that Brooked No Argument, because she shot back, "If you think I'm going to cower in my drawing room and leave the important work to the menfolk, then you don't remember me at all."

"I'm not asking you to cower—"

"We were equal partners growing up, Michael. *Equal*." Her hands were clenched into fists, and she was blinking back tears. "We did everything *together*. I took every rail you took. I climbed every tree. I've jumped that gap in the battlements of Cranfield Castle a thousand times. You never suggested I was less capable than you just because I'm a girl." She rubbed at her cheek with the back of one hand. "It's what I *like* about you. Or maybe I should say *liked*. Because clearly you don't feel that way anymore."

It was like a knife to the heart, to hear her say that. And she wasn't wrong, regarding their childhood. But the boy she had taken those fences with was gone. Experiencing the agony of losing her had scarred him. He couldn't just snap his fingers and go back to those carefree days before he knew what it was to have to live without her.

Michael crossed the room in two strides and stroked a hand along her cheek. "I know how capable you are, Anne. But Gladstone and whatever henchmen he's employing... they're dangerous. They killed Smithers, and they would kill again to save themselves. I just don't want to watch the only woman I've ever loved get stabbed to death in front of my eyes."

"How is it any different if you go alone? Do you not think I would worry just as much about you?"

Michael locked his jaw. "That's different. That's completely different."

"I should like to know how!"

Michael groaned. Whereas he would very much prefer not to explain. Discussing your inner scars, your fears—this was not something an Englishman did. It went against every tenet by which his father had raised him. "It just is."

"Don't you give me that, Michael Cranfield." She jabbed one finger into his chest. "I'm trying to give you the benefit of the doubt, trying to assume my best friend, the person who respects me, is still in there somewhere. I get glimpses of him every now and then, like when you were telling off Mr. Hewitt. But half an hour later, *you're* the one dismissing me, insisting that I need to hide in my parlor and leave the important work to you. I don't know what to think."

He tilted his head back all the way toward the ceiling and squeezed his eyes shut. When he dared to peer down at Anne, he found her looking at him expectantly. "You're not really going to make me say it, are you?"

"Apparently I am, because I have absolutely no idea what 'it' is."

Michael swallowed, fixing his eyes on the wall behind Anne. "My... my mother died, Anne. She died, and—" He broke off.

He felt her take one of his hands and squeeze it. "I remember, Michael. I remember how awful it was for you."

"It was awful for me, but I'm not talking about myself. I'm talking about my father."

He chanced a glance down at her and saw that the anger had gone out of her, that there was nothing but sympathy in her eyes.

He looked away. It was going to be hard enough for him to get through this. "It was like half his soul had died. My mother was his world. He loved her the exact same way I love you. The Cranfield way, it would seem. And a man is supposed to protect his wife. But he... he just had to sit there and hold her hand while she bled to death." He swallowed. "He's never really recovered. I doubt he ever will."

At some point during his speech, Anne had wrapped her arms around his waist, pressing her head against his chest.

"That's why I can't risk you, Anne. Because I never thought that would happen to me. But then, I... I *lost you*, Anne." His voice broke, and he had to stop for a moment. "Or at least, I thought I did. When you married Wynters. And I —" He broke off, trying to push back the gulf of blackness that accompanied that particular memory. When he spoke again, his voice shook. "I can't do that again. I *can't*. Please don't ask me to. There wasn't anything my father could do to save my mother. But this, we can prevent."

He caressed her beautiful face. "My not wanting you to go has *nothing* to do with thinking you incapable, and every-thing to do with my inability to live without you. I'll go look for Nick. I'll do it gladly. I don't care if I die, as long as I don't have to live without you. Please, Anne, let me go alone. Please just let me protect you."

"Oh, Michael." Anne rubbed his back, and they stood that way for a moment, just holding each other.

Anne leaned back and met his eye. "Just to be clear, your position is that I shouldn't go to Lambeth tonight, even in your company, because it's too dangerous."

"Correct."

"Yet you want me to accompany you to Canada. I'll be the first to acknowledge that there is some danger in my participating in this investigation, even with you there to protect me. But I'll warrant the risk is comparable to that ocean crossing."

Michael gazed at her, struggling to summon up a counterargument. In truth, she was probably right.

"And then," Anne continued, "once we reach Canada, there are a host of potential dangers. Disease. Frostbite. Why, I'm given to understand there's a rather spectacular story of you being charged by a bear that I'm yet to hear."

"I can protect you from bears."

"You cannot be with me every second of the day. Nor can you wrap me up in cotton gauze and put me on a high shelf for safekeeping."

"I wish I could," he grumbled.

She squeezed his waist. "I know you do. But I refuse to hide in my parlor all day drinking tea and embroidering flowers. You have accepted the risks inherent in bringing me to Canada because your work there is important. It's the same for me. I have accepted a small degree of risk in order to run my society. Because the work I'm doing is important, too."

She leaned back to look up at him. "I know you don't

mean badly. But you have to find a way to get past this. It's important. For *us*. Because this is every bit as big an obstacle to our having a future together as figuring out where we're going to live."

Michael bowed his head. "It's hard for me, Anne. But"—he swallowed—"if this is truly what you want—"

"It is."

He peered down at her. "And there is no possibility you could want something else?"

"Absolutely none."

He sighed. "I had the feeling that was the case. I will try, Anne."

"Thank you for that. And look at the situation I find myself in tonight. I've got to go to Lambeth and search for Nick, but I'll be honest—I don't want to do it alone." She looped her arms around his neck. "You're the only one who can help me. Won't you please do this, Michael?" She looked up at him beseechingly. "For me?"

In an instant he was defeated. Routed by a pair of gorgeous brown eyes.

That didn't mean he had to like it. "That's—that's not fair!"

"Does that mean it's working?" she asked brightly.

"You know full well it is," he grumbled. "I would have thought such techniques were beneath you. Where did you learn to manipulate a man like this, anyways?"

"From my mother. She does it to my father all the time."

"Dear God, you learned from the master."

She twined her fingers in the hair at the nape of his neck. "Come now, don't look so grumpy about it. After all, if you help me, I'm bound to be feeling very *grateful* when we get back home."

This got his attention. "Grateful, you say? Just how grateful do you think you'll be?"

She smiled as she leaned forward, pressing her breasts into his chest. "Very, very, extremely grateful. So grateful that I will doubtless be searching for some appropriate means through which to express my gratitude."

"I'll have some suggestions, should you require them," he said before he captured her lips with his own.

CHAPTER 32

A half hour later they alighted from a hackney carriage on the east bank of Westminster Bridge.

Michael felt a trickle of hope as they approached a smart building with four columns, each topped with a statue in the classical style. The words "Coade and Sealy's" were carved into the stone facade. Although the windows were darkened at this hour, the neighborhood was clearly a respectable one. "Is this it, then?" he whispered to Anne.

She shook her head. "That's the gallery. The kiln is five hundred yards downriver."

He grunted. Of course it was. Knowing his luck, it was probably between a row of basement gin shops and a cock-fighting ring.

Once they cleared the handful of houses near the bridge, the landscape opened up. Truth be told, it wasn't as bad as Michael had feared. It was industrial, to be sure, but not especially seedy, with deserted timber yards to their left and open fields to their right.

Not that he was letting his guard down. Someone called

out from the nearby timber yard, and Michael whirled around, fists raised.

It proved to be an owl.

Anne gave him a sideways look but said nothing. "We'll start by sweeping the area around the kiln," she whispered, "looking for anything suspicious. We should question anyone we encounter, so long as they don't look disreputable. Some people are likely to recognize me, so I'll keep my head down and let you lead the questioning, at least to start. If anyone seems wary, we'll use the cover Sarah suggested the other day, that you're a young man out on the town, and I'm your—"

He cut her off, not particularly wanting to hear Anne refer to herself in those terms. "I remember." He lifted his head. "It smells like we're getting closer."

"It does," Anne agreed.

Indeed, as a row of cramped houses sprang up on their right, not only did the smell of charcoal become thicker, Michael began to detect a faint glow emanating from a building in the distance.

The open fields ended, and they entered a small neighborhood with a few streets of houses and a brewery. They passed what looked to be a basement gin shop. A couple of women lingering on the corner cast Michael suggestive smiles, which he ignored.

"This should be it on our left," Anne whispered.

They made a quick circuit of the kiln, finally finding the entrance to its yard on the far side of the building. Michael was given to understand that Eleanor Coade's company made bespoke statues for the wealthy out of some sort of ceramic material (the exact composition was a closely guarded secret), that looked like marble and were completely weatherproof. He saw examples of Mrs. Coade's handiwork strewn about the yard as they approached the kiln—a recumbent lion here, an urn there, a statue of Poseidon that seemed destined for a fountain in the far corner. It was disconcerting to see statues that looked like they could be ancient treasures sitting in the mud, but there they were.

"Oy," a sharp voice called, "what're you two doing?"

Michael wheeled around and saw a night guard approaching. He immediately stepped in front of Anne. She squeezed his arm. "Question him," she whispered.

Michael nodded. "Good evening. Apologies for having startled you—"

"You can't tup her here," the man said, cutting straight to the chase. "Go find someplace else."

Michael's hands clenched into fists. He willed himself to calm down. Although he hated the insinuation the guard had just made, it was their cover story, after all. "That's not why we're here. We're looking for a little boy who's been kidnapped. We've reason to believe he might have been brought to this neighborhood. Have you seen anything suspicious? Say, men bringing young boys to one of the nearby houses at all hours?"

The guard snorted. "A wise man don't see nothing he's not meant to. Now get out of here."

Anne was already tugging at his arm. Michael let her lead him away. "We'll get nothing from him," she whispered as they stepped back into the street.

They continued north past more houses and more industrial yards. There came the sound of footsteps against the cobblestones, and a little old woman clutching a basket to her chest emerged from the shadows.

Before he even realized her intention, Anne had slipped her hand from his arm and crossed the narrow street. "Anne!" he hissed, hastening after her.

She stepped directly into the woman's path, pushing back the oversized flaps of her cap. "Forgive me for detaining you, but I was wondering if you could help me. I'm Lady Wynters—"

"Lady *Wynters*?" The woman's eyes flew to Anne's face. "Blimey, it really is you."

"Would you mind if I asked you some questions?" Anne asked.

The woman gave a nervous chuckle. "Can't imagine what use I'd be to the great Lady Wynters, but ask away."

"I'm looking for a boy who's been kidnapped. I'm trying to track down a man who's been selling little orphans as apprentices to chimney sweeps. Have you seen any boys being brought to a particular house? We think they're delivered in a shiny black carriage with a crest of two wild boars."

The woman's expression turned stony. "I don't know nothing about any of that," she said, staggering back a step before hurrying past Anne. "Beg pardon, m'lady," she called, already ten feet down the street.

"Can we just leave?" Michael muttered. "We're not going to learn anything here."

"I wonder if we just did." At Michael's quizzical look, Anne added, "She was glad to talk to me. She seemed eager to help... until I brought up Lord Gladstone's carriage. It makes me wonder if she *has* seen it."

"Even so, we can't knock on every door within smelling distance of the kiln." He steered Anne around a man who was lying against a building, reeking of gin and muttering to himself. "And this isn't the best neighborhood."

"We'll look just a bit longer," Anne said, turning toward a narrow alleyway. "Let's check in here."

"I'm going first," Michael muttered.

After a few feet, the side street opened up into a tiny brick courtyard. Little light filtered down to street level due to all the washing hung between the rows of buildings. Most of the windows were either boarded up or covered with paper and rags. Michael knew this was a common practice to get out of paying the window tax, but the ubiquity of the practice also provided a convenient cover for those who didn't want anyone to see inside.

They had almost reached the end of the courtyard when a door opened. A thin, fair-haired man who was only an inch or two shorter than Michael came ambling down the steps.

The man started at their presence. "Who're you? What're you doing here?" he growled.

Anne buried her face in Michael's shoulder. Her grip on his arm was steel. He knew what she was trying to remind him—act casual and keep to their plan. God, how he hated doing this, hated referring to Anne in the terms he was about to use.

"Nothing much," he said, trying to sound tipsy and unconcerned. "Just looking for somewhere to take this prime article." He gave Anne a squeeze.

The man turned to Anne. "Say, I ain't seen her before. I like a Long Meg, I do, but they're hard enough to find. Most bunters ain't tall enough for a Tuppenny Upright. I fancy you know what I mean, being a jack of legs yourself."

It took every ounce of Michael's self-control not to throttle him. Anne squeezed his arm. *Stay calm.* He strove for a jovial tone as he replied, "Indeed I do." It came out sounding a bit strangled, but the man didn't seem to notice.

"Why don't you take her around that corner?" The man nodded to the building behind them. "There's a little alley-way, nice and private. I fancy a turn with her after you've done. As tall as she is, she'll do nicely for me even up against the wall."

"This one's mine," Michael snapped. "Why don't you find someone else and take her inside?" He nodded toward the door through which the man had come.

"Because my boss is a right cunt, he is, and he won't let me bring no one inside."

"But he doesn't mind you loitering in the alley, looking for a fancy piece?"

The man looked affronted. "Well, he ain't there *now*."

Michael was inching back toward the main street, ignoring Anne's attempts to dig in her heels. "You can find someone to bring inside, then, can't you?"

"I'm telling you, I can't. If they tell him I brought a moll in there, he'll skin me alive."

Michael peered at him. "*They*? Who exactly are *they*?"

For a split second the man's eyes went wide before he schooled his features. "N-never you mind. The point is, I ain't had a swive in three days, and unless I can find a cat tall enough to do it up against the wall, I won't be getting one."

"Well, you'll have to keep looking," Michael snapped.

"Hey, now. Don't be like that. Like I said, I'll wait 'til you've finished with her. Head 'round that corner. You'll find a nice spot. There's a good fellow."

Michael was debating the merits of strangling the man with his bare hands when he felt a sharp pinch on the inside of his arm. He glanced down at Anne.

Her expression was unmistakable, even in the near darkness. *Don't you dare.* He gave her a petulant look, and she very subtly shook her head.

He drew in another breath. "Around the corner, you say?" He led Anne the direction the man had indicated, glad at least to be getting her away from that cretin.

Anne pulled him into a nook, then looped her arms around his neck and began kissing his jaw. "That was good, Michael," she whispered. "Very convincing."

"We've got to get out of here," he muttered.

"Not yet. I wonder who's hiding inside, who would tell on him to his boss? Let's see if we can get him to say."

"That could be anyone. It's probably just his criminal associates. I don't want you anywhere near him. We need to—"

"I say," the man said, peeking around the corner, "here I was, coming to see if you was close to done, and what do I find but you haven't even started! I'm on a tight schedule here, so get on with it."

Anne buried her head in Michael's chest to hide her face. "That's more like it," the lanky man said. "I'll be back in a few minutes to check your progress." He disappeared again.

"Anne!" Michael hissed. "We're leaving. Now!"

"But Michael—"

"Now!" He grabbed Anne's hand and pulled her deeper into the alleyway, only to find that the way was blocked by a pile of broken crates.

Cursing, Michael led Anne back the way they had come. "All done, then?" the lanky man asked. Michael didn't respond but positioned himself between him and Anne as they hurried past.

Michael felt the man grab his arm from behind. "Where do you think you're going? I said I wanted a go with her."

Michael shook him off. "I've decided I want her for the entire night."

Unable to take the hint, the man began jogging after them. "That's fine and good but let me have a turn with her first." He eyed Anne's figure appreciatively. "Aren't you a rum piece? Lift up your skirts for me, little squirrel, this won't take me but a minute."

That was when the lanky man made a crucial mistake. After another fruitless attempt to arrest Michael's progress, he reached out and grabbed Anne by the arm, jerking her to a halt. Her eyes went wide.

"Unhand her," Michael growled. "*Now.*"

A scowl crossed the blond man's face, and this time he yanked Anne's arm. "The hell I will! Not until I've—"

Michael's fist took the man square in the left eye. The punch would have been enough to knock most men out cold, but it appeared this man's one redeeming quality was that he knew how to take a punch.

The quality was redeeming only because it afforded Michael the pleasure of hitting him again. A hook to the right temple followed by an uppercut beneath his chin and the man's body went limp, then crumpled to the ground in a heap.

Anne was staring slack-jawed at the man's collapsed form. Michael grabbed her around the waist and lifted her over the man's inert body. "Let's go," he growled, hauling her back toward the main road.

CHAPTER 33

They jogged back to Westminster Bridge, where Michael managed to flag down a hackney carriage. Inside, he found that his hands were shaking. He had lived on the frontier. He'd been charged by a bear. He was no stranger to life-or-death situations.

But seeing Anne in danger was something different altogether.

Watching that cretin lay hands on her, knowing that, had he not been there, that worthless piece of trash would probably have raped her... Michael finally understood the true meaning of things that had only been words before. Words like bloodlust and battle rage. He was furious, but in the moment, he'd felt fear such as he had never experienced before. The threat of getting mauled to death by a bear was nothing, *nothing*, next to the terror of something bad happening to Anne.

And even though she was out of immediate danger, Michael felt like a gunpowder wagon bumping along the road, ready to explode if a wheel threw up a single spark. He didn't trust himself to say one word to Anne right now. He wasn't mad at her, but there was no possibility of him speaking without shouting.

On the seat opposite him, Anne pulled off her cap, and her hair came tumbling out of its knot. God, she looked beautiful in the moonlight, with her hair falling all around her and that high color in her cheeks. She looked... freshly tumbled.

Just like that, all the violent emotions thrashing around inside of him transformed into pure, unadulterated lust. He wanted to bury his hands in her hair, bury his face in her neck, and then bury his cock inside her. He wanted to reassure himself that she was alive, she was well, and she was *his*.

He curled his fingers around the edge of the seat to stop himself from grabbing her and hauling her into his lap. He was in no condition to touch her; she deserved gentle caresses, and right now all he wanted to do was pound into her like a rutting animal. Hell, he hardly even dared to look at her.

But as she tossed her cap aside, he noticed that her fingers were trembling. He seized her hand. "What's this?" he demanded in a voice that shook. "Are you hurt? Upset? Overwrought?"

Anne gave him a look. "Overwrought?"

"Your hands are shaking."

"So are yours!"

He released her as if he'd been singed. "You don't want to know why my hands are shaking," he said darkly.

"Yes, I do," Anne said, and that was when he noticed she was panting.

"Don't push me right now, Anne."

"Do you not know me at all? Telling me not to ask makes me all the more determined to know. You may as well go ahead and—"

He grabbed her with a snarl, hauling her into his lap so

that she straddled him. His lips crashed down on hers, and then he was devouring her. His hands were not gentle, for all that they shook as he ran them absolutely everywhere over her body.

God, he needed to get control of himself. This was Anne, *his* Anne, his future lady wife, and here he was, mauling her like a rabid animal. Although she was tolerating it stoically. She was kissing him back, her arms around his neck, her hands stroking over his shoulders, and if he didn't know better, he would have said that her hips… that her hips…

That her hips were grinding against his rock-hard cock.

He jerked his lips from hers, his hands coming up to frame her face in shock. "Anne?"

He could read her face, even in the near-darkness, and what he saw there was *lust*. Without breaking eye contact, she reached down and stroked his straining erection through his trousers. "Is this why your hands are shaking, Michael?" she asked breathily.

"Yes," he replied, his voice guttural.

She gave a shaky laugh. "Then I have good news for you. It's the reason my hands are shaking, too."

It was like throwing oil upon a flame. He had no reason to hold back now. He claimed her mouth in a searing kiss as he struggled to pull up her skirts with hands that trembled. He couldn't get them untangled, and yet the bunched fabric yielded, and Anne settled deeper against him. He realized with a shock of pleasure that she was helping him.

He reached between her legs and found her already slick. She cried out at his touch, and he could tell she was already close. He started rubbing her with his thumb, and—

She was almost thrown from his lap as the hackney jerked to a stop in front of her house. She mewled in protest as Michael withdrew his hand. He all but ripped the door off and climbed out with Anne in his arms.

He set her down just long enough to throw some coin at the driver. It was probably ten times their fare, given the driver's low whistle and enthusiastic, "Thank you, m'lord!" But Michael could not have possibly cared less. He had already swooped Anne up in his arms and was sprinting up the steps.

Hugh opened the door, and Michael had an impression of the befuddled expression on his face melting into amusement as Michael charged toward the stairs, taking them three at a time.

As soon as Michael crossed the threshold into Anne's sitting room she kicked her legs free. She looped her arms around his neck and strained up for a kiss, and Michael was right there with her, falling upon her like a starving man. They were tearing at each other's clothes; he heard a button pop off his jacket and hit the wall. By the time Michael got Anne down to her shift, she had stripped him to the waist.

He moved to sweep her up and carry her through to her bedchamber, but she swatted his hands aside and began struggling with the buttons on the placket of his trousers.

"I need you now, Michael," she panted.

"*Yes.* I'll take you through to the—"

"*Now,*" she said again, pulling open his trousers and shoving them down. "Right here. Right now. Against this wall, if we have to."

"Anne," he said in a strangled voice.

Her face flew to his with wide eyes. "Oh—am I too heavy? Can you not do that?"

He gave her a Look.

She smiled wryly. "Of course you can." She lifted the hem of her chemise, then jumped up and locked her legs around his waist. He instinctively caught her as she wrapped her arms around his neck.

He struggled to form a coherent sentence as she began

kissing his neck. "It's just—pregnant. You don't want to get pregnant. And—*God, Anne*—I—"

"I don't care. I'll take the chance. I need you. *Right now, Michael.*" She attempted to slide down over him.

"I can't be gentle—"

"I don't want gentle!"

Her searching attempts to guide his cock to her entrance finally succeeded, and Michael shuddered with pleasure as he slid inside her. He heard a feral groan emerge from his own throat. She was wet and slick and hot and tight and *perfect*, and more than that, she was alive and she was *his*, and nothing had ever felt so good.

He swung her around so her back was against the wall, and then he was pounding into her, his last threads of control destroyed. He had no thought but of chasing the climax that was bearing down upon him, but the sensation of Anne's fingernails digging into his shoulders was able to pierce his lust-filled haze. He glanced down and saw an expression of ecstasy so pure it looked almost like pain crossing her face, and then she was screaming his name as he experienced the delicious sensation of her passage throbbing and trembling and squeezing his cock.

Seeing her climax sent Michael into a frenzy. He wouldn't have thought he could have thrust faster or harder, but suddenly he was doing it. God, nothing had ever felt this good, he was desperate to find his own peak, he was—

He was interrupted by Anne screaming his name again, another orgasm coming fast on the heels of her first one. Michael made a strangled sound, and then it was his turn to cry out her name, as he was almost blinded by the intensity of his own climax.

He finally stopped with a shudder, still holding Anne aloft, his forehead coming to rest upon the wall just above her head. He was breathing as hard as if he'd sprinted all the way from Lambeth.

Once the room stopped spinning, he smiled at Anne, hoisted her up, and prepared to carry her to the bed, her legs still wrapped around his waist.

He made it exactly one step before he started to trip, as his trousers were down around his knees. His discovery was met with a bright giggle from Anne.

He shifted her onto one of his arms so he could use the other to haul his trousers up but didn't bother to button them. They were coming off.

"You think that's funny, do you?" he asked, carrying her into the bedchamber.

"Yes, actually, I do." Her smile was coy as he laid her down upon the bed.

He tried and failed to keep his features stern. "Quit making me laugh." He peeled Anne's shift up over her head, groaning as the beautiful sight of her naked body came into view. "I'm still cross with you for having put yourself in danger."

She mewled as she began to caress his chest. "You don't seem cross. If I didn't know better, I would say you were in an excellent mood."

"It is constitutionally impossible for a man not to be in an excellent mood after such an explosive orgasm."

She laughed. "I'll remember that."

"I hope you will have *many* occasions to put this information to good use in the future. But don't let my supremely well-pleasured grin fool you. I am vexed, extremely vexed. I could have killed that man I was so furious when he grabbed you."

"Mmmmm," Anne purred. "I've never seen you quite so close to the edge before."

Michael grinned. "You liked that, didn't you? Seeing me punch him."

She squirmed uncomfortably. Or maybe her squirming was because he had turned to caressing her breasts. "Michael!"

He brought his fingers to her nipples, which made her squirm even more. "There is absolutely no point in lying to me, Anne Astley. I can read your face. And even if I couldn't, it would be fairly obvious from the way you just climbed me like a tree."

Now she was definitely blushing. "Perhaps," she allowed. Michael arched an eyebrow. She sighed. "You were just like the gallant knight in a fairy tale defending my honor. I didn't expect it, but I suppose it was a bit, er, stimulating."

Michael's hand drifted lower. "A *bit* stimulating? You expect me to believe that?"

"Yes." Anne sat up suddenly, pushing him down on the bed, and climbed up to straddle him. "And might I point out that I wasn't the only one *growing* excited there in the carriage. Explain that, Michael Cranfield!"

Michael grinned, stroking his hands over her hips. "Oh, I was as randy as a stag in October. Everyone knows men get all charged up by fighting."

"I didn't know that," Anne muttered.

"I don't suppose it's the sort of thing your governess would tell you. But it's true. At least now you know how to get back in my good graces the next time I have to punch someone in the face for you."

"Hopefully there won't be a next time."

"Indeed, although what followed was most enjoyable, even if *someone* was barking orders at me like a fishwife. 'Right here, Michael. Right now, Michael. Against the wall, Michael.'"

Anne huffed. "I don't seem to recall you complaining."

"Not at all. I've always liked your commanding side." He brought his hand to the juncture of Anne's legs, where he gave an experimental caress. Surely enough, she was warm and wet and ready for him again. "In fact," he said, lifting her up to position her right over his cock, which had once again risen to the occasion, "why don't you boss me around some more? Your wish is my command."

Unsurprisingly, Anne was able to come up with some additional tasks for him. And even less surprisingly, Michael was happy to perform each and every one.

CHAPTER 34

The following morning, Anne and Michael headed
back to the Bow Street Offices. Samuel was due in
court, but he'd sent Anne a note confirming he didn't find
anything of interest on Pottery Lane last night.

The good news, Anne mused, was that the condescending
clerk, Mr. Hewitt, now saw fit to receive them immediately.

The bad news was that neither the Bow Street Foot Patrol
nor Anne's footmen had discovered anything of value while
out canvassing last night.

"And so we see," Mr. Hewitt said, "that the exercise was a
complete waste of time."

Michael moved into looming range. "I beg your pardon?"

"That is…" Mr. Hewitt stepped back and busied himself
straightening his jacket.

Anne stepped up to the counter. "What are your plans to
continue the investigation?"

Mr. Hewitt shook his head. "We can make no progress
with our investigation while Lord Gladstone remains in
hiding."

"I agree," Michael said.

"You do?" Mr. Hewitt said, his head snapping toward Michael. "I mean, good. Once he is located, we shall question him."

Michael leaned in, causing Mr. Hewitt to recoil. "I believe what you *meant* to say is that Bow Street will therefore exhaust every effort to locate Gladstone. What have you done so far?"

Mr. Hewitt looked affronted. "We have questioned his servants, as well as his particular friend Lord Scudamore."

"Did you speak with Mrs. Mariah Brownlee, who is his aunt? With Lord Ryland, his godfather? He's also good friends with Andrew Tomlinson, Matthew Beckett, and Percival Thistlethwaite. I'm given to understand he boxes at Gentleman Jackson's, gambles at Brooks's, and takes coffee every afternoon at the Cocoa Tree. If I was able to learn all of that with a single note sent to a mutual friend, imagine what leads the famed investigators of Bow Street will be able to uncover if they give the matter the proper attention."

Mr. Hewitt was scowling, but he pulled out a sheet of paper and took up a quill. "Would you mind repeating all of that, my lord?"

A few minutes later, having extracted a promise from Mr. Hewitt to send a runner 'round to question Lord Gladstone's intimates, Michael handed Anne into her carriage and climbed in behind her. "What a windbag," he grumbled.

Anne slumped against the cushions. She was trying to keep up hope, trying not to listen to that little voice in the back of her head kept saying none of it mattered because Nick was probably dead. "I'm used to much worse."

"I don't see how you hold your tongue."

"Out of necessity, more than anything. No one would donate to the Ladies' Society if I said what I was really thinking. I constantly remind myself to hold my temper. But I do appreciate the way you supported me."

Michael took her hand in his. "Of course. It is my intention to support you every single day for the rest of our lives."

Anne swallowed. That sounded wonderful, truth be told. It had been less than a week since his return, but already she had grown so used to having Michael in her life again. She didn't know how she was going to survive without him.

Don't think about that now.

"Thank you, Michael. What do you have planned for today? My mother has invited us to dinner tonight. I need to spend today getting caught up on Ladies' Society business. I hate to even imagine the mountain of correspondence I'm bound to have."

"You receive a lot of mail, then?"

"I do."

"And you handle it all yourself?"

"Yes. Why do you ask?"

"I've been trying to figure out how we're going to make things work when we're married—"

"*If* we marry," she amended.

"*When* we're married," he said, giving her his full Obstinate Face, "and there are a few questions I need to ask you."

Anne gestured for him to proceed.

"You see," Michael said, "I had always assumed I knew what you wanted your future to be like. I see now that there's been a lot I've missed. Perhaps your wishes have changed over the years. So, let there be no further confusion between us. When we were younger, we always used to talk about all the adventures we wanted to have, the places we wanted to go, the things we wanted to see." He smiled wistfully. "When I was passing through Niagara, all I could think about was how much you'd always wanted to see the Falls."

Anne grabbed his forearm. "Did you truly see Niagara Falls? What was it like, Michael? Is it as spectacular as everyone says?"

"It's almost indescribable. It kicks up so much water, you get soaked to the skin just looking at it." His smile was wistful. "I stared at it for hours while I was waiting for that last ferry to take me to my uncle, wishing so badly you were there with me." He cleared his throat. "I take it that you still want to see Niagara Falls?"

"Yes."

"And the lakes?"

"Yes."

"And the northern lights?"

"*Yes.*"

"And yet, you will never see any of those things if you continue with your current schedule."

Anne sighed. "So many people are depending on me."

"I understand that. But let us continue. You wanted to have children. A whole pack of them, you always used to say. Is that still your desire?"

"It's what I want more than anything."

"And do you wish to spend time with your children? Or do you plan to hand them off to the nurse and inspect them once a week?"

Anne's mouth fell open. "Of course I want to spend time with them! Hand them off to the nurse—how could you even ask such a thing?"

He held up both hands. "I ask only because your current schedule does not seem to allow time for anything else." He continued over her sputtering protest, "You currently spend upwards of twelve hours a day on your charity work. What do you plan to do once our first child comes along?"

Anne rubbed her forehead. "I... I don't know. I suppose I'll have to scale back. But if I cut back on fundraising, I'll have no choice but to reduce the size of the Ladies' Society. And I hate to even consider that."

Michael was studying her face. "It would make you sad."

"It would make me sad," Anne agreed.

Michael took her hand. "I cannot bear for you to be sad."

"I don't see any way around it. I'll have to either give up my dream of starting a family or gut the Ladies' Society."

"I refuse to have you do either."

"But Michael—"

"Which is why the first thing you need to do is hire a secretary." Anne blinked up at him in surprise. He continued, "Do you think Archibald Nettlethorpe-Ogilvy opens his own mail? Of course he doesn't. He employs a secretary. You must have the same."

Anne sighed. It wasn't as if the idea had never occurred to her before. "Secretaries don't work for free. And the Ladies' Society runs on a tight budget."

"Money will be less tight after my father makes his donation."

"Donation?" Anne frowned. "What donation? Your father has a subscription."

"Oh, did I forget to mention it? My father is planning a donation to the Ladies' Society in honor of our marriage. For twenty thousand pounds."

Anne blanched. "Twenty… did you say *twenty thousand pounds?*"

"I did." Michael laughed at her gobsmacked expression. "How much do you want to marry me now?"

Anne rolled her eyes. "As much good use as I could find for twenty thousand pounds, it ranks very low on the list of reasons I wish to marry you."

"You have a list, do you? Allow me to speculate what's pushing my twenty thousand pounds out of the top spot— perhaps that thing I did to you last night, with my tongue?"

Anne swatted at his arm. "Fishing for compliments, Michael Cranfield? I suppose you deserve one, because that thing you did last night with your tongue was rather spectacular. But it's not at the top of my list."

"Then what is?"

She swallowed. "Spending every day of the rest of my life with my favorite person in the world."

Michael pulled her into his lap and started kissing her. And there they were, driving through the streets of Mayfair at ten o'clock in the morning, and anyone who happened to look through the carriage window would have seen them kissing as if the world were about to end.

She felt a tear sliding down her cheek. Michael pulled back. "What's all this?" he asked, brushing it away with his thumb.

"I don't want to lose you. I didn't realize how much I've missed you until you came back. And now—" Anne broke off, unable to speak around the lump that had suddenly appeared in her throat.

Michael rested his forehead against hers. "We're going to work everything out. I refuse to consider any other possibility."

"I don't see how we can. If you're still bent on returning to Canada—"

"Which I am."

"—then it's impossible."

The carriage came to a halt. Glancing out the window, Anne saw that they had arrived at Cranfield House. She hastily slid off Michael's lap.

"It's not impossible. Don't look so glum. I'm going to figure something out. You'll see." He pressed a kiss into her palm. "I'll come and collect you tonight, and we can drive to your parents' house together."

Anne forced a smile to her lips. "Tonight, then."

CHAPTER 35

That evening, Anne gasped when the door to Astley House was opened by none other than her little sister Caroline.

"Caro!" Anne cried, enveloping her in a hug. "What are you doing here? I thought you meant to take a month or more for your bridal trip."

Caro looked affronted. "You did not seriously believe I was going to miss Morsley's return? I had Henry order the horses the moment I received Mama's letter."

"How wonderful," Anne said, "that you were so eager to see an old friend."

Caro rolled her eyes. "I didn't interrupt my bridal trip to see *Morsley*. No offense, Morsley."

Michael smiled amiably. "None taken."

"What I wanted," Caro said, taking Anne's arm and steering her into the foyer, "was to be there to witness you finally coming to your senses. I only regret that I got back so late. I had to rely on Harrington and Edward for a description of the proposal, and their scope for the romantic is sadly limited."

Anne blanched. "What do you mean, a description of the proposal?" She glanced up at Michael, and his expression confirmed the worst. "They... they were spying on us?" She paused, considering. "Although... I cannot honestly say I'm surprised."

Caro looped her arm through Anne's and led them toward the parlor. "You don't know how long I've been waiting for this day. What has it been, about nine years, Morsley?"

From behind them, Michael gave an audible sigh. "Nine years," he confirmed.

"How is it," Anne asked, "that everyone seems to have known but me?"

"La, I have no idea!" Caro said. "How you remained oblivious for so long is utterly beyond me. He was so very obvious about it. Every time you walked into the room, he would look at you like this." She made her eyes huge and full of longing. "And his gaze would follow you wherever you went."

"I wasn't that bad," Michael grumbled.

Caro rounded on him, pointing a finger. "You most certainly were! I always knew this day would come." She gave a dreamy sigh. "'Anne Cranfield, Lady Morsley.'"

"Well," Anne said crisply, "I do hope Michael and I will be able to marry. But there are some issues still to be resolved."

"We're getting married," Michael said firmly.

"Of course you are. Don't be *ridiculous*, Anne. Obviously you're going to marry him." She made a sweeping gesture. "Just look at him!"

Michael's smile was all smugness. "Just look at me, Anne."

"Yes, see how well Morsley looks, now that he's grown into his hands and feet?" Caro took Anne's hand and deliberately placed it on Michael's arm, posing them together. "And look how *divine* the two of you look together. She has this

297

ridiculous idea," she said to Michael, "that she's too tall. I have told her and *told* her that I would eat a bucket of leeches to have such an elegant figure, but does she listen to me? Of course not. And why should she? I'm just the leading authority on fashion in the *haute ton*, what would I know about it?" Caro shook her head. "Really, Anne, how you could even consider not marrying him is beyond me. If you think you'll find another man in all of Europe who cuts half so dashing a figure, you are sadly mistaken."

Anne felt Michael nudge her with his elbow. "You should listen to your sister."

Anne raised her eyes heavenwards. "Because everyone knows that the basis of every successful marriage is a fine figure and the best tailoring."

"Well," Caro retorted, "it can't hurt. Now, where is my husband? You know Lord Thetford, don't you, Morsley?"

"Of course."

"He will be getting into the brandy with Harrington, I imagine. I'd best check the library."

Anne started to trail after her sister, but Michael held her back. "You remember our conversation this morning. About the issues we need to resolve?"

"Yes?"

He grinned. "I've found the solution."

It took Anne a few seconds to process his words, then she said in a rush, "Truly, Michael? Tell me!"

"It's perfect. It came to me during my afternoon ride. I always think better out of doors, and, well, the point is, you *can* go to Canada, Anne. I've figured out—"

"Morsley." Caro's new husband, Henry Greville, the Viscount Thetford, emerged from the library. Anne bit her lip to hold in the sharp retort she had been on the cusp of uttering. Perhaps Michael would let her borrow the battle-axe from Cranfield House. That might be the only means by which she could club it through his thick skull that she could *not* go to Canada. If his notion of a solution involved her giving up her charity so he could get everything he wanted…

Lord Thetford pumped Michael's hand. "It's deuced good to see you again." He turned to Anne, bowing over her hand. "I understand congratulations are in order."

Anne's two older brothers trailed down the hall after Lord Thetford. Edward herded everyone into the parlor, where they found a gathering that could have taken place at Harrington Hall back in Gloucestershire—Anne's family, Michael's father, and Cecilia Chenoweth.

Caro plucked a sheet of paper from the writing desk in the corner. "Have you seen this, Lord Redditch?" she asked. "*The Times* featured Anne in a cartoon just last week."

"Do you have it there?" Lord Redditch asked, pulling a pair of spectacles from his pocket and perching them on his nose. "I've been wanting to see it."

"Caro!" Anne said. "Must you pass that around?"

Caro smiled and shook her head. "Modest Anne. If *The Times* ever printed a cartoon that made me look half that pretty, I would hang it in every room."

"They called me a *virago*," Anne hissed.

Caro made a show of fanning herself. "I know—I almost *expired* of jealousy!"

Edward strolled over. "You know, Anne, in the original Latin, virago isn't a disparagement. It shares a root with the word *virtus*, which refers to the highest set of ideals a man can embody—valor, heroism, and the like. Adding *-ago* makes it feminine. So virago simply refers to a superior woman, great in courage and character."

"I don't think that's how they meant it," Anne muttered.

"I do," Edward said quietly. "I wish you wouldn't assume otherwise."

Anne gave Edward a half smile. He really was the best

brother anyone could ask for. She was about to tell him as much when Yarwood announced that dinner was served.

Anne wound up seated between Harrington and Michael, which would have been lovely but for the fact that she had been hoping to discretely question Michael about his supposedly brilliant plan for them to move to Canada. Knowing Harrington, not only would he eavesdrop, but he would also announce whatever they said to the whole table.

Anne sighed. Michael had won a reprieve. For now.

CHAPTER 36

*I*t was a delightful evening in which old friends and neighbors were reunited after far too long apart. Dinner was followed by parlor games, and it was after midnight when Michael and Anne prepared to leave.

The Astley brothers were bickering as they saw their guests out, Harrington basking in the glow of having defeated his older brother at charades. "Don't feel bad, Edward, just because you sealed your team's defeat by failing on the last word."

Edward bristled, his shoulder giving a twitch. "I should like to have seen you enact the word *posthumously*. I thought I made a creditable effort."

"I enjoyed watching you die on the carpet again and again, to be sure," Harrington said.

"You were probably the one to place that word in the bowl," Edward grumbled.

"Well, of course," Harrington said.

Her brothers wandered outside with Michael. Anne leaned in to kiss her mother's cheek but winced slightly when her mother accompanied the gesture with a hug.

It did not escape her mother's notice. "What is it, Anne?"

"It's nothing, I'm sure," Anne said, tugging at her gown. She dropped her voice to a whisper. "My chest has been exquisitely tender all day. I must be about to get my courses, although it's strange—I've never felt close to this sore before."

Her mother gasped and brought both hands to her mouth. She looked positively giddy, which was odd, because the Countess of Cheltenham was not the giddy sort. "That *marvelous* boy!"

"Mama? What are you talking about?"

Her mother seized her arm and tugged Anne's ear to her mouth. "I am talking about the fact that I am going to be a grandmother!"

Anne blinked at her mother, shock and horror swirling in her stomach. "But—but—you can't know that. I haven't missed my courses or—"

The countess snorted. "Really, Anne! You doubt the woman who's borne eight children? That tenderness you describe is always the earliest sign. Mark my words, you're increasing."

"Oh, my *gracious*!" The room suddenly swayed, and she felt her mother grab her by the arm. She let her mother lead her to a padded bench. "Oh, Mama, this is terrible!"

Her mother sat beside her, brow furrowed. "Really, darling! You've nothing to worry about." She took Anne's hand and squeezed it. "Morsley will come up to scratch. We've always known that. He would probably marry you right this instant."

"I know he would. That's… that's not the problem." Anne felt tears streaking down her face.

"Anne!" Her mother fished a handkerchief from her pocket and pressed it into Anne's hand. "Darling, there's nothing to cry about." She studied Anne, bewildered. "If it makes you feel embarrassed, we won't tell anyone that the happy event took place before your wedding. So long as you marry in the next week or so, no one will suspect a thing."

Anne found she was unable to speak. Which was fortunate, because how could she explain to her mother the real problem—that she now had no choice but to marry Michael. He had her backed into a corner. If she didn't marry him, she would be ruined, and nobody would donate to a charity founded by a scandalous woman.

And if she did marry him, he was going to drag her off to Canada.

Either way, she was going to lose her charity, the thing she'd worked so hard for, her pride, her joy, her purpose. And all of those women and children were going to be back on the streets.

Michael poked his head in the door. "Are you ready, Anne? The carriage is—" It wasn't difficult to mark the moment he noticed her distress. He was across the room in three long strides, then collapsed to his knees before her. "Anne? What on earth is wrong, darling?"

She looked down, unable to speak. Michael turned to the countess expectantly, and she cleared her throat. "She is... unwell."

She felt Michael take her hand. "What can I do?"

"Just take me home," Anne said, her voice breaking.

Michael obeyed at once, scooping her into his arms and carrying her straight out the door. He did not pause at her brothers' alarmed inquiries, explaining, "She's unwell, and she wants to go home," then boosted Anne easily into the phaeton.

As soon as they had pulled away from Astley House, Michael said, "What is it, Anne?"

She didn't yet trust her powers of speech. "I'll tell you once we arrive."

Michael pushed the horses faster than was probably wise, given that Mayfair was crowded with carriages at this hour, as the *ton* made their way from one entertainment to the next. They arrived at Anne's house within minutes. Anne insisted she could walk and led Michael past a startled Hugh and into the parlor.

She rubbed her forehead as she settled on the sofa. At least her sobbing had subsided. Michael wasn't quite pacing the room, but he was radiating tension as he visibly struggled to figure out what to do with himself.

After half a minute, he could take it no longer. "For the love of God, Anne, tell me what's going on."

Anne clenched two fistfuls of her skirts. "Based on what my mother tells me," she said, her voice quavering, "I'm fairly certain that I'm pregnant."

For an instant, Michael froze, his eyes wide. He rushed across the room and sat beside her, taking her hand. "But Anne, that's—that's wonderful news." He studied her face, brow creased. "Isn't it?"

"It should be. It should be the happiest moment of my life. Except—" Her voice broke. When she managed to speak, she was unable to conceal a note of bitterness. "Except now you have me exactly where you want me, don't you? I have no choice but to marry you, and you're going to drag me off to C-Canada." Anne dabbed at her cheeks with her handkerchief. "I might as well go ahead and shutter the Ladies' Society."

"Anne," Michael groaned. He dropped to his knees before her and took both of her hands in his. His green eyes held a trace of bewilderment. "Don't you know me at all?" She said nothing. "Have you not noticed that nobody else seems worried I'm going to drag you off to Canada?"

She frowned. "Are they not?"

He laughed ruefully. "I wish you could have seen your

brothers, and my own father, mocking me yesterday. Because they all know something you haven't seemed to figure out yet. They all know that you have me right here." He released one of her hands in order to wrap his huge fist around her little finger. "*You're* the one who has *me* exactly where you want me. You always have. All you have to do is crook your finger and I'll be falling over myself to do your bidding. It is agony for me to see you crying, and to know that you're crying because of me?" He shuddered. "It's unbearable. So please, let us have no more talk of me dragging you to Canada against your will. Because any plan that would result in you being sad every day is the exact opposite of what I want."

"But… but you said you'd figured out how *I* could go to Canada. You just said it tonight."

"I did, but hear me out, Anne. My plan doesn't involve us going to Canada for another two years, and it certainly doesn't involve you shuttering your charity. Quite the opposite. You're going to expand it."

"E-expand it?" Anne asked, startled.

"Expand it," Michael said, rising to sit beside her on the sofa. "What I realized today is that, if you take a step back, our goals aren't mutually exclusive. Your goal isn't really to live in London. It's to help as many people as possible. And my goal isn't really to live in Canada, although I do love it there. It's to do something meaningful with my days. Well, I can do meaningful work here in London." His green eyes were bright as they met hers. "Because you're doing meaningful work right now. And I can help you."

Anne felt tears springing to her eyes for a different reason this time. Michael squeezed her hands. "Is there room for a gentleman in the Ladies' Society? Because I'd like to apply. And I have an idea that I believe might be of interest to its president."

Anne dabbed at her eyes. "What's that?"

"It's time for the Ladies' Society to expand overseas. You see—"

The door burst open, and Lord Scudamore rushed into the room, followed by Mr. Hewitt, the clerk from the Bow Street offices.

Michael glowered. "What the hell, Scudamore?"

"Gladstone's back," he said, panting.

"He is?" Anne asked.

"How do you know this?" Michael demanded.

"I arranged for a watch to be kept on his house. I feel responsible for this whole miserable business." Scudamore nodded toward Mr. Hewitt. "I just received word."

"He only stayed for a few minutes," Mr. Hewitt said, "then he set out again. He went west. Our patrolman tracked him as far as Notting Hill before he gave him the slip."

"That's when I remembered," Scudamore said, "one of the few assets Gladstone still owns is a string of tenement houses near Pottery Lane."

Anne gasped. "Pottery Lane! That's got to be it, Michael. That's where he's holding Nick."

"Come on, Morsley," Scudamore said. "Bow Street is marshalling patrolmen, but it will take time to round them up. We'll get there faster. God willing, we won't be too late."

Michael froze. His jaw was locked, and his expression was that of someone who had just swallowed a spoonful of vinegar. Anne watched him take a deep breath, then turn to her. "Do you want to come?" he asked.

Mr. Hewitt had just stepped through the door; Lord Scudamore, who had been right behind him, whipped around. "What's this nonsense? This is no place for a lady—"

Michael's eyes didn't stray from Anne's face. She could see his struggle, how much he really didn't want her to be there, either. But what he said was, "That is for Lady Anne to decide."

Anne felt her throat constrict, for all that she was smiling. Because this was the proof she needed that Michael wasn't going to walk all over her. He was going to respect what she wanted, even when it was hard.

She reached out and took his hand. "Someone has to stay here and coordinate the response. You go. I'll summon reinforcements and send them after you."

Michael's shoulders sagged as he gave a great exhale. "You're sure?"

She pressed his hand. "I'm sure. But thank you." She rose and went to the door. "Hugh," she called, "gather all of the footmen. You're going with Lord Morsley to rescue Nick."

Hugh bowed. "At once, my lady."

Lord Scudamore frowned. "Hewitt and I came in my curricle. There won't be room for any of your footmen. It'll be a squeeze with just the three of us."

"They'll follow in my carriage, then." Anne crossed the room to her desk and pulled out the case containing her flintlock pistol. "You should take this, Michael."

"Is that a *gun?*" Scudamore said, hurrying over. "Um, good idea!"

Anne pulled out a sheet of paper and slid it across the desk toward Lord Scudamore. "Write out the address of Lord Gladstone's buildings."

"Very good," Lord Scudamore said, scrawling down an address while Anne loaded her pistol.

They hurried out the door. While Lord Scudamore climbed into his curricle, Michael paused to give Anne a quick kiss.

"Be careful," she whispered.

"I will be," he promised. He caressed her cheek. "And as soon as I get back, we've got a wedding to plan."

"Yes," Anne said, smiling up at him through the tears that had suddenly welled up. "Yes, we do."

He climbed up beside Lord Scudamore, and Anne stood for a moment staring after the curricle as it clattered down the street.

Then she gathered her skirts and ran back inside. She had work to do.

CHAPTER 37

he three men said little to each other during the drive. Michael could hear Hewitt shifting around on the rumble seat behind him. Michael didn't have much to say to Scudamore. They had never liked each other, truth be told. Michael had always thought Scudamore was a bit of a snake, the type of fellow who would sell his own mother if it would net him twenty pounds.

He shook his head. Apparently the man had turned over a new leaf. He shouldn't hold old schoolyard grudges against him.

Scudamore reined in the horses then turned to face his companions. "We'll burst in on them unawares. I'll go first, then Hewitt, then Morsley."

"Why don't I go first, since I'm the one who's armed?" Michael asked.

Scudamore shook his head. "No. I really feel like it should be me. I'm the one who caused this mess. It's my responsibility."

Michael shrugged. "As you like."

"Here," Scudamore said, "since I'm going first, let me have the pistol."

Michael handed it over and they all climbed down from the curricle.

Scudamore led them toward the nearest house. Something about the plain grey brick buildings, the laundry overhead obscuring the moonlight, felt strangely familiar.

Michael dragged his gaze back to the house before him. Those features were probably common to every row of tenement houses in London.

Scudamore grasped the knob with one hand, pistol gripped in the other. "All right, here we go!" He turned the knob and charged through the door with Hewitt and Michael right behind him.

The room was quiet. There was a battered table and a pair of chairs to one side, and a narrow bed along the opposite wall. The dirty plates atop the table were the only signs of habitation. The mantelpiece was bare and save for a few rags hanging from a clothesline above the bed, there were no possessions.

"I'll check upstairs," Scudamore said, striding toward a staircase at the back of the room.

Michael was about to follow when he heard a muffled groan coming from a dark corner.

He hurried over and found a willow-thin boy of about eight years of age. He was lying on the wooden floor, bound and gagged.

Michael knelt down and began picking at the knots. He removed the gag first, and the boy took a few gasping breaths.

"What's your name?" Michael asked, starting to work on the bindings at the boy's wrists.

"Nick, sir."

Michael's eyes flew to his face. "Nick? Are you the same Nick who was kidnapped from Lady Anne's lodging house?"

Nick nodded. "Yes, sir."

"*Thank God*," Michael said as the knot gave way. "We were afraid Gladstone would have killed you already. I'm Lord Morsley. Lady Anne sent me to rescue you."

Nick used his newly freed hands to grip two fistfuls of Michael's coat. "You're in terrible danger, my lord."

"Yes," Michael said, moving to work on the bindings at Nick's ankles. "We've got to get out of here before Gladstone arrives. Are there any other boys here?"

"Yes, six or seven, but—" Nick shook his head. "What do you mean, *before he arrives*? The man who first took me—the man from the black carriage—he's already here. He came here with—"

Nick froze at the metallic click of a pistol being cocked. Michael looked over his shoulder and saw Scudamore standing near the stairs.

Except now he was flanked by four men.

One of those men was Mr. Hewitt from Bow Street. Another, Michael realized with a start, was the man they had encountered last night, the tall, skinny cretin who had grabbed Anne. He was now sporting an impressive black eye.

Something clicked into place. *This isn't Pottery Lane.* No wonder the row of tenement houses had felt familiar.

Warily, Michael dragged his eyes back to Scudamore. The viscount smiled at him, but it wasn't a nice sort of smile.

And he was pointing Anne's pistol at Michael's heart.

ANNE WASTED no time in dispatching notes—to Samuel, to the men guarding her lodging house, to everyone she could think of who might be able to assist. She sent them the address Lord Scudamore had indicated in Notting Hill, and requested they go reinforce Michael with all possible speed.

She had just sent the last one off when the sound of someone clearing his throat made her start.

It proved to be *Lord Gladstone*, standing in the doorway.

Anne's heart started racing. How... how could he be here? He was supposed to be over by Pottery Lane, and—

Anne swallowed. The carriage bearing all of her footmen had just departed. There were a couple of maids in the house, but...

But she was alone. Unprotected.

And face-to-face with a murderer.

"Pardon the late hour," Lord Gladstone said, wandering into the room. "I could see you at your writing desk through the front window, so I knew you were up."

"What... what are you doing here?" Anne asked, struggling to tamp down her rising panic.

"I never gave back your handkerchief." At Anne's blank look, he elaborated. "You handed it to me after the punch spilled on my glove. I thought, since I was riding by, I might as well return it." He dropped a freshly laundered square of white linen on Anne's desk, then pointed to the decanter. "Do you mind if I help myself?"

"N-not at all." Anne squinted at Lord Gladstone, trying to parse his bizarre behavior. He was certainly a good actor; he gave every appearance of being completely at ease. She cleared her throat. "Lord Scudamore mentioned you've been away. Where have you been these past few days?"

"Wait, do you mean Scudy's in town?" he said, pouring himself four fingers of brandy. "He was supposed to meet me at this house party in Somerset. He was so excited about it—he insisted we leave the Sunderland ball right after our dance to go pack, and then he loaded me onto the mail coach at the crack of dawn. Said he would join me in a day or two. We got set upon by a pair of highwaymen a half hour outside of London. They both came after me—I guess my clothing marked me as a gentleman—but one of them missed, and the other's gun jammed. It was quite the adventure, let me tell you!"

He paused to take a swig of his drink. "And do you know what? When I got to Somerset, I couldn't even find the house party! Everyone told me they'd never heard of a Lord Warklesworth, and the place I was supposed to be, Dumbtree Manor, didn't exist." He shook his head. "I must've gotten it mixed up. It's not like Scudy to make that sort of mistake. He's the organized one."

Anne peered at the baron. Her heart was still racing, but now she was feeling a mixture of terror and befuddlement. It seemed that Scudamore had been trying to protect his friend after all, taking steps to get him out of town before he could be arrested. Did Gladstone truly not realize the net was closing in around him?

Something occurred to Anne. "Wait, you took the mail coach? Why not take your carriage?"

"Oh... uh..." Lord Gladstone trailed off, his ears reddening. "Mail coach is faster."

"Faster, and significantly less comfortable." Anne took a step forward. "And tonight you said you were *riding* by. Did you have another use for your carriage this evening?"

"No! Uh, that is—"

Anne cornered him next to the decanter. "What are you doing with your carriage? What? I demand you tell me!"

"I... I had to pawn it!" he confessed, his eyes wide with alarm and confusion.

Anne recoiled. "Pawn it? What do you mean, you had to pawn it?"

He ducked his head. "It's not the sort of thing a man likes

to admit, but—well—it's no secret that I'm not exactly plump in the pocket. I had to pawn my carriage."

Anne's heartbeat had kicked up again, for a different reason. "To whom did you pawn your carriage?"

"To Scudamore." Gladstone laughed. "It's the perfect arrangement, you see. The cost of storing it alone is crippling here in London. Had to get it off my hands. And Scudy will let me buy it back someday. Assuming I can raise the funds, that is."

"So, Lord Scudamore has possession of your carriage." Anne huffed. "I don't suppose you also pawned him your signet ring?"

The baron flinched hard enough that brandy sloshed over the rim of his glass. "How did you know?"

"Do... do you mean to tell me it's true?"

Gladstone tugged at his cravat. "No one knows about that. *No one.* I mean," he pulled off his glove, "this ring has been in my family for more than two hundred years. To have to sell a family heirloom like that... my grandfather probably turned in his grave."

Anne was staring at his hand. "Your carriage is in Lord Scudamore's possession. But you still have your ring."

"Yes. Scudy let me hold onto it. Should he ever ask for it, though, I'd have to give it to him."

Something occurred to Anne. "And has he ever asked for it?"

"Only once. He said he needed to take it 'round to the appraiser for insurance purposes." He laughed. "I don't know what kind of appraiser he used, he came and demanded it at seven o'clock at night and had it back to me by the next morning. But that's the only time he's ever asked for it."

Anne's heart was in her throat. "When was this?"

"Oh, I don't know. Four years ago, maybe five."

Oh God. It fit. It all fit perfectly. Scudamore had possession of Lord Gladstone's carriage. He had demanded use of his signet ring right around the time he came to collect Nick, the one and only time he knew he would be seen!

A final question occurred to Anne. "Tell me, my lord. You're the secretary of the R.M.A." She looked at him, gaze piercing. "Do you handle its correspondence?"

"I'm supposed to. It's just that I've never been much good at that sort of thing." He shook his head. "I told Scudy I was useless at keeping track of letters and what not, back when he was badgering me to join the R.M.A.'s board. He was insistent, though. Said I needed to make connections if I wanted to improve my fortunes." He snorted. "Well, that hasn't happened. But at least Scudy takes care of the correspondence, just like he promised."

Anne felt like she might be physically ill. Scudamore hadn't been protecting Gladstone.

He'd been framing him.

Scudamore was the real villain.

And he'd just taken Michael off into the night.

Michael had no idea of the danger he was in. The whole thing had been a trap. Anne would bet anything they weren't really headed to Pottery Lane.

The problem was, she had no idea where they *were* heading.

She slumped into the chair behind her desk. "I don't suppose Lord Scudamore owns any property near a kiln."

"Do you mean like that row of tenement houses he owns over by the Coade Stone manufactory?"

Anne's gaze flew to Lord Gladstone's face. "He owns some houses near the Coade Stone manufactory? Truly?"

"Yes—it was after he bought them that his fortunes really started turning around." Lord Gladstone shook his head. "I've got to buy me some of those tenement houses. Whoa, there—what are you doing?"

Anne had pulled her other gun, her little Queen Anne pistol, out of her desk drawer. She began unscrewing the barrel.

"I need to borrow your horse," she said as she loaded the gun.

"Borrow my horse? But I—" Lord Gladstone looked even more perplexed than usual. "I didn't ride here on, you know. A sidesaddle."

"I had not supposed that you did," Anne said, rising from her desk and striding from the room.

Lord Gladstone jogged after her as she hurried out the front door. "But—but what's going on?"

There was no mounting block, but Anne was tall enough that she was able to get her left foot into the stirrup. She managed to pull herself up into the saddle. She had to hike her skirts almost to her knees in order to sit astride in her dress, but considering Michael was about to die, she had far greater concerns than whether someone saw her ankle.

She wheeled Lord Gladstone's bay gelding around. "It's a bit complex. I'll explain everything when I get back."

Lord Gladstone asked another question, but Anne couldn't hear it over the horse's thundering hooves as she galloped south toward Westminster bridge.

CHAPTER 38

*M*ichael straightened and slowly turned. Nick scrambled to his feet beside him, rubbing at his recently bound wrists. Without tearing his eyes away from the pistol, Michael placed a hand on Nick's shoulder and pushed the boy behind him.

"To answer your question, Morsley, the reason I haven't killed Nick is because he's worth nothing to me dead. Alive, on the other hand, I can sell him to a ship captain I know who makes sail four days hence. I'll be eight pounds richer, and he'll be far enough away that he can't go squealing to Bow Street. Considering my friend runs the West India route, he'll probably be dead soon enough from some hideous tropical disease. It's the ideal solution."

Michael glowered at Scudamore. "The West India route—do you mean a slave ship? You disgust me, that you would count such a man as your friend."

Scudamore sneered. "Ah, yes—there's the sanctimonious prig I remember from school. Always sticking up for some sniveling first-year and ruining my bit of sport."

"If that's how you remember me, then I'm glad not to have changed."

"Oh, but you're about to." Scudamore grinned. "You're about to be transformed. Into a corpse."

Michael's mind raced, trying to come up with any sort of strategy. "You're not going to kill me," he said, even though he was fairly certain that was wrong. The only thing he could think of was to keep Scudamore talking.

"Dim, as always, Morsley. Of course I'm going to kill you. You know that I'm the one who had Smithers killed. You therefore have to die." He waved to his henchmen, who began fanning out into the room. "Besides, I need you out of the way so I can marry Lady Wynters."

"You will *never* marry Anne," Michael growled.

"She'll need someone to console her after the tragic death of her childhood sweetheart. As the only one who can describe your final moments, I'll be well positioned. Then I'll get her thirty-five thousand pounds and access to that lucrative charity of hers." He grinned even bigger, clearly enjoying himself. "To say nothing of getting her flat on her back for me every night."

Michael started forward with no thought in his mind but ripping Scudamore's head from his worthless body. Nick grabbed his arm. "Don't listen to him, m'lord," he murmured.

Michael drew in a breath. Nick was right. The situation was bad enough without him going off half-cocked.

He turned to the man from Bow Street who'd accompanied them. "Hewitt, listen to me. You work for Bow Street. You swore an oath to uphold the law." Hewitt looked away and shifted his weight uneasily but said nothing. Michael tried again. "You're better than this. It's not too late—"

"Of course it's too late," Scudamore said. "Who do you think quashed the investigation before you went and appealed to Lord Hobart? He took his thirty pieces of silver, now he has to see this through."

The man with the black eye stepped forward. "Can we have some fun with him before you shoot him? I owe his lordship here a facer."

"You know, I would quite enjoy seeing that." Scudamore took a step back but didn't lower Anne's pistol. "Enjoy yourselves."

The last thing Michael did before two of the thugs seized his arms was to shove Nick back toward the corner. He scarcely had time to brace himself before the man with the black eye punched him in the gut.

Getting punched wasn't particularly comfortable, but after four years on the Canadian frontier, he was used to uncomfortable.

He ignored the pain, ran through his options, and made a decision.

Giving a great roar, he surged forward, trying to headbutt the man who'd punched him.

It didn't work, but that was all right.

He hadn't intended for it to.

It did cause the two thugs holding his arms to pull as hard as they could, struggling to restrain him.

That was what Michael had wanted.

He abruptly relaxed his right arm. This had the effect of sending the man to his right, who'd been expecting his resistance, stumbling off-balance. Michael followed this up by reversing course and pulling in the same direction as the man on his left, which sent him careening into the wall.

They wound up in a tangle, causing just enough confusion for Michael to wrench his arms free.

Now that he was loose, he figured Scudamore would try to shoot him, so Michael dove for the wall. Surely enough, the report of a pistol filled the room, accompanied by the sound of a shattering windowpane.

He caught a glimpse of Scudamore scowling at him through a haze of smoke, but he didn't have time to gloat, because there were four men closing in on him.

There was a ladderback chair by the wall. Michael snatched it up and wheeled to face his opponents.

He began swinging the chair. It was old and rickety, but it made a reasonably good weapon, even if he was still taking blows. That was unavoidable fighting four against one.

He managed to lay a well-placed strike upside Hewitt's temple. The Bow Street clerk dropped to the floor, unconscious, just as Michael took a fist in his left eye that sent him staggering backwards.

The man he'd punched last night charged, and Michael was able to catch him square in the chest with his boot, launching him into the air and sending him crashing into the wall. There was a squeal and two young boys emerged from the shadows and went scrambling out of the way.

One of them ran straight into one of the assailants. The thug rounded on the boy, raising his fist. "Out of my way, brat!"

The boy froze, his eyes huge, as the man started to swing a backfist toward his head. Michael dove forward, terrified he wouldn't get there in time.

He barely managed to shove the chair in the way of the thug's arcing fist. The man gave a howl of pain and sank to the floor, clutching his hand to his chest. "Get back!" Michael called, but the boy stood there, frozen. Suddenly Nick emerged from a corner, grabbed the little one, and hustled him out of the way.

Michael took a hasty step back, assessing the situation. Scudamore, having used up his only shot, was cowering by the stairs like the worthless piece of trash that he was. Two out of the four ruffians were still standing, and they resumed the attack. Fatigue was starting to set in, and what was worse, as Michael parried a blow, he heard the sickening sound of splintering wood. A lower cross slat had broken, and it spelled the beginning of the end for the chair. Michael kept swinging it, but he took a fist to his ribs and another to his right cheek. He raised the chair to block a stinger aimed at his left temple and another slat gave way, then another, until all he was left with was one long stile with a few splintered bits of wood hanging off.

His two remaining attackers were circling him, looking for an opening. Just as he started to raise the chair, someone stole up behind him and grabbed him in a bear hug. It proved to be Scudamore.

Michael lost his grip on the remnants of the chair. He struggled to get an arm free, but exhaustion was starting to set in. Scudamore twisted Michael's arms up behind his back, locking them in place.

And then Michael felt something cold and thin pressed against his neck.

A knife.

Everyone in the room froze, as they waited to see if Scudamore was going to do it, if he was going to kill Michael in cold blood.

Michael was half-tempted to turn around and throttle him with his bare hands. With the knife at his throat, he knew he would die in the process. But he was about to die either way; maybe he could send Scudamore down to hell before he did.

No. *No.* He couldn't think like that.

He had to live. He *had* to. He was going to spend the rest of his life with Anne. He just needed one idea. Something. *Anything*.

But... he had nothing.

Michael felt Scudamore tense behind him. The viscount sucked in a tight breath, as if he was steeling himself for the kill. And then—

And then the door swung open with a creak.

Whoever had arrived didn't enter right away, and it was dark enough that Michael couldn't make out their face.

What he could make out was the gleaming tip of a pistol.

Michael didn't have long to wonder who had arrived, or whose side they were on, because at that moment the newcomer spoke. It was a voice Michael would know anywhere, a voice that was dearer to him than any other sound on the face of this earth.

"Let. Him. *Go*."

CHAPTER 39

*A*nne had felt resolute galloping through the darkened streets of London. But as she guided Lord Gladstone's horse into the dim alley just past the Coade Stone manufactory, she heard sounds—crashes, thumps, and grunts—coming from one of the houses, and reality snaked its way through her chest like a vein of ice.

Someone was in a fight for his life, and she was fairly certain that someone was Michael.

She swung off the horse and rushed up to the door. She frantically inspected the front windows but could find no chink in their coverings through which she could peek.

Suddenly she heard, distinct amongst the commotion inside, a groan. It wasn't a loud groan, or a long one, nor was it particularly agonizing.

But it was Michael's voice. She knew it was. Michael was in there, and he was in danger.

She swallowed. There was nothing for it; she'd have to go straight through the front door, with no idea what she might find on the other side, and hope for the best.

She raised her little pistol with hands that shook and

swung the door open. The scene that came into view was worse than anything she could've imagined. Michael was horribly battered. His left eye was red and all but swollen shut, and blood was caked around a wound on his forehead. But worst of all, Scudamore had him pinned, his arms twisted behind his back, and a gleaming silver knife pressed against his throat.

All it would take was a mere flick of Scudamore's wrist, and Michael would die. There would be nothing she could do, nothing except cradle his beautiful face in her arms as he bled to death on the floor. Her knees started to buckle, and she caught herself with her shoulder against the doorframe. She managed to straighten, able to hear nothing but the roar of her own heartbeat thundering in her ears.

The thought of Michael dying was agonizing. It was unbearable. It was a thousand times worse than dying herself. She didn't want to live without him, she—she *couldn't* live without him, she—

Oh, God.

An image sprang to mind, as clear as if it had happened yesterday, of that fateful picnic from all those years ago, and of fifteen-year-old Michael smiling as he rolled on top of her. In an instant of clarity, she finally understood, finally admitted to herself that when she had closed her eyes, she hadn't just been *thinking* he was going to kiss her, but *hoping* that he would.

... my favorite person in the whole entire world...

... I can't survive without you...

... the very finest man I know...

And all these years, she had told herself he was her *best friend.*

How could she have been so unbearably stupid?

And now she was the only one who could save him. Oh, God, why could it not be anyone but her? This was exactly like one of Harrington's horrible shooting exercises, the ones she always failed, except it was a thousand times worse, because it was real, and it was Michael. Her hands were shaking with terror, and her palms were so slick she almost dropped her pistol as she pulled back the hammer.

"Let. Him. *Go*," she said, with as much conviction as she could muster as she strode through the door.

"Well, well, well," Scudamore said. "Lady Wynters. Isn't this touching? It's a shame, because I was planning on marrying you. And now I'll have to kill you instead."

"I would rather be dead than married to the likes of you," Anne said, her voice quavering.

"That can be arranged, just as soon as I've dispatched Morsley here."

Anne tried to line up her shot, but it was hard, given that Scudamore was cowering behind Michael, using him as a shield. She started as she realized—that was why he hadn't done it, why he hadn't cut Michael's throat. Because as soon as he did, she would have a clear shot.

He wouldn't kill Michael so long as she had her gun trained on him. He *couldn't*.

She had a chance.

All she had to do was make this shot.

She peered at Scudamore, searching for a target. Michael was tall enough that he blocked him completely. The only parts of Scudamore's body that were exposed were the hand that held the knife and his forearm, which was wrapped around Michael's shoulder. Even if she made the shot to the arm, the bullet might very well pass through Scudamore and go straight into Michael's chest.

She could target his hand, which hovered just above Michael's shoulder. But if her aim was the tiniest fraction off, she might very well shoot Michael in the throat.

Her shoulders slumped. Oh, God, she couldn't do this. No

matter how hard she tried, she never came through when it really mattered. She was going to fail, and the price of her failure would be Michael's life.

She looked at his beautiful face through her tears, wanting to memorize it.

What she saw brought her up short. Because Michael's face didn't hold any of the things she had been expecting—regret, farewell, and sorrow for the lifetime they wouldn't get to spend together after all.

Instead, she saw joy. Relief. Confidence.

He—he trusted her to take the shot. There wasn't a doubt in his mind.

He believed in her.

And in that moment, she decided she wasn't going to be that person anymore, the one who failed, the one everyone dismissed, the one who always missed the shot. More precisely, she realized she had never been that person in the first place. Who she had always been was the heroine Michael trusted to save the day, the lady Archibald Nettlethorpe-Ogilvy respected, the woman the people of London called a virago, *their* virago, the one they summoned in their darkest moments, because they knew she would always fight for them. She was not the one who stumbled; she was the one who got back up, the one who tried again, the one who *never* gave up.

The one who won in the end.

That was who Michael saw when he looked at her, and she realized that he was right. That was who she was, who she had really been all along.

A calmness descended over her. The hands that had shaken just seconds ago were steady. She could not fail Michael. She *would* not fail Michael. She refused to live without him, and how dare Scudamore hold that knife to his throat! She focused everything on her target, squeezed the trigger...

... and watched the lead ball fly true, catching Scudamore just where she had aimed, right in the hand that held the knife.

He screamed and dropped the blade, clutching his hand. Michael was on him in a second, kicking the knife clear, then shoving him up against the wall.

But two of Scudamore's thugs were still sensible. One of them grabbed Anne's arm. As she struggled to free herself, she watched in horror as the second man stole up behind Michael, fists raised. Anne tried to scream but her throat had gone dry with terror.

That was when the door flew open, and Samuel and Lord Gladstone came charging into the room. Samuel ripped the man holding Anne's arm off of her, smashing his head against the wall for good measure.

Meanwhile Lord Gladstone charged the man creeping up behind Michael and took him out with a ferocious headbutt.

Anne blinked at them in confusion, then noticed a third person coming through the door—a shirtless, soot-streaked Nick.

"Nick!" She pressed a hand to her chest. "Thank God you're alive." She caught him in a hug as she turned to Samuel. "What are you doing here?"

"I received your note. Having spent most of last night searching Notting Hill, I happen to know that it does not feature a"—he pulled Anne's note from his pocket and consulted it—"Butterfield Lane. I went to your house seeking clarification, and who should I find sitting on your front step but this fellow, looking more than a little confused." He clapped Lord Gladstone on the shoulder. "Once Gladstone recounted your conversation, I was able to put two and two together." He nodded toward Nick. "We were trying to figure out which house you were in when this intrepid young man came scrambling down a gutter pipe, shouting for help."

Anne turned to Nick. "Scrambling down a gutter pipe? But how did you get out? *We* were coming to rescue *you*."

"I went up the chimney, naturally," Nick said, retrieving his shirt from the floor by the fireplace. "I did it the first night, too, but they caught me and dragged me back. That's why they were keeping me tied up."

"But why did you remove your shirt?" Anne asked.

Nick thumped his concave stomach. "I'm getting downright stocky, what with those two rolls at breakfast. Figured I'd better buff it."

Anne laughed as Samuel stepped forward. "Lord Scudamore, you're coming with me. I'm taking you straight to Bow Street."

Scudamore made a vain attempt to jerk from Michael's grasp. "I am a peer of the realm. You cannot lay hands on me."

Lord Gladstone stepped forward. "Then allow me to do the honors." He stripped off his cravat and proceeded to bind Scudamore's wrists.

"Look, Gladstone," Scudamore said, "I can explain—"

"You're a bad person and an even worse friend," Lord Gladstone said, jerking the knot tight. He leveled a glare at Scudamore. "Even I'm smart enough to figure that one out."

Michael surrendered Scudamore to Lord Gladstone, who hustled him across the room, making a point to steer his former friend into the doorframe on their way out.

Anne's eyes met Michael's, and she flew across the room, throwing her arms around his waist. Suddenly she was crying uncontrollably.

After a few moments she pulled back, and gently raised a hand to his battered face. He might be bruised and bleeding, but he was alive, which made him the most beautiful sight in the world as far as Anne was concerned. "Oh, Michael," she said, burying her face in his chest.

"Now I really do look like I wrestled a bear," he said. He ran his thumb over the top of her head, frowning. "Er, I'm afraid I bled on you."

Anne hugged him closer. "I could not possibly care less."

She was distracted by a rustling sound. Glancing around, Anne saw half a dozen little boys emerging from dark corners and beneath the furniture. She smiled as Nick herded them together.

Anne ruffled Nick's hair. "Come, and I mean the lot of you. Let's go home."

CHAPTER 40

*A*nd so it was that they squeezed inside a hackney carriage (Scudamore's curricle having been commandeered to transport its owner to gaol) and made their way to Anne's lodging house. Anne hated to rouse the whole house in the middle of the night, but that was exactly what ended up happening, as nobody wanted to miss the excitement. Mrs. Godfrey supervised the bathing of their new arrivals (as well as Nick, over his protestations that he wasn't *that* sooty.)

The children were peering up at Michael with a touch of hero worship. He ducked his head and demurred when asked how he had received such impressive injuries.

Unfortunately for him, the tiny witnesses who had been peering out from the darkened corners of the room were much less circumspect.

"T'was four against one, battle royale—"

"Took a fist right in the eye and didn't even blink—"

"And then his lordship gave it to him plump in the breadbox—"

"He's an out and outer, all right—"

"A nonesuch, is what he is—"

"And then her ladyship shot him!"

"What?" Mrs. Godfrey cried, turning to Anne. "You *shot* someone, my lady?"

Anne started to duck her head, but she stopped herself. Instead, she lifted her chin. "Why, yes. Yes, I did."

"Aye," Nick said with an air of authority, "her ladyship is bang up to the mark. Don't be letting nobody tell you any different."

It was four in the morning by the time Anne and Michael found themselves climbing the steps to her town house.

They made their way to Anne's room. Word had gotten back to the household about their exploits, and there was a copper tub set out before the fire in Anne's room. Anne waved off her maid's offer of assistance, and Hugh's as well. She wanted to tend to Michael herself.

But first, there was something she needed to tell him.

"God, that bath looks divine," Michael was saying as he unbuttoned his jacket. "I've sore muscles in places I didn't even know existed."

"Michael," Anne said.

He groaned as he shrugged out of his jacket. "I'm going to need some help getting my boots off. I don't think I can bend over."

"Michael," Anne said again.

He started at the sight of a hole in the shoulder of his jacket, which was also marred with bloodstains. "Look at this —I think it's a bullet hole. That bastard almost shot me!" He groaned as he tossed it aside. "Fighting off four thugs will be nothing compared to your brother's tailor when he sees this. Pinkerton is definitely going to kill me."

"Michael, there's something I need to tell you."

"Of course, darling," he said, pulling his shirt up over his head. "Just let me get out of these bloodstained clothes and into that tub."

She winced as the mess of rapidly darkening bruises covering Michael's chest and arms came into view. She crossed the room and took his hands. "No, Michael. I need to tell you right now."

He glanced at her as he turned toward the tub, and what he saw caused him to jerk his head back around. Because, of course, he could read her face, and she could read his, and she saw the exact moment he realized that the thing she needed to tell him so urgently was that she loved him. Incandescent happiness radiated from his eyes (or at least, from the one that wasn't swollen shut).

"Michael," she began, "I—"

She didn't get to finish because his lips crashed down on hers.

She tried again when he lifted his head. "I—"

He lifted her up and began spinning her in a circle.

"Michael!" she protested. "Put me down. I want to look you in the eyes when I tell you."

After a moment he complied, a huge grin on his face. She tried again, but only got as far as, "M—" before he started kissing her again.

"Will you stop that?" she said when he finally lifted his head. "I want to say it!"

"And you're going to say it. A thousand times today, and another thousand tomorrow, and a thousand the day after. You're going to grow so sick of saying it."

"No, I won't. I can think of nothing I would rather do than tell you that I love you, Michael Cranfield, a thousand times a day for the rest of our lives."

He drank her words in, basked in them, treasured them. When he spoke, his voice was a trifle unsteady. "And I love you, my darling Anne."

Then he was kissing her again, and it didn't matter that he had pulled one of his wounds open and was bleeding on the carpet, or that she smelled of horse. The moment was simply perfect.

They were still smiling as she helped him finish undressing and ease himself into the tub.

"As soon as I saw that knife at your throat, I knew," she said as she lathered his back. "I knew, and I felt like such a fool for not having realized it until I was going to lose you. After the incident at the picnic, I told myself it didn't matter that you felt nothing for me but friendship, because that was what I felt for you, too. And I repeated that to myself so many times, I managed to convince myself it was true. I see now that it was really denial. You've always been in a separate category from everyone else. You're my best friend, my favorite person, the one I can't live without, the very finest man I know."

She was now rubbing the washcloth over his chest, and that look of supreme masculine satisfaction settled over his features. "Please, go on," he said, leaning back. "As exhausted as I am, I find that I could listen to your praise for several more hours. Preferably whilst you continue to give me a sponge bath."

"If there was even one inch of you that wasn't covered in bruises, I would poke you there. But my point is, I've felt that way about you for so long, I had come to think of it as 'the way I feel about Michael.' It wasn't until that horrible moment that I realized that 'the way I feel about Michael' isn't just friendship. It's love." She laughed. "I've loved you for years, Michael. Certainly, since that summer when we were fifteen. I just didn't admit it to myself until tonight."

He groaned with pleasure as she began to lather his hair. "Then I am glad to have been beaten black and blue and held at knifepoint. If that's what it took to make you realize that you love me, I would do it all again."

"Oh, God, never again—I was so terrified, Michael. I honestly don't know how I made that shot. If you could have seen how much my hands were shaking—"

"I never doubted you. I knew you would save me."

"You were actually what gave me the confidence to take the shot. I saw in your eyes that you believed in me, and—I somehow knew I could do it."

"Of course you could. It's something I've noticed—you don't seem to understand how amazing you are. But don't worry, I intend to remind you of it every day for the rest of our lives. Now, there are two things that we need to do before we can go to bed and sleep for the next twelve hours."

"Oh? And what would those be?"

"You need a bath, and we need to make love. Conveniently, we can accomplish them both at the same time," he said, reaching for the ties of her dress.

"Is that so?' she asked. She tried to make her expression stern, but couldn't suppress her smile. "I don't think we'll both fit in that tub. Indeed, *you* don't even fit in that tub."

"Which is why you will have to climb on top of me," he said with a wolfish grin, "for your sponge bath, and for what will immediately follow." He winced and rubbed his back ruefully. "I'm not moving as well as I'd like. I fear you're going to have to be on top for the better part of a week."

She smiled as she peeled off the remainder of her garments and climbed on top of him. "My darling Michael," she said, smoothing her hands over his chest, "I have absolutely no objections."

CHAPTER 41

*T*he day Michael finally married Anne was exceptionally beautiful, with crisp blue skies and a soft spring breeze. It was as if even the English weather did not dare deny him his perfect day. As they alighted from the carriage, he even heard a woodlark singing nearby (a woodlark—in London!).

Anne wore a white gown that Caro informed him was embellished with Honiton lace and seed pearls (although she could've worn sack cloth and he still would've thought she looked perfect). On her head she wore a crown of blush-pink roses, rich with greenery. Pinkerton sent Michael to the altar in a coat of midnight blue with a dove grey waistcoat and cream breeches. A week had passed since their clash with Lord Scudamore and his thugs, and although Michael's eye was still more purple than not, at least it was no longer swollen shut.

And the moment Michael kissed his bride, and at long last made Anne his wife?

Well, there could never be any words to describe what he

felt in that moment. But Anne could read his face, so she knew.

After the ceremony, their friends and family mingled at the back of the church. Caro gave Anne a congratulatory kiss on the cheek, then glanced around. "Is this a wedding, or a meeting of the Ladies' Society? I believe the entire board is present."

It was true. Expanding the Ladies' Society's board had been part of Michael's plan, and everyone Anne had asked to take on a new role had accepted with pleasure.

"Vice president of fundraising," Caro mused. "I cannot wait to get started. I daresay I will raise more in six months than you ever raised in a year, Anne. Just see if I don't."

"You very well might, darling," Lady Cheltenham said, strolling over. "But don't forget that Anne has appointed *two* vice presidents of fundraising. And if you think you'll be able to raise more than me, you are in for a very unpleasant surprise."

Instead of one vice president, Anne's society now had eight: Caro and Lady Cheltenham as vice presidents of fundraising, Cecilia Chenoweth in charge of special events, Archibald Nettlethorpe-Ogilvy overseeing employment, Samuel Branton in charge of legal affairs, Michael overseeing construction, Mrs. Wriothesley as vice president of operations, and Lord Graverley as vice president general.

Beside him, Anne was tearing up. "Truly, I cannot thank you all enough for helping me. Especially you, Mrs. Wriothesley. I fear you will come to regret it when you see what a commitment it will be."

"My dear girl," Mrs. Wriothesley said, "it is my pleasure. Well do I remember what it's like when you're first starting a family. You have been so selfless these past four years, but you won't have time for that now. Meanwhile my youngest daughter married three years ago, which has left me with too much time on my hands and too little to occupy it. I am glad to become more involved."

"So, let's see," Thetford said, taking his wife's arm, "there are two vice presidents of fundraising, and one each of operations, special events, employment, legal affairs, and construction. What does that make you?" he asked Graverley.

"I am vice president general," Graverley said.

"And what exactly do you *do*?" Thetford pressed.

"Lady Morsley," Graverley said, "if you would be so kind as to remind me—what was the effect on subscriptions when you announced me as your new vice president?"

"They tripled overnight," Anne said.

Graverley's smile was smug. "I believe my work here is complete."

"It's starting to feel like Edward and I are the only ones who aren't on the board," Harrington said.

"Not so," Fauconbridge said. "Anne has asked me to serve as treasurer."

Harrington's head snapped toward his brother. "Really? You didn't tell me that."

Fauconbridge shrugged. "I'm glad to do it. I know my way around an account book well enough."

Harrington threw his hands up. "Oh, I see the way it is— I'm the only one you didn't ask to help."

"Of course I would love to have your help, Harrington," Anne said, clearly distressed to have insulted her brother. "Tell me, what would you like to do?"

"Let's see," Caro mused, "what is he good at? Vice president of sarcasm?"

"Vice president of debauchery?" Thetford offered.

"Oh, *you're* one to talk," Harrington said, glaring at his friend. "Besides, it's not as if you have a position, either."

"Certainly I do. I am the special assistant to the vice president of fundraising," Thetford said, smiling at Caro.

Archibald Nettlethorpe-Ogilvy moved next to Michael. "I understand you'll be overseeing the construction of some new buildings. We keep an architect on staff. Feel free to make use of him."

"I will," Michael said. "Thank you."

The architect was going to be busy. Donations may have tripled after Graverley was announced as vice president, but they had doubled again after Scudamore's arrest. Anne's heroics had once again been memorialized in a cartoon, this time showing her galloping through the streets of London on Lord Gladstone's horse, gun in hand, with the caption, "Our virago rides to save the day!" Michael now understood her embarrassment, as *The Times* had also run one featuring him heroically protecting a flock of terrified children from four thugs with the caption, "The only man who could possibly deserve her." As embarrassing as it was, donations were up, and they were now looking to build not one new lodging house, but three, and that was just for starters.

"And let me know how much iron you'll need," Mr. Nettlethorpe-Ogilvy continued. "I'll arrange it as a dona—" He broke off as Graverley, who had stolen up behind him, began prodding him in the shoulder. "A donation," he finished. He arched an eyebrow as he turned to Graverley. "May I help you?"

Graverley was staring at his coat, transfixed. "I was just seeing if this was made from an actual potato sack. Remarkably, it seems it is not."

Mr. Nettlethorpe-Ogilvy took a step back, straightening his jacket. "And this is relevant because?"

"Because if we are to serve on the board of the Ladies' Society together," Graverley said, "then *you* are a reflection upon *me*. And this"—he made a cringing gesture to Mr. Nettlethorpe-Ogilvy's attire—"will not do. You'll have to see my tailor, Pinkerton."

Mr. Nettlethorpe-Ogilvy gave an unmistakable shudder. Michael leaned in. "Look, they made me go to Pinkerton, too. It was horrible, but you'll survive. Just tell him to make you whatever he thinks is best and run out the door the second he's done with your measurements."

"So," Caro said, "when are you two leaving for Canada?"

"Not for another two years."

That was the core of Michael's proposal—they would alternate time between England and Canada. In the early years they would spend the majority of their time in England, travelling to Canada only every other year, and only for six months at a time. If Michael was indeed appointed governor general one day, they would spend five years in Canada, after which time he would resign his post.

But the real genius of Michael's idea was the merging of their goals. In his new position, Michael would be responsible for overseeing the construction of the Ladies' Society's new lodging houses. That would give him something important to do each day and would provide the sense of meaning and accomplishment he had come to crave.

As for what the Ladies' Society would get out of the arrangement, Anne happened to be explaining it to Mrs. Wriothesley.

"... here there are so many war widows and relatively few men, as so many are off fighting. But in Canada, the situation is reversed. Michael tells me there is such an excess of men that an unmarried woman is like to receive half a dozen proposals within her first month on the frontier. And it's considered a boon if she already has children 'ready-made,' as they say over there, as you can never have too many hands to work the farm. Of course I wouldn't dream of recommending it to my residents until I have seen exactly what the conditions are like. It is a hard life, and they must have an unflinching portrait of it before they make such an important decision. But I'm excited to be able to give them the option to become landowners, which they would never have here. And just think how many additional families the Ladies' Society will be able to help!"

"How wonderful," Mrs. Wriothesley said. "But why wait two years? Why not head over immediately?"

Michael tilted his head toward his father, who was conversing with Lord Cheltenham in the corner. "I've been gone for so long, it's good to be back. I'm not in such a great hurry to return." He ducked his head. "And it occurred to me that I probably ought to build a house a bit more suitable for my lady wife."

Lady Cheltenham regarded him sharply. "I should like to know what you mean by that, Michael Cranfield. You didn't expect one of my daughters to live in some frontier shanty?"

"Not a shanty," Michael hastened to say. "It's a square log cabin—"

"A square log cabin?" Lady Cheltenham smacked Michael in the shoulder with her fan. "You expected *your countess* to live in a *square log cabin?*"

"I thought better of it," he grumbled.

Thirteen-year-old Freddie Astley strolled over. "Congratulations, Morsley. I'm glad you finally managed to marry her."

Michael tilted his head to the side. "Finally? What do you mean, finally?"

Freddie waved his hand. "I felt so bad for you four years ago, when you were so horribly in love with her, and you didn't manage to propose."

Michael blanched. "I didn't realize that you knew, Freddie. You didn't say anything."

Freddie gaped at him. "What was there to say? Did you really want to talk about it?"

An extremely fair point. "But how did you know?"

Freddie rolled his eyes. "I was nine. I wasn't stupid."

They made their way to the doors of the church, where they were surrounded by even more friends—the residents of the Ladies' Society's lodging house had attended as a group.

Mrs. Godfrey stepped forward. "Congratulations, Lady Morsley." She paused, wringing her hands. "I must warn you about something."

"Warn me? About what?" Anne asked.

Mrs. Godfrey swallowed. "You see, when the neighbors saw us leaving to go to the church en masse, they guessed where we must be going. And word spread like wildfire through the neighborhood that today was the day of your wedding. I'm afraid a bit of a crowd has formed outside."

Michael smiled. "A bit of a crowd won't bother us in the least, Mrs. Godfrey." He turned and opened the door for Anne.

Only to be greeted by a roar from the mob that had gathered in Hanover Square, stretching as far as the eye could see.

He immediately stepped in front of Anne. But then he relaxed as he saw that those assembled were cheering, not braying for blood, and that children were strewing the portico of the church with flowers.

"I'm so sorry about this, my lady," Mrs. Godfrey said. "It's just that you've become a folk hero. Both of you have. And nobody was about to miss your wedding."

Michael glanced at Anne, whose mouth was hanging open. He laughed. "Well, there's only one thing for it. Come, Anne, let's give them what they want." He took Anne's hand and led her to the very front of the portico of St George's, right between the two central columns.

And that was how Michael Cranfield came to be kissing his new wife in front of several thousand cheering witnesses.

An event which was, once again, immortalized in the papers in the form of a cartoon.

Although this time, Michael didn't mind.

∽

KEEP READING **for a special preview of Book Three in the Astley Chronicles, *The Sea Siren of Broadwater Bottom*!**

∽

AS ALWAYS, **subscribers to my newsletter will receive a free second epilogue short story for each of my books.** Anne and Michael's second epilogue contains a love scene, and I'm gonna be honest—**I think it's the hottest love scene I've ever written!** Here's what it's about:

Four years into their marriage, Michael is embarrassed when he accidentally reveals his ultimate fantasy to Anne. But Anne is… intrigued. Can Anne make Michael's wildest dreams come true?

If that sounds like something you'd like to read, **visit my website, www.courtneymccaskill.com, and sign up today!**

∽

WOULD you be willing to help me by taking a moment to write me a review? Reviews are very helpful to new authors like me because they help people discover my books and give potential readers an idea what to expect. I would appreciate it so much, thank you!

∽

COMING SOON: **The Astley Chronicles, Book Three:** *The Sea Siren of Broadwater Bottom*:

Two scholars. One contest. Only one can be the winner...

Edward Astley has to win the classical translation contest being held at Oxford in two weeks. Literally, he has to, because his little brother, Harrington, got drunk and bet fifteen thousand pounds that he would, and their father will cut Harrington off if he finds out about his imprudent wager. Edward would never let his brother down, but he cannot possibly win this stupid contest. Not only will he be competing against fifty other scholars, but one of them is the latest star on the literary scene, the anonymous translator whose rendition of *On the Sublime* is taking Britain by storm. Meanwhile Edward hasn't opened a Greek lexicon in years, because he secretly hates classical poetry following his grueling years at Cambridge.

Now he's supposed to be studying, but all he can seem to think about is Elissa St. Cyr, the redheaded daughter of his former tutor, who's every bit as brainy as she is delectable.

Elissa St. Cyr has problems of her own. She has to win that classical poetry contest, too. It's her only chance to earn an academic credential so she'll be taken seriously as a scholar. And with her father's health failing, Elissa, her mother, and her three sisters will be left destitute unless Elissa can support them through her translation work.

To make matters worse, she managed to get stuck in the middle of a pond during a thunderstorm, and the person who happened along to rescue her, witnessing her in the most humiliating moment of her remarkably humiliating life, was her ultimate *beau idéal*, the brilliant Edward Astley. Now Elissa keeps bumping into Edward everywhere she goes. Which would normally be wonderful…

… except she's worried he's going to figure out that *she* is the anonymous translator everyone is talking about.

PREVIEW: THE SEA SIREN OF BROADWATER BOTTOM

G loucestershire, England
March 1803

THE SECOND HE STEPPED OUTSIDE, the wind ripped the hat from Edward Astley's head and carried it to the top of a nearby elm tree, where it became lodged. He bit back a curse as he crossed the small yard to his horse. Wasn't that just the kind of week he was having? In addition to the impending disaster bearing down on him, he'd ridden all the way out here, to the house of his former tutor, Mr. Julian St. Cyr, and he hadn't even learned what he'd hoped to find out.

And, judging by the rapidly darkening sky, now he was going to get drenched to the bone.

He urged his mount into a canter, hoping to cover as much ground as he could before the skies opened. This had been his best shot, his only shot, really, at learning something useful. Edward wasn't the type to panic, but he only had two weeks to figure this out, and if he couldn't…

If he couldn't, his brother would be left hanging in the wind, exposed to both their father's wrath and society's scorn. And although, in truth, this whole ridiculous situation was Harrington's fault, Edward would never allow that to occur. There was nothing he would not do for his brother. Edward would lay down in a muddy ditch and die for Harrington without a second's hesitation.

The thought sounded strangely appealing, compared to what he was now going to have to do instead.

He was riding through a grove of cherry trees when something caught his eye, a blur of pale blue just visible through the branches. He squinted and saw a flash of copper.

Suddenly every hair on the back of his neck was standing on end. Although he knew he needed to return home with all possible haste, he found himself reining his horse in. Even as he chastised himself for being ridiculous, he steered his gelding through the cherry trees, and a pond came into view.

That was when he saw her.

A single ray of light penetrated the gathering clouds, and no subject of a Raphael painting had ever been better illuminated. She was floating on a rowboat in the middle of the pond like a water nymph surveying her demesne. She wore a simple gown of pale blue, and a cascade of red curls tumbled down her back.

God, he had always been so partial to redheads, and she was the most beautiful woman he had ever seen, by a very wide margin. She had a heart-shaped face and perfectly shaped coral-pink lips, the bottom just a hair fuller than the top. She was biting that full bottom lip in consternation. Edward also could not help but notice that his nymph had a figure that would tempt any ancient god who stumbled across her bathing in her pool to sin, with breasts that were neither large nor small, but which suddenly struck him as being precisely the right size. The outlines of her nipples, clearly visible through the thin fabric, were both tantalizing and tempting. She looked to be neither tall nor short, with delicate shoulders and a lithe waist, which led to the delightful swell of her hips.

He could see... *everything*. Hell, that dress fit her like a second skin...

Wait. It was difficult to think when his senses were being bombarded with so much female gorgeousness, but some-where deep in the recesses of his mind the thought emerged that the reason her dress fit her like a second skin was because it was soaking wet. That the delicate shoulders were drawn up and subtly quivering, and those lush, full lips were a bit... blue.

He shook himself. How disgraceful, to be gawking at the poor girl when she was freezing to death. He nudged his horse to the edge of the pond and opened his mouth to offer his assistance.

But the words died on his lips as it hit him—this wasn't just any gorgeous woman.

He knew this girl. It had been ten years since last he saw her, ten years since he had sat caddy-corner to her in her father's classroom, but he was sure of it.

"Miss Elissa?" he asked in shock.

ELISSA ST. CYR had done it this time.

She was hardly a stranger to calamity; one might say it was her stock in trade. Nor was this the first time reading out of doors had been the cause of her downfall. There had been the time when she was ten and had thought she could finish the last few pages of Xenophon's *Anabasis* during the short walk to church. She had wandered straight into Mrs. Naesmith's blackberry bramble, and it had taken a quarter of

347

an hour to disentangle herself. She could still recall the way the preacher fell silent, and everyone turned to stare as she slunk into church with her dress torn and her arms covered in scratches.

There had been another incident when she was twelve. It must have been a Wednesday, because Wednesday was the day the village shop received a box of books from the big circulating library at Cheltenham to supplement the two shelves they kept behind the counter for lending. Elissa never missed a Wednesday and, besides, she had to return the book she had out, Francis Fawkes's translation of *Argonautica*. She had been reading a favorite passage one final time as she walked along.

That was when she tripped over the pig (because of course there happened to be a pig just wandering by) and fell flat on her face in the middle of the road.

She was unharmed, but the incident was unfortunate in that it was witnessed by William Ricketts, one of her father's students. More specifically, William Rickets was the worst of her many tormentors inside the classroom. The Unfortunate Pig Incident had given him years' worth of fodder.

Then there was the Bicklebury Bog Debacle.

Elissa still did not like to think about the Bicklebury Bog Debacle. She'd had to wait until Farmer Broadwater had fetched his plough horse to pull her out, by which time a crowd had gathered to point and laugh.

That had been when Elissa finally swore off reading and walking, but she still loved to read outdoors. There was nothing like a picturesque spot to truly stir the imagination. Farmer Broadwater, her rescuer all those years ago, didn't mind if she borrowed his rowboat, and when she was reading something set on the water, she liked to lie in it. The gentle bobbing gave her the feeling of being aboard a ship, right there amongst the ancient heroes who sprang right off the page and into her imagination.

She always kept the boat tied to the dock. She had never dreamed that anything could go wrong.

Today had been the first day of the year that had truly felt like spring, and she just had to get outside. She had grabbed Plutarch's *Life of Theseus* from the library and set out after luncheon. As always, she had become lost in the tale, and must have read for the better part of three hours.

She sat up when she saw the clouds rolling in. She ran a hand over her opposite arm and was startled to find goose-flesh; she had been so caught up in the story, she only now noticed that the temperature had dropped by ten degrees. And that was when she noticed what had happened.

At some point, the rowboat had come untied from the dock and drifted into the center of the pond. A quick search revealed that there wasn't an oar in the boat, but no matter— the pond was small enough that she could use her hand to paddle back to shore.

It was when she failed to make any progress that she noticed the rope had become entangled in an underwater tree that had been left in place when they flooded the hollow. Try as she might, Elissa was unable to work the rope free. And although she picked at it until her fingers bled, she wasn't able to loosen the knot.

By this time, the weather was really starting to turn, and she shouted as loudly as she could for Farmer Broadwater, whose house was just over the rise. This was to no avail, and that was when she began to grow fearful. A storm was coming, a bad one, and she knew she couldn't be stuck on the water with absolutely no protection.

The only option she could come up with was to wade to shore. Although she couldn't swim, the pond was small, and most of it wasn't very deep. Perhaps she could touch bottom.

She lowered herself, trembling, into the water, and was quickly disabused of that hope. The outside of the boat was slimy with moss, and she immediately lost her grip. Her chest seized with panic as her head went under, but she managed to grab a tree limb with a flailing arm and pull her head back out of the water. It was a struggle to get back into the slippery boat, especially after her hair became snarled in the tree, and she tried and failed so many times it began to feel like she was never going to make it out of the frigid water. By the time she finally collapsed into the bottom of the boat, her hair had unraveled from its pins, and her whole body was shaking with fatigue and terror.

That had been perhaps an hour ago, an hour in which the temperature had continued to plummet. The thin muslin gown that had seemed perfect for a sunny spring afternoon was grossly inadequate for the current conditions, and between her sodden state and the way her thoughts were becoming muddled, she was fairly certain she was growing hypothermic.

She had mumbled every prayer her frozen brain could dredge from her memory. Elissa had always prided herself on being self-reliant. She may have her head stuck in the clouds, but she had never been the type to sit around and wait for someone to come to her rescue. Life had taught her there was no such thing as a prince on a white horse.

But if ever she had needed someone to be her hero, it was right now.

And then she heard it—the cadence of hoofbeats on the nearby path. She tried to cry out, but she was so cold she could only manage a sad little croak.

The hoofbeats slowed, and she could see something moving through the trees.

It proved to be a man.

A man on a white horse.

And—oh, God, surely this could not be happening...

Although Elissa knew she needed help, and had in fact just spent the better part of two hours praying fervently for someone, anyone, to happen along, she could not believe her terrible luck.

Because if there was anyone on the face of this earth she did not want to witness her in this, the most humiliating moment of her remarkably humiliating life, it was *Edward Astley.*

It had been ten years since last she saw him. He had been seventeen, as she recalled ("as she recalled"—as if she did not recall it all perfectly!) At an age when most boys had been spotty-faced and awkward, Edward Astley was already breathtakingly handsome, showing every indication that he would become this outstanding specimen of the male species, whom the newspapers reported that the tittering ladies of London had dubbed "Prince Charming."

Certainly, he deserved it. Although he looked much the same as she remembered, his shoulders were broader, his jaw squarer, and he appeared to have grown even taller. He looked the part of the ideal country lord. He was riding a gorgeous white Irish Hunter and was impeccably turned out in buff breeches and glossy top boots, with a cream waistcoat and flawlessly white linen. His coat was the color considered most suitable for the country, a pale brown shade called drab. On anyone else, it would have looked, well, *drab*, but on Edward Astley the dull color only served to make his thick, glossy, dark brown hair look richer by contrast. And as for his eyes...

They called them the Astley eyes. She had heard that his mother had them, and four of his six siblings. They were huge and as blue as... Elissa didn't even know how to finish that sentence, because she had never seen anything as blue as

Edward Astley's eyes. Even from fifteen yards away, she could make out their color.

Those eyes were currently staring at her in shock. Oh, but this was mortifying!

Get a hold of yourself, Elissa. It wasn't that bad. He didn't seem to recognize her. Gracious, after all these years, he probably didn't even remember her!

"Miss Elissa?"

Well—er—so much for that hope. She cleared her rusty throat. "Lord Fauconbridge," she replied, using his title (because as the heir to the Earl of Cheltenham, he was known by the courtesy title Viscount Fauconbridge). She sifted through her brain for the appropriate manner in which to converse with a viscount whilst one was floating on a pond in a gathering thunderstorm, wearing a translucent dress. "How—er—lovely to see you again."

"Yes, what an unexpected plea—" He was interrupted by a rumble from the sky above. "Forgive me, Miss Elissa, but are you perhaps in need of some assistance?"

"Indeed I am." She could hear her own voice trembling with gratitude. She gestured to the front of the boat. "The rope has become entangled in this tree, and I cannot free it. I fear I am stuck. I—I cannot swim, you see."

He swung down off his horse. "I see," he said, draping the reins over a branch.

"If you would be so kind, Farmer Broadwater's house is just over that rise," she said, gesturing. "If you would alert him, he can fetch the neighbor's boat."

"Ah," he said, brightening, "there is another boat. Where is it? I am sure that, given the circumstances, the owner would not object to my commandeering it."

Elissa flushed. "I wouldn't want you to go to such trouble."

"It is no trouble at all."

She swallowed. "It is a mile, maybe a mile and a half, down the road."

"A mile and a half—" He broke off, looking affronted, and began peeling off his coat.

"What—what are you doing?"

"You cannot wait that long," he said firmly. He hung his coat from another branch and began tugging at one of his boots.

Oh, dear God, he meant to come in after her! "Please, my lord," she sputtered, "I would never expect for you to—"

"You should," he said, grunting as the boot slid free. "What kind of blackguard would leave you there with a storm coming?"

He had never seemed to understand that she wasn't the kind of girl who received such solicitude. "I'm not worth the trouble," she said ruefully.

He looked up, shocked that she would even suggest such a thing. "Of course you are."

She sighed. This was why Edward Astley would always be her *beau idéal*. Not because he was devastatingly handsome (which he was), or because he was rich, or because he was heir to an earldom. Not even because he was so smart (although she had always found that even more appealing than his good looks). After leaving her father's tutelage, he had gone on to win just about every award the University of Cambridge gave out, including its most prestigious, Senior Wrangler, which was given to the best student in mathematics. He had also been named second Classical Medalist, having completed the near-impossible feat of being a top student in both mathematics and classics.

But more than any of those things, the reason Edward Astley had always made Elissa a bit weak about the knees was because he had always been so kind to her.

By the time Elissa had been old enough to join her

father's classroom, Edward had gone off to Eton. But during school breaks, he would ride over twice a week to take some additional lessons. The days when he was there had been completely different. Her father's other students seemed to be universally of the opinion that it was unnatural for a girl to study Greek and Latin. Mostly they would ignore her, but there were a few, led by William Ricketts, who seemed affronted by her mere existence, and were constantly making remarks just skirting the inappropriate, trying to get a rise out of her.

But Edward would not brook any boorish behavior in her presence. As soon as William Ricketts started in on her, he would clear his throat, say, "Come, Ricketts," and nod toward Elissa with a genial smile. He always assumed the best about everyone, assumed that Ricketts was a good sort who had momentarily forgotten himself (Elissa could have disabused him of that notion).

It hadn't been anything extraordinary, just little things like the way he would smile and say, 'Good morning, Miss Elissa,' when she walked into the classroom. He often made an interested observation after she read her translation aloud (an event that was usually followed by the sound of crickets, at best). Once she had broken the nib of her pen, and he had immediately handed her his spare.

She knew very well that he didn't *like* her, at least, not in the same way she liked him, nor did she expect him to. But he had treated her like his fellow student, at a point in her life when everyone else had treated her like an oddity. It was a small thing, but one that head meant a tremendous amount to her.

From the bank of the pond, he cleared his throat. "And it is obvious that you are rather cold."

Oh dear—he had caught her woolgathering. "I cannot deny it," she said, hugging her arms around her chest.

He divested himself of his second boot and waded into the pond. Once he was waist-deep, he leaned forward and began slicing through the water with smooth, precise strokes.

He made three attempts to disentangle the rope, twice diving down under the water and not resurfacing for what seemed like too long. After the last attempt he ran a hand through his hair, pushing it back from his forehead (gracious, she had never seen a man with such thick hair in her life). "You are right," he said, "it is well and truly tangled. I fear there's nothing for it—we'll have to swim. Please don't worry. I am confident in my ability to convey you safely to shore."

She had no concerns on that front; she had seen how efficiently he cut through the water. The only question was as to the mechanics of how this was to be accomplished. "Thank you, my lord," she said, and she could hear her own voice trembling with sincerity. "Um, how should I, er—"

"Let's see," he said quickly. "I can pull down on the side of the boat. Can you—"

"Yes, let me just—"

Her dress snagged on the lip of the boat as she slid into the water. She felt a rush of cold air all the way up to her thighs as her skirts were pulled up. Oh dear—well, she was into the water so quickly, he probably didn't see any higher than her knees. At least, that was what she was going to tell herself. She was gripping the side of the boat with both hands, in the water up to her collarbone, when he wrapped a warm, strong arm around her waist, pulling her body flush against his.

Even in the icy chill of the pond, he was so warm beneath his thin linen shirt, and she instinctively curled into him, a groan of pleasure escaping from her throat. She had never been this close to a man. Never. Her breasts were pressing into the firm planes of his chest, her stomach was flush with his, and their legs tangled intimately beneath the water. She peered shyly into his face, which was mere inches from her own. "All right?" he asked.

"All right," she confirmed, her voice a squeak, and he was leaning back to push away from the rowboat when she remembered. "Oh—wait—I almost forgot my book!"

"Your book?" he asked, his brow wrinkling.

She reached over the side of the rowboat, feeling around. "You know how my father is about his library. I'll never hear the end of it if I leave one of his books out in a rainstorm— here it is," she said, pulling it from the boat.

His face broke into a broad grin as he took in the title. "You read Plutarch in a rowboat?"

"I—er—yes." She cleared her throat. "You know, it's the ship of Theseus, and the rocking of the rowboat makes you feel like you're on the water, and… and…"

She trailed off, ducking her head. Edward was studying her, a soft smile upon his face. His face was so close to hers, she could feel his breath brushing her lips. "That strikes me," he said slowly, "as the ideal place to read it."

The sky gave another rumble, and he glanced heaven-wards, serious again. "I'll need at least one hand to swim. Can you hold the book up out of the water? Perhaps if you wrap your other arm around my neck—"

The only advantage of being half frozen was that it prevented her cheeks from bursting into flames as she hooked her arm up around his shoulders. Now her entire body was pressed against his, and she felt a shudder ripple through her.

"We must get you out of this cold water," he said, misinterpreting the reason for her trembling. He shifted so that he was floating on his back, pulling her on top of him, one arm wrapping around her back, his hand resting gently on her waist. "Is that all right?"

Was that all right? She was lying on top of *Edward Astley* with naught but a few layers of wet muslin to separate them. She might feel mortified now, but she had a feeling this would go down as the best moment of her whole entire life.

She cleared her throat and nodded her assent, and he let go of the boat. He floated along on his back making slow, smooth strokes with his free arm, propelling them steadily toward the shore.

Mere seconds later his arm scraped the bottom. "Ah," he said, putting his feet down, "here we are." He grasped her about the waist again and helped her rise to standing.

"And we even managed to keep Plutarch dry," she said, holding the book up. "More or less," she laughed, holding it between two fingers, trying to keep it from being soaked by her wet hands.

He grinned. "Excellent." He released her waist and offered his arm. "Now, let's get you back home before—"

She started to sway as soon as he withdrew his hands. She hadn't realized she was that cold, but it was clear her legs wouldn't hold her. He immediately snatched her up about the waist, pulling her body flush against his, preventing her from falling.

Plutarch was not so fortunate. The book slipped from her tenuous grasp and plunged into the pond.

"Oh, no!" she cried. "Father is going to *kill* me."

"I'm terribly sorry," he said, somehow managing to hold her upright while bending down to fish the book out of the water. "That was my fault."

"It absolutely was not." She gave a bleak chuckle. "Disaster is my signature. It has a way of following me wherever I go."

"Are you all right now?" he asked.

"I think so," she said, taking a step forward. "I just—"

Her knees promptly buckled. Edward was on her in an instant, scooping her up in his arms and living up to his nickname as he carried her to shore.

He seated her on a log and immediately draped his coat around her shoulders, solicitously making sure she was well wrapped before taking up his boots. As soon as his back was turned, she buried her nose in the collar. *Bergamot.* It was the same shaving tonic he had started to use when he'd been around sixteen years old. She could remember catching a hint of that fresh citrus as she rounded the corner toward the classroom, and how a shudder would run up her spine, because she would know before she even saw him that he was in attendance that day…

All semblance of rational thought fled from her mind as Edward scooped her up again and carried her to his horse. He lifted her up onto the saddle as if she weighed nothing, then adjusted the stirrup so she could insert her foot. She was seated sideways, even though it was not a sidesaddle. "I won't go faster than a walk," he said. "Do you think you can manage?"

"Of course," she replied, grabbing the pommel for purchase.

She really thought she could, but as soon as he started leading the horse, she began to sway at even that much motion, and came close to tumbling off.

He immediately drew his gelding to a halt. "Miss Elissa?" he asked, his expression sincerely.

She felt mortified. "I'm so terribly sorry. I—I guess I'm colder than I realized."

"It's no trouble." He studied her a beat. "I apologize—this is not going to be entirely proper. But I can't think how else to get you home before this storm breaks."

He led his horse slowly, watching her the whole time,

back to the log, which he used to climb up behind her. He then lifted her just enough to scoot up into the saddle and settled her on his lap. He wrapped one arm securely about her waist, holding her firmly against him, and took the reins in the other.

"Is this all right?" he asked tentatively.

All right? Of course Edward Astley sweeping her up in his arms and carrying her away on his white charger was not "all right."

It was her every schoolgirl fantasy come true, is what it was.

But she could hardly tell him that, so what she said was, "It's all right."

"Come," he said, "let's get you home."

THE SEA SIREN OF BROADWATER BOTTOM **will be available spring of 2022—preorder your copy today!**

AUTHOR'S NOTE

I did quite a bit of research into both women's employment conditions and Regency charitable organizations while writing this novel, and I'm sorry to report that the deplorable practices I described were indeed common to the era. It was the prevailing opinion that women should not work, and a common assumption was that while male "breadwinners" sought wages so they could support their families, women, by contrast, wanted wages in order to purchase bonnets and other fripperies. This poem written by Arthur Smith during a labor dispute involving the Carpet Weaving and Trade Union dates from the 1890s, but the prevailing attitude was the same:

> Mary had a little loom and unto it did go.
> And every Saturday afternoon you should have
>   seen the show.
> With veil, kid gloves and gaiters too, she goes
>   out on the mash.
> She fairly knocks the men out now because she
>   gets the cash.

It was common practice to bar women from holding the better-paying jobs, and the male unions struck over and over again to prevent women from being hired into them. This was both to preserve those jobs for men and also because they knew that as soon as something became "women's work," their own wages would be slashed. In the rare instances when women were allowed to hold the same jobs as men, it was common practice to pay them a lower wage solely on the basis that they were women (similar to the example I cited in the book about painters who decorated Wedgwood china,) and the rationale that women deserved lower pay simply because they were women was openly discussed in a way that honestly startled me as a modern reader.

These days, I sometimes see an article suggesting that our modern-day wage gap is because women choose to go into lower-paid professions and wondering why more women don't become welders instead of daycare workers. I would turn that around and ask why it is that welders are paid so much better than daycare workers and suggest that this might be a chicken-and-egg problem that dates back hundreds of years. Daycare workers are poorly paid today because they have always been poorly paid, and if you go back two hundred years, everyone openly acknowledged that the reason they were poorly paid was because they were women. I am far from the first person to muse upon this topic—in 1915, social scientist B.L. Hutchins wrote, "There is no reason, save custom and lack of organization, why a nursery-maid should be paid less than a coal miner. He is not one whit more capable of taking her place than she is of taking his."

Still, there were examples of people pushing back against the prevailing attitudes, and I would like to share one of my favorites with you. At a Parliamentary Commission Hearing into the Working of the Factory and Workshops Act in 1876, a Miss Sloane from Birmingham went on the record stating, "If a woman is cleverer than a man and she can go out and earn as much as her husband, I do not see why she should be prevented from earning what she can to bring up her children in a better way... I can do it and do it, and would very much rather do it than stay at home and scrub." This is one of those quotes that just leaps out of the historical record. It's a great reminder that, just like today, there is no one thing that everyone believes, that people have always held a range of attitudes, and that at all points in history there were those who rejected the prevailing way of thinking.

By the late Regency to early Victorian period, the idea of model lodging houses, an early form of affordable public housing, was beginning to appear. Thomas Beames discusses them in his 1850 book *The Rookeries of London*, by which point they were popular enough that many parishes ran their own, as well as some individuals including the Earl of Ellesmere and Lord Kinnard. These were my inspiration for The Ladies' Society's lodging house, and Beames's book was the source of many of my facts regarding the particular challenges faced by the poor in this era.

I would also like to give credit to George Smart, inventor of a "Chimney Cleansing Machine" very similar to the one I described as having been invented by Archibald Nettlethorpe-Ogilvy. Smart won a prize contest in 1803 seeking to find a machine that could take the place of climbing boys. Much like Mr. Nettlethorpe Ogilvy, Smart thought up his invention one evening, stayed up all night building it, and tested it on every chimney in his house before his servants woke up (much to their delight, I'm sure!). The story was so good, I couldn't resist including a version of it, and hope that Mr. Smart's descendants will not mind my attributing their forebear's invention to Archibald

Nettlethorpe-Ogilvy. Unfortunately, Smart's machine never caught on, as it remained cheaper to use climbing boys. It wasn't until 1840 that a law was passed forbidding those under the age of 21 from climbing and cleaning flues, and not until 1875 that the law was given enough teeth that the use of climbing boys finally ended.

Finally, if anyone was surprised to see a Black gentleman barrister featured as a character in a book set in England in 1802, allow me to reassure you that this is well supported by the historical record. Please visit my website (https://courtneymccaskill.com/a-note-on-researching-whats-an-earl-gotta-do/) if you would like to learn about Nathaniel Wells, Julius Soubise, George Bridgetower, Robert Morse, William Ansah Sessarakoo, and other Black Britons who were members of the most refined circles during the late 18th and early 19th centuries. Anyone who is interested can also find a list of some of the research references I consulted in writing this book.

ABOUT THE AUTHOR

After reading Black Beauty for the 1,497th time, Courtney McCaskill was inspired to write her own stories. Reviews of her early work were mixed, with her fourth grade teacher, Ms. Compton, saying, "Please stop writing all of your assignments from the point of view of a horse."

Today, Courtney lives in Austin, Texas with the hero of her own story, who holds the distinction of being the world's most sarcastic pediatrician. She is reliably informed by her six-year-old son that she gives THE BEST hugs, "because you're so squishy, Mommy." When she's not busy almost burning her house down while attempting to make a traditional Christmas pudding, she enjoys playing the piano, learning everything there is to know about Kodiak bears, and of course, curling up with a great book. Visit her online at www.courtneymccaskill.com.

ACKNOWLEDGMENTS

Many thanks go to my wonderful editors, Megan Records and Victoria Curran, as well as to my beta readers, Carole, Amy, Bliss, Karen, Ricky, and Susan. I am so grateful to Bailey McGinn for creating the most beautiful covers, and for tolerating my obsession with getting the collar points at *just* the right height. I would also be remiss not to mention the University of Texas Library, as it's pretty much the only thing standing between me and bankruptcy via research books.

I would also like to thank my family—my parents and my son, and especially my amazing husband, who has been nothing but supportive of me on this crazy journey. I love you all so very much! I also want to give a shout-out to all of my fabulous writing friends! Your support and encouragement means everything to me, and I never would have made it this far without you.

Many people have older sisters, but vanishingly few have an older sister as wonderful as Anne. I am happy to count myself in this exclusive group and would like to dedicate this book to my own big sis, Gennie (who, much like Anne, is terrified of spiders!) Just for you, I didn't even put a bassoon joke in this one, but don't go getting used to it. There are *loads* of bassoon jokes in book three. Thank you for not telling Mom about that time I spilled a gallon of orange paint on her brand-new carpet. I will always be your ride or die when it comes to removing tarantulas and recapturing your many evil hamsters. But if you ever decide to take out another wasp nest, you're on your own.

www.ingramcontent.com/pod-product-compliance
Lightning Source LLC
Chambersburg PA
CBHW050505110726
47899CB00005B/1340